LEGIONARY

Quintus Roman Thrillers
Book One

Neil Denby

SAPERE
BOOKS

LEGIONARY

Published by Sapere Books.

24 Trafalgar Road, Ilkley, LS29 8HH

saperebooks.com

ISBN: 978-1-80055-889-2

To Eileen, of course

ACKNOWLEDGEMENTS

I could not have written this novel had I not read Mary Beard's masterful and thorough (and very readable) *SPQR*; Tom Holland's equally readable and knowledgeable *Rubicon* and Guy de la Bédoyère's *Gladius*, a comprehensive description of the lives of Roman soldiers, based on the evidence they left behind.

I: DECIMATIO

The man stared at the white stone in the palm of his hand with more than a degree of incomprehension. It had been hidden in his fist until this moment. The men around him had all, on a count, opened their fingers at the same time. He looked around, dazed; of course it was just him, no one else. The others were at once overjoyed with the fate revealed to them. Two had embraced each other; most wore smiles. All had opened their own hands to find a shiny black stone — a symbol of safety, of reprieve.

The condemned man looked at the other groups on either side of him, drawn up in a rough line away from the camp. They were mostly contubernia — groups of eight men who had marched together, camped together and cooked together, and who slept in the same tent. They were now augmented with legionaries from groups whose own men had fallen in the action that morning, so each was now a group of ten.

Ten soldiers. Ten comrades. Ten stones.

Where they could, the men of a tent party had stayed together, seeking comfort in companionship, like children hiding from a storm. They had embraced each other and wished each other well, though surely in their hearts they only wished no ill for themselves. The groups had squatted on the ground in a rough circle to draw their lots, their fates. Ursus the bear, an affectionate nickname for the hairy man who stared at the white stone, had organised his own group just so.

Men were rising now, their noise reaching him. Congratulations were in the air, but also wails of anguish and in some cases arguments. There were cries that the draw had somehow been manipulated, that fate was compromised, that the gods had not intended for the stones to fall so.

Each group found just a single white stone, for they had been carefully divided before being distributed amongst the cohort and counted out for each section of ten. Ursus' would be the only one in his group. He continued to focus on the shiny marble pebble, its veins strangely beautiful, while everything on the edge of his vision became a blur. The noisy celebration from his comrades grew dull and distant.

He remained silent, stunned by the enormity of what he held. It was not possible. He was an optio, second-in-command in his century, promoted from the ranks. A twenty-year veteran, he was ready to claim his bounty and his land and see out his days as a citizen and a farmer, respected, comfortable and at peace. He had a wife, a child, a home. He should live to become a retiree, a taleteller, a greybeard at the fireside — not just a father, but a grandfather too. Had he not fought with honour at the general's side and received an armband of copper for his bravery, when he'd been part of the detachment that had chased the Egyptian queen to Alexandria? Had he not done his duty?

His comrades jerked him upwards, but he could not rise from his knees. As the order to carry out the sentence was repeated down the line, he felt strong hands take his wrists and tug his arms backwards. Other hands grabbed his head, his ears and his wild black hair, pulling his gaze downward so that all he could see was the beaten earth beneath him. He was about to protest when he felt the cold edge of a blade against the nape of his neck. He shivered involuntarily, felt a searing pain, then all was darkness.

Ursus was lucky — not with the lot that he had drawn, but with the men of his tent party. He had been valiant in the action, had urged the legionaries to keep on fighting and had protected some of the spear-carriers, the boys he'd been charged with training. A man who dwelled on what the white stone meant might try to run or might even soil himself in panic. Ursus could not escape his fate, but his comrades could offer him a swift death. This was a mercy reserved for those few comrades who were popular, well thought-of and brave.

Ursus had a gladius plunged into his neck as he knelt. The blade had been concealed under faggots in the centre of the circle, as it should not have been there.

Not all the condemned men had been as fortunate as the optio. Some had been less than courageous in the action, had tried to run, had abandoned comrades, had turned their backs on the enemy and, even worse, had encouraged others to run. These were suffering slow and violent deaths, being beaten with stones, clubbed with sticks, pounded and pummelled with knees, and smashed with tight fists wrapped in leather bindings.

And when they were allowed to fall to the ground, feet came into play — heavy, nail-studded leather sandals, caligae, kicking ribs, stomachs, backs and livers, increasing the agony until they chose to deal the death blow. Men vomited, whimpering through bloodied teeth, instinctively trying to protect themselves with their arms and crawl away. They finally felt the life drain from them as yet another heel landed on their neck, or they took another kick to the face.

No blades were used, for they were not allowed to wear them. Belts were also forbidden, so that shamed men had to wear their tunics hung low and baggy to their knees, like a woman's garb. Some men found rocks or hid a few weapons away so that they could kill more efficiently, or extinguish their own shame. The sword that had cut off the optio's existence had been well concealed and was swiftly hidden again before any officer could see it and use it on the men.

Night was beginning to fall as the moans and screams subsided. The condemned men, now mostly dead, were dragged to the place set aside for the funerary pyre. They were stripped — many unrecognisable as the legionaries they had been, many barely recognisable even as men, now nothing more than a mass of blood, flesh and bone. Slaves had been detailed to remove the heavy open-toed boots and anything else that might be of value, though the men had already divided their weapons and possessions before the draw. It was their comrades, their executioners, who were made to drag them to the fire, as part of the punishment.

If these deaths had resulted from battle, the officers would have collected the men's last wishes and sent word to loved ones at home in Rome. They would have sent tablets telling of how Quirinus or Casca or Maximus had fallen bravely, so that the Senate could celebrate at least some of them, the Vestals could light fragrant fires for them, and the citizenry could share in their honour and glory, drinking to their shades and pouring libations to the gods for their selfless sacrifice.

But not today. The names of these bloody bodies would not appear on any roll of noble dead. They had been punished for cowardice in the face of the enemy. The cohort had failed to advance, many of its soldiers instead seeking safety. The legion's own cavalry had had to be turned on the men to force them back to the field, but even this had not been enough. When the cohort had ignored orders and fallen back, the prefect had not had any choice but to order a general retreat, away from battle. He had ordered the centurions to regroup the men here, in this fold of the hills that still seemed to echo with the screams of the dying as the flames shot up against the darkening sky.

The general had been furious. The cohort's shame was magnified by the fact that not only were their enemy just tribesmen — natives, already defeated, escaped slaves in effect — but they were led by a woman who was fast becoming a legend, somehow undefeatable. The blame fell squarely on the prefect, who was inexperienced and fresh from Rome. It had been a political appointment, and he'd been stupid enough to trail his wife with him into what, after all, was still wilderness. But the punishment could not fall on him; it had to fall on the cohort that had defied the order to advance and had instead returned to camp.

The river pebbles had been found, counted out and bagged carefully. There were enough for the survivors of each cohort, far less than the almost five hundred men that had set out that morning. Each centurion was entrusted with a bag for what remained of his century. There would be no cheating; the gods watched over all, but so did the general and his staff. Centurions were not exempt and had to draw a lot themselves. Even cohort commanders were considered answerable, whether or not they were patricians — though the gods had smiled on them and favoured them with luck. Of the centurions, only two had chosen white stones. They had both died badly.

The youth Julius Quintus Quirinius, from the most junior of the rural tribes of the ancient city, had enrolled as a common soldier, a legionary. He'd been placed in a reserve troop, barely battle-trained, though at least he was no longer a probationer. He'd watched the violent deaths in a daze, a sort of detachment. This was not his first action, but it was his first taste of bitter defeat. He was fresh-faced, like many of those recruited with him, and very tall and thin. He had dark eyes and light brown hair that he had allowed to grow long and flop across his forehead. His cheeks were barely troubling a blade as yet, though he had his chin scraped as often as he could. Many of his fellow recruits looked older than he, and they shaved often already, spoke like gruff veterans, and told ribald jokes and stories as if they had been a part of them. Quintus had gained a nickname already — 'Mac', short for 'macilentus' because of his skinny frame. His comrades were not being unkind, though the name was hardly complimentary. He was the target of jokes about turning sideways so that the enemy should not see him; the other men also suggested playing a tune on his ribs as a distraction.

'Ursus was kind to me,' Quintus said under his breath, not realising that he spoke out loud until Crassus, the blacksmith, turned to him.

'He was as guilty as the rest of us,' Crassus said firmly, his eyes narrowing above his flat nose. 'He was just unlucky. We should be glad that it is only one of ten.'

'I know,' Quintus nodded, speaking softly and regretfully. He was glad that at least his voice had broken long since, otherwise it might have betrayed him. 'I know, but he was kind.' He took a deep breath, squared his shoulders, and shook the emotion from his head and heart, becoming brisk. 'What now?' His question was directed at the blacksmith, but it was others of the new recruits who answered.

'We will be moved, sent away.'

'We cannot infect the rest of the troops with our shame.'

'We cannot be allowed to.'

'Where to, when…?' Quintus looked around, hoping for an answer, but it had already come. The veterans had started marching, heads drooping, the officers herding the others to join them.

The column was vanishing along the valley of the river, through the trees and bushes. Quintus, Crassus and their little group hastened down the bank to join them, not wanting to feel the lash of an officer's tongue, or worse, the flat of his sword or the butt of his spear. As Quintus joined the column, head bowed in shame, the thought returned to him: Ursus had been kind. He had told him that his time would come, that his height would be an advantage, as would his reach, and that he just needed to train more, to eat more meat. He'd slapped him on the shoulder with a laugh, almost tipping him over. Now the man was but a memory, and Quintus wiped the unbidden tear from his eye before anyone could see it.

He was envious of the blacksmith who walked alongside him, who shaved often and was full of muscle. Still, he had to look down to speak to him. 'Where are we going?' he whispered.

'I don't know,' Crassus replied hoarsely, keeping his head down. 'It cannot be far. We have no weapons, no provisions, and no tents.'

'No mules, no slaves,' added another soldier.

'No forgiveness as yet,' interjected a veteran, a bald man, many lines converging above an oft-broken nose. 'We have not yet been judged.'

A call to silence, a barked order, left Quintus' question frozen on his lips, wondering how far they would have to march before they were considered cleansed. He braced himself for many hours on the road.

But it was not a long march, at least not by the standards the men had grown used to. The river track turned away from the water and into a low-lying field. It was almost a marsh, with the ground turning to liquid beneath their feet as they trooped through the narrow entrance, mud splashing their calves and tunics. A rotten stench hung in the air.

Once a halt was called, the men stood around, many still shocked by what they had not only witnessed, but been a part of. Others were used to violent death and barely gave it a second thought. Instead, they began to think of their own survival and comfort.

Quintus had two advantages. He was very tall, so he could see over the heads of many of his fellow soldiers, and more importantly, he was of farming stock. He knew the land and the way it lay; he knew that the water must drain to the west, into the crook of the valley, the lowest point, even though the river did not quite flow in that direction. He saw how the grass grew, the subtle change in its composition, and he spied the small rise to the east long before anyone else.

Quintus shouted at the nearest two of his contubernium, a handsome young man who'd been recruited at the same time as him and one of the veterans. 'Sextus, Marcus! See that patch, where it looks like shadow?'

'I see it,' Marcus, the veteran, responded.

Quintus waited until the two approached him before he spoke, trying to make sure only they heard. 'It is dry,' he said. 'Believe me.'

'I trust you, Mac,' said Marcus, dragging the boy with him. 'So does he.'

'Claim it,' Quintus ordered. 'Tell the others, if you can find them. Crassus?'

'I am here.'

'The carts there,' Quintus urged, his voice low, pointing to the few carts being pulled into the field, 'they must have weapons, food, maybe even cooking pots and tents. The dry ground, there —' he pointed to where Marcus and Sextus now stood guard over the little patch of land that they had decided to claim — 'that is where we camp.'

'I understand,' Crassus responded, 'but I will need help.'

'I will find the others,' said Quintus, wading into the crowd of men, calling the names of his contubernium as Crassus made for the carts.

'Help me,' a thin man moaned, grabbing Crassus by the arm.

Crassus recognised him as one of the two strangers who had been allocated to their group. 'You are not one of us,' he said. 'None of you are.'

The man continued to whine, but he had underestimated the blacksmith's strength; Crassus kept going, in spite of the claw-like fingers gripping his wrist.

'I do not deserve this. I did not run — I should not be punished for the faults of others.'

He had not managed to stop Crassus but had slowed him down. Other men were heading for the carts and would reach them before he did.

'Quintus!' Crassus called after his friend. 'Help me!'

Quintus turned. His head was above many of the men, so he could see what was happening, but he was trapped in the midst of them. 'Strike him!' he shouted, his voice imperious. 'Strike him down!'

Crassus did not hesitate, but hit the man's wrist and then struck him across the cheek with the back of his hand, the full force of his arm behind the blow. 'We are one!' he yelled as his knuckles made contact, sending the man reeling. 'We are all one, praised or punished the same! You should know that.'

The man fell, vanishing into the melee, under the boots of all those who were now heading down the little hill towards the carts. Crassus still managed to be near the front, orders and admonishments ringing behind him, all of which he ignored.

Quintus and Crassus were not the only ones to seek order. Though the officers who had driven them here were gone, their own centurions, each with a bustling optio, were already by the carts, detailing some men to push them to more solid ground, others to unload them and divide up the meagre provisions they carried. There were no tents and not enough cooking pots for each tent-party, but at least the men's belts and cloaks were there. There were some swords and spears, which were soon stacked neatly. There was enough to defend the camp, if it should need defending, though not enough for everyone. They had just enough barley to feed them, but no wheat, and there was water in the stream, but no wine.

Their punishment was clearly not over.

II: EXTRA MUROS

Crassus lifted a cooking pot onto the ground, quickly hoisted a sack of barley, put it in the pot and stood over it, daring anyone to challenge him. Red-haired Rufus, another of their contubernium, stood to one side of him, while Quintus stood on the other. But there was no need — discipline had returned to the ranks, growing in the men like the warmth from a hot bath. Old hands restrained impetuous young ones, and a few sharp blows jerked the recalcitrant into line. There was order. Officers were able to issue commands, cloaks and weapons were distributed, and men found their comrades and took solace from familiarity.

The mood of the men was black, but for the most part their rage had dissipated in the violence. Their shame at their punishment was manifest — not because they had been forced to kill their comrades, which was a necessary lesson, but because they had been found wanting. This, now, was the true test. They would have to survive on ground that quaked and on rations that would not feed a squirrel. They had few weapons and their shelters were constructed from willow and birch, with no means to make fire unless someone managed to strike a spark and then shared it. But once a single flame was kindled, the light was offered to others and several small fires sprang into being. Pots were shared, barley doled out, a guard posted, and measure and method was restored.

Two men, members of the contubernium, stood a little apart from the ground that Marcus and Sextus held as the others returned with food and equipment.

'We could have helped,' said the dark one quietly. 'We are willing to help.' He offered a bundle of small twigs, while the fair one, himself holding a larger branch, nodded enthusiastically. Both were hoping for a positive reply.

'Come,' said Quintus briskly, a glance at his companions being enough to confirm the decision, 'you are still one with us.' He beckoned them forward, and the two dumped their meagre collection of firewood on the ground with some relief.

That night, more than one man died by his companions' hands — cowards, thieves, and some who moaned about the inequity of it all. Crassus' attacker was one such. He rolled slowly down the hill and into the muddy field at the bottom, his neck broken, though Crassus had had no hand in it.

He and Quintus slept fitfully under the open sky, wrapped in the same cloak and lying as near to the dying embers of the fire as they could. Though they had managed to secure dry ground, it was broken and uncomfortable, and they shared it with the others of their contubernium that they had found and a small group of veterans who made a claim as valid as theirs had been. The visitors had quietly but forcefully settled on the ground alongside them, rather than taking it outright.

The men's bellies were empty, and other aches and pains were magnified now that the excitement had drained. Unfamiliar noises of the night replaced the usual comforting rhythm of their camp, and this made them nervous. Apprehension had given way to emptiness rather than relief; now, there was the smell of threat and sweat, and the acid tang of fear.

They, along with the others, had been made to drag their own comrades to the pyre before being marched from camp, and many had sustained cuts, bruises and burns. Many of the legionaries had also suffered with broken and battered hands and feet from the force with which they had despatched their compatriots. They were now prey to night terrors as the shades of the dead visited, displaying their torn flesh and crushed bones and pleading for mercy, their voices pathetic. They had not gone to their rest, and they would not let their killers go to theirs.

Eventually Quintus gave up any attempt at sleep and sat up, rubbing his eyes. Crassus, who had also been struggling against wights and djinns in his nightmares, was happy to sit up with him — he had been lying awkwardly, afraid to move in case he disturbed his friend. They sat shoulder to shoulder now, drawing the cloak around both of them and watching the false dawn lighten the line of hills in the east. They listened to the morning sounds of the camp — men moving, grumbling, snoring, talking, arguing and pissing — all at a low volume, as if they did not wish to disturb the night.

'Mac, we are not even supposed to be at war,' Crassus offered quietly, with a slight shake of his head. 'That action should never have happened.'

'We are always at war,' said Quintus glumly, 'even when we are not meant to be.'

'But the gates of the Temple of Janus are closed, or at least they were closed when we set out. We are meant to be settling here, not fighting,' Crassus complained. His voice was quiet but forceful.

'I know, my friend,' said Quintus, allowing himself a bitter half-smile. 'Things are not always what they seem. You should know this.'

Crassus tried to pull the cloak tighter around his own shoulders, and Quintus resisted with a tug. He shivered as he replied sulkily, 'Ursus would still live if these Cantabrians would just acknowledge that they have been defeated.'

Quintus stared at the growing light, waiting for the birds to start singing to signal the start of true dawn. Both boys faced east, not looking at each other as they spoke, even though they were sharing a cloak. He replied in a low whisper, as if to himself, 'How should they know? Victory was never officially declared — there was no triumph for the emperor, no public holiday, no arms of war dedicated to Victorious Jove. If Rome does not know, how would they?'

'Everyone knows that the war has ended,' Crassus insisted. 'Everyone knows that the emperor did not order a triumph because the Astures and Cantabrians had all killed themselves in honour of their own gods. There were no prisoners, and despite the tales of silver and gold, there was no plunder. There were no weapons to dedicate at Jove's feet. There were not even any slaves.'

'I am told that even their women are ugly,' Quintus added, with disappointment. 'What sort of a triumph would it have been with no prisoners and ugly women?'

Crassus sighed. 'Surely we could have brought some prisoners back. We could have let them take their own lives publicly and watched them fall onto blades, throw themselves into fires — that is what they did, you know. They made bonfires and threw on their women and children, then themselves. And they sang all the while.' He threw a stick at the remnants of their own fire. 'We could do with a Cantabrian fire right now.'

'Most of them poisoned themselves,' said Quintus, breaking Crassus' little reverie, 'so that wouldn't have been much of a spectacle. Yew is apparently holy to them, like it is to those heathen bastards that attacked us.' He half-turned his own head, stroking his non-existent beard. 'Some were crucified,' he added matter-of-factly, 'but even then, they sang.'

'And the ones that attacked us, waving their tree branches — why are they not dead?'

'They do not know that they have lost. Their tribal leaders never surrendered and never conceded that Rome had beaten them.' Quintus shrugged the cloak from his shoulders as the red light of dawn appeared tentatively behind the dark shapes of the hills. He heard loud, confident birdsong — a thrush, he thought, or even a pair. He stood up, unwinding his body, twisting and turning to lessen the aches. 'They are remnants,' he went on disconsolately, kicking the fire in a feeble attempt to bring some life to it, 'remnants who bite and get under the skin like lice. They rob and burn Roman settlements, destroy farms, attack marching columns and steal animals, food and baggage trains. They are led by a woman who manages to keep three full legions battened down, and they fight like wasps instead of men, in little swarms that sting and fly away. Yesterday we found a nest and it stung us badly. We were not prepared; it only took a few of us to break for all of us to fail.'

'We could not have known they were there,' muttered Crassus as he drew the cloak more tightly around him. 'It was not our fault. They hid — they did not offer open battle.'

He was right. The marching column had stopped so that the surveyors could investigate some interesting hump, riverbed, or pile of stones. The men had been allowed to break out rations, but not to light fires, and they had not unloaded the mules. A guard had been posted, but it was a desultory one — after all, they would not be here long. This was a fault of command, of the politicians and rich fools in charge rather than soldiers. The tribesmen had sprung up, it would seem, out of the ground, wearing leaves and branches to disguise their presence — mostly yew, of course. They rushed at the column, shouting and calling on their gods in their grating tongue. They swung long-handled axes, setting the mules running. But there was method here. The first to fall were those centurions who had not removed their plumed helmets. They were followed by the cornicines, the trumpeters, who were alongside them, so few were left to issue orders and even fewer to sound them to the men.

Some centurions survived the first charge and managed to get a semblance of defensive order formed. They contained the initial shock, but the enemy melted away. The tribesmen did not want to face spears, swords and shields that were organised. They had done what they'd set out to do: they had inflicted a defeat of sorts on the invader and had jeered at their enemy from the hillside above the track. The order to follow, to attack, was called by a centurion and played by a cornicen, but by now there was no enemy to be seen. Another cornicen managed to sound a retreat, and confusion followed.

'They were probably youths,' said Crassus slowly, 'no older than us, untrained, and hot with shame at their country being conquered.'

'They were led,' said Quintus flatly. 'There was method. She was there. You cannot make excuses for them.'

Crassus put his hands up. 'I do not excuse them,' he insisted.

'The guard would have had their throats cut — a quick death and a quiet one,' said Quintus, his voice rising, 'unlike that of our comrades.' He was becoming angrier and louder. 'It is as if a little tribe of rabbits or squirrels sharpened some sticks and sent a pack of fierce wolves running down the hill, tails between their legs, howling that they had been hard done by. No wonder the general was furious. No wonder the whip had to crack.'

A strong hand landed gently on his shoulder, though its owner had to reach upwards to do so. 'Do not dwell on it,' said Marcus softly. His voice belied the solid frame behind it. Marcus was reasonably tall, but also squat and muscular, with square shoulders and a broad chest. It was no surprise that, with his low centre of gravity, he was a fearsome wrestler.

'We are being punished,' he continued, deep-set eyes peering out from below his bushy black hair as he turned Quintus to face him, 'but do not worry. In a day or two we will be back at camp and it will all be forgotten — maybe even by nightfall today.' The lines on his brow, his crooked nose, his immaculately shaved chin and the scars on his forearms and legs all told of long service as a soldier. The men therefore trusted his knowledge of such things.

'Have you been here before?' asked Publius, the pale boy who looked to be the youngest of the group. He had also risen as the light had begun to turn from red to pink to white. 'Have you survived more than one punishment such as this?'

Publius was standing with his friend, Cato. Cato was tanned and heavy, and dark-skinned enough to have Egyptian or Nubian blood amongst his ancestors. He was of the Esquilina, an urban tribe of mostly poorer craftsmen. He might even have been descended from a freedman, though his citizenship was not in doubt. He had deep-set brown eyes, bushy eyebrows that were tangled as a thorn thicket, and wiry black hair. He was Night to Publius' Day, and they carried the nicknames Lux and Nox within the cohort.

'Not such as this, no,' answered Marcus, putting his other hand on Publius' shoulder so that the three of them stood connected. 'No, not such as this, boys. This does not happen often. The general needs to be very … shamed for decimation to be called down upon a unit.'

Most of the others were stirring now. They had been soldiers long enough to wake with the morning light, though few had slept well this night. Some, veterans who had learned to sleep while standing guard with their eyes open — or so legend would have it — claimed to have slept like babes, though most had not. Sextus, still as fresh-faced as the day he'd been recruited, seemed to be the only one enjoying untroubled sleep, curled up with his back to them. For the moment, they left him.

A dozen of them shared the dry ground: Quintus and the others of his party, plus four veterans. Between them there were eight cloaks, one cooking pot and half a sack of barley, for Crassus had not been allowed to depart the cart with the whole of his haul. All were at least partially armed, with either sword, dagger or spear, very few with all three. All at least had belts, and could now wear their tunics properly; the humiliation they'd felt at not being able to do so still ran deep. Quintus loosened his shoulders and held a hand out to Crassus.

'Up,' he urged, helping the blacksmith to his feet with a pull. 'I thought we were sharing that cloak.'

'It will be warm enough soon,' replied Crassus, looking up at the clear sky, already turning blue, but still holding the cloak around himself. 'Your turn will come.'

Quintus and Crassus had formed a bond before the events of yesterday, one only strengthened by the passage of fire they had just endured. Quintus was primus amicus, first friend, to Crassus, and the blacksmith the same to him; they held each other's last wishes, the names of those who should be told of their deaths, the places to where their final letters should be sent, and their last possessions if there were any. These details had been cached on tablets and stowed in the cart that had belonged to the tent party, and so they were lost — at least for now. It did not weaken the bond. Marcus had been primus amicus to Ursus. He had kept the optio's last prayers and wishes hidden in a leather pouch tied ingeniously beneath his tunic. Marcus had not yet had the heart to read them. Many others had also taken possession of such wills and concealed them.

It was Ursus who had arranged to hide the gladius, and it was Marcus who had plunged it into his neck while Crassus had gripped his head. Rufus and Sextus had grabbed and held his arms while Quintus had kept watch, to make sure that there would be a clean execution rather than a lingering death, and that there would be no interference from officers. Publius and Cato each faced one of the new men, making sure that they did not intervene. These men had been told what was planned, but once they had drawn black stones they felt they had no part in it. The Fates had placed them with these companions, but they felt no affinity with them.

All ten legionaries had agreed that whoever drew death, the others had a role to play in making that end as swift as possible, even though their officers — their general in particular — would deeply disapprove of such plans. The officers believed that the restoration of discipline through violence was more effective than through comradeship and friendship. Had Marcus drawn white, then Ursus would have delivered the blow, risking his own command. Had it been Quintus, Crassus would have despatched him. Had it been one of the new men, it was expected that the other would have killed him, though none knew the trustworthiness of these two. The rest of the contubernium had accepted what they had told them — that they had not run, not been guilty of cowardice.

They all knew that such actions were against orders, against the spirit of the punishment, but they recognised that they had become more than just marching companions. They were not the only contubernium to choose mercy and risk further discipline.

'A fire,' said Rufus, who was squatting behind the trio. 'Come, Crassus, some magic of the forge, if you please, or must we pray to Vulcan?'

Rufus was, of course, red-headed, freckled and florid-faced. Once he had had a real name, but that had been buried under the nickname before he could even walk. He thought his mother might know it, but few else. His hair was thick and unruly, his pale orange eyebrows met above a long nose, and his lips were framed with a drooping moustache, cut in a style he had seen as a boy on Gaulish prisoners in one of great Caesar's triumphs. He too was tall, though neither as broad as Marcus nor as long and thin as Quintus — few were as skinny as Macilentus. He had served sixteen years, long enough to have fought the Cantabrians beneath the snowy mountains of the Picos, long enough to have seen prisoners sing victory hymns whilst bound to crosses or walking into pyres, and long enough to know that the general, the emperor as he was now, would not abide the shame of defeat.

'You are right, of course,' he said to Marcus. 'Shame is the right word. Still, we need a fire.' Rufus had served enough time to lose two previous partners. He'd had to send meagre possessions in the case of one, and nothing in the case of the other. Almost nothing had remained of his second partner; there were only tablets with loving thoughts and wills that passed on possessions that no longer existed. Rufus had sent his loved ones a message saying how honourably the man had died, scrawled in his own poor hand.

He looked across with affection to Sextus, his third primus amicus in as many years. The young man's features were still composed in sleep, and Rufus thanked the gods that he had not lost his latest companion.

III: VERBERATIO

As light spilled onto the field, revealing the ragtag arrangements of the remains of a cohort, Publius and Cato were sent for water, whilst Crassus tended to the fire. An ember or two had survived the night and a little breath, a little coaxing, and maybe a prayer or two to the lame god of the forge, made flames appear. Quintus had managed to find dry kindling — another talent of the farm-boy — and soon the pot was warming. Barley and water would be their breakfast, but at least it would not be cold. Other groups looked at them with envy. Marcus — now belted, armed and cloaked — scowled at those who would have taken their flame, whilst those who requested it were given it freely.

Discipline was survival; where thieves and murderers might have flourished, so did summary justice, and so did the quiet blade in the dead of night. Most knew that the only thing that separated them from animals was discipline, applied from without and enforced from within. They knew that Marcus would protect his own and had the right to do so. They also knew that survival often lay in sharing — a bowl of food, a cloak, a shield even. They had learned to look out for each other.

Not all the men were of Ursus' tent party, so not all were known to Marcus, but the extras, the four who had shared the ground with them, were welcomed nonetheless. They were allowed to take a share of the gruel before they withdrew back to their own camp, a little higher up the slope.

'Wake up, son, or you will miss what little breakfast there is.' Rufus aimed a friendly kick at Sextus' exposed rump.

The young man rolled over lazily. 'What is it?' he asked innocently. 'I was having such a wonderful dream — a dream of long-legged girls with golden hair and...' As he spoke, his hands made curved shapes in the air.

'We do not want to know,' Rufus cut him off sharply, 'and if you wish to share our gruel, you will leave the dreams behind.' He thrust a wooden bowl at the legionary, barely half filled with a gritty paste.

Sextus looked at it with a grimace, asking plaintively, 'Will we soon be back at camp?'

'We will,' Marcus reassured him. 'Look.'

There was movement at the muddy entrance to the field, where the cart had stood the night before. There were men marching, and there were animals being herded, some seemingly carrying timber, others what looked like grain. There were officers, their plumes marking them, and high on a dark horse, surrounded by his own guards and carrying a white staff of office, there was a man of importance, a prefect.

Quintus sighed. He had seen such a thing before, within the first few weeks of his arrival to the legion — the only time that he had seen Octavius, now Caesar Augustus and Imperator, in person. He had seemed impossibly young to hold so much power, and his curly golden hair had glinted in the Spanish sunshine as he had taken his helmet off. Quintus remembered the hair, but he did not remember what had been said.

'A platform, Marcus,' he said dully. 'We are to be lectured, not fed.'

'Maybe we are to be lectured, then fed,' said Sextus hopefully.

Somehow, though the last to rise, he had a cloak to himself and a gladius at his side, and he was leaning on a spear. He was also chewing. Quintus narrowed his eyes at him, suspicious —

no-one else had had anything that might have needed chewing. Sextus shrugged his shoulders and smiled.

They all turned back to watch the platform party. A cornicen called the men to attention. There was a group of well-trained guards with polished spears and shields and plumed helmets, centurions fussing and complaining, and at least one signifer who was carrying a banner with the name of the cohort and the number of the legion written on it. The banner was black on yellow and was decorated with tassels and ribbons, but no eagle — there would be no eagle for a disgraced cohort. Finally, there was a single man of importance, in this case a prefect. He would speak softly to the centurion who possessed the loudest voice, and he in turn would shout exactly what the man had said, losing all of its nuance and careful intonation in a monotone yell.

'I have seen this before,' said Quintus knowledgeably. 'I helped build the platform for Octavius when I first arrived.'

'As did I,' said Sextus, stepping forward.

'You did little or nothing, as I recall,' Quintus scoffed. 'Were you not in charge of nails?'

'I was in charge of keeping out of the sun and sipping the general's wine,' grinned Sextus, 'better than mere carpentry.'

'It was ever thus,' Crassus added, joining them. He had been recruited at the same time as Quintus, neither of them in the 'first rank'. He and Quintus always managed to secure the hard detail, Sextus the easiest.

The three of them had arrived with a group of two hundred recruits, allocated to the Old Ninth by luck — poor or good, they could not judge, though they knew others of their age and standing had been sent as far away as Parthia, Armenia and even Egypt, now that the queen and her lover were dead by their own hand.

The Ninth had played a part in that; it was one of great Caesar's favourite legions and had been with him against Pompey in Africa, remaining loyal to Octavian, his heir. Now it helped hold Hispania Ulterior, the land that had once been home to the Cantabrians and Astures. The legion held it from their camp, which was named in honour of the emperor, Lucus Augustus, and already had a small town growing around it. It stood on a hilltop surrounded by three rivers, commanding a view over the woods and fields, away to the mountains. It was near enough to the coast to bring the salty tang of the sea to the nostrils of the men when the wind blew warm and southerly. The enemy had occupied this hilltop once, dug their own defences and dedicated it to their own gods, but now only Roman tents and fortifications stood, and the flags and pennants, the vexilla, of Roman forces flew.

On the Campus Martius, Quintus had not been the first choice, either for his quartet or for the legions recruiting. The boys and young men volunteering for service were divided into groups of four and each legion had first choice of the four in turn. They knew nothing of the skill of the recruits — how well they could throw the pilum, the javelin, or how good their stamina was. Quintus could fight, this he knew — he had watched the training from the edges of the Campus Martius whenever he had travelled to the market with his father. When he'd turned seven or so, he had started to copy the movements, the thrusts and parries with a wooden sword and a wicker shield, the complex dance steps practised by the young men daily.

On his thirteenth birthday he had donned his toga virilis, his 'manly gown' and had been allowed to join in at least some of the exercises. His father wished it so, though his mother, had she been alive still, would not have. His younger brother, named Proculus as he'd been born whilst his father was at war, was envious. Quintus was the fifth child, the first to live, three boys and a girl having passed away before they were even named. Proculus was the next and final one, his mother succumbing shortly after the child had been cut from her. Both boys wanted to join the army. They understood it to be their duty, though their father knew that if they did not, they could be charged with desertion, so it was hardly a choice. To his wife he had always maintained the fiction of choice, as did the state. You had to be rich or powerful to avoid the army — most people were neither.

Quintus thought he might be chosen first, as he was the tallest — but it was not so. There were no small boys here, and there were many that looked stronger and fitter than he — deeper of chest, broader of shoulder, more muscular of thigh. Being skinny, he was the last choice, his future falling to the Ninth whether he — or they — liked it or not.

The next to be allocated to the Ninth was Sextus, who stood nearby, still chewing, still with that half-smile on his lips. Sextus looked younger than he was, but he had wisdom beyond his years. He was barely a citizen, though he had a tribe. He had been a runner for a whorehouse in the dank and steamy valley of the Suburra, and he was saddled with debts that were not his. Sextus had therefore escaped to the army — not unusual for one born into poverty. He was lucky, for he had charm and seemed to be blessed with good fortune that somehow rubbed off on his comrades. He was a favourite with the young women — he was pretty, rather than handsome, and had large brown eyes, a clear forehead and a long straight nose. He could have been a by-blow of Marcus Antonius for all anyone knew.

They had all arrived from Rome just over half a year since, expecting comradeship, honour, and glorious battle alongside the contemporaries with whom they had trained on the Campus Martius. Instead, Quintus had gained a hammer and a saw and a back loaded with timber, while Sextus had somehow gained a light duty, handing out tools and nails. Quintus had not practised carpentry; he had practised running and wrestling, slinging shots and throwing spears, cutting and parrying with a wooden sword. It was his duty, after all; he had come willingly. He knew he could be counted on to support the great general now that all opposition was finally crushed and Rome could embark once more on its historical mission of civilisation and glory, of wrapping the world in its reforming embrace.

Quintus also brought agricultural skills — he knew how to keep animals, so he was made responsible for the mule that carried the contubernium's tent and cooking pots. It was a lowly position — one some of his companions thought more suited to a slave than a soldier, though they were keen enough to turn to him when they wanted meat butchered.

Sextus brought other skills — most importantly a confidence, a way of doing things. These were not necessarily soldierly skills, but certainly skills that were of use to soldiers. If you needed a chicken or a pig, he could obtain it by charming the dark-eyed local women with his own doe-like gaze. If you needed an advocate, he had a glib tongue; if you needed money, he seemed able to obtain silver by snapping his fingers. He drew men to him with a kind of magnetism, engendering loyalty and trust. He brought luck, and that was more important than skill. He, of course, had already slept with the prefect's wife. Though Quintus regarded him with suspicion, he still looked on him with affection.

The men below were building a platform, the man on the horse destined to mount it. But there was something else. A pillar, a stake, had been driven into the ground in the space beyond the platform, whilst shouts went up from centurions and their optiones, busying themselves up the hillside.

'Form up!' was the order. 'Look like you are soldiers. Form battle order as centuries — whatever is left of them.' For the centuries had already lost men in the shameful action before being reduced by a tenth. The ranks were therefore much thinner than they should have been, though there were still three or four hundred men here, able to form centuries of a sort.

Once they were standing, with outstretched arms to even out the spaces, the rabble of the night before began to look like a Roman unit once more. Most were armed with spears, and some had shields. All were facing the stake whilst the work of building the platform continued down on their right. The field was eerily quiet but for the banging of nails, the men knowing that to speak now could bring further punishment on their heads.

An optio stepped forward in front of the men and began to declaim, reading from a tablet he held: 'Cassius Maecenas, once of the tribe of Collina, cornicen, did yesterday sound a retreat without orders, bringing shame and disgrace on his fellows. A coward, he attempted to desert, hiding out until the cohort's punishment was over. He has been found, and will now be punished as a foreigner, his citizenship revoked with his desertion.'

A murmur, an unasked question, passed through the assembled men. It was quickly quelled as the officers turned their gaze upon them, but the whispers were correct. They were to witness a flogging: *verberatio*.

From beyond where the construction was taking place, two legionaries approached, dragging between them a man. He was half-naked, with no tunic on his back nor boots on his feet. His hands were held wide above his head, each tightly bound to the curve of a trumpet, its battered bell pointed uselessly at the ground: the badge of his shame. Now the purpose of the stake became clear as he and the instrument were tied to it, his arms high, the taut muscles of his back facing the assembly. His two guards each drew a switch, a wicked implement of many knotted leather thongs plaited together into a handle. At a signal from the optio who had read out the charge, they began to lay open the man's skin, taking it in turns to apply the lash.

The first blow merely caused welts to rise, the mark of the thongs spread across his back; the second opened the flesh so that blood began to flow. After that, each subsequent blow brought more flesh away, until the white of bone could be seen through the sticky red gore.

On the first few blows the man cried out, though it was clear from the strangled sound that he was trying to contain them. After that, his head dropped, and he merely moaned, though water was thrown over him twice when it seemed that he had passed out. It seemed that there was no count, and the guards appeared not to tire. But finally, at a signal from the man on the horse, the punishment ceased, the soldiers stowed the switches in their belts and the victim was cut down by slaves.

As he was taken away, Marcus whispered, 'He will not survive.'

'He was not meant to,' hissed back Sextus. 'This was not about him. It is an example for us. I doubt that was even the man.'

'Silence,' ordered the centurion nearest to them, 'or I will have your tongues cut out.'

Their attention was taken by the prefect, now on the platform rather than on his horse, and by the carts that had been brought in. They were covered, leaving the men curious about their contents. The prefect spoke to the centurion on the platform next to him, the centurion yelling out the words in a parade ground voice.

'Men!' the officer shouted. 'Legionaries of the Ninth!' He indicated the carts with an outstretched arm. 'These wagons contain enough to make you whole once more — cloaks, swords, spears, shields, even boots.' Many grimaced at the thought of the pile of bloody leather they had seen yesterday. 'There are also your tents and pots, as well as mules to carry them and slaves to care for them.'

Sextus managed a sideways glance at Quintus, and a brief smile. Quintus scowled. But it was true: a line of pack animals, accompanied by slaves, could be seen on the track leading to the field. They were going to be re-equipped.

'Forgiven,' Crassus whispered to himself with a prayer of thanks to Vulcan, his personal deity.

'We are not the only legion present here in Hispania,' the centurion continued, repeating what the prefect said. He spoke the truth: though the Ninth was stationed here in Ulterior Hispania, it was not the only force. The Tenth Gemina was here also, further south, and the Fourth Macedonia was further west. All were needed to fight the Cantabrians and Astures, who would not accept that they were defeated.

'But we are the only legion with soldiers brave enough to fight this enemy and defeat them once and for all,' declared the centurion.

Despite the discipline, this brought a few murmurs from the men. Clearly this was some sort of sick jest regarding their previous behaviour — for which they had been punished. Crassus cut short his prayer.

But it was no jest. The prefect was clear: the cohort was not to return to camp, not now, possibly not ever. Instead, it was to chase the Astures and Cantabrians into their mountain strongholds, to defeat them utterly, capture their chieftains, especially the talismanic female, and destroy their gods. His words were lost amongst high-flown language about the glories of Rome, of the empire, and of the ambitions of divine Caesar, which the prefect had no doubt spent many long hours composing, and which the hoarse tones of the centurion now rendered comedic.

Finally dismissed, each group began to make its way back to its own temporary camp, animatedly discussing what this meant. The cohort was to be made whole, it would seem. New officers would replace the fallen, new men would replace their lost comrades, and they would receive sufficient equipment and arms. But no-one completely understood what it was they were to do.

As they made their way back up the hill, Marcus took Quintus by the arm, leading him away from the others.

'What is it?' Quintus asked. 'Where are we going?'

'Out of earshot,' said Marcus urgently. 'I must do this before we regroup.'

'Do what?' Quintus halted.

'Ursus was my primus amicus. I hold his will.'

'I know. What of it?'

'Mac, I read it last night. You are in it. I have something to give you.' He reached inside his tunic and pulled out a leather pouch, unwrapping it to reveal a copper armband. 'This was his.'

'I never knew,' said Quintus. He had seen such armbands awarded for bravery, but not often. He half reached towards it, then drew back.

'It is yours now.' Marcus held the armband out.

Quintus made no move to touch it. 'It is not mine,' he said, shaking his head. 'I did not win such a thing.'

'Ursus won it in Africa. Caesar gave it to him himself after defeating Sextus Pompeius. He has carried it ever since, even when recalled.'

'Recalled?' Quintus was confused.

'Ursus has always served with the Ninth,' Marcus explained, 'but when Caesar was killed, they were disbanded, discharged with honour and pensions as Caesar had promised, and given land and farms near Picenum. But the civil wars proved too much for the state, and the Ninth were recalled by Octavius. Ursus had to leave his retirement behind: the farm, his land and his wife, heavy with child.'

'What has this to do with me?' Quintus asked.

'He has left it all to you, if the child is a girl. If it's a boy, he gives you stewardship, and asks you to be like a father to him until he dons his manly gown. This proves your claim.' Marcus held out the armband.

This time Quintus took it, feeling the cold metal against his fingers and peering at the inscription on it, unable as yet to read what it said. 'I cannot take this charge,' he said softly, making to hand the armband back.

'You must,' finished Marcus. 'It is my duty, and it is as he wished. There is more…'

'More?'

'He charges you with keeping his friends safe. He says he sees leadership in you. It is written here.' Marcus thrust a tightly folded paper into Quintus' hand, then looked quizzically at him. 'I will not mention it if you do not want me to,' he offered. 'Can you read?'

Quintus nodded as he placed the paper in its pouch and concealed both it and the armband inside his tunic. Marcus, duty done, set off up the hill, leaving Quintus fixed where he stood.

IV: MAL FORTUNA

They had been told to send two men: he who they had elected leader or decanus, and one other to collect from the quartermaster what was required to make up their contubernium, be it men, weapons or materials. Ursus had been decanus to Quintus and his companions, so they needed to elect another. Marcus at once suggested Quintus, in an effort to cheer him as much as anything.

'You gained us the dry ground, sent Crassus for supplies, found Publius and Cato and set them their tasks.' Marcus clearly seemed impressed, patting Quintus on the back. 'Yours was the voice of command,' he insisted.

'Dry ground, maybe,' Quintus smiled, 'but the food was doled out by the centurions, and the water was freely available. It is too soon for me. It should be you, Marcus. You are senior.'

'Or Sextus,' offered Crassus, laughing. 'He would be able to get us wheat instead of barley, a stallion instead of a mule, and sheepskin-lined undershorts.'

'Not I,' said Sextus quickly and firmly, holding his hand up as if to ward off the responsibility, though it had not seriously been offered. He made wave signs with his open palm. 'I work better below the water than above it,' he added with a wry smile. 'You would not wish to see my methods.'

'It should be you, Marcus. You have served longest,' said Rufus. He turned to the others for support. 'Publius, Cato?'

They looked up quickly and nodded in unison.

'Quintus, Crassus?' asked Rufus.

'We agree,' said Quintus swiftly, speaking for both of them.

'Then it is settled.' Rufus turned to the new decanus. 'You will need an amicus; we need one to make up our number.'

Of the men who had joined the group in their makeshift campsite, only one remained, the others having found their own, or new, companions. This one had been listening and now stood, his face serious. He was a veteran, a man as old as Marcus. He had a long, straight scar that divided his beard, running down his weather-beaten cheek from his right eye almost to his jawline. The jagged edge of his right ear looked like a bite — from a wolf, perhaps. A glint of bronze betrayed the earring he wore in the lobe, the little that was left of it. His dark brown hair had all but gone; just a short ring of chestnut lingered above his ears and the back of his neck. His eyes were hooded, his lips full, his nose wide. Yet he was confident and seemed to carry authority. His chin tilted upwards to the man who was half a head taller than he.

'I have lost my primus amicus,' Marcus said swiftly to him. 'Ill luck, but someone had to draw the white stone.'

'It was not the draw that took my own friend,' said the man softly. 'It was a fault with a trumpet...'

Sextus gasped, his eyes straying to the post that still stood, a stark reminder.

'Yes,' the man repeated, his gaze deliberately not following. Instead, he looked directly at Marcus, asking, 'Perhaps it is I who am cursed by poor luck?'

'Not so,' said Marcus, his wrestler's firm grip grasping the forearm of the man. 'You are welcome.' He looked at the other six for confirmation, though he knew he did not need it, and all nodded.

'Come,' said Quintus, 'introduce yourself.'

'I should go,' said Marcus, looking at the men who were already making their way down to where carts and beasts and legionaries were assembling.

'Introductions can wait,' said the newcomer, smiling just a little, white teeth showing through his scrubby brown beard. 'I will introduce myself to this man first,' he added, indicating Marcus, 'whilst I help him with his task.'

'No,' said Sextus, laconically, still chewing on something. 'Quintus should help. I would hear at least a brief history of why you think yourself ill-fated.'

'If we are late or last, there will be nothing left,' Marcus warned.

'Then go,' said Quintus. 'I will follow you shortly.'

Marcus set off quickly down the muddy slope.

'I spoke true,' the new man said, standing. His audience was seated in a semi-circle, all but Quintus and Sextus, who stood also. 'Perhaps I am a bringer of ill-fortune,' he continued. 'You should know and judge before you accept me.'

'We should know your name before anything else,' Sextus said firmly.

'I am Postumus Tullius Surus of the Suburana,' said the man, chest puffed out, shoulders squared proudly and once more offering his forearm, this time to Sextus.

Sextus ignored the gesture, but Quintus stepped forward and took hold.

'Well, Tullius, I am known plainly as Quintus, sometimes Mac,' he smiled, 'though I, too, have a history, as do we all.'

'My father died in battle, my mother in childbirth soon after...' began Tullius tentatively.

'I guessed as much,' said Quintus matter-of-factly. 'Mine did too. It is a common way for parents to die. Surely this is not why you claim to be a bringer of ill-luck?'

'No,' said Tullius, 'there is more.'

Sextus indicated that the stage belonged to Tullius, who put his hands on his hips and began. The men would discover soon enough that this was a very long speech for their new companion. He did not talk much.

'I was decanus of my own tent-party, elected by my men, well liked, and looked upon favourably by officers. Clearly the gods did not like this situation, Fortuna in particular.' He shrugged and sighed. 'Such is luck. A month ago, we lost five of our number, good men, experienced soldiers, but caught in an ambush that barely registered as a fleabite on the legion. They were unlucky to be foraging in a dangerous area, and they were caught in woodland by a roaming band of native tribesmen, barely missed by anyone but me. They were replaced with new men — boys, really...' He could not stop his eyes from flicking to Publius and Cato.

Publius noticed. 'I am not as young as I look, just fair,' he said softly, flicking his straw-coloured hair. 'I have seen action.'

'As have I,' added Crassus, 'and not just in the forest.'

'We all have,' said Quintus. 'We are not raw.'

'Your pardon. These were raw boys,' Tullius went on, 'newly arrived from Rome, and still complaining of the march.' He took a deep breath. 'Their first action was the one in the forest for which the cohort is punished. They did not flee. They were brave, but young and foolhardy. They died at the enemy's hand, unlike two of the veterans, men on whom I thought I could rely, but who died with javelins in their backs as they fled.' He shook his head. 'Of my contubernium, only I and my amicus survived. On our return to camp, we were divided and sent to other parties to make up numbers.' His voice dropped. 'We thought our luck had changed when at nightfall we found each other and embraced, joyful that neither of us had chosen the white stone.'

His voice dropped even further, so that the listeners had to strain to hear.

'We were among the last to leave that place. As we left, an officer, waiting on the bank of the river with half a dozen men, pointed to Marius, my companion, and his men grabbed him, marching him back towards the still burning pyres. They urged me on, away from them, and said something about a special task for him.' He paused, his voice now little more than a whisper. 'The next time I saw him he was being dragged, bound to a trumpet, and tied to a stake. I watched them flog him to death.'

'Then...' began Sextus.

'Then he was no trumpeter, no traitor,' said Tullius. 'He was an example, and that was his special duty. It seems an example was needed, and it was he.'

The group were quiet, not really knowing how to react. Though Sextus had said that the victim was probably not the guilty party, he had not wholly believed it. Now they knew that an innocent man had been scourged beyond survival just to make a point. And before them stood the innocent man's primus amicus.

As if picking up on the sombre mood, rain began to fall, more of a drizzle than a downpour. Quintus breathed deeply and was transported by it; it was a spring rain redolent of grass and grain, of his family's farm.

'You are one with us.' Sextus' assertion broke the silence. He turned to Quintus. 'Is he not?'

'He is,' said Quintus firmly, his reverie broken.

This time, it was Sextus who held out his hand to grip Tullius' forearm. 'You are welcome,' he said, his eyes meeting those of the older man. 'You are not a bringer of ill fortune, but one who has had more than his share of it. I think you may bring us luck.'

Quintus nodded. 'Make him at home,' he said to the seated men. 'Tell him your names and histories; he is one with us.' He half-laughed. 'I must run and catch Marcus, or I will not be.'

He turned to peer down the slope as the others pulled themselves up from the ground, ready to welcome Tullius.

'There, to the right,' said Rufus. 'Do you see him?'

'I do,' replied Quintus, setting off at a jog down the hill.

Before he reached Marcus, he had passed the detail that was already taking the platform apart and had to barge his way through others with apologies and explanations. Finally, he joined the decanus in the middle of the ragged line.

'So, is he ill-fated?' Marcus asked.

'He has had his share of bad luck — but, with your approval, he is one with us,' said Quintus. He looked around furtively. 'I will not go into detail where others can hear us.'

'His name, at least?'

'Postumus Tullius, of an urban tribe — a true citizen and, I think, an honest man.'

'If you approve, that is good enough for me,' Marcus chuckled. 'There are not many honest men left.'

The head of the line was marked by two junior officers who were not of their cohort. They were stern-faced and in full armour. Behind them, at the muddy bottom of the field, was a ragged troop of legionaries, somehow managing to project discontent by the set of their shoulders and the disappointment on their faces. A centurion, wearing helmet and plumes, stood nearby, whilst other men, each armed with twin javelins and with short swords drawn, guarded the line of carts.

'As if, after yesterday, anyone would dare to steal,' said Quintus under his breath.

'And yet...' added Marcus, raising an eyebrow as a scuffle broke out at the head of the queue. Over what, they did not know. It was quickly quashed with a barked reprimand from the officer that any sign of indiscipline would be dealt with harshly.

Finally, they reached the front to find that they were standing in thick mud, churned by the many feet that had preceded them. They stood on a small, raised area, like a rostrum. Marcus lifted his sandals out of the mire and shook them, glancing disapprovingly from under his brows at his companion.

Quintus saw the look. 'You blame me for the conditions?' he asked.

'Not the conditions, no, for who can control the weather?' Marcus held his hand out to test how much light spring rain still fell. 'But for the delay, yes, and for our place in this line. I fear the best of everything will be gone.'

'I thought we needed to know his history,' Quintus said.

'Don't worry. We did,' Marcus replied. As he spoke, he pointed towards the dwindling number of legionaries still waiting by the officer. They were being allocated at random to any contubernium that lacked a full complement. They were the ones who would bring the cohort back to near full strength.

'They are not the best of us,' said Marcus dismissively, waving his arm at them. 'Why would a commander give us his best? They are sick, or criminal in some way, or unblooded boys. Look at them.' He patted Quintus' shoulder. 'I am glad we do not need them,' he went on with a smile. 'That is your doing.'

As he spoke, two of the men were detailed to join the head of the queue. One looked about fourteen, fresh-faced and eager, but with a vacant look. The other was around forty, with a scowl and a limp. They were questioned briefly, and a mark was made on a tablet.

'You are the decanus?' one of the officers asked.

'Not I,' said Quintus, jerking his thumb at Marcus. 'He.'

They had not realised that they had reached the front as they watched the boy and the veteran depart, along with two of the contubernium they were joining, leading a mule and cart between them.

'I am Appius Marcus Saturninus.'

The legionary was not interested in the name. 'How many men do you have left in your contubernium?'

As he said this, the other officer started to beckon to the remaining legionaries. Two of them, both gruff and odious-looking, detached themselves slowly.

'We are complete,' Marcus said quickly. 'We have our eight. We need equipment and slaves, not men.'

The soldier scowled and waved the men back into line; they complied reluctantly.

'Tell him what you need,' said the officer, indicating a clerk standing with a tablet near the carts. 'He will record it.'

They approached the man.

'A cart and a beast, a tent and a millstone,' said Marcus. 'We have a cooking pot.'

'Wheat instead of barley,' dared Quintus.

'Unlikely,' said the clerk disdainfully, 'at least not yet.' He signalled to his left and a cart was trundled forward.

Quintus immediately stepped across and assessed the animal pulling it, looking into its eyes and its mouth, investigating its ears for mites and lice, its jaw for signs of weakness. The mule resisted, shaking its head — a good sign. Quintus nodded to Marcus, although in truth they had no choice but to accept the beast.

'Weapons, clothes, armour?' the clerk asked, unable to suppress a smile at Quintus' inspection.

Marcus said, 'For the most part we have our armour, but we need weapons.'

'So, choose.' The clerk indicated a pile of blades, some nicked, some showing signs of poor maintenance, but he seemed unconcerned about how many were taken. Spears were leant against each other in pyramid shapes, points upward. Quintus grabbed a bundle, flinging them into the cart.

'And slaves,' said Marcus, pointing at the group of unarmoured men trying not to shiver in the rain. Their plain and undyed tunics clung to them, their legs were bare and they wore thin leather shoes. He squinted at the group, trying to pick out features. 'Ours are not here,' he said.

'They have all been reallocated,' explained the clerk, wearily. 'There is no loyalty amongst slaves.'

'There was,' Marcus said under his breath, remembering those with whom he had shared laughter.

'Two,' ordered the clerk, and two men stepped forward as he bent to make a mark on his tablet.

The first of the pair seemed to stumble, knocking into his companion, who lost his balance and his footing, dropping to one knee in the mud. As he fell, another man pushed forward and past him, joining the one who had caused the fall. Marcus and Quintus witnessed this little episode, whilst the clerk, his attention elsewhere, failed to see anything amiss. Marcus was about to speak, but Quintus placed a restraining hand on his arm as he saw the pleading look in the slaves' eyes and the similarity in the two men's faces.

'They may be brothers,' he said quietly.

'Or lovers,' smiled Marcus. 'All right, we will accept them as the will of the gods.'

'They are Macedonian,' said the clerk conversationally. 'None of the Iberian tribes wanted to be of service. Even when captured, they still managed to poison themselves — or make such a nuisance of themselves that they were more trouble than use.'

As they made their way back up the hill, one of the slaves leading the mule, Quintus asked their names. The taller one, who had the beast's sparse mane under his hand, said, 'I am Maxim, and he is Jovan. We had other names when we were free, but they are forgotten until we are free once more.' Without being asked, he continued with his history. 'I was a farmer, and now I cook as well; Jovan was an educated man, a factor who could read and write and calculate.'

'For now, you are still an animal keeper and a cook,' said Marcus flatly, 'though there is little here for you to show your skill.' He tapped the half sack of barley that bounced in the cart along with the weapons. As he did so, Quintus noticed a few leather packages in the bottom of the cart, which he picked up with curiosity. 'They look like...' he began.

'They are,' confirmed Marcus. 'Personal wills, messages for home, those that a partner did not manage to grab before we were marched away.'

'They are sacred,' whispered Quintus, as he turned one over with his fingers, 'and they should be returned.'

'They should,' said Marcus. 'We will find a way.'

V: OPTIO

'Your friend says you can read,' Marcus said to the slave walking beside the cart.

'I read, master,' said Jovan flatly, 'but it is not a skill that has been called on for a long time. I am more used to manual labour.' He was a dark man, with black hair, a black beard and dusky skin, while his hands, Quintus noticed, were long-fingered and expressive — more expressive than either his face or voice.

'When we are settled,' said Marcus, pointing to the rest of the tent-party who were waiting higher up the slope, 'you will read the names on the leather packages and try to find the owners in the camp. Can you do that?'

'I can,' Jovan said. He indicated the other slave. 'May I speak with him?'

'If it does not interfere with your duties,' Marcus replied with mock solemnity.

'Are you brothers?' Quintus asked as Jovan walked to the other side of the mule's head. 'You look very similar.' Maxim was also tanned, with dark hair, the same shaped face and nose, and the same black beard — though his was just a little shorter.

'Cousins,' said Jovan. 'Our fathers were brothers, both killed fighting in the Roman wars.' Quintus noted that to the Romans it was always this or that campaign, or expedition, or conquest. To everyone else, the words 'war' and 'Roman' were enough to describe any conflict of the past forty years.

'We were raised by a Greek relative, a distant cousin, but one who appreciated the value of literature, mathematics and art.' Jovan became pensive and added quietly, 'He too was killed by the invader.'

'At least we have managed to stay together,' said Maxim, 'though only just.' He touched the fingertips and palms of his hands together in a gesture of thanks.

Quintus acknowledged the action with a nod. Marcus said nothing but dropped back behind the cart and beckoned to Quintus to join him.

'Tell me about Tullius,' he said in a low voice. 'What is his story?'

By the time they'd reached their patch of dry grass, hardly touched by the brief rain shower, Quintus had told him the tale of the lost contubernium and the cornicen that was no trumpeter. Marcus listened impassively and then greeted Tullius as an old friend, saying, 'You are welcome and one with us, though we are diminished.'

Tullius raised his eyebrows inquiringly.

'We lost the best of us,' said Marcus sadly, in response to the implied question. 'Our leader, my friend,' he went on with more than a little anger. He took a deep breath and continued to speak with feeling. 'A man with a wife and a child in Rome; a man who had served more than his time with the Ninth and had served with great Caesar; a man who should have been released from service long since.' He lifted his chin and looked directly at Tullius. 'You and I have seen service, and we may be fated to never leave, but he had left. He had his farm, his woman, his life. He deserved to snooze in the sun.' He shook his head, and opened his arms, encompassing in the gesture Publius and Cato, who were laughing as they unfolded the tent.

'I do not know which is worse — losing the young, with all their optimism, innocence and enthusiasm…'

Tullius interrupted, jerking his thumb at Sextus, who seemed to be industriously managing to do nothing. 'Not all of them are enthusiastic,' he said.

'I think he has seen some of life's sting,' said Marcus sympathetically. 'Even so, is it worse to lose the likes of him, lazy but young, or those like Ursus, who have earned their rest?' His voice tailed off and his eyes momentarily glazed over at the memory of his friend.

Tullius opened his mouth, closed it again, and then spoke softly, more to himself than to Marcus. 'My amicus was taken in circumstances as bad, if not worse — though I did not have to deal the blow myself.'

'I know,' said Marcus. 'Mac told me all. I do not need to hear it again.'

'Mac?' Tullius queried.

'Macilentus, a nickname — perhaps you should have one? Mal Fortuna seems appropriate, but…' Marcus shook his head and smiled. 'It is a little cruel. Mac at least deserves his — look at him!'

'Skinny, indeed,' said Tullius and the two, already understanding one another, smiled at their lanky fellow soldier.

'Accept it all as the will of the gods,' said Marcus, with finality. 'We can do no more; we live or die at their behest. The past is gone. We start afresh today. Come…'

They set to with the younger men to help pitch the tent.

They waited for three days, whilst half-hearted curtains of light rain pulsed across from the west — enough to irritate but not enough to confine the legionaries to their tents. The rain caused fires to spit, and there was only wet wood and green wood to feed them. As a result, the field was obscured by smudges of smoke, regularly whipped away by the swirling breeze.

The men still trained. Many were morose, still smarting from their shame. Others shrugged their shoulders in acceptance: this was just how it was, being a soldier. The gods smiled upon you or they laughed at you; you could not predict which.

The cohort, though still understrength, had quickly been organised into a proper military camp. Officers had moved tents, so that the members of each century were together and in proper order. Marcus and Quintus' contubernium had, through this process, lost their little patch of dry ground and were now closer to the base of the hill and to the river. The favoured — the command tent with the prefect in the centre — were at the top of the field. Latrines were dug, rules enforced, order maintained and training resumed.

Quintus and Crassus were sparring partners and fought each other regularly, sometimes with encouragement from one of the older legionaries. They practised striking, thrusting and parrying, the hops and sidesteps as familiar to them as the steps of a wood pigeon's mating ritual.

Crassus was older than Quintus and more experienced, though like most men he was shorter than him. He was stronger, but not as quick, so they made a good match for each other. Crassus was also dark and muscular, the evidence of his exertion quickly manifesting itself as perspiration. Sweat oozed swiftly from his scalp, saturating his thick curly hair and prickling the back of his neck, which was as solid as a bull's.

He jabbed with loud, frenetic energy. Each thrust and cut was accompanied by a shout, often an imprecation directed at himself, or a curse to the gods and fates.

Quintus was fair, lithe and lanky. He moved smoothly, like a cat, with the minimum expenditure of energy. Every move was quiet and calculated; he did not even draw harsh breaths, and seemingly only a little sweat spotted his pale brow. They fought with pairs of javelins, short spears, or with swords and shields. When not sparring, they practised throwing the pilum. Crassus was better at this than Quintus, so he became his trainer.

Around them others also practised in pairs, wearing full kit and working up a lather of sweat. At the end of the day, they splashed river water, fetched by the slaves, on their heads and necks. Then they gambled, ate the poor rations that were on offer, and slept fitfully, many plagued by nightmares and dark visions.

Throughout this time, they subsisted on barley, with no meat, no garlic, little salt, and little olive oil. The slaves could not bake flatbread in the fickle flames, so morning, noon and night the men ate gruel. Quintus took Maxim with him along the riverbank, and together the farmer and cook managed to find herbs and roots for flavouring. Sextus, bored with the diet, vanished on the morning of the third day and returned a few hours later with a duck, its neck broken and its head swinging dolefully. It wasn't a lot to share between eight men, but it was better than most were eating.

Jovan read the names on the five leather-wrapped packets that had been found in the cart and moved around the camp, calling them out to each tent-party. Two were pronounced dead by comrades, and for only one of these did anyone offer to take charge of the message. Two more were claimed by their owners, the last identified by none. The following night another slave, following Jovan's example, appeared by their own tent, reciting names.

'None of us,' Marcus was glad to be able to say. 'Our contubernium stayed mostly whole.'

Somehow word of this was relayed to the prefect, and Marcus found himself the object of unwanted attention. A centurion approached their fire, flanked by four men. 'You are the decanus?' he demanded. Then, not waiting for an answer, he went on, 'You kept your party together?'

'For the most part,' Marcus said cautiously. 'We lost our previous leader in the … punishment.'

'He was an optio?'

'He was — a good man and a good trainer. Ursus, he was called.'

The centurion was not interested in the name; instead, he ordered Marcus to follow him. Quintus and the others had seen the detail at their tent, ceased their training and returned to their little area. They were concerned that their new decanus had been singled out for some extra punishment.

Night was falling by the time Marcus returned — whole and undamaged, to the relief of the others. Quintus was first with the question they all had on their lips.

Marcus gave a harsh laugh. 'I have been given Ursus' rank,' he said sourly. 'The prefect rewards me for killing my friend. I am now the optio of our century.'

The men wanted to congratulate him, but they held back awkwardly, realising that this honour came with a bitter taste. Finally, while fiddling with his wrecked ear and the ring that hung from it, Tullius mumbled in embarrassment, 'You will grow into it, my friend.' He ushered the others away, leaving Marcus staring dejectedly into the petulant fire.

Early on the morning of the fourth day, from their position near the entrance to the field through which they had originally come, a party appeared, led by an aquilifer. He was carrying one of the legion's eagles and wore a lionskin cloak, the head of the animal covering his own. He was flanked by two officers and accompanied by six legionaries carrying a pole on which was slung a live goat, bleating pathetically. They marched towards the commander's quarters as the officers of the cohort roused the men and ordered them into a square.

Quintus noted that it was a smaller square than it should be. There were no longer six full centuries, and there appeared to be few mounted men. 'I hope that we are not going into battle without reinforcements or reserves,' he said in an aside to Sextus.

'Some cavalry, at least,' came the response.

'We will march to battle tomorrow, whatever the entrails say,' Tullius offered cynically. 'It is a full moon, the ides of the month — sacred to Jupiter.'

'I think we will go hunting, remember, not into battle,' said Marcus.

'Surely a hunt requires horses?' Sextus' question went unanswered as their centurion looked sideways at Marcus. He clearly thought he should have been keeping discipline, not adding to idle talk.

'Silence!' the centurion bellowed. 'The prefect speaks.'

The prefect, again raised on a platform, though this one was smaller than the last — more of a podium than a platform — spoke at a conversational level to the men, and his words were shouted by the centurion who stood on the ground at his side.

'Men,' he said, 'if the auguries are favourable, we march tomorrow.' When the men cheered, he added, 'And you will march on wheat, not barley.'

No-one knew who the prefect's household gods were, or who was his own special favourite in the pantheon — though it was rumoured he was a Flavian, so Mars would not be far away. But all knew that, as priest and prefect, this sacrifice would primarily be to Capitoline Jove. Clearly a white lamb was unavailable, so a scrubby brown goat would have to do.

There was little ceremony. A tripod had already been set up, and smoke and flame could be seen rising from it. The sudden silencing of the bleats told the men who could not see that the goat's throat had been cut, while the sizzle and rising smoke indicated that the entrails had been offered to Jove on the fire.

The pronouncement that the omens were good came as no surprise to the older soldiers, or to those who had been watching the growth of the moon. The order to break camp and march at first light the following day followed shortly. The men were dismissed, their stomachs growling at the smell of the roasted goat meat that was wafting from the prefect's tent.

In the uncertain first light of the morning, before the sun had risen, the tent, cooking pot and millstone were loaded aboard the cart. What grain they had, along with some of the personal gear of the legionaries, was tied to the mule. Little other equipment was to be allowed to follow, other than that required by the prefect and officers. Their abrupt departure meant that, though the slaves and carts would bring up the rear, there would be none of the usual camp followers. So they would have no wine merchants, no moneylenders, no barbers or hair-pluckers, and, saddest of all, no women.

Most of the equipment would be carried by the legionaries themselves. Each of them stood with their bundles of small weapons, spades, mattocks, tools and eating utensils tied to their crosspieces, ready to hoist them onto their shoulders when ordered. These were heavy packs, but learning to carry them easily was part of their training. They had eaten earlier — the usual barley gruel flavoured with river herbs.

'Typical — barley, not wheat as promised,' Sextus had complained, as he cleaned his bowl with his spoon.

'Tonight, with the help of the gods, I will make bread,' offered Maxim, as he began to douse the fire.

'Never mind the gods — use the wheat,' Rufus laughed, slapping the slave on the back just a little too roughly.

The slave staggered but managed to smile and nod.

'Rufus,' said Quintus, 'why do you treat him so?'

'I lost friends in his country,' the redhead replied dourly. 'Perhaps he killed them.'

'And how do you manage that?' Quintus asked Sextus in mock amazement, wanting to deflect Rufus' ire. Sextus was just fitting his helmet, polished and shining, onto a head that looked like it had spent the past few days at the barbers and bathhouse rather than in a muddy field. He was clean-shaven and his hair was combed and tidy, without so much as a smudge of dirt on his healthy, shining face.

'I have people,' he grinned, 'or people skills. You choose.'

'Look,' said Cato. He was already prepared to leave and was helping Publius with his straps. At the entrance to the field, a small troop of horses was trotting in, leading a few spare ponies. 'We have scouts, if not cavalry.'

'But no eagle,' said Publius sadly. 'They took it back.'

'Hopefully they did not take our luck with it,' said Marcus. 'Come, we march.'

They began by shadowing the bubbling river south. This part was easy going, though boggy in places and narrow in others, where trees strode down to the water's edge. They started quietly, still in the half light of early morning, getting used to the weight of their armour, the familiar burden of their helmets and the way they made them look only forward, obscuring whatever happened left and right. They shook out the knots in their shoulders and backs, and adjusted the balance of their swords, shields, spears and marching packs. They had quickly turned into soldiers once more, knowing that they were not yet forgiven and still had to wipe away the taint of their shame.

The sun cleared the hills and trees, and the breeze strengthened. The morning was becoming blustery, with a pale blue sky and small clouds, and there was the smell of rain on the wind but none yet falling. As the light grew, one legionary started a song. His deep baritone voice carried well, and the simple call and response quickened the men's pace. Slowly, their heads rose and they became a unit, marching and singing bawdy songs. There was flat land to either side of the river, some of it cultivated, and the sound of the running water lifted their spirits.

'Are you not happy to be on the move?' Quintus asked Tullius, who marched alongside him but did not join them in song. He looked despondent.

'I cannot be merry until Appius is avenged,' he muttered.

'Appius?'

'My murdered friend,' he snapped.

Quintus had not truly forgotten, but for the moment he had put Appius out of his mind. It was also the first time in days that he had heard the man named. He was about to apologise but then thought better of it; it might rub salt into Tullius' wounds. He did not dare to continue singing whilst this man simmered beside him. Eventually, he asked in a low voice, 'What vengeance do you seek, my friend?'

Tullius replied simply, 'The centurion who gave the order still lives. I would see him dead.' He turned to face Quintus, his scar catching the light. 'Sing, boy.' He smiled just a little, a crooked smile. 'It is not your problem. Sing.'

With the camps and fires, with the songs and the marching feet, the rumour of the Roman advance echoed far up the mountainside.

Many warriors — Cantabrians, Astures, and others from tribes who the legion thought were defeated — had fled to the mountains and established camps and rough settlements for the winter. They had braved the raw winds and swirling snows so that now, when the spring came and the invaders set foot on their mountains, they were ready. Some of these warriors had allegiance to kings and chieftains now dead, some to gods of war and carnage. Some had cousins in the settlements that the Roman troops had burned. Some had wives from families on the plain or in the coastal regions. Many had sons and daughters married into the ancient tribes.

Some of them, it was rumoured, were led by a female warrior who had been captured by the invaders, enslaved and separated from her husband. He had been sold into a life at sea and had met death still pining for his mountains and his family. His son and daughter were also dead by Roman hands. Only his grandson, still a boy, remained. It was he who had risked his life to rescue his grandmother, spiriting her back to the mountains, where she had become the point of the rebellion's spear and the needle in the Ninth's side. She had tactical and strategic nous, was rumoured to be tall and impossibly beautiful, and was certainly a sorceress — she might even have been a goddess. Stena was her name and her reputation, her legend, caused at least as much fear as her presence.

Not only did the tribes have leadership, arms and determination, but they were also willing to die. They were determined to punish the Romans, take back the land they had stolen and free their slaves.

But determination and resolve were never going to be sufficient to regain their lost lands. Most of the tribes knew that all they could ask for was a measure of revenge, and it was for this that they prayed to their gods. They stayed out of sight, below the skyline and behind the rocks and rises of the mountain, stealthily tracking the marching column and waiting for an opportunity to strike.

VI: GNAEUS CRASSUS MALLEOLUS

After a day's tramp, the cohort had stopped to set up camp by the river. The last few miles had been difficult. It had become impossible to march. The soldiers had stumbled over boulders and stony tracks, which often narrowed as the forest strode down almost to the water's edge, threatening to pitch the men into the fast-flowing water. Many of the more experienced legionaries found themselves using the pole of their crosspiece as a walking aid. Whilst this was not as efficient as marching with it slung over a shoulder, it was the best way to make progress on such terrain — and the best way to keep feet dry.

Now, as any evidence of the sun vanished into cloud and the day cooled noticeably, they had found a bend in the river. Within it was flat ground and grass, a place to stop.

By the time the men had unwrapped their packs, established a perimeter, dug trenches and levelled the ground for their commander, their slaves and mules had caught up, bringing cooking pots, utensils, ropes and tents. The slaves were detailed to collect firewood — abundant here and, miraculously, dry under the forest canopy. Meanwhile, some legionaries mounted guard and others pitched tents. Instructions and orders echoed around the space.

Quintus' contubernium lacked its leader. Marcus, as optio, had been given other duties by their centurion. There were still many of what the veterans dismissively referred to as 'rabbits' — new recruits, young and untried. They were less than four months out of Rome and needed training. Marcus was running them through drills and formations, sometimes using his voice to encourage and cajole, sometimes using the trumpeter who stood close to him, so that he could blow the command.

The men — or boys, as the other soldiers would have it — were all in full kit and lathered in sweat. They were desperate to see an end to their day, to pull off the hard leather of their heavy hobnailed caligae and soak their feet in the cooling waters of the river. Even though the light was fading, their shadows could be seen in the gloaming, going through the drills of striking, thrusting and parrying with the gladius while manoeuvring the tall, curved shield. The gathering dark eventually came to their rescue.

'That could be us,' Quintus smiled to Crassus as they helped to erect the heavy tent. The first two inches of ground yielded easily, but the deeper ground still hard from winter.

'I learned those manoeuvres on the Campus Martius,' Crassus replied as he took the heavy mallet from Quintus and hammered the peg he had been working on into the ground with ease. 'They should have done the same.'

'I think they did,' Quintus said, turning down Crassus' offer to return the mallet with a raised palm. 'They have just not had time to make it second nature.'

'My father always said that it was better to learn drills patiently, somewhere where you were not about to be killed if you got it wrong, rather than in the noise and dust of battle.' Crassus became more thoughtful. 'I suspect it was these rabbits who ran.'

'Or who obeyed the call of the trumpet,' Quintus excused them.

'My father obeyed the call of the trumpet,' Crassus mused as they fixed the last of the guy ropes and stood back to admire their handiwork.

The slaves Jovan and Maxim had worked in tandem to unload the mule and to light and feed the fire, so that the flames were now high. They had fetched water and were even now in the process of making decent bread and a store of the thrice-baked biscuits that sustained the men on the march, Maxim instructing his cousin.

Sextus and Rufus were a little way off, pretending to take care of the mule and probably plotting some way of avoiding duty. Tullius was humming softly to himself as he sat on a rock, cleaning his equipment.

Cato was morose and quiet, his bottom lip thrust out in a sulk. He refused to see the funny side of a joke played on him by Publius. The large green and brown frog he had found in his helmet had hopped away unperturbed, but on discovering it the legionary had stepped back and fallen over one of the taut guy ropes, sitting down hard, an easy target for the men's laughter. Publius played practical jokes on Cato that he took in good humour for the most part. He seldom lost patience, but sometimes he found Publius' humour just a little too wearing. At this moment, it was making him mutter and frown. But everyone knew that they would soon have their arms around each other's shoulders once more.

Later, Quintus and Crassus sat near the fire, bellies for once full now that wheat was restored. They were also warmed by the flask of wine that Sextus had triumphantly produced.

'Where did your father serve?' Quintus asked Crassus, resuming their earlier conversation.

'He was here first, in Hispania, then later in Greece and Macedonia. He managed to come home a couple of times, hence me and my brother,' Crassus replied dismissively, as if he had no interest in the doings of his father.

'Are you not proud of him?'

'Not really, no. He did his duty to the state — not to his family.'

Quintus sensed that there was more to be told, but that it would not be forthcoming if he did not listen with subtlety. He did not seek to look into men's souls, but for some reason others opened up to him and he had learned to lend his ear sympathetically. He asked, in as offhand a way as he could manage, 'Did he serve with a famous legion? Fight in any battles?'

Crassus sniffed scornfully. 'A famous legion, indeed — the Equestris. Great Caesar's favourite. A legion of traitors and back-stabbers.' He turned his face to Quintus, the flickering flames lighting only half of it. His eyes narrowed under deep brows. 'He was in the Tenth — recruited to the Old Tenth that mutinied against Caesar.'

Everyone knew the story. The Tenth had been raised by Caesar and had been with him throughout the Gallic wars, and even when he marched on Rome. They had been heroes until they had turned on him and the citizenry, demanding their back pay. Caesar had persuaded them to fight on in the civil war, promising them land, farms and livestock. They had redeemed their honour by wiping out the army of the republic near Osuna on the plains of Munda, destroying Caesar's last opponents — though, to some, they had tarnished their eagles by being too barbaric and bloodthirsty. They had a palisade out of captured weapons and bodies, mounting severed heads on swords to face what remained of the enemy.

'Was he at Munda?' Quintus asked with awe. The battle was famous for its ferocity. No prisoners had been taken; some thirty thousand men under the command of Pompey's sons had been killed.

'It was a bloody slaughter about which he would not speak,' Crassus said softly. 'I think even he was ashamed.'

'But Caesar was true to his promise?'

'He was. My father was demobbed with the rest and offered land in Gaul.' Crassus spoke with disappointment. 'But he turned it down and ignored the needs of his family. He said he could not farm — he was a blacksmith, from a line of blacksmiths; he needed to work with metal. We even carry the name Malleolus. But he had no forge and no smithy, so instead he joined the new Tenth, raised by Lepidus, the legion dedicated to Venus. He did not want to come home.'

'Perhaps he did,' said Quintus kindly. 'We legionaries do not always have a choice.'

'Oh, he had a choice all right,' Crassus sighed scornfully. 'He turned down land in Gaul, and he turned down discharge in Rome.' He spoke quickly, angry now. 'He won an armband for bravery at the battle of Actium and was offered an honourable discharge by Octavius after the legion switched sides. Three fingers were gone from one hand, and he had a deep spear wound in his thigh that made him lame. By then, my mother had bought the smithy — she was a smart businesswoman.' He said it with pride, then continued to despair at his other parent. 'He could have come home and been Vulcan of the Forge. Three times he turned down honourable discharge. Three times. Instead, he stayed with the Tenth, was complicit in their next rebellion, and was dishonourably discharged. He was denied his pension and was lucky to keep his life.' Then, with a tinge of regret, he added, 'He missed my childhood almost completely.'

Quintus, realising that Crassus was hurting, tried to steer the conversation onto another course, asking, 'Did he not want you to join the army?'

Crassus stared into the flickering fire, the slaves still flitting around it, making preparations for the next meal. 'What choice, in truth, do we have? What does the state care what anyone wants?'

'I know.' Quintus put an arm around his friend's shoulder, feeling that he needed to give him comfort. 'But fathers can make it happen sooner or later, can encourage or discourage, and can even keep their sons away from war altogether if they try hard enough.'

'Or if they have too much or too little money,' Crassus scoffed. He was thinking of those ancient families whose sons would only ever be commanders or generals. Such men could sit atop a horse, well away from death or injury until their legions were victorious and they could enjoy a triumph. Some families could even keep their precious boys out of uniform altogether. 'The rich will avoid danger if they can.'

Quintus nodded in agreement, adding, 'As will the poor — those who scavenge, beg for food, sleep under the open sky. Those whose names and citizenship are in doubt.'

Crassus looked across to where Sextus was smiling at some in-joke with Rufus. 'For them, the army can be an escape. There are boys in the city who run errands, who load and unload on the wharves, and who act as go-betweens for gamblers and criminals. Boys like Sextus, there, who are runners for whores and can even climb into the beds of Roman matrons.' They both knew that Sextus had bedded the prefect's wife almost on the day that she had arrived, the first of many. He added darkly, 'There are others who avoid service entirely.'

Quintus was about to ask who, but Crassus continued bitterly, shrugging off the arm on his back and shaking out his dark curls. 'Those boys die in the winter cold, or by a felon's knife. They fall into the Tiber or are spirited away to become a slave, or worse, an old man's catamite. They are swept away unmourned with the detritus of the night, as if they had never drawn breath.'

He paused. Quintus could hear him breathing hard and guessed that this outburst was linked to a memory, a painful one. The noises of the night, the shouts of soldiers gambling and joking, all seemed far away. Only the crackling of the fire seemed to fill the silence. He asked gently, 'Who did you lose?'

Crassus took a deep swallow from the wineskin and spoke in a whisper, facing the fire rather than his friend. 'I had an older brother, seven years older than me. My father put him in charge of the forge when he went to war, when I was but this high.' He indicated a point about four feet from the ground. 'He was foolish — no, not foolish, stupid, really. He became a young man with no-one to offer him a guiding hand. He turned into a tyrant to me and our mother, and he drank and caroused too much. He got into debt. There were men in the city that he owed money to. They could have taken it in blood if they had wished.'

He looked up, the firelight reflecting off a tear in his eye. 'But they wanted payment, not blood. They took him from the forge; they laughed and said that he was pretty — he was dark, like me, with hair like mine.' He twisted a curl in his fingers. 'They said that he would fetch a good price. My mother understood more than I what they said, and she screamed. They silenced her with a blow, took him and left me crying. As they left, they knocked a red-hot iron to the floor.'

He shook his head sadly. 'Clumsiness and the fires of the forge do not make good companions. The man was burned, as the iron fell across his ankle and foot. I like to think it festered, that he killed himself, but that is but a dream.' He took a deep breath. 'Only by the will of the gods did the forge not burn down — myself and my mother in it.'

He offered the wine to Quintus, who took it. Thinking of his own favoured brother, he said, 'Yet you survived…'

'We survived,' Crassus confirmed unemotionally. 'The men never returned, but nor did we see my brother again. We comforted each other and, before I had even put on my manly gown, I became the blacksmith. I had always helped, so I knew the secrets of the forge. My mother had always been the one who dealt with the customers — smiling at them and giving them greater respect than they deserved. She also kept the accounts. It was, for both of us, a time of peace.'

'Yet here you are. Could you not have avoided service and remained the blacksmith?' Quintus drank from the wineskin, wiped his mouth and gave it back to Crassus. He knew that some — with influence, with money, maybe with trades and skills, could avoid the army.

'Not once my father returned,' Crassus confirmed acidly, as he accepted the drink. 'He was bitter, broken and would never again be himself. He blamed me for the disappearance of my brother. He wanted to know why I had not sought out the criminals.' He now looked directly at Quintus, as if challenging him to gainsay him. 'I had. I had spent time in the stews and pits of the city, too much time. My father thought I was gambling, drinking and whoring. He could not believe it of my brother, but he happily believed it of me.' He lowered his eyes, drank, and passed the flask back. 'In time, he was right.'

'I clearly never knew the city,' said Quintus quietly, taking only a sip before lowering the wineskin. 'I only saw it on market and festival days.'

'I learned to know it well.' Crassus' attention wandered. 'There were women…' He snapped back to himself. 'But mostly I did not like it.' In a stronger voice, he took up the tale again. 'My father did not make staying at home a pleasant experience. To begin with, he wanted me there, working the bellows, fetching and carrying, delivering orders. In the end, he wanted me gone.'

Crassus pursed his lips and shook his head. 'I was never his favourite. He was frustrated by the loss of his eldest and the loss of his pension, and he took out his frustration on my mother. When I tried to stop him, he took it out on me. But I was no longer a little boy — I was faster and stronger than him, though he was more cunning and better trained than me. It took months but, eventually, we fought each other to a standstill. It was then that he was keen to see me gone. He took me to the Campus Martius each day, whilst at night I gave myself over to the cesspits of the city.'

He opened his arms wide and gave a sad half-chuckle. 'And that is how I joined up! During a night of drunkenness, I was robbed by a harlot. I came home to be scourged by my father's tongue and saddened by the bruises on my mother's face. It was on a whim that I stood beside you that day on the Campus Martius and was assigned to the Ninth. Before I left, I had one last blazing argument with my father. In his heart, he did not want me to go — but nor did he want me to stay. He was torn. He sobbed like a child on my shoulder and then cursed me out of the door, telling me that I would never return.' Crassus held out his hand for the wineskin, took one last pull and gave a hollow laugh. 'He cursed me to die in service. I have nothing to go back to. I can never return.'

Quintus was quiet. His own childhood had not been an easy one.

72

'Never return?' The deep voice of Marcus, unnecessarily loud, crashed into the space between the two legionaries. 'Why would you wish to? Don't you have everything you need here?'

'Except peace and quiet,' laughed Crassus.

'And gold and silver,' added Quintus.

'And wine,' offered Rufus, joining them and tipping the wineskin up to show that it was empty.

'And the soft curves of the fairer sex.' Sextus had also stepped across whilst outlining the shape of his dream girl, sadly absent, with two expressive hands.

'But we shall have battle,' insisted Marcus. 'What could be better?'

Cato and Publius had also joined the group, appearing from out of the shadows, apparently reconciled after the frog incident. Tullius continued to sit on his rock, cleaning his weapons diligently. Though all the contubernium sat near enough to the fire, eating, drinking and talking, each had been enjoying private moments or private conversation. They were all undoubtedly within earshot of one another, but when men lived in such close proximity, they learned to close their ears to those conversations that did not concern them.

Marcus had deliberately broken the spell. He had eaten with the centurion and other officers and had returned to urge the men to sleep, for, he told them, they would dismantle the camp before first light. Tomorrow they would choose a battlefield; tomorrow they would engage with the enemy.

VII: INSIDIAE

The men were used to having to rise before the dawn. The slaves were up and about even earlier; a fire was their first task, then water — and for those of their charges who wanted to shave, hot water.

One of the few things they could not do for their masters was perform their bodily functions, so the legionaries had to make their way to the river or latrines to relieve themselves. If they found they were leaving the camp, even temporarily, they would require the call and response password provided by the guard commander, the tesserarius. This password often echoed events that had just passed or foreshadowed events that were to come. The watchword on this dull morning was 'the storm is breaking', which seemed to refer to the unsettled skies, mottled with clouds that hid the dawn. The response of 'over our enemies' heads' let the men know that it was not weather-related, but more an indication that there would be action this day.

Quintus looked up from his ablutions at the sound of horsemen approaching the camp entrance and being challenged. His instinct was to grab his sword and armour, but he knew to listen first, to see if the arrivals were friends or enemies. They had some cavalry with them, a small troop which, thinking itself better than foot soldiers, marked out its own portion of the camp. A glance confirmed that, as far as Quintus could see, these horses were still in place. He waved away the bowl, and the patient slave with it.

'What is it?' asked Sextus, as he rolled back the heavy leather flaps of the tent. Though barely risen, he was immaculate —

clean-shaven, not a hair out of place, tunic looking newly washed, belt and its leather apron straps polished, silver ends shining. He called out to Jovan to bring his armour.

'Don't know yet,' responded Quintus, still wondering how Sextus did it. 'Seems like information rather than trouble.'

They could now see the small troop of horsemen. The ponies were blowing hard, their breath white on the morning air. Their riders were but lightly armed and armoured; they were clearly fast horsemen, used for scouting, pickets and guarding flanks.

'Our allies,' Quintus responded, without conviction — 'allies' were notoriously fickle, even more so when they were in their own lands. 'They have been scouting.'

The messengers were Iberian auxiliaries from tribes now supposedly loyal to Rome. They had been defeated, conquered and enslaved. Then they had rebelled and fought, almost winning a famous victory against Augustus' own kin, but they had been defeated again and severely punished. It was no wonder their loyalty was always in question. Still, they remained proud and would not pass their intelligence on to any common soldier, or even any officer.

They needed to report directly to the prefect, whose own tent — much larger and roomier than the men's — was already being rolled up by slaves under the pompous guidance of one of the Flavian's freedmen.

The leader of the troop dismounted and spoke with the commander, flanked by centurions and framed by the banners of the cohort. Fragments of the message could be heard by those close enough — words such as 'enemy', 'difficult', 'rough terrain', 'tracks', and 'climb'.

'Can you make anything out?' Cato had joined them with a couple of strides, not minding that he was towing Jovan, who was struggling to fasten the buckles and laces of the legionary's armour.

'Not really,' said Quintus. 'We will have to wait for Marcus to report to us. He is busy with our newer recruits.' He pointed to where Marcus was directing his trainees in dismantling their century's part of the camp.

'We will know soon enough,' said Cato, as he held his arms out to the side for Jovan to fasten his straps, whilst upbraiding the slave for his inefficiency.

As latrines and ditches were filled in, stakes removed, tents folded and lashed to mules, fires extinguished and the packs of the legionaries once more tied, the camp gradually vanished. They left little but circular scorch marks from their fires and flattened grass. Even the ditch and rampart that enclosed it all was destroyed, and the timber of the fortifications was fired. Nothing would be left for an enemy to use — everything was either carried away or destroyed.

And all this was done with an efficiency and order that was ingrained. Marcus had his trainees comb the ground for anything of use that might have been left, then released them to form up with their comrades, whilst he joined the group around the prefect and the messengers.

The prefect and his officers had already begun to discuss the reports. Some voices were more experienced than others, some just louder. Some claimed to have been in vaguely similar situations and could tell the rest what had succeeded, while others could offer little but speculation. The final decision would be made by the senior centurion, though it would need to seem to come from the politician. It would be announced as his strategy, though the legionaries knew otherwise.

The men themselves did not need to know what was happening; they had no part in strategy. Their role was to wait and obey. The scouts had brought valuable information — if it was true. The tracks of their quarry led away from the river into mountainous lands, rough underfoot and with steep-sided valleys. The terrain, Quintus heard the officers say, would be difficult if not impossible for the horses, mules and baggage carts. The troops could attempt to find a way around the mountains, but this would be slower, and they would be less certain of catching the enemy. But if they followed them, there would be no room for horsemen or scouts on the flank, so they would need to be wary.

It was a difficult decision, with some of the officers urging caution, knowing that these mountains were home to the tribes, and others supposing that, if these passes were so rugged, the Astures could not mount an effective attack.

The decision was made to try and follow. The centuries were ordered into a narrow marching formation — just four legionaries side by side, warned by their officers that even this might not be sustainable. Then came the mules, carts and equipment. The cavalry, who would kick up a cloud of dust, brought up the rear.

As the legionaries marched, the hills rose up on either side of them and underfoot it became narrower, rockier and more difficult. Soon the gullies became too cramped for four men, so they reduced to three. Then, as the hills became mountains and paths twisted and turned, they were forced to break formation completely. The mules, carts and slaves were strung out behind them. A decision should have been made to break the march and for legionaries to help with the baggage, but no-one of authority was looking behind. The cavalry came on at a mere walking pace.

The men were relieved when they came out of these uncertain ways into a wide area of flat earth, though the mountain hemmed it in and the sky above looked small. Ahead of them the path divided, going steeply up either side of a jagged outcrop. Rough steps had been cut into the rock, the centres of them smoothed with the passage of time. A halt was called, and the centuries were formed up on the flat ground.

'What do you think?' Quintus asked Rufus, who stood next to him. He was, in Quintus' eyes, one of the most experienced here.

'I think we should have found a way around,' said the older man emphatically. 'I think the idea to go through the mountains was madness.'

'But if we had gone around, we might never have caught them.'

'We haven't caught them yet, Mac,' grumbled Crassus, on his other shoulder.

'Do we go back and go around, or do we climb?' Quintus asked.

'We climb,' said the other two in unison, and in a tone that clearly accused Quintus of being at least naive, if not an idiot.

'Whilst we climb, we are exposed. Once we've climbed, we are safe — that is the logic, at least,' said Crassus.

Marcus, Rufus and Tullius, veterans all, did not like the part about being 'exposed'. They were worried — this was not their way of waging war.

Still, the centurions and the prefect discussed the possibilities at length, with the auxiliaries assuring them that above this climb was an area at least as broad and, more importantly, defendable.

The men could see that climbing was the only option anyway, and quietly wondered how it had taken a lengthy discussion for the officers to reach the same conclusion.

It meant dividing the cohort, reducing the advantage of numbers, and rendering the men unable to carry out any sort of manoeuvre. The centurion of the First, a big man who was popular, argued for his own century to take the lead. They were better climbers, better fighters, and would be able to hold the ground above. They would climb swiftly and lightly, with no support, relying on speed to keep them out of danger. Once they had dug in, the others could follow, escorting the mules and manhandling the carts. They would be slower, but the First could offer them protection. The cavalry would protect the rear, and their horses would be led up last. It would be a long few hours.

Tullius cursed as he scraped the back of his hand on a rocky crevice that he was having to grab to haul himself up. He would have preferred to have his sword held and ready, but this was not possible, and his shield was strapped to his back while he climbed with both hands.

Rufus was muttering — he did not like any of Rome's newly won allies and did not trust them. He was not convinced that these Iberians had not sent them into a trap. His route — he chose the right-hand side for luck — was particularly steep and, though he did not want to, he was forced to hand his pack up to the next man whilst he used both hands and knees to climb. Quintus was ahead of him, making good progress.

Marcus had gained the next level on the left — he was no believer in superstition; he just thought this side looked easier. He held out his hand to Cato, who was following him whilst surveying the scene below. The remaining legionaries were waiting to start the ascent, standing in as good order as they could manage. Jumbled together behind them were mules and slaves and carts. To the rear, the cavalry horses champed. The shadows thrown by the weak sun had already begun to lengthen and the temperature had dropped, though this made no difference to the sweat that dripped and dampened the neck-scarves of the climbers.

Most of Marcus' attention was on his comrades, although a small portion bemoaned the fact that tonight there would likely be no tents, no slaves to cook for them, and no warm food — the mules, though better equipped for mountains than the horses, would never make it to the top before dark. Whilst they were hardy and sure-footed, they would not manage this climb speedily. Marcus shook his head; the cohort would be vulnerable, split between top and bottom — an outcome that he had fervently hoped would not happen.

The cavalry would be the last to climb. Therefore, as protectors of the baggage, they would gain whatever comforts the slaves could supply if they stayed at the base. At the very least they would get hot food, and at best they would unpack some of the tents. Those above would not have such luxuries if the mules did not make it in daylight, although the various parts of the prefect's headquarters tent had already been manhandled up the slope.

Marcus shook his head — legionaries were exposed everywhere, unable to carry weapons in their hands and climbing over boulders and outcrops. Their comrades were doing their best to protect them with shields held high and eyes searching for enemies. The last of each group to be helped up was the most exposed, with no-one to provide them with protection. These men scrambled quickly, sometimes tripping in their haste.

Quintus had seen dim shapes shadowing them far above, phantoms on the skyline. As yet, there had been no solid evidence of their presence, but the legionaries could feel them and sensed that there were eyes — unfriendly eyes — on them.

The shadow men did as they had been instructed by their captain; they bided their time, waiting. They set their own watches, flitted from hiding place to hiding place, and spoke quietly or signalled to each other with silent hand gestures. They were patient, ready to take advantage when the opportunity arose. An arrow here, a spear there, and the Romans would have lost a man. But these tribesmen were disciplined. They did not want to take out one or two Romans and have the cohort turn on them; they wanted to stop the pursuit, so they prayed that a chance to do more would present itself. Maybe the enemy would be exposed by the lie of the land, a fallen tree, an incident, a betrayal...

Unexpectedly, it was the weather.

The sunlight had not been strong and there was a slight drizzle in the air, drifting in and out on a capricious breeze, but there was no sign of worse weather — at least not to those unversed in mountain craft. The weak sun flitted in and out of grey and white clouds that did not look to be a threat.

The storm first appeared as an innocuous small dark cloud at the end of the steep valley, a smudge almost, incongruous against the sky. The tribesmen had seen such weather before. They knew exactly what would happen as this little black cloud twisted and grew, coming closer and bouncing from one side of the narrow gorge to the other. It would pick up energy along the way, eventually blocking all light, as if a blanket had been thrown over the sky. Within its Stygian core, lightning flashed and the noise of its approach grew louder and louder. It was like an animal released from long captivity, thundering towards its helpless prey. A swirling wind was its harbinger, buffeting and battering the climbers as they clung to the rocks and outcrops. Hailstones stung wherever skin was exposed, and visibility was diminishing by the second. Then came the rain, a solid wall of water, driven hard by the gale.

The legionaries used the backs of their hands to wipe the rivers of water from their eyes. Instantly they were soaking wet, comforted only by the solid presence of their weapons and armour. They could see little through the driving downpour, which seemed to join ground and sky into one. The two routes, left and right, had no view of each other.

Valerius, centurion of the Sixth century — a decent climber who wanted to be an example to his men, recognisable by the plumes he wore on his helmet — never heard the swish and whisper of the spear that skewered him, nor saw the tribesman that had flung it. He drew a deep breath, transfixed by shock before he could lift his shield or draw his sword and turn to face his attacker.

The man next to him watched as his companion fell slowly, dropping his shield for no reason that he could immediately glean until he saw the weapon deeply embedded in the back of his neck, in the only vulnerable space between the base of his helmet and the top of his overlapping body armour. At once he thought of treachery, or sorcery, and would have shouted a warning had a spear not thudded into his own thigh. The javelin that had plucked the centurion from the rock face was perhaps a miraculous throw, but it was not the only one that had found a mark. A hail of spears hurtled towards the scattered legionaries, some finding thighs, some arms, some not finding flesh but instead knocking men from precarious positions.

Over the hammering of the wind and rain, shouts were heard. The strident note of a trumpet was cut short. The men knew that arms would be raised, urging men to form up, to turn and fight, and that centurions and optiones would be telling them what to do. But no orders could be heard, so though the men knew what was being asked of them and drew swords, they did not know what formations should be made. Unable to detect any commands or trumpets, they squinted through the curtains of rain, but they could see few of their comrades, and certainly no enemy.

The men crouched down behind shields and outcrops in small groups where possible, ready to fight. But this was not their sort of combat. They preferred a wide, flat expanse where they could outmanoeuvre an enemy, where they could hinder the foe's advance with the pilum, where they could wheel and march and change formation as a unit, protected by shields, comrades and discipline.

One minute the rain was lashing down, thunder rumbling, lightning streaking and it was as if night had fallen in the midst of day. Next minute, the storm rose over their heads, passed them by and continued its journey down the valley, still crashing from one side to the other.

The rain stopped as suddenly as it had started; the wind dropped and a deathly quiet descended. The sudden stillness was rent by a multitude of raised voices and screams of pain and suffering.

In moments a pale blue sky re-emerged, along with fluffy white clouds and a sun that seemed too bright to be true.

The sun — Helios, Apollo, the chariot of flame — promised warmth, light and life. It shone benevolently on pain, injury and death.

It shone on the deadly aftermath of the *insidiae*: the ambush.

VIII: DEDUCERE VELATOS FORTUNA

It was as if a maddened troop of bears had charged through an olive grove and these were the remnants. Legionaries were lying in various impossible positions, some killed and many injured by the spears, the fall or, to the amazement of the survivors who examined the bodies, by cuts to their throats beneath their helmets. It was hard to believe that the Asturian tribesmen had been so close, for there was no sign of them now. They seemed to have vanished entirely.

The cohort had been below full strength, and to lose so many men made it even weaker. Losing officers undermined it further. The Astures had, like the attackers in the wood, known who to target from their plumed helmets, their wolfskin cloaks or, in the case of the cornicines, the curve of their instruments. Whilst they had not managed to touch the cohort commander or his personal guard, and the banner of the cohort remained safe, they had slain signiferi, tesserarii, at least two centurions and two trumpeters — all vital to discipline and to passing on battle orders and tactics.

The ground, which just moments ago had been hidden in darkness with rain falling so hard that it bounced back up to knee height, was already drying. The remaining men looked with trepidation at the retreating black cloud with no knowledge of how such storms behaved. It appeared once again unthreatening, moving away from them, a smudge of smoke that grew smaller and smaller as it disappeared into the distance. Most had never seen such a phenomenon. Many feared witchcraft of some kind and called on their family gods and the gods of their legion to protect them. More than a few blamed the storm and the deaths on their lack of an eagle, though in their hearts they knew they were not entitled to one.

Quintus checked whether his comrades lived or died. Sextus, for once, failed to look immaculate. He had fallen down a steep slope, grazing both elbows. His highly polished helmet was missing, and his curly brown hair and handsome face were both streaked with ochre mud. Crassus sat at his feet. They had been together, and the legionary seemed to have suffered an injury, though Quintus did not know what. His amicus had waved him away impatiently with a lavish curse for good measure, so Quintus did not think it serious.

Tullius and Rufus could be seen with arms around each other's shoulders, helping one another to climb a rough track on the left. Quintus could not see the others, but nor did he recognise them amongst the dead and wounded at the foot of the climb. He remembered the charge that he had accepted from Ursus and shook his head, asking himself, 'How could I possibly keep them safe in such a situation?'

'Publius, my helmet!' Sextus shouted down the slope. 'It is there, by your feet.'

Quintus saw Publius now, standing with his back to the slope, hands on his knees, as if winded. He stood up slowly, sword in his hand, revealing an Asturian warrior beneath him, the red stain of death still spreading from his body.

'You got one!' shouted Quintus. 'Good work!'

'Not I, Mac!' Publius shouted back, shaking his head. 'I had him captured for information. He grabbed my dagger and killed himself.'

The two legionaries looked around to see if there were any captives at all, but though many Astures were now lying amongst the dead and dying of the cohort, none appeared to have survived. Some, with no sign of injury, had a yellow-green foam around their lips — lips that were curled back to reveal teeth in a terrifying rictus grin.

'Poison,' Publius said, gesturing at them as he replaced his dagger in its sheath. 'Yew, I would think.' Turning to face Quintus and Sextus, he asked softly, 'Cato?'

'I cannot see him amongst the dead and injured,' Quintus said, 'and I am able to see much from up here. Nor have I yet found Marcus, dead or alive.'

He could see a dead centurion and one of the trumpeters, his instrument reflecting the sun. Cato's dark skin would make him easy to spot.

'Nor I,' added Sextus. 'My helmet, Publius?'

Publius smiled and picked up the helmet, distinguished by its lustre through the dirt that marred it. He prepared to throw it up to Sextus.

'No, bring it,' Sextus said quickly. 'If the Astures have not managed to dent it, I would hate you to do so!' Like much of the soldier's gear, the helmet had known at least two previous owners, and their initials and the letters DVF were stamped into it. The helmet was still undented and Sextus was still alive, a situation he put down to the inscription '*deducere velatos fortuna*' — 'bring the wearer luck' — next to which he had incised his own initials.

Publius grim chuckle at the quip was drowned out by the many other raised voices. Some offered greetings, some asked questions, and some wailed in grief at a discovered loss. Woven into this tapestry were the cries of the injured and the echoing rumble from the storm as it dissolved into the distance.

A voice of command from the very top of the slope cut through — a centurion. 'Look to your comrades, collect the injured and report to me here.'

Another voice followed from behind the officer. What it said was indistinguishable to the men, but whatever it was, it made him change his mind. Someone had made a decision.

The centurion cupped his hands and called down the slope. 'All of you leave the dead, collect the walking wounded, and help everyone who will survive up here. I want all medics to me now. One of you bring me a tally of the dead and injured. The rest of you, climb up here.' He paused, had words with the other to whom he spoke, then took to yelling again. 'The barbarian will not return! He has fled.'

But this was clearly a report being delivered. It did not carry the ring of conviction.

'You men near the top…' He pointed to those that were still clinging on, frozen halfway up the climb. 'Get up here. There is work to be done.' He leant forward and called to the men further down. 'You men near the bottom, go down and help with the mules.'

There was some confusion towards the centre of the climb as men had to decide whether to go up or down, but within minutes legionaries were crawling across the red rock like ants, half climbing, half descending. They were not convinced by the centurion, but they would obey. The injured — at least the not too badly injured — were helped upwards to where they could be treated. The others, those beyond help, would each depart in his own way. Some took their own lives, some faded away in stoic silence, and some, though they would have wished it otherwise, screamed in agony.

Quintus, already at the top of the slope, was picked out by the officer.

'You,' the centurion said, 'are you a good climber?'

'Fair,' he called back.

87

'Then get down there and find the decurion. Tell him to use the auxiliaries as guides to find another way through these passes. There is another climb beyond this one that the horses will not manage.'

Quintus saluted and turned to start the descent.

'Leave your gear!' the centurion shouted. 'I want speed. Collect it when you report back to me.'

As Quintus dropped his pack and shield, he was one of the few able to hear what the centurion said next, speaking to whoever was standing behind him. 'At least this time they did not run. I suppose that is an improvement.'

There was confusion for a short time as men scuttled up or down the slope. The climb was difficult enough, the descent even more so, and more than one of them slipped and swore as he obeyed the command.

Quintus was no exception, grazing elbows and knees and, most annoyingly, the soft skin on the back of his legs as he slid down the slope. He had not thought it wise to remove his helmet, so he was sweating profusely by the time he reached the base and found the cavalry, still with much of the baggage train and still unmounted.

'Your decurion?' he demanded. 'I bear a message.'

On foot the horse soldiers were less haughty than when they sat a cubit or more above even a tall man.

'Behind,' said one of the riders, pointing. He held his helmet under his arm and gently stroked his horse's nose.

'A good mount?' Quintus asked quietly, the farmer in him coming to the fore as he cupped the horse's jaw in his hand.

'An expensive mount,' replied the cavalryman bleakly. Then he smiled and went on, 'But I love him.' Professional again, he gestured towards the decurion. 'There, the black crest.'

Quintus acknowledged his duty with a nod and carried the message to the commander.

'The baggage, the mules?' the officer asked tersely.

'They are to go on. The horses must find a way around.' At least, this was what Quintus had understood. 'The men will help.'

All the legionaries were helped up or cursed their way down, and they were organised into their centuries. The tally of the dead and injured and the severity of their injuries was now completed. By the time Quintus once more climbed the rocky slope to report his mission accomplished, the memory of the day was already starting to fade.

There was some good news: though signiferi had fallen — they were easy targets, after all — the enemy had not taken any of the standards, so the ill will of the gods had not fallen on the cohort. Some legionaries scratched their heads as to why such important trophies had been left behind, but the wise knew that, for this enemy, the speed and surprise of the attack and the ability to vanish into the mountains were more important than mere symbols.

All the Asturian tribesmen had left behind were the dead, either killed by Roman legionaries, or by their own hand, or by the ingestion of poison. Those killed should have had arms to strip, but there appeared to be no blades on them, and their poor coverings were of no use to a real soldier. The legionaries did not wish to touch the suicides, except to gingerly roll them to one side, their lips and faces already turning black. There was deep suspicion of an action such as poisoning on a battlefield, and many were concerned that whatever disease they had visited on themselves could be contagious.

The men were sanguine about who would live and who would die. Some wounds would take a man's shade at once, while others would cause a lingering and painful death. The medically trained in the cohort knew who would not see the morning and who would live to fight again. They, skilled in healing, would have to be as the Fates, deciding who could be saved and who should be allowed to drift away. They assessed wounds, cleaned them, sewed those that could be sewn, made those men who would not last the night as comfortable as they could, and quietly released some to end their suffering.

By the time all this was done, the sun had lost any warmth it had offered and was rapidly sinking towards the west. The last of the mules were resisting their masters' entreaties to move with loud complaints, but they were moved anyway. Slowly, all of the remainder of the cohort, bar the cavalry, travelled away from the danger that the exposed hillside still offered.

Night would come early in these mountains, the light of the day still kissing high peaks whilst the valleys were already cloaked in darkness. The sky had cleared, the clouds had melted, and the sun's afternoon heat had dried up any trace of the storm, but tonight it would be cold.

Makeshift shelters had been made from spears, shields and cloaks for the treatment of the injured, and the commander's pavilion was already pegged out in the centre of the space. It was a smaller area than they had camped on by the river, but the same principles applied. A number of men paced carefully over the space, driving in wooden stakes at regular intervals. As soon as these were marked out for each century, the slaves began to unpack the leather tents and to start fires. Each contubernium found its own tent, its own gear and its own slaves. Only then did some find that comrades had fallen.

Legionaries had also been tasked, by the centurion who had issued commands immediately after the action, to dig in and create a perimeter. At this level they were above the treeline and there was brushwood only, so a fortification or platform was not possible. A deep ditch would have to suffice.

Quintus and his companions grouped together with the rest of what remained of their century, which seemed to be now at less than half strength. They worried about the fate of Marcus and Cato, still missing. Neither had mustered with the rest of the legionaries; neither had been mentioned in the tally of the dead and injured. They were the only two numbered amongst the missing and had possibly been captured, though many suspected them of desertion.

Quintus was amongst those hacking at the hard ground with their trenching tools, the two-headed metal implements that all legionaries carried that had a digging blade on one side and a pickaxe on the other. Progress was slow; the ground, to their surprise, had not been softened by the deluge and resisted their efforts, so the men spent much of their time picking out rocks with the sharpened metal points of their tools.

This was not, Quintus thought, where any sensible commander would have chosen to camp. Much of it was bare rock, making the construction of a ditch and rampart impossible, and it was overlooked by more jagged outcrops and huge boulders — ideal ambush conditions.

At the western end of the campground one squad, who were working the section next to Quintus' contubernium, dared to ask their decanus if they had done enough. He, who continued to dig alongside them, took one look at their efforts and rewarded them with a string of oaths. Sullenly, they went back to work.

'That went well,' offered Rufus sarcastically, to no-one in particular.

'See to your own,' shot back the soldier nearest to him. 'It looks no better.'

'Nor is it,' Sextus admitted, 'but we did not ask for approval.'

'At least our decanus is neither a deserter nor dead.'

'Ours has not yet proven to be either,' Rufus replied slowly, clearly holding back his anger but also worrying about Marcus.

The man harrumphed and continued attacking the earth before pausing and leaning on his mattock, in the time-honoured way of resting workmen everywhere. 'How many years?' he asked Rufus.

'Sixteen,' said the veteran, 'though it feels like longer.'

'A mere ten,' said the other, without being asked. 'What do you think of our position?'

Rufus stopped work. He had his veteran's head on. 'I think the commander is stupid. Last time I had a stupid commander I was nearly killed, and the legion was nearly lost. It was not that long ago, not that far from here, and against these same tribesmen, though at that time they were not led by a woman. They are good fighters — clever, even.'

Quintus, who was standing on the other side of the redhead, pricked up his ears at this. Soldiers did not like talking of defeat, and if a legion was almost lost — but saved — it would be a disaster averted, and newsworthy. Where had Rufus been?

But the opportunity to ask the question was lost, as Rufus continued, 'I think he is foolish to divide his forces. It is not a rational military decision to send the cavalry elsewhere.' He was not above the infantryman's traditional contempt for his mounted comrades. 'They may be of little use, but they do guard the flanks,' he admitted.

'What would you have done?' Quintus asked.

'Regroup at the base, camp on softer ground and attempt the climb again on the following day, without the injured.' Rufus had clearly thought it through.

Tullius, joining them, disagreed. 'This climb itself is foolish,' he said, stroking his scar in his habitual way. 'What does it gain us? We should go down and not attempt the climb again — that slope is a death-trap. We should find a way around, cavalry too, even if it means going all the way back to the riverside campsite. I'll wager there are wolves in these mountains, bears too, and despite what was said after the attack, it is possible for the Astures to return. There is still a little light left in this day; there could yet be another assault.'

No-one really disagreed, though other voices offered opinions as they set to digging again. They were all working towards a common aim: the protection of comrades. Gradually, the rough red earth was transformed into a camp. Only when a guard was mounted did they rest.

IX: PILUS PRIOR

The list of the dead and injured had been brought to the commander, but each contubernium already knew who was missing of their own. The dead officers included Quintus' own centurion, a grizzled, evil-eyed veteran, little missed or mourned. He had served in Egypt and Greece, had often found himself on the losing side in the civil wars, and had carried the unfortunate nickname of 'bring-me-another' from his habit of calling for a fresh birch rod every time he broke his across a legionary's back — which was often. Others whose rank or duty were revealed by their uniforms — such as the signiferi and the cornicines — also seemed to have been targeted.

The veteran's demise meant Marcus, as optio, would have commanded the Fifth, becoming centurion at least temporarily. His absence was thus a blow to both his contubernium and century.

The commander of the First, the pilus prior, had been at the front of the climb but was found at the base of the rock. He and his men were among the most experienced of the cohort. The centurion, who, rather than the Flavian, had been the real commander, had been found on his back with his throat cut. He was a big man and had proudly worn the bright plumes along the ridge of his helmet that marked his rank. He had died with his sword in his hand, but, though there were dead enemy warriors lying near him, there was no blood on his blade, no sign that he had taken any of them with him to the afterlife.

The Second and Third centuries, diminished by the defeat in the woods and further whittled down by the decimation, had new and inexperienced officers. Antoninus, who had at least been an optio before, became centurion of the Second, while Galba was promoted to centurion of the Third from the rank of tessararius. Antoninus had taken a javelin in the calf, a deep wound but a clean one that would heal. He would find marching difficult, climbing even more so. Galba was at least uninjured, perhaps due to the fact that, shamefully, he had lost the helmet that marked his rank during the climb. Before the attack he had removed it to see better, then dropped it from beneath his arm as the storm broke. It had been returned, but the story was already being told throughout the camp and his reputation for carelessness established.

The other centurion out of action, Valerius, was a popular leader with much promise, one loved by his charges. He had commanded the Sixth century, the younger and less experienced men, but he had been shaping them into a formidable force. He had been three parts of the way up the ragged climb, exhorting his men onward, when he had taken that first spear. He lived, but he had head wounds from the subsequent plummet to the base of the rocks. He had been made comfortable but was not expected to survive the night. A legionary in his state would have been left, possibly helped on his way or at the very least given a blade to do the job himself. Valerius had been carried by his men to the medics in the camp, though there was little hope for him. The men of his century held a vigil for him, exhorting their comrades to work quietly lest they disturb him.

Sextus was, as might be expected, nowhere near the sweat and toil where Quintus and the others were struggling with the hard ground. His injuries were superficial and more a blow to his pride than a threat to his survival, his condition immediately self-assessed as not life threatening. He had not even needed to trouble the medical tent. His grazes had been roughly washed and bound by Rufus, after which he had vanished, apparently to relieve himself.

Marcus' absence meant that Quintus' century had no officers of its own, so it was being commanded by the centurion with the loud voice.

'You,' he demanded of the group working around Quintus, 'who is your decanus?'

Before any other could respond, Rufus pointed to Quintus. 'It is he for the present,' he said, knowing that the others would not disagree.

'Then make these fortifications better, the trenches deeper, and pile the rocks higher,' the centurion ordered Quintus. He then stomped off to have words with the prefect.

'Why me?' Quintus asked Rufus.

'Why not?' Publius interjected. 'You could have been elected when we were eating barley.'

Quintus knew it was true; Marcus had become their leader by default when he had avoided the responsibility. He shrugged. It would be short-lived; Marcus would be back.

Though Sextus had returned and taken his entrenching tool from his pack, it would be notable to an unbiased observer how little use he seemed to make of it and how his effect on the progress of the work was not just minimal but increasingly negative. He conversed easily with other legionaries, preventing them from working. Men swatted him away until there were no more left for him to annoy, and he squatted on the ground near his own contubernium.

As dusk fell and the fortifications were deemed, by the men at least, to be complete, men from Sextus' own century squatted with him and a larger group of men, wrapped in cloaks, came to listen to his news. They chewed on hard biscuit and drank water or, if they were lucky, heavily watered wine.

The slaves had, along with men of the Second, been tasked with manhandling the empty carts up the right-hand slope, itself flattened and smoothed by the many boots that had passed over it. On their return they set to building fires out of the brushwood — poor fires, but at least bread and biscuit had been made. Now that the tents, in neat lines, were erected, Maxim and Jovan busied themselves keeping the fire lit, replenishing drinking vessels, and looking after the mules that had struggled up the mountain. Though the rock retained some of the heat of the latter part of the day, the air was soon mountain-crisp.

Had there been officers, no doubt other tasks would have been ordered — but, for now, Sextus had his audience gathered. Standing up, he prepared to tell them what he had heard. Quintus shook his head in puzzlement at the young man's abilities. He had only been gone for a short while, yet he had returned not only with clean armour, clean bandages and a clean face, but with intelligence.

'Well, my friends,' Sextus said quietly but confidently, 'we are to be further divided.'

This was met with a murmur of doubt and discontent, along with questions as to how likely such a foolish move would be — and how would he know anyway?

'I know because I have ears,' Sextus responded, tweaking his lobes with his fingertips, 'and, unlike some of you, I have a brain to interpret what I hear.' The sarcastic tone caused a mild ripple of laughter but seemed to be enough to silence the hecklers.

'Carry on,' Tullius directed, lifting his head briefly from the incessant cleaning regime he turned to whenever they were at ease. This time, it was his helmet. 'Tell what you know.'

Sextus bowed his head in mock obeisance to his comrade. 'The cavalry is all kept at the base of this mountain, tasked with using the auxiliaries, and any locals they can capture, to find a way around. We stay here but a single night, and early tomorrow we set off climbing again, there.' He pointed to a steep and rocky trail that wound its way up until it disappeared into the darkness.

'That is worse than we have just climbed…' a voice began.

'It looks narrower,' said another.

'And it is overlooked,' added a third.

All heads had turned to look at their path, with some already starting to work out possible routes and lines.

Maxim, from his position by the tent, waiting to serve, dared to ask Sextus in a small voice, 'Are we to attempt this with the mules and carts?'

'You are,' said Sextus, adding sternly, 'and you had better look after everything.' The wry smile on his face belied his tone, and the slave knew he was not being unkind. 'Worse,' continued Sextus, 'I think our centuries will be reformed.'

This caused a storm of questions and comments — surely they would not be weakened further? They operated better with their own people. There was definite dissent in the air.

Sextus jabbed a thumb in the direction of the headquarters tent. 'The one who yells,' he said, not a little scornfully, 'is now our cohort commander. He it is that has the ear of our prefect, our Flavian politician. He is reorganising the troops to, I would say, his own safety and advantage.'

'Who would ever do otherwise, given the opportunity?' Rufus asked with heavy sarcasm.

Sextus ignored him and continued, 'Our own century has no centurion, old "bring-me-another" having fallen. And we have no optio, Marcus having … gone missing, no tesserarius, so no passwords, no signifer…'

A young man, tall and broad-chested, his fair hair betraying some of his ancestry, interrupted him. 'Here!' he shouted, lifting the cohort's standard. It seemed that some had already been detailed to carry the vexilla that the slain signiferi had let fall.

Those stepping up for this role had to be brave men, proven men, although this one looked young. He was cloaked in the courage of youth and in the youthful conceit of immortality.

'I wonder if he wipes his own arse yet?' Tullius muttered to himself as he twiddled his earring, loud enough for the young man to hear and for those in his contubernium to begin to stand in his defence. Some of the listeners were unhappy with Tullius' obvious disapproval, while others nodded in agreement. Sextus quickly raised his hand, palm open, whilst glaring at Tullius.

'You are brave,' said Quintus to the man pointedly.

'I have proven it,' the legionary shot back with unexpected fervour. 'I may look young — I am fair — but I have served for more than ten years. My comrades know my worth.'

So saying, he sank back to the ground, though he left the standard upright. His comrades patted him on the back and murmured quiet words of praise. Most men were understandably nervous about being so easily identified by the enemy — an enemy that seemed to know to remove officers before it bothered removing men — and about carrying a vital and sacred object that was, unfortunately, neither a sword nor a shield. The magical properties of protection that came with the wolfskin cloak and the raging bull symbol of the Ninth Legion had not appeared to be very effective.

Urged on by the men, all wanting to know what lay in store for them, Sextus picked up the thread. 'He — I have yet to learn his name — is to remain centurion of the Fourth, but he will join it to us. We are to be a combined unit of the Fourth and Fifth — so,' he laughed as he opened his hands in a gesture of helplessness, 'we will gain officers, whether we like it or not.'

'He is Marius!' shouted one man.

'And a bastard,' added another. 'You will wish you had "bring-me-another" still.'

Sextus spoke with not a little irony. 'He will lead our combined century into the mountains as hunters, up that track, us at the front and mules following, a combined century — along with the Third...'

He did not have time to finish before voices were raised.

'Galba!'

'Big and stupid.' One legionary hunched his shoulders, swinging long arms in imitation of a monkey.

'And slow.' Another made the one fingered gesture that indicated slowness of thought, diseases of the mind.

'Slippery fingers,' offered another, miming the catching and dropping of a ball, then pretending to throw it to a comrade, who patted the air ineffectually.

'Galba gallina,' said another, laughing at his own wit.

'Enough,' snapped Crassus, looking around apprehensively. There was only so far you could take insulting an officer before someone reported you and you earned yourself a flogging. 'You cannot accuse a man of cowardice for being careless.' He subsided, his quick temper just as quickly controlled. 'Like it or not, tomorrow he leads you, so you better watch what you think — and say.'

But nicknames stuck easily. 'Galba gallina' — Galba the chicken — already had reach and currency. It would not be easily shaken off.

Sextus stood languidly, leaning to one side, a cup of wine having miraculously appeared in his hand. He decided he had been patient enough. He asked with mock solemnity, 'Should I resume?'

The noise of the men subsided; their attention was once more on him.

He carried on. 'So, we lead. The other centuries — the First commanded by its optio, the Second with a centurion who can barely walk, the Sixth with one who barely breathes — will bring up the rear, to protect the baggage. The prefect will be who knows where, but I guarantee will be well protected.'

'The Sixth is bringing up the rear?' Quintus complained. 'They are some of our best fighters.'

'Indeed, and loyal to their commander,' said Sextus, 'who lies in the hospital tent with a spear wound in his back, a hole in his head and a crooked smile on his face. He will not last the night. If he does, they will carry him with them.'

'Perhaps he will be more use as a talisman than anything else,' muttered Tullius, to the amusement of those near enough to hear him.

'The mules?' Maxim asked, the wineskin in his hand betraying from where Sextus had gained his drink.

'Oh, you will be quite safe.' Sextus' sarcasm was biting. 'You will be in the middle of this idiotic snake, three centuries ahead of you, three behind.'

Initially, his audience was quiet, weighing up the curious nature of this division, most judging it to be folly. Dividing their troops on a narrow path would not protect anyone. The formation would slow them down and would expose the equipment. Voices began to be raised in question and indignation when many of the legionaries realised that this Marius sought glory; he had organised the centuries so that he could lead them into action against the enemy.

'We will be undermanned and exposed,' said Tullius, a verdict with which many other veterans, with sage nods and knowing grunts, agreed.

'Is there more?' Quintus asked. 'I think I am weary of sharing my fire, and I see we have provisions.' He cocked an eye at Maxim, who returned a sheepish look, having been caught attempting to hide the wineskin behind his back.

'No more,' said Sextus, 'unless they change their minds.' He bobbed his head towards the pavilion where he knew Marius and the prefect to be.

'Or unless the Astures wipe us all out tonight,' said one of the men, laughing.

The assembly broke up, carrying the rumour of what they would be tasked with back to comrades — for, whatever Sextus said, it was still a rumour, not yet confirmed. Quintus managed to put a reassuring hand on the shoulder of the new signifer as he passed, and to whisper encouragement. Tullius saw and shrugged.

Once more they were left in their own little group, by their own fire. Crassus was impressed with what Sextus had brought and asked eagerly, 'What else can you tell us about our future? Do you read it in the stars?'

'When they emerge, these will not be my stars,' Sextus responded in all seriousness, looking up at the darkening but currently almost starless heavens. 'I may not be able to read them as well as the stars in Rome.'

Quintus and Crassus exchanged glances; they were not at all sure whether Sextus was joking with them. Crassus wore a sort of scowl, as if he were trying to make out something far away — a ship on the ocean, perhaps, or a light in the distance.

'Tell us,' he said, as solemnly as he could, 'do you know where our comrades are? Do they live?'

Sextus, for once, looked grave. The half-smile that perennially played around his mouth dissolved, and his face composed itself into a look of intense concentration. He pursed his full lips. 'I do not feel that they are dead,' he said thoughtfully. 'I think I would know if they were, and it does not seem so. I think they will return.'

They were strangely reassured by his certainty and felt better as they prepared for what could be a long night.

The other men of what remained of the cohort were more concerned with those who would now command, with so many officers down, and with what tasks they would be given. To them, possibly the easiest task — forming the rearguard — had already been given to some of the best of them, the young men of the Sixth who, though they did not yet mourn their commander, expected to do so soon enough. His death made them keen to chase and kill the tribesmen.

The new combined century of the Fourth and Fifth contained mostly men of experience, holding many memories of both brave decisions and foolish ones.

The survivors of the First, mostly long-serving veterans, accepted orders, however foolish they seemed. They had served long enough to seek neither safety nor glory. Amongst them were men who had fought in Africa, Gaul, Greece and Macedonia, and had served under the Dictator Caesar, Marcus Antonius or Lepidus. Some had served with the general Agrippa, or Pompey the Great and his sons, some even in the armies of Cleopatra Philopator. Now they all belonged to the Ninth, and a few days of fighting Iberian tribesmen held no menace for them.

They shrugged their shoulders and prepared to obey.

X: QUO VADIS

The camp, though as well protected as it could be, was on edge. The torches at the four corners and those marking the prefect's quarters were fretful in the uncertain wind. In the window of sky that could be seen between the mountain tops, there was enough cloud to block out the stars and moon. There was rain in the air, the darkness and the dampness compromising visibility.

The two figures that approached from the north knew that the pickets would be apprehensive, expecting an attack. They boldly called out their names, their full citizen names, all the while staying low and ready to run. At the sound, torches moved along the perimeter, gathering at the nearest place to them. Marcus shook his head. These must be some of his untrained rabbits, judging by the way they would have provided a target for the enemy if they had been such.

'*Quo vadis?*' The traditional challenge was issued, to which the legionaries repeated their names. It was not enough. Though it was to be only an overnight camp it was still protected, and the pickets demanded a response to the question set by the man who had been promoted to tessararius. Of course, they could not oblige.

On being asked to prove that they were who they said they were, one of the men admitted to being Nox to another's Lux — nicknames that would be known only to those of their own contubernium. It was only then that Publius was summoned, and the rest of the group followed. If it was indeed Nox — Cato — then his companion, they reasoned, must be their own decanus and the century's optio, Marcus — the two men whom many thought had deserted.

Though they were finally identified and allowed into the camp, the pilus prior did not want to interrogate them until there was full daylight. They were therefore bound at the wrists and left lying uncomfortably on the hard ground, quietly furious.

Their comrades — all but Publius, who was ordered to stay to confirm their identities to the prefect — were dismissed. However, Quintus, in spite of being imperiously waved away by one who appeared even younger than himself, insisted on also staying.

'You can see who we are,' Marcus had complained vociferously. 'Do you think that we stole this armour? Do you think we are tribesmen dressed up as Romans? Do you think tribesmen shave?'

However, he soon fell silent; he had served for too long and had seen too much stupidity to bother wasting much energy on their unjustified plight. Cato shrugged — whatever fate threw at him, he would bear it stoically, though he was close to losing his temper at this level of ineptitude. Their information, as far as they could both judge, was vital, and the sooner it was acted on the better. This delay just gave their enemy more time to regroup, more time to vanish into the depths of the mountains.

Publius and Quintus sat on the hard ground, not sure if they were prisoners or not. Quintus decided that he had made the wrong decision, following his heart instead of his head, and now wished he had returned with the others. Of course, there was no way he could go now. Publius, still naive though he pretended not to be, could not quite reconcile the treatment of his friends with his own vision of the Roman army. For him, the good always outweighed the bad and he looked around in hope, thinking that maybe this was some sort of jest. Had Publius been the officer, it would have been a practical joke; Quintus knew this and wished it were so.

'Are we truly to sit here until morning?' Publius asked innocently of no-one in particular. Cato harrumphed. Quintus said nothing, but sadly nodded his head. Marcus began to speak, then thought better of it, and instead also gave a resigned nod.

Quintus rose and walked towards the guards, intending to stroll past them. Surely they would not take this unnecessary confinement seriously. He recognised them as two more of Marcus' trainees and assumed they would let him pass. Gently, but surely, they did not.

'It looks like we are,' said Publius.

It had not been the usual raucous notes of the trumpet that had woken the camp before dawn; it had instead been the rumoured return of the two 'deserters'.

After several false starts, dawn had finally broken — a sullen red sky in the valley in the east, with clouds above lowering over the mountains. They were only just darker than the mists into which the peaks soared and vanished. There was much bustling in the camp and their guard was changed, but the new men brought no news of their fate. Indeed, there seemed to be little urgency in talking to the prisoners. Around them they could hear the sounds of the camp being dismantled, the bark of orders, the flapping of leather, the hiss as fires were extinguished, the braying and complaining of mules as they were loaded.

No food was brought for them, and it seemed another age before two more legionaries came to dismiss the guards and collect them. Their orders were clearly to bring the 'prisoners' or 'deserters', obvious by their bonds. The status of Publius and Quintus was less certain, leading to a short, muttered discussion between the men of the escort before they shrugged and told them to follow, reasoning that it would be better to arrive with two extra than to be two short.

The prefect — or at least those around him — had set up a sprawling command post, one which included both shelter and fire. At the centre was his own tent, so the men found themselves being escorted inside just as cold waves of drizzle started to blow across the exposed site. The slaves and freedmen of the junior senator, commander and politician, Titus Flavius Pusio, huddled in the lee of the tent, waiting for the command to dismantle it.

Inside, an argument was taking place between the prefect and Marius, the loud-voiced centurion who had become pilus prior.

'At least one of them should be lashed,' Marius was insisting. 'They have none of their gear; they were at least careless, if not wilfully treacherous.'

'We were ambushed,' replied the prefect laconically, 'and we need them fit. Centurion Galba lost his own helmet, remember.'

Marius had no answer to this and merely grunted. Galba would never have been his choice as a centurion, imposing as he was once armed and armoured. Big, he might be, but not the brightest.

The prefect was an unassuming man in, Quintus supposed, his late twenties. He was clean-shaven with prematurely thinning hair and what looked like old boxing injuries to his nose and ear. His attitude to his new commander seemed less than fully supportive. Marcus guessed — from his experience — that the prefect would not have chosen to be led by this man.

He exchanged a swift glance with Cato, wondering if this conversation applied to them. Quintus and Publius were trying to make themselves less obvious. They really wished that they were not there.

Marius tried again, indicating Marcus and Cato, still bound at the wrists. 'There will be no discipline without open demonstrations of it,' he argued. 'Otherwise, the men will become slack. These two will do as well as any — they ran away from battle and were recaptured — what more do we need to know?'

Flavius asked softly, 'Why did they come back?'

'Warmth and food, I would think,' scoffed the centurion. 'They still ran.'

'They did not run,' blurted Publius indignantly, forgetting himself, unaware that such an interruption could bring punishment on his own head. 'And all their gear is with us. It is not lost; it was passed up first.'

'Be silent!' the centurion roared. 'Who are you, his advocate?'

'I was sent to identify them,' said Publius in a small voice. 'This is my amicus.'

There was an awkward silence as Publius realised that he should not have spoken once, let alone twice. Cato gave him what might have been an encouraging smile, but it was accompanied by the slightest shake of his head. He prayed inwardly that Lux would say no more.

The prefect spoke first, at which Quintus gave out a little exhalation. He had judged that whoever broke the silence would decide the fate of all of them. He was relieved that it was the Flavian, rather than the centurion. He asked Cato softly, ignoring Publius, 'Did you run?'

'We ran...' he began to reply.

'See, they admit it!' interrupted Marius.

'We ran to follow the enemy, to find out where they are hidden, to discover their lair!' Marcus had finally lost patience and had spoken, though he had not been asked to.

The prefect held up a hand, silencing all of them. 'Let's do this as it should be done,' he said, his tone authoritative. 'You,' he went on, addressing Publius, 'is this the man you say he is, and one of us? A nod will do.'

Publius nodded glumly.

'You,' the prefect said to Quintus, 'who or what are you?'

'I am second in the contubernium; this man is both our decanus and friend.' Then he added meekly, 'I think I should not be here.'

'So do I,' said the Flavian, but he did not dismiss him.

'Guards, if they are not deserters, unbind them,' Marius ordered. He had seen which way the prefect was leaning. There would come a time when he could oppose, he reasoned, and that time was not now.

The guards untied the two men. Each then saluted with a fist to the heart and left.

'Stand forward,' the centurion ordered Marcus and Cato. 'Speak your tale to your commanding officer.'

The Flavian preened just a little — Marius knew how to handle him — and repeated, 'Yes, speak your tale.'

Marcus, ruefully rubbing the place where his bonds had been, looked at Cato, who nodded, happy to let the older man speak first.

'I am Appius Marcus Saturninus, optio of the Fifth,' he said, standing especially tall and straight and saluting the commander. 'We were halfway up the climb on the left, where the big rock jutted out. It protected us from the first onslaught. We drew swords, ready to fight — our shields and packs had already been handed up — but in the darkness of the rain, we

110

could find no enemy warriors. Cato, Cornelius Cato Petronius — this man here,' he went on, tapping Cato on the shoulder, 'he was close and called to me that the attackers were getting away. So, we gave chase.'

'Is that it?' Marius demanded harshly. 'Others did the same and did not take a day and a night to return.'

'That is not all,' said Cato, quickly. 'We did not return at once because we followed them and sought their lair.'

Marcus continued, 'We nearly stumbled into their camp in the dark, and it was only by fortune that we were not taken. We had been descending. There were scant trees, but enough to offer us protection. The men, those who attacked us, were gathered in a grove, where the trees were thicker. They had no fires or shelter, but they did have a few torches and loud voices. Clearly, they thought themselves safe. We crouched low and listened.'

'Sitting in the place of honour on a flat rock,' said Cato excitedly, 'was the chieftain, the woman…'

'…the one whom we are never sure is real or legend.'

'She is real,' Cato confirmed. 'She was there. She is old, yes. White-haired, yes. But when she stood, she stood lithely, and with little sign of age.'

Marcus, seeing the eyebrows of the centurion shoot up, thought this perhaps too much. He attempted to intercede on Cato's behalf, to soften the picture. 'There was some frailty, I think, when she arose. She leaned on a youth, a strong, wide-shouldered youth with long black hair, tied at the nape. We think him her grandson.'

The prefect was uninterested. 'Carry on,' he ordered. 'What did you hear?'

'Cato understands some of their tongue from time spent in the town. I, too, understand a little. Much could be guessed from tone and gesture.'

The centurion harrumphed at such nonsense, but the prefect waved them on before he could object. The two legionaries looked at each other, Cato indicating that Marcus should carry on with a small nod.

'We heard that they are close to some sort of headquarters, some sort of command centre or religious site — a temple to their heathen gods, perhaps. She urged them not to delay, to reach it quickly so that they would be safe in the valley. There were voices raised in objection. Some wanted to attack our camp. Others wanted to celebrate what they called a victory. But she said no. She was very forceful; she said it would be too well defended, that we would be expecting an attack. She said that they must rely on surprise and subterfuge and their knowledge of the mountains. She silenced her critics.'

'You sound like you admire her, optio,' Marius sneered.

'Who would not admire a warrior leader, whether man or woman, sir?' Cato replied honestly — but stupidly.

Marcus quickly carried on: 'They must have made the decision to continue down. They had not lit any fires or erected any shelter. It was an easy decision, I think, if it was an easy journey. We shadowed them through the trees and down into a hidden valley.'

'They went noisily,' said Cato. 'It was not difficult.'

'We watched them enter their temple,' Marcus continued with pride and excitement. 'She led them in. We have found where they hide in the mountains and can lead the cohort there to wipe them out completely. We can offer you, sir,' he said, bowing his head in deference to the prefect's rank, 'complete victory.'

The Flavian looked at the centurion, his thin lips pursed. He was no coward, but he was minded to be cautious. He did not wish to risk too much, or too many men. He had become even more wary after the ambush.

The centurion read his thoughts and asked, 'Is it well defended?'

'Sir, I think not,' said Marcus, this time addressing the centurion — whom he knew to be the true military commander. 'Though there are many tribesmen, there appear to be few defences. I think that they think their mountains protect them.'

'And you?' he barked at Cato.

'I think it is more than the mountains. I think there is a shrine or temple to one of their gods; I think that is what they feel gives them protection. We climbed high above them and looked down on where they were. I think it was some sort of sacrifice or ceremony.'

'A good place to put an end to them,' said the centurion quietly to the Flavian.

'Agreed,' he responded, 'and to wipe the stain of yesterday's defeat.'

Marius shivered involuntarily and nearly cursed, but he bit it back. He did not like talk of defeat; he did not like ambushes and hit-and-run tactics. He wanted a battle. Maybe he would get one. 'Where is this place?' he asked, directing his sharp eyes at Marcus.

'I would say perhaps a day's march away,' Marcus said, calculating. 'We did not go right down to it but looked at it from a high vantage point. The initial climb is not where you would think.'

'Show me,' ordered Marius, striding outside.

Marcus followed confidently, the rest — the Flavian included — wondering if they should follow also.

'Come, come,' barked the centurion to all of them, then added with mock humour, 'If I am to get wet, then we all should.' He turned to the prefect. 'Perhaps, sir,' he said, waving an arm at the shivering slaves, 'we should let them get on.'

'Yes, yes,' agreed Flavius. He turned to the waiting men. 'Take it down and pack it away.'

The drizzle was not too cold, but the wind driving it was sharp and easterly. It blurred visibility, but not so much that the track they intended to take was hidden.

'Up there?' asked Marius, pointing.

'No, sir,' said Marcus. 'I think that is where they would have you think it is — it looks inviting.' He instead indicated a bare hillside further to the north, a hillside that looked impassable. 'We followed them on narrow trails that weave through the base of those boulders —' he pointed at the bottom of the slope — 'but beyond they join together to form a wider path, at least as wide as that one. Even better, it is one on which we will not be expected.'

'You are certain?'

'On my honour,' Marcus insisted, fist automatically touching his heart.

'And mine,' repeated Cato, with a similar salute.

'Then we need not change our plan,' the centurion said to Flavius, 'just its direction.'

The prefect nodded.

'You are optio of the Fifth?' Marius asked Marcus.

'Yes, sir.'

'You have a new century, the Fourth and Fifth combined, and a new centurion, me. You will be second to me.'

'Yes, sir,' repeated Marcus, automatically saluting.

'Both of you,' Marius said, pointing to Marcus and Cato, 'will show us the way.' He then addressed Quintus and Publius. 'You two can count yourselves lucky that you have escaped without punishment. Go and tell the trumpeters to sound the assembly.' He did not give the men time to respond — indignation at a false accusation would help no-one — nor did he give the Flavian time or space to react. This, he had decided, would be his command, and it was time to march.

By now it was as if the camp had never been. It was all dismantled, packed away or burned. The poor rampart that had been raised from the stones and soil hacked out of the ditch with such expenditure of effort had been returned to where it had come from. The soldiers did not think it a waste, for they had not been attacked in the night. Those not on guard duty had slept soundly — as had some of those who had been on duty. They were accustomed to it.

Not long afterwards the combined Fourth and Fifth — with greater strength than a single century, but significantly less than two — stood in lines in the now incessant drizzle, ready to receive orders. Galba and the Third stood behind them. Most of the mules and carts had already been loaded, the rest being hurriedly dragged or pushed across to stand between these men and the other centuries. The commander of the Sixth had, against the odds, survived the night, and was being carried on a stretcher, the poles on the shoulders of legionaries. They intended to rotate this duty so that fatigue would not compromise their pace. Marius shook his head. Given the choice, he would have left the centurion to die, but the men were not giving him the choice.

Antoninus, the centurion with the leg injury, could be seen upright, refusing to be carried, but leaning on the shoulder of a brawny trooper. Marius gave the commands directly, the prefect standing by him. The orders were to follow Marcus and Cato, who would lead.

'Look to your feet,' he said. 'The trail will be narrow and rocky to begin with, but I can promise you that, at the end of it, and before the end of the day, you shall have a battle.'

He held both arms aloft as he shouted this, and the men cheered and stamped their feet. Tullius was only half aware of their exultation, even though he applauded with the rest. Then he was suddenly jolted to full consciousness.

The man, Marius, to whom he had given little notice up to now, stomped away from them with a limp, favouring his right leg.

Tullius prayed quietly to Nemesis, goddess of vengeance.

XI: NEMESIS

The column had followed the route that Marcus and Cato had taken and had expected little or no resistance, assuming the tribesmen were still in their valley. But the natives had been watching the camp and had seen the legionaries depart. They knew that they had to pass this place.

They had been travelling through a high, narrow gorge. Though the trees were not thick here, they were numerous, and provided sufficient cover to allow the Astures to approach to within a spear's throw before emerging, with much roaring and shouting. They knew the ground, its folds and pitfalls, its slips and traps; the Romans did not. However, the enemy could not come close enough to stop the Roman legionaries forming up, line abreast and shield to shield, ready to repel each attack. But the line was spread out and thin in places, and the foolishness of placing the equipment train in the centre was quickly exposed by the tribesmen. Once the natives had realised which track was being taken, many mules, many slaves and much gear had been lost on the climb.

Though the enemy had fled, yet again, Marcus was certain that they had not gone for good. They would be lurking amongst the trees as they had already lurked amongst the rocks and boulders, ready to charge once more as they climbed, once a flank was exposed, or a mule or legionary was left unprotected.

Quintus did not see the blade pierce Marius, but he did see blood running down the centurion's leg and also that Tullius held his blade curiously, backwards. He saw the centurion's shield slowly fall as he grasped at the wetness that suddenly spread across his thigh, and he saw him stumble and hit the floor heavily.

In shock, Quintus forgot his training and turned towards Tullius, who was already striding forward, trampling the centurion's feathers into the dirt. 'Tullius, what...?' was as far as he got before the urgent yells of Marcus brought him back to his senses.

'Quintus, wake yourself!' screamed Marcus, parrying a blow that Quintus should have taken with his shield. 'Look to Crassus! There, to your left! Remember what Ursus taught you!' He swung his sword again and the enemy tribesman fell, a great gash across his neck. Quintus' head cleared at once and his arm stiffened. He lifted his shield. He looked quickly where Marcus had indicated and acted instinctively.

Crassus crouched on one knee, his head down and his shield somehow knocked from his hand. The enemy was above him and about to strike. Quintus took two steps, the second to stand astride his amicus, and forcefully thrust and smashed the tribesman in the chin with his shield, knocking him from his feet. As the enemy warrior tried to rise, he once more slammed the shield into him, driving him backwards. Seeing swords strike from comrades on his right, his own sword arm was finally brought into action, slashing and stabbing as he yelled angrily, furious at himself for losing concentration.

Crassus had pulled himself to his feet, dazed but carrying no serious injury. He was able to grin at Quintus, his bright white teeth dazzling in his dark and bloodstained face. 'Step!' he bellowed.

'Step!' yelled Quintus in return, both of them remembering their time on the Campus Martius. They had fallen slightly behind the battle line.

'Close up, close up!' Marcus ordered stridently. 'Close up and step forward!'

Many had seen Marius fall, so they knew that Marcus, as optio, now commanded. The line responded, Romans going shield to shield as they stepped rhythmically, like the inexorable tide marching up the shore, the very essence of the power of Rome. Discipline. Comradeship. Honour.

'Step, step, step!' the men thundered in time, reaching through the barest of gaps between the shields to find enemy flesh, lunging and stabbing, again and again until arms ran with blood. 'Step, step, step!' *Tramp, tramp, tramp*. 'Step, step, step…'

It was the rhythm that filled their dreams, the rhythm that they awoke to when the trumpets sounded. It was the breath in their lungs and the beating of their hearts.

And the enemy inevitably stumbled, fell back, broke and ran.

Quintus was tying a bandage — cloth torn from a dead man's tunic — around a comrade's arm. He was uninjured and trying to build a picture of what had happened in the skirmish, and of how Marius had fallen, before the essentials faded.

The Roman dead had been hauled to one side, not without respect, although anything of use had been taken from them. Amongst them lay Marius, the putative pilus prior. His helmet, sword and shield were all gone, and he'd bled out, it would seem, from a lucky strike to the leg.

Quintus watched Tullius, seeing the scar, the ragged ear, the lines of age and stress etched into his forehead. As was his habit, he sat slightly apart from the others, cleaning his blade and humming tunelessly to himself. Like most of his colleagues, Quintus could parade, stand guard and march with his mind elsewhere. He tended to think of green fields and ripe corn — but he was ready to snap into action on an order or a signal, instantly vigilant.

He had no idea where Tullius' thoughts took him. He had witnessed three versions of the legionary: he had seen — and admired — the soldier, who was alert and obeyed orders without question. He had also seen this fugue state, where Tullius seemed to inhabit a dream world and the life in his eyes dimmed. When he spoke of Appius, his dead amicus, Quintus saw another state: a spark of humour, signs of warmth.

It did not seem like the right moment to question Tullius about his actions, especially as Quintus was not sure of what he had seen — or not seen. He knew Marius had toppled, pitching forward like a felled tree, clutching his thigh. He knew that Tullius had been at the man's side when he'd fallen. He knew that no enemy had been near and no spear had been flung. He could not connect the pieces together to make sense.

'Ow!' The man Quintus was tending complained loudly as the bandage was tied too tight, dragging him back from his reverie. His hands were not surgeon's hands, but he had handled animals, including young ones, and he was usually gentler than this. He apologised, tied the bandage properly and sent the man, still grumbling, on his way. Another, no more than a boy, began to rise, deciding to seek a different comrade to tend his wound.

'No, no,' said Quintus, shaking his head. 'Come here. I will not be so harsh with you.'

'It is my first injury,' said the boy, with a touch of pride. He was clearly one of the latest arrivals, one of Marcus' trainees, a rabbit with a cut on his leg that was long but not deep.

'It will not be your last,' muttered Quintus. The boy flinched as he began to clean the wound.

They had taken no Asturian prisoners, and the tribesmen had managed to leave few bodies behind. They seemed to make a point of ensuring that their own injured and dead were removed, whilst any held captive immediately pulled themselves onto a blade, or ingested poison. Their tactic of rushing out, killing or injuring a few Romans, and then melting back into the trees was wearying the men. It was like being stung again and again by some flying insect that you could not swat. The legionaries had become frustrated, lashing out in exasperation and growing careless — this time they had lost not just the centurion, but half a dozen others. It had been the fourth or fifth such action of the day — the men had ceased to count. Each had taken place in one of the many sharp, cold showers of rain that blew in on the northern winds, as if the Astures knew when these were approaching and timed their attacks accordingly.

In this encounter some men, including Crassus and Quintus, had lost concentration and had almost let the tribesmen break through the line. Quintus knew that Marcus had seen the danger and had dragged them back, but there had been losses. Quintus was ashamed that Marcus had had to yell at him to save his comrade and get back in formation. He sighed and shook his head; it should not be so.

In between bandaging and ministering hard advice and little sympathy, he found a moment to pull the small leather pouch from beneath his tunic and to unfold its contents. He also made sure that the copper armband was still in place. Though it lived next to his skin, he had to check that it was still there regularly, convinced that something terrible would happen to him if it was lost.

Ursus' writing was still clear, though he doubted it was in the veteran's own hand. Again Quintus read the charge to look after his comrades, to keep them from harm. He had done so with Crassus, although his own lapse of attention might have been at least a partial cause of his friend's jeopardy.

'Take more care,' he advised himself quietly, 'or you will never be true to Ursus.'

He scratched his head, trying to recall what had caught his attention. *What had Tullius been doing?*

XII: PILUS ET MANUS

The men sat morosely in the damp air, their tunics clinging to their bare legs and their sleeves sodden against their arms. Even their shoulders were wet and cold, the rain having seeped under their armour.

'I have been drier in the baths at home,' complained Rufus. His moustache was dripping and his bright hair was plastered to his head. He looked sadly at the small pile of dead. 'There is nowhere to bury or burn them,' he went on. 'Who will help them cross the river?'

'It does not matter,' Sextus said. 'They are protected.'

'Protected?' Quintus asked. 'How?'

'In Rome,' Sextus explained, always the wellspring of knowledge, 'it has been decreed by the Vestals themselves that legionaries who die honourably in battle will not suffer in death, but be welcomed into Hades as heroes, that Mercury himself pays Charon their fare for the ferry, and that a special place is reserved for them.'

'Well, if the Vestals say it is so,' began Crassus, without conviction, knowing he had been very close to joining the pile.

'Then it is so,' Marcus finished his sentence for him. The attacks had separated them from the prefect and the other centuries, who were slowed by the baggage. Marcus was the only figure of authority. Though he wore none of the regalia of a centurion, the legionaries knew him to be their officer, and respected him as both a veteran and a fighter. He raised his voice to address them. 'We move out quickly — take anything of use and leave the rest. Quintus, for now be my optio. We will see what happens officially when we are safe.'

Quintus nodded; now was not the time to argue. Neither Galba nor the men of his century objected.

They all knew that there was no point in creating any sort of grave. They would not have time to dig a deep enough pit before they moved on, and so the bodies would still be vulnerable to scavengers. Though there were many trees, the day's unabating rain had soaked the timber, so there could be no pyre. Funeral rites on a battlefield were a waste of time and energy. There would be no fires for the dead — and there would be no fires for the living either, unless they cleaned out this hornet's nest.

It was still afternoon, and Marcus felt that one last push might take them down to the temple, or whatever it was that these Astures protected with such ferocity and determination. They needed to move swiftly, away from these trees, to give the enemy less cover in which to hide. He ordered the advance. He was willing to offer the men warmth and comfort if they destroyed the enemy temple.

'Do we wait for the prefect and the other centuries?' Tullius asked laconically, looking up.

'It's too late to wait.' Marcus was adamant. 'We cannot keep being bitten and stung until we lose our minds,' he continued, 'and nor do I think it safe for us to wait here for the rest to form up. They are constrained by the baggage, and no doubt repelling their own attacks. I think the snakes will strike less without the tree cover. I have sent Cato and Publius forward to find the position that we found last night — the place from where we saw their smoke — and to scout a way down. We must bring them to battle — proper battle.'

The men nodded and grunted their agreement.

'This is our battle. Tonight, we will sleep within their temple and feast on their sacrifices, or we will test Sextus' knowledge of the underworld!' Marcus slapped the legionary on the back, almost knocking him over.

Sextus did not take kindly to being treated so, but said nothing, moving away from Marcus to be with his primus amicus, Rufus. 'Idiot,' he spat as he squatted next to the redhead.

Quintus was close, as was Crassus. Quintus heard Rufus ask, 'Idiot? Why, Sextus? Explain.'

'You should not speak thus of what you do not understand,' Sextus said, his face sombre and unsmiling.

'You are wearing your serious face,' said Crassus. His half-smile was quickly suppressed as Sextus turned his gaze on him.

'These are serious things,' said Sextus gravely. 'You cannot mock their gods. You cannot mock *any* gods without risking their ire.'

'I appreciate what the Vestals have done for me,' said Crassus lightly, 'though I did not ask them to.'

'They protect you whether you ask them to or not.' Sextus was almost angry. 'They have always protected me, even before I knew they existed.'

'Then we should just leave this place?' Marcus interrupted. None of them had seen him join them. 'We should just let them carry on with their rituals to whatever god it is they worship?'

'It may be the same as ours,' said Sextus sulkily. 'They could be sacrificing to Candamius, chieftain of the gods, ruler of heaven, flinger of thunderbolts! Do you recognise him?' His voice had risen in anger.

Marcus shook his head. He did not care what the gods said or did not say, though he did pray to them. For now, he prayed to Mars that Nox and Lux would return soon, so that they would have time to take the fight to the Astures that day. He had a job to do.

'Look, Sextus,' he said, not unkindly. 'Look there.' He pointed at the pile of Roman bodies. 'That is why we cannot leave them be — or leave them to worship their own gods. Within a season they would be back at the walls of Lucus Augustus, battering and burning. They have done it before. I know that is not what you want.'

'Sir!' A shout interrupted their discussion. 'Men approach. I think they are our scouts.'

Publius and Cato looked like grey ghosts through the drizzle. Publius was lithe and smooth in his movements. Cato moved more like a wolf, confident and implacable.

'We have found it,' reported Publius, 'and it is not far away.'

'An hour at most,' added Cato. 'It's a short climb first, which takes us out of this wretched cloud. Then there is a clear track down to the shrine.'

'Best of all,' said Publius, 'there is a broad clearing before the shrine where the ground is flat and the trees are gone.'

'Then we fight,' said Sextus quietly and resignedly to Crassus and Quintus before either could intervene, 'but understand that it is not what the gods want. All I can do is feel their displeasure.' He waved his arms around. 'I feel it in the weather, in the tone of the wind, in the voices of the trees. I feel ill will and bad fortune.' He took a deep breath. 'I know we have a job to do. I will not fail us. But I cannot help what I feel.'

'Then we fight under an uncertain sky,' said Crassus, as he moved away. 'So be it. It is as the gods will it. I will still pray to Vulcan.'

'Come,' Quintus said, standing and offering a hand to Sextus to help him up.

Marcus had raised his voice to address all the men. 'Soldiers,' he said, 'we shall have battle and avenge our comrades before the sun is set.' He looked at the leaden sky and laughed. 'If indeed there is ever a sun in these parts!' He threw a sideways glance at Sextus, then called out, 'Pray to Vulcan of the forge, if you will, but also pray to your own gods. Pray to your household gods, pray to Mars and Jupiter, and pray to your ancestors if you have any. Pray that Sextus here was right about the Vestals, for today we have only victory or death. I do not intend to walk these paths again.'

The men picked themselves up from their various groupings, lifted arms and armour and shook water off themselves like wolves drying their fur. All were keen to see an end to this day, preferably one that involved victory and a warm place to eat and sleep. If not, they would accept death, with their fare already paid.

'We must make haste,' ordered Marcus. 'There is no time to waste. Cato, Publius, take the lead.'

The three centuries — or what was left of them — were used to travelling fast when they had to. Where the ground was flat and firm, they marched in double-time, and when they had to climb, they broke formation and scrambled upwards, comrades guarding their backs and flanks.

They soon forgot the cold of their damp tunics as they marched. The basic training of the Roman legionaries meant that they were all fit, and even those carrying minor injuries were able to move. Those with major injuries had been left behind to fend for themselves as best they could, and to follow when they were able. They knew that they were paused rather than abandoned.

In less than an hour Publius, dancing from rock to rock ahead of Cato, raised his hand, and the column came to a halt.

They looked down at a wide expanse of flat ground, beaten hard by men's feet and accessible via a track. It was broader than the one that they had been on and not as steep, and it wound down from their vantage point. At the far end of this ground was what might have once been a building, though it looked more like a series of rocks piled on top of one another to make a sort of wall. Behind it, a passage had been cut into the rock face, leading to tunnels or caves. Smoke rose lazily from one spot behind the wall — a sacrificial brazier, perhaps — but there was no sign of the enemy. To the rear of the wall, the mountain rose and vanished into the heavens.

It had finally stopped raining, and the lowering cloud that had squatted on the landscape for so long was beginning to thin. Already it was lighter, enough to lift the spirits of the men. The sun, should it make an appearance, would be at their backs.

'Go down the track silently,' Marcus whispered. 'We form up at the base. If we do it right, the enemy will still be in their temple. My contubernium will lead and form a guard.' He looked over his shoulder to make sure they were there, even though he was confident that they would be. 'Quintus, Crassus, you lead.'

The squad helped each other with their spears and shields so that the descent was silent. The wind helped to cover any sound. It was rising and dispersing the cloud, whistling eerily through the gaps in the rock and rustling the tops of the trees that edged the open ground. Once down, the small group formed a semi-circle facing the temple, shields locked, protecting those that already followed stealthily behind.

It did not take long for the whole force, the three undermanned centuries — including some of the ones bandaged by Quintus and others — to make their way down the track and to form up, twenty shields across and four deep as far as they could. They would make a shorter line if they had to, but they would leave no gaps. The new signifer, the brave youth, stood proudly at one end with the standard of the Fifth. Another, a veteran in a wolfskin pelt, stood at the other end, holding aloft the emblem of the Fourth. There were two signiferi of the Third, each carrying the tall pole on which the flag and number of the century were borne, along with the pilus and manus, the spear and hand, the symbols of Rome's legions. They stood a little way behind the centre, either side of Galba, almost as if preventing any independent action. Marcus, smiling wryly, approved. He himself stood to one side — he would fight, of course, but he needed to also issue orders. His commands would be simple: find the enemy, draw them out, and wipe them out.

'Do not be drawn in — if you enter those caves whilst the enemy occupies them, you will die,' he warned. They had no cornicen, but Marcus' voice carried. 'Now go forward slowly; step on my command.' He paused. 'The time for silence is over, so make yourselves heard. Step!'

Each legionary took one step forward, leading by the right. Shields were lifted and crashed on the ground in unison, spears then clashing against them. The left foot followed in time, and then they were still.

Though the sound echoed from the surrounding mountains and birds flew up in fright, there was no sign of movement from the temple. All was once more eerily quiet; the legionaries could hear each other's breathing.

'This time,' Marcus commanded, 'we keep going, and we sing.' He called Rufus' name. 'You will know a song or two, I think,' he said.

Rufus began a chant. It was well known to the veterans of the century, though likely to burn the delicate ears of some of the younger men. It described — in great detail — the sexual prowess of the Dictator, Julius Caesar, as he brought all the beasts of the animal kingdom to their knees with the size of his manhood, his ultimate goal being to satisfy the insatiable queen of Egypt.

It was repetitive, a call and response that was soon picked up by all, so that slowly the legionaries made their way across the ground to the rhythm: step, call, response, repeat.

After ten steps, Caesar had finished with the domestic beasts of Italy and barely started on the animals of Africa, and the Astures began to emerge from their mountain fastness.

At the head of them came a tall figure, dressed in the skins of wolves and bears, her white hair emerging from the shawl tied across her head. She was still strong and vibrant, though the white hair betrayed her age. Her face was in shadow, but her whole body shouted anger and resistance, the long sword and round shield with which she was armed confirming it. At her side, partly clothed in stolen Roman armour and carrying a spear as well as a sword was what Quintus took to be her grandson. He was no boy, but a young man — bearded, broad-shouldered and bareheaded, his long black hair tied at his back.

She shook her sword at the approaching legionaries and yelled something incomprehensible. She turned and spoke to the young man, and it seemed a short argument ensued. Whatever it was that was said, she prevailed, and the young man retreated into the temple. She was no coward, and her people outnumbered the Romans but, Quintus reckoned, they had sacred things to protect, and this was the young man's errand.

Within minutes, he had to revise his guess, as the man emerged from the mountain's maw with many warriors. They poured out of the stronghold with axes, swords and a fierce determination to protect this place.

The seemingly ceaseless drizzle had finally stopped. Behind the tribesmen the mountain glowed a deep orange, whilst the legionaries finally felt the warm touch of Apollo on their backs.

While the tribesmen, led by the woman who stood to the front and centre of them, jumped up and down and waved their weapons in the air, the Roman soldiers now stood stock-still, silent, listening for further orders.

There was space between the two sets of forces, and the tribesmen did not immediately attack. They paused, apparently waiting for guidance. Quintus saw the woman's stern face as she raised her eyes to the heavens, and he assumed that she was praying to her gods. He quietly prayed to his, but especially to Mars. All the time more men were emerging from the mountain, pushing the first ones forward.

Quintus, standing in his place close to Marcus, was glad that their half of the cohort had finally trapped a large force. There would be a pitched battle, a battle they had been seeking for days. There were fewer than two hundred Romans and over three hundred of the tribesmen, he estimated. He smiled at the odds; he was not unduly perturbed. This was what he did, this was what the Roman war machine was trained for.

XIII: CONTENDITE VESTRA SPONTE

The state asked three things of every recruit. It did not ask for a man's head, or his heart, but it demanded that the soldier care for his equipment, that he trained and exercised diligently, and that he obeyed orders, instantly and without question. All obligations were sealed with a sacred oath.

At the lowest levels, if your cohort was ordered to go first to take a stronghold, even into certain death, you obeyed, following your standard bearers with your head high and honour intact. In the higher echelons, the same rules applied — if a general ordered a commander to take his own life, he had to fall on his sword and head for the afterlife in defence of his honour and that of the state. You should never be captured alive, never disgrace your standards. It was better to die heroically than to live as a slave.

The tribesmen continued to shout and scream as their numbers and confidence grew. The woman at their head held them back, arms wide, willing the Romans to come to them. Her voice was distinctive: loud, gravelly and full of authority. The legionaries guessed that they were being insulted in the Asturian tongue — a waste, as few but those flinging the curses understood them.

There seemed to be an invisible barrier that the Astures would not cross — the precincts of the temple, perhaps. Marcus knew he needed to draw them out. They had to attack; the Roman force was smaller and better suited to defending itself. He also held the narrower part of the valley, with trees on either side. The enemy could only bring limited numbers to bear if he held this ground. Of course, his force was also more disciplined.

The men looked at each other along the line, reading determination in each other's faces and drawing strength from the bonds of comradeship.

'Stand and wait!' ordered Marcus loudly. Then he shouted, 'Javelins, prepare!'

The younger and less experienced men that he had been training, who each carried two of the lighter throwing spears, gripped one of the javelins in their right hand. The front ranks ducked down behind their shields to give them space.

'Loose!' Marcus ordered.

The spears were thrown in quick succession, enough to temporarily darken the evening sky, whistling as they flew overhead. Some found flesh, but their primary purpose was not to kill; it was to disrupt and goad. They fixed themselves to shields, to the leather worn by the tribesmen, and quivered on the ground in front of the enemy. This had the desired effect, for in trying to remove them or step over them, the tribesmen found that the light weapon hampered their movements. It was enough to enrage them and, screaming in defiance, they at last broke through the invisible barrier and ran towards the Romans.

The battle was now on Roman terms. As the Astures swarmed past her, their female chief turned and headed back towards the temple. An admission of defeat, Quintus thought at first, but then he realised that she was more likely to be fetching reinforcements — either men or gods.

At a command from Marcus, each man in the front rank braced himself, shield thrust forward with his left arm, ready to absorb the first shock of the charge. Their concentration was absolute. They had to stop the enemy, kill the enemy, and repeat until no more came at them.

The Astures wielded mostly axes and long swords for slashing and cutting, whilst the legionaries' short swords stabbed, each stab felling an enemy warrior. The Astures climbed on top of each other and leapt at the Roman shields, throwing axes in frustration. They even tried to clamber over the shields, screaming and cursing as they bled and died.

The Dictator had taught the Romans well against the Gauls: when faced with a line of enemy warriors, they knew not to stab at their direct opponent, for that was what would be expected. The enemy would be trying to parry the blow and strike back. No, the legionaries were to look to the man who stood beside their opponent, at their right hand that would be preparing to stab down. They were to then thrust their blade under the armpit of this man while it was exposed and vulnerable. Caesar's surgeons had discovered that a wound there would often be fatal, that a man would bleed out from the soft flesh.

'Second rank, on the standard, forward!' Marcus ordered, over the cacophony of clashing metal, relying on the men to relay the order.

'Second rank, prepare!' yelled Quintus. 'Look to the signifer!'

Crassus repeated the command, as did other men down the line. Marcus could only judge that word had passed and, as he ordered the signifer to dip the standard, that the ranks would change. As the standard was briefly lowered and quickly held upright again, the front rank turned their shields ninety degrees and stepped backwards as the second rank moved through the gaps created and braced their own shields against the enemy. What had been the first rank passed to the rear, where they could rest and reform.

The Astures, to their astonishment and consternation, faced fresh soldiers. They renewed the attack, the noise of battle now reverberating from the mountainsides, the clash of iron and steel now mixed with the groans of the wounded and dying.

As the wave of attackers broke on the implacable wall again and again, the number of their dead meant that their lines were broken. The Astures' attack relied on force — flinging everything at the invader, leaving nothing in reserve, whereas the Roman line had repeated its manoeuvre and had reformed with a third, not giving even a handspan of ground. Those who had been on the front line first returned to it, rested and fresh. Marcus was impressed by their discipline.

Quintus and Crassus fought shoulder to shoulder, pointing out danger, encouraging each other and relaying orders. Quintus' height had given him a long reach, enough to cut a throat or pierce a heart whilst the enemy's arm was still drawn back to fling a javelin or strike with the edge of a long sword. Crassus was quick and methodical, and protected Quintus' long arm when it became vulnerable.

As the noise of battle began to abate, Marcus realised that it was time to move on to the attack, to force the enemy on to the defensive and break them utterly.

'On the signiferi,' he yelled, 'follow the banners!' Then he turned to the standard-bearer nearest to him, the new one, and said forcefully, 'You, young man, on my command, step. I am with you.'

Marcus took up position before the front rank, near the centre. He had stood forward to lead, as was expected, and fought off tribesmen almost as an afterthought, thrusting and killing with his sword, smashing and maiming with his shield, wielding it as if it were made of kid leather rather than metal and thick hide.

'On my command, step!' he yelled at the other signifer.

The men heard their centurion and listened for the command. Quintus put an arm out to stop Crassus, a movement repeated by many along the front line, keeping the formation solid. It was like holding back water that yearned to rush over a cataract.

'Step!' Marcus ordered. 'Step!' As he shouted, each standard, along with himself in the centre, moved a single step forward. Each signifer was careless of his own fate, and each symbol was held high and proud.

On the order, men and weapons moved across the ground as one. As the standards continued to move forward and Marcus repeated the order, the century advanced and the enemy in front of them slashed and stabbed. The iron and salt tang of blood filled the air, fine droplets spraying upwards in a scarlet mist. Quintus and Crassus, each splashed with bright red spots, held one another back. They were straining to go but obeyed Marcus' order. The steps became faster and faster.

'Step, step, step!'

The enemy were pushed further and further back. Some stood to battle on, apparently determined to die fighting and to take Romans with them to the afterlife. Many fled into the trees and some ran towards the temple, but on the whole they seemed to be trying to lead the soldiers away from it. The woman had vanished.

Many warriors fought hand to hand, but the odds were against the tribesmen. Fights turned into two to one, as a legionary gave assistance to a comrade in the form of the swing of a sword or the thrust of a spear. Sometimes, three or four came together to dispatch a single enemy who refused to fall. The space between the advancing forces and the low, dull orange wall that marked the entrance to the temple became smaller and smaller, the Astures finding less and less room to manoeuvre.

Quintus thrust his sword into the soft belly of a man who had lifted an axe to him. The man was already dying from wounds to his head and neck but did not seem to know it. Quintus could see Crassus next to him, also pausing, for once with no enemy to engage. Both looked up.

'Crassus!' Quintus warned, as an Asturian stumbled towards his friend.

But there was no strength in the attack; the man carried many wounds and no weapon. Crassus swatted him out of the way, the soldier on the other side of him despatching him with a single thrust.

'I am fine,' Crassus said hoarsely, lifting his bloodied gladius in salute to Quintus.

Marcus looked around and saw that the Astures were trying to escape. He gave a sigh of relief and shouted one final command: '*Contendite vestra sponte!*' This meant that the formation could at last be broken and that each legionary could fight the enemy that was closest to him. The Third could finally engage.

Quintus and Crassus lowered their arms, standing close to each other as the fresh legionaries of the Third surged past them. They did not need to fight anymore; they could now let the Third have their moment.

This general order, Marcus knew, meant that some of the enemy warriors might escape, but he reasoned that a few were needed to carry the message to others that the fight was over.

'Quintus, Crassus, I need captives,' Marcus ordered. 'I need some of them alive. And I need the queen, or whatever she is, and the grandson. We need hostages.'

The friends waved their acknowledgement.

'It will not be easy,' said Crassus in Quintus' ear.

'Sextus, Rufus!' Quintus called their comrades. 'Follow — we need captives, live ones.'

Moving through the few individual fights that still continued, they found their way to the edge of the trees at the side of the clearing. Quintus observed that this was where most of those wishing to escape were fleeing.

Capturing them was not easy. It took the four of them to take just one captive: as soon as an enemy was held, he stabbed himself or pushed poison into his mouth. The first they caught had lost his weapon and they managed to pin his arms behind his back before he could swallow anything. They trussed his arms and legs using his own clothing, then moved to catch another, knowing to disarm them and keep their hands away from their faces, even if they had to break their arms to do so.

'There!' Quintus called excitedly, and they all turned to where he pointed. A bloodstained warrior stood, shieldless but still wielding his axe, blinded by blood and rage. His long black locks betrayed him: the grandson.

Crassus leapt, disregarding his own safety, and grabbed the man by the hair, pulling him down. Rufus punched the man hard in the face with the hilt of his sword — a blow that caused an explosion of blood and much disorientation.

Quintus and Sextus held an arm each as Rufus struck again, making the man drop his axe. Desperately, he tried to reach something at his belt — perhaps a sword, a dagger or poison — but Quintus tightened his grip to prevent him.

'Bind him tight,' he said. 'He is important.'

They only managed to capture six men in total, including the grandson, before there were no more left. The men of the Third had not heard the order for captives and were intent on slaughter.

One of their captives clearly would not survive his injuries, so they sent him on his way to whatever god had been worshipped here. The other five, though they moaned, would survive. The prize was the long-haired grandson, whose fiery black eyes were full of hatred.

The operation was now no more than a clean-up. Some of the men had taken their own captives, perhaps hoping for plunder, but Marcus ordered their death. He did not wish to waste resources on them and thought the five trussed by the wood would suffice. The badly injured were summarily killed; even the uninjured were of little use, as they would likely make poor and disobedient slaves.

'We keep high-status captives only,' Marcus said.

The men assumed that the chieftains would be those who wore torcs and rings of precious metals, but there appeared to be only one of these left alive. He was injured, though not seriously, and was dumped alongside the five surviving captives. Parties of legionaries began moving around the battlefield, separating injured Romans from fallen enemy warriors and deciding who might recover and who should die. Others took whatever weapons and trophies they could from the dead, then dragged the bodies to the edge of the wood that lined the killing ground, where the animals of the night could feast on them.

Marcus placed a guard on the entrance to the temple but, considering the tribesmen's reluctance to be captured, he assumed they would all have sacrificed themselves to whatever god they worshipped here. The structure at the front of the site now revealed itself to be rough walls, long and low, with rounded tops. It was made from the same stone as the mountains, which now glowed in the setting sun.

Quintus, having made certain that their captives were secured, was keen to investigate the temple now, in the last of the light, especially since the caves might provide warmth and shelter for the men. He left his companions on guard and walked into the enclosure.

Behind the wall, the earth was beaten flat, but with many gullies and trenches cut into it. There were also low stone structures that looked like basins, with open conduits running into them. The smoke did not rise from a brazier, but from beneath a bowl, raised on a tripod. Quintus scratched his head, having never seen a temple structure of this type.

He called to Marcus, who was busy sending runners to see how far behind the baggage train was. He came over to look at the strange courtyard, then enrolled Sextus in the investigation. 'Genius,' he called to him, 'come and tell us what this is!'

Sextus, still feeling that the place was accursed, was reluctant and insisted that Crassus accompanied him, leaving just Rufus guarding the prisoners. Rufus waved them away, grinning and brandishing his sword. He could look after the captives, now lying trussed uncomfortably on the ground.

'This is like no temple I have ever seen,' Sextus offered, having looked at the various bowls and basins and channels. 'Perhaps whatever happens, happens further inside the mountain.' He was clearly perplexed.

'It looks like these are meant to carry water,' said Quintus, 'and there are remnants of some sort of sludge in some of the basins.'

Crassus' gaze turned from the men to the mountain and back, a look of concentration on his face. 'I know what this is,' he explained in a hoarse whisper. 'I am a blacksmith, but not everything we made was practical. Sometimes, if the client wanted a design worked into a piece, or some embellishment on the hilt of a dagger, for example, we would work with the goldsmith.' He paused and opened his hand to the mountain. 'That is what this is, my friends: gold, hidden in the deposits that this stream is bringing down the mountain. And these pits and pans are nothing to do with sacrifice or religion, Sextus, but are designed to allow the gold to be extracted.'

He looked at the dark entrance to the caves and then allowed the slurry to run through his fingers, a few bright beads of metal remaining in his palm. 'There is a lot of gold here,' he said, in hushed tones. 'This could be *mons auri*, a whole mountain of gold.'

XIV: MONS AURI

The four of them stared in wonder at the tiny, bright objects in Crassus' hands. They were blacksmith's hands, big and strong, and the dirt of battle made the shining nuggets look even brighter. He closed his fingers over them, making a fierce and bony fist that hid the wealth beneath.

Marcus had decisions to make. Night was falling and outside, the legionaries were still moving across the killing ground, seeking comrades, dead or alive. The Roman losses had not been great, but there were some. Marcus needed to assemble the men, order their disposition for the night, and clear out the caves — and now, he had to guard what seemed to be a goldmine. He sighed.

He had explored the wide opening into the mountain with the last of the daylight and had found a food store just inside. Grain, vegetables, some things that he did not recognise but assumed were foodstuffs, and, of course, fresh water, running down from somewhere inside the mountain.

'Keep this information to yourselves,' Marcus told his little group, then nodded his head towards the rest. 'I will tell them when the time is right.'

'But surely it is ours,' said Crassus, quickly. 'Surely this belongs to the men that won it?' He held out the fist that contained what he saw as his prize.

'It is not ours.' Sextus shook his head. His face was long, his smile extinguished. 'It belongs to the gods of this mountain. Maybe *that* is what I felt,' he added, almost to himself, 'a curse, a malediction. Maybe it is the gold that is cursed, not the place.'

'You are too superstitious,' Quintus offered, putting an arm lightly over his comrade's shoulder. 'Surely you can see that this is good fortune, not bad? This is wealth.'

Sextus was unappeased and shrugged the arm off, muttering under his breath.

'And how would you use it? To escape your service?' Marcus asked, raising an eyebrow. 'Would you desert? Or would you maybe lead a revolt and become a fugitive?' He waved his hand at the mountain. 'If what Crassus says is true, there is too much for us. Sadly, this will belong to Rome. We could not take a share even if we wished it. It will be the emperor's.'

'Then should I not keep even this?' asked the blacksmith pleadingly, opening his fist.

'I think that is safe.' Marcus closed the blacksmith's fingers. 'I think perhaps even a little more — enough for a drink and a woman is a fair reward for all of us.'

'But not so much as to draw attention.' Quintus understood and smiled.

'I will have none of it,' said Sextus, turning away. 'I still think it cursed.'

'Yet you will obey my order and tell no one,' Marcus said sternly.

'They will find out anyway,' Sextus sniffed, holding his hands up quickly as Marcus bridled. 'Not from me,' he added swiftly. 'But we have more than one Crassus in this company, more than one who will recognise this for what it is.'

Quintus had been considering possibilities and said thoughtfully, 'Marcus, surely the information itself is precious — at least as valuable as the gold. We should take it as high as we can, to the emperor himself if possible. Those who bring this to the ear of Augustus will receive a reward. It should be us.'

'And what makes you think you could get within a hundred paces of the emperor without his praetorians cutting you down?' scoffed Marcus. 'It is not for the likes of us to be heard in his presence.'

'Perhaps you are right,' said Crassus, slowly. 'Perhaps the emperor is aiming too high.' He paused. 'The legate in Lucus Augustus, at least. He would listen; he would be able to speak to the emperor on our behalf.'

'On his own behalf, more likely, and take all the glory,' said Sextus dismissively. 'Whoever carries this information will want the credit — and any reward — for themselves. I tell you it is accursed.'

'You would plan to cut our Flavian out?' Marcus asked Crassus, ignoring Sextus' warnings. 'How do you think that would go?'

Crassus shrugged. Sextus was silent. Quintus remained thoughtful, trying to think of a way to capitalise on their discovery and failing. Clearly the discussion was at an end, even if it wasn't resolved.

'My orders stand,' said Marcus, 'until I decide otherwise. In the meantime, guard the entrance.'

Marcus needed to know as soon as possible how far away the baggage train was, along with the other three depleted centuries and the politician that was their commander. He had taken an enormous risk by going into battle without them. A loss would have meant certain death, either by his own hand or that of the state. But the dice had fallen on 'Venus' and, with the permission of the prefect, he could be a hero. He doubted that such permission would be granted, but he hoped to at least keep his rank.

He had sent what he hoped were swift runners, reasonably fresh men of the Third, with Galba's permission. The big man

— or chicken, Marcus smiled — was directing men to collect all the weapons from the field, to make space for camp. In other words, thought Marcus wryly, he was telling them to do all the things that they were doing anyway.

He wanted the rest of the cohort here to protect his position. Most of all he wanted to share the responsibility with someone, which, he thought, would have to be the prefect. He had also decided that he did not trust Sextus not to 'warn' the men about the gold. Knowledge that there were riches here could, if not handled properly, cause unrest.

Night was closing in quickly and he needed light to investigate the mountain. It was provided by Crassus, who, peering inside the cave from where he guarded it, found a basket of torches, clearly for the use of those who worked here.

Marcus was keen to explore the mountain but did not know if an enemy lay within. He wanted knowledge before the prefect arrived.

Quintus took the burning brand from the blacksmith and peered inside the opening. 'There is food here,' he said, 'and perhaps offerings.'

Marcus followed his gaze. 'Not offerings,' he said, 'supplies.' He took another torch from Crassus and ignited it, passing it to Sextus, and then he became brisk. 'Quintus, bring the cohort's signiferi to me,' he ordered.

Quintus, drilled to obey without question when a voice held authority, headed out to the flat ground. The sharpness of the air after the day's rain sent a shiver down his spine. He was also wary of the shadowy figures on the battlefield, some of which could easily be the shades of the dead.

'And bring the rest of our contubernium!' Marcus shouted after him. 'Bring Galba too. Show him respect, Quintus.' He paused. 'But make sure he has his helmet,' he added under his breath.

Quintus grinned.

Publius and Cato were already close, curious to know what their companions were discussing with such intensity.

'Nox, Lux!' called Quintus. 'Find the others; we are missing Tullius and Rufus. Report to the mountain. Rufus is guarding the captives. I don't know about Tullius. Rufus will have to find another to relieve him.'

Cato signalled his understanding with a wave whilst Quintus went in search of Galba. He found him picking over the pile of broken and bloody weapons claimed by the Third.

'Sir,' Quintus said as he saluted smartly, jolting the centurion out of his reverie, 'you are needed at the mountain.' It was not his place — nor that of Marcus — to give orders to the man, but Galba seemed happy to take it as a summons. He rose, saluted in return, and was about to set off when Quintus saluted again and said, 'Sir…'

The centurion frowned, then realised that Quintus was pointing to his helmet, which was still on the floor. He grunted, picked it up, placed it over his bald crown, and departed.

Quintus had more authority with the signiferi. One was a scarred veteran, clearly a survivor, and the other was the brave young man who had taken on the responsibility, no doubt urged to it because of his courage. Quintus remembered that although he looked like a youth, he was a ten-year veteran, more experienced than himself and worthy of respect.

'You are summoned,' he told them. 'Our once optio, now centurion, calls you.'

Both had already planted their standards on the field of the dead, the fair-skinned man standing proudly by his, the veteran

146

squatting on the ground. Though bearing a standard had its dangers, as you were expected to lead where the troops would follow, it had its benefits too. These two were amongst the immunes — those who did not have to take part in the mundane tasks of the legion. They could watch as comrades cleared enough space for a camp and began erecting defences.

'Bring those,' ordered Quintus.

As the standards were lifted and moved, a number of heads were raised, eyes following them. These were the hearts of the two centuries; the men would follow them wherever they led.

'Set up the standards here,' Marcus told them as they approached, 'then spread the word to the men to send one from each contubernium for food. There is not much — just grain and vegetables — but it is better than nothing. There is fresh water, too. Centurion Galba will oversee its distribution.'

The big man smiled and nodded.

'He will then oversee the building of a marching camp.' Though Marcus spoke to the signiferi, it was clear to any who witnessed that in fact he was instructing Galba. 'Tonight, the men will be able to light fires,' he continued, 'but must camp in the open. We need a ditch and a rampart: there is soft ground and there is timber. Mount a guard. The enemy may yet return — they may even lurk in the trees. There are some in the cave that we intend to flush out.' He turned to look at Galba, to check that he was taking all this in. It should have been second nature to any legionary, and, indeed, the men were already marking out a perimeter, but he did not know how far to trust this centurion.

Galba was nodding sagely, Marcus was pleased to see. He continued, 'Tell them to keep watch. The baggage train may be close, so tents and food could arrive at any time. If it fails to come, we'll see out the night and we'll muster at dawn.' He added, almost as an afterthought, 'The prisoners can have enough water and food to survive, but no more.'

Galba seemed about to speak, but then shook his head.

'Sir?' Marcus asked, knowing the man outranked him.

'Nothing,' Galba said, in that soft voice that belied his frame. 'Carry on. You are managing very well here. I will see to the camp.'

As he left, Marcus spoke to the signiferi. 'You can see to the distribution of the provisions?'

'Yes, sir,' the standard bearers answered in unison.

Marcus made an approving noise.

He did not want any more of the men seeing the workings of this mine. He wanted to tell them what they had found himself, and at a time of his own choosing. In fact, he did not even know if he should tell them — perhaps he should wait until the prefect arrived and tell only him. Then at least it would not be his decision. He detailed Cato and Publius to bring the provisions to the gap in the wall. The signiferi thrust the standards into the ground on either side of the entrance, then told the nearest of the men to come and collect food.

Marcus turned to Quintus and spoke quietly to him. 'I want you to take our contubernium into the mountain, with your swords drawn.' In reality he wanted these legionaries out of the way, especially Sextus, but he also knew that a few Astures had fled into the mountain, including the queen, for that was how he thought of the female chieftain. They could be hiding themselves, moving wealth, or fetching reinforcements, and they would need to be flushed out. 'Be careful,' Marcus added in an undertone. 'The queen went this way.'

Quintus gathered up the others and, armed and ready, with the flickering torches casting uncertain light, they prepared to investigate. 'Keep your wits about you. Remember, that woman must be in here somewhere. She would make a fine captive.'

It seemed that new responsibilities were beginning to fall into place, now that their decanus was likely to be confirmed as centurion. Marcus, friend though he was, would billet apart from them and would no longer be in their group, and Quintus would be expected to lead. He did not wish it, but he could see no way of refusing.

Of the seven legionaries, six took a torch, all lit from the fire or from the one that Publius held. Quintus held no torch but carried his sword in his right hand, balancing his shield on his left forearm. In his belt he had tucked not only his dagger, but also a longer blade borrowed from the dead. He worried that the queen would not have fled without warriors with her. He did not doubt his companions' courage or honour, but he did harbour doubts about Tullius — and what he may have seen him do on the battlefield.

They could see five clear tunnels leading into the mountain from where they stood, though Quintus was aware that there could be others not yet illuminated by their meagre lights. None of these looked like a natural feature, and all had tell-tale tool marks along their walls. The two nearest to them were narrow — crawl spaces, really. Publius and Cato thrust a torch into each, revealing them to be short and incapable of hiding any enemy warriors. The other three openings were all at least the height and width of a man, one clearly used much more than the others, judging by the way the floor was beaten down.

'That one last,' decided Quintus.

'This is more a cave than a tunnel,' Crassus said, emerging from one of the other openings. 'Though it is man-sized, it hardly goes back far enough to hide anything. I think it has only just been started.'

'This one looks more dangerous,' said Quintus, as he took the first steps into the opening. 'Take care.'

This passage was larger. They could enter it two abreast. Crassus would have joined Quintus, but Tullius elbowed past, leaving Quintus behind. 'It will need light — two torches,' he explained. He held his own flaming brand high.

Quintus let him pass, but stayed right behind, at his shoulder. The initial opening, broad as it was, widened out further and seemed about to fork, but both legs of it ended abruptly after the separation. It was obviously unfinished.

'There is nothing here,' said Tullius, clearly disappointed.

'And no-one,' agreed Rufus, equally unhappy that there was no enemy to fight.

As they turned around and led the way out, ready to explore the remaining passage, Crassus grabbed Quintus' arm. 'There is something,' he whispered urgently.

XV: DRACO

Quintus recognised the confidential tone and held back to let the others move out of earshot.

'I did not know if you wished to share it, but look,' Crassus whispered.

Halfway down the wall of one of the dead ends, there was a clear horizontal line and below it was darker stone. He kicked the darker section, and the wall moved.

'Again,' breathed Quintus. 'Kick it again.'

Crassus did so, with the toe of his sandal. A gap appeared and the wall crumbled around it, debris falling to the floor.

'What is it?' Tullius shouted, turning to come back up the opening.

Quintus stepped across and waved him away. 'Nothing,' he said quickly, 'just a rockfall, and Crassus stumbled. Go on, we are following.'

After Tullius left, Crassus put his torch close to the opening he had created, peering in wonderment at the nugget upon nugget of gold piled within. This wall had been made very recently and had not had time to dry, hence its discolouration, but it was clearly intended to hide what had been mined this day or this week — or maybe this month. If it was this day or this week, then this was indeed a mountain of gold. Crassus reached in and grabbed a couple of larger nuggets.

'No,' insisted Quintus. 'Remember, it is the emperor's…'

'He does not know it yet.' Crassus' face was alive with the joy of possession: his dark eyes sparkled. As he spoke, he shoved the nuggets inside his clothing.

'No,' said Quintus again, but less forcefully.

Crassus thrust a scant handful into Quintus' palm, closing his fist over it. 'These are yours,' he said. 'Think of Ursus — he would have used them for the common good.'

Quintus did not refuse; he could not, though in his heart he wished to. He did not know what Ursus would have done, but the memory of him had been enough to give Crassus time to fill his hand and close his fingers over the shiny metal. It should be cold, he knew, but it felt warm, like it belonged there.

'I will keep just a little,' he said, hesitating, 'for the common good.' He looked at his palm briefly. Three bright nuggets nestled there. He quickly thrust them under his tunic, out of sight.

The two friends looked into each other's eyes. What they were seeking, neither quite knew — a shared crime, perhaps, or just a shared secret. Both jumped guiltily when a voice spoke near to them. This time it was Sextus calling, suspicious of what was happening.

'Quintus, Crassus, come on,' Sextus said. 'What are you doing?'

'Cover it up,' Quintus ordered urgently, flapping his hands at the cracked wall.

Crassus hurried to close the gap with the still soft clay, then both of them strode purposefully towards Sextus, the wall behind them receding into the shadows as Crassus' torch was carried away from it.

'What is it?' Sextus asked cautiously, trying to peer beyond the two who now came towards him. Being clever and wily enough to flourish in Rome, he clearly knew that something was amiss.

'Nothing, nothing,' said Quintus. 'Come, let's see what the last passage holds.'

Soon they were all back together in the main 'hall', looking down the biggest and darkest of the tunnels, ready to explore it.

'This passage looks older than the rest,' Quintus said. 'The sides and floor are worn smooth. Many feet have passed this way.'

'It widens out, too,' said Rufus, who, with Tullius, had taken the lead. 'Be wary, there could be hiding places here.'

The tunnel twisted and turned, so that they could no longer see even a faint light from where they had come. It became wide enough for them to go as many as three abreast. The air seemed somehow empty. Quintus was sure he would have detected any hidden Astures by now. It was impossible to hide your footsteps, however softly you tried to tread. He was convinced that no escapees would be found here.

Although there appeared to be small side tunnels and explorations, none were of a size that could have fitted a man. Finally, the main passage became wider still, so that they could no longer feel the sides. They could not touch the ceiling and their light did not reach it. It was an underground cavern. It opened into even deeper darkness, so that they had to hold the torches at arm's length in front of them and move slowly and cautiously, lest there be traps or pits.

'Work your way to the side,' said Quintus, 'so that we can follow the wall. There is no hiding place, I am sure.'

'So there must be an exit,' said Sextus.

They moved cautiously to the left, feeling for the wall, Cato putting his hand on it first.

'Here,' he said, waving his torch, 'to me.'

'Keep one hand on the wall,' said Quintus, 'then at least we will know we are moving forwards.'

They moved in single file, each with one hand brushing the wall. Quintus, his free hand still clutching his weapon, had taken the lead. Suddenly Sextus, directly behind him, stopped. His nose was twitching. 'Wait,' he said, and the column halted.

'What is it?' asked Publius, who had only just avoided crashing into him.

'I smell the night air.'

'Move on,' said Quintus, quietly.

They moved forward again, and soon they could all feel a light breeze. An opening appeared ahead of them. It was a way out.

'There is starlight there,' said Cato, turning to Publius in amazement. 'I have never seen starlight inside a mountain.'

'Is it inside the mountain?' Lux asked incredulously. 'Or is it outside? Have we passed right through?'

They had all been talking in whispers, but Publius had spoken loudly. Though Quintus turned to him with an urgent 'hush', it was too late. They realised that there were no Astures lying in wait, and that this was how those that had fled had escaped from the mountain.

Cautiously, they began to move outside, their torches wavering in the cold evening air. There was no moon, but early stars had risen above the open pasture, enclosed by the mountain on one side and by small trees and hedgerows on the other three sides. They raised weapons and braced themselves for combat as a noise disturbed the night, but they relaxed as they saw a small troop of ponies cantering towards them, no doubt expecting to be fed. It was hard to see in the dim light, and they wondered if this was some sort of ruse. But the beasts began to crop the grass and no enemy emerged.

Publius spoke gently and musically, coaxing the ponies to his hand.

'Leave them be, you fool,' snapped Rufus, pulling him away.

'What...' began Publius, sword already unsheathed, ready to defend himself.

Rufus raised a hand to stop him. 'I have seen riders hide under the bellies of horses,' he said quickly. 'You should take more care.'

'There is no enemy here,' said Cato gently, putting an arm around Publius. 'They have fled.'

'Come,' said Quintus, 'stay in formation. There could be enemy yet. Keep together.'

Their eyes had quickly grown accustomed to the dark and, with the aid of starlight, they were able to make out the edges of the field and the small troop of ponies in its corner. There was woodland opposite the mountain, deeper darkness and the spectral silhouettes of trees, but even this felt safe — it was certainly too far away for any tribesmen to mount a surprise attack.

'But there are stars,' said Sextus, removing his helmet and tipping his head back to face the brightly patterned heavens.

'There are,' Tullius agreed, 'many, many stars.' He, too, took off his headgear, to better see the heavens. 'They are different to the ones back home, though I think I recognise some of them.' He turned to Sextus, asking, 'Can you read them?'

'Maybe,' Sextus admitted slowly, 'if we are sure this place is safe.' He had lowered his weapon and stood his shield upon the ground, as had they all. The place felt peaceful.

'Still...' said Quintus.

They knew what to do. Reluctantly Sextus and Rufus replaced their helmets and picked up their shields. The squad was thorough, investigating twenty-five paces in each direction, quartering the field in pairs, torches revealing nothing but grass and the odd bush, nothing but night animals that rustled and fled at this unwarranted disturbance. There was no sign of the enemy, though they could only speculate on why they might have left perfectly sound ponies behind.

'Perhaps they only took what they needed,' said Publius.

'Or they were in too much of a hurry to catch the rest,' said Cato. 'Anyway, they are not here.' He held his torch high, and it flickered in the cool evening breeze.

The horses, finding that they were not about to be fed, had moved away from the lights. The legionaries stood in a semi-circle, each casting around with his eyes to make sure they were safe. It was quiet, with just the wind rustling the leaves, the fire crackling in the torches, and a slight whinnying from the darkness into which the horses had vanished.

'I think we are safe,' Quintus announced as he took off his helmet, the others following suit.

They stood or squatted in a small circle, shields forming its circumference, torches planted firmly in the ground. Sextus' eyes were once more fixed on the sky above: there was no moon, so the stars were bright.

'What do you see?' Publius asked him, respect in his tone.

Though he pushed the thought back from where it had risen, Sextus knew how easily he would have been able to take this man for everything he had if he had ever come across him in Rome. 'There, up and to the right.' He pointed to a group of stars. 'That is Ursa Minor, the Little Bear. You see the four stars together, then those leading from them? That is the North Star, the lodestar, the one that allows ships to navigate at night. Around it, there and there —' with each word he stabbed his sword at a star — 'and there, and there — that is Draco, the dragon or serpent. At times he threatens the Little Bear with his coils and great maw.'

'Where is the Great Bear? Is he here?' Quintus asked, thinking that this was where Ursus' shade would most likely have taken up residence.

'He is beneath Draco, there.' Sextus pointed out a double line of stars. 'That is his body. That,' he said, pointing further, 'is his nose, and there,' he went on, gesturing vaguely, 'would be his tail — but he is difficult to see in this sky, or he has not risen yet…' His voice trailed away.

He turned his eyes on Quintus, who noticed the smudges on his comrade's face. His eyes glistened slightly, as if he had wiped a tear away, but Sextus would never have admitted to such a sadness. Quintus thought that there had been sorrow in his expression, perhaps because Ursus was not with them in the stars. The memory of his death flashed back to him in painfully vivid detail, and he grew solemn. 'The future?' he dared to ask.

'I see betrayal, dishonesty,' said Sextus, making Quintus and Crassus both shiver, whether with guilt or from the cold night air, neither knew. 'See Draco? He smiles; he only smiles when he sees ill deeds.'

A cloud had paused in front of the constellation, which did indeed make it look as if the dragon sneered. Publius looked around quickly, as if evil would arise from the short grass or emerge bellowing from the mountain.

'It is just what might be,' Sextus calmed him gently. 'It may happen, and it may not; it may be long in the future.' Though his voice soothed Publius, his eyes were still fixed on Quintus and Crassus. 'I see murder, too, an execution; the Little Bear has blood dripping from his mouth.' Sextus pointed heavenward, though none of the others could see what he meant.

'We have captives,' said Tullius flatly. 'I think we may see an execution.'

This appeared to be sufficient explanation to stop further speculation, although all now looked at the stars to see what they might interpret for themselves.

XVI: TITUS FLAVIUS PUSO

Quintus and the rest of the group stayed for longer than they really needed to, staring at the night sky and seeing what other shapes or legends they could conjure. They watched the ghostly shapes of the ponies gently cropping the grass, thinking of their executed companion and of the executions that were to come, but eventually the cool of the night began to seep into their bones and, one by one, they sought the entrance to the cave.

Rufus and Tullius had been exploring the area either side of this entrance, each looking for, and finding, a similar thing.

'I have one this side — I think it's the smaller one,' called Rufus.

'And I have one here, the larger.'

'Can you manage it yourself?'

'It will take two.'

'What is it?' Quintus asked. 'What have you found?'

'They would not leave this entrance unguarded if they could not seal it,' said Tullius, 'so we were looking for the "doors". There are stones to roll across to stop up the cave.'

Rufus, drawing on his long experience, added, 'We thought there would be something. If we go, we should not leave it open.'

The field was pleasant, the stars instructive, the wind cool but friendly. They were away from noise and battle — and responsibilities.

Quintus spoke as much to himself as to anyone else. 'We must return,' he said, sadly.

'Five minutes more,' pleaded Publius, almost like a child asking to have his bedtime extended.

The others laughed. Quintus added, like a stern father, 'We must report back.'

'What about the ponies?' Publius asked. 'Should we not take them with us?'

'I think not,' Quintus decided after a little thought. 'Catching them in the dark will be difficult, as will leading them through the twists and turns of the tunnel with no rope or harness.'

'And even if we did get them back, we have no feed for them,' said Cato, seeing his friend's disappointment. 'Here, they have grass and open air.'

'They stay,' Quintus confirmed, 'but the passage must be shut.'

The legionaries rolled first one and then the other stone across the entrance. One was large and blocked much of the opening, and the other was smaller. They dropped into place in clear indentations where they had obviously been before, leaving just enough space for one man to pass between them.

Rufus looked around inside the cave and found a long stone, a perfect fit for the opening. Tullius found the final part of the puzzle, a thick branch, sharpened at one end to go into a slot cut into the floor, and tapered at the other to wedge against the central stone. The 'door' was secure and could not now be opened from the outside.

This job complete, the squad waited a few moments for their eyes to adjust to the torchlight then set off again in single file, right shoulders next to the wall of the cave.

When they had navigated the large cave and reached the passage through which they had originally entered, there appeared to be some jostling for position, Sextus trying to make sure that he was at the front.

Quintus realised why and allowed the fortune-teller to slip into the side passage that he and Crassus had explored. He did not think his comrade would find anything, certainly not in the short time he was going to give him to look. Sextus had time to wave his torch from side to side in the passage, but failed to look low and failed to see the discolouration of the wall.

'Wrong way!' Quintus called, laughing, before Sextus could explore more thoroughly.

Sextus turned and came back, laughing unconvincingly at his 'mistake'.

A very different scene was waiting for them at the site of the battle. In the few hours that they had been gone, the prefect had arrived with the other three centuries, led by Antoninus, centurion of the Second, who immediately began issuing orders. Galba was happy to listen to him, Marcus less so, but they knew that on Marius' demise this man had claimed pilus prior.

Quintus, emerging with his squad from the mountain, blinked at the edifice that had been so quickly erected. The men were well drilled and already there was a gate, a headquarters area, accommodation for the prefect, tents for the officers, latrines, an exercise area, a tribunal platform, a central place of honour for the standards and vexilla, guards, and above all, order and familiarity. Trees had been felled to clear a larger space, and the timber had been used for the fortifications. A wide ditch had been dug all around, and pickets had been posted at all possible approaches.

The squad were challenged by a rough-voiced sentry as they exited the mountain, the head of eight legionaries guarding the opening. There was a tessararius, so there were passwords already, but the sentries knew the men emerging from the mountain would not know them.

'We do not report to you,' Quintus insisted, as the man asked him to explain where he had been. 'We report to our centurion, to Marcus.'

One of the sentries asked, 'Is that the idiot one?'

'No,' said his superior, 'it is the other, the optio.' He turned to Quintus. 'He is with the prefect.'

'Then it's even more important that we report our findings to him personally,' insisted Quintus.

'Just you, then,' said the man, reluctantly. 'The rest of you stay here until I am told otherwise.'

Quintus' sword and dagger were taken from him, and his shield and helmet were handed to Rufus.

'Apparently the enemy went into the caves. You could be spies; we must take care,' explained the sentry.

Quintus was paraded across what would be the exercise area, where holes were being dug to set up posts, for what purpose he could not yet guess. Two sentries guarded the door of the headquarters tent, throwing it back to admit Quintus and his escort when told to do so. Inside, Quintus could see slaves and freedmen, wine, fruit, the remnants of some sort of meat, papers, uniforms and, at the far end, lit by flickering torchlight, Marcus and the prefect in intense conversation, their heads close together. There was a scribe of some sort standing near to them.

He had no idea what Marcus was telling the Flavian, although he thought that he could make a fairly accurate guess. This was no description of a battle. This was something more: a secret being imparted, valuable information — less valuable, thought Quintus resignedly, the more people knew of it.

It was the first time that Quintus had been close enough to the prefect to properly study him. The commander had been a long way from him, resplendent in uniform and flanked by signiferi and centurions when he had first seen him, standing on a box on a podium and addressing the men. He expected nobility — though he wasn't quite sure what that meant. After all, the prefect was a Flavian, Titus Flavius Pusio, a member of one of Rome's ruling families, of ancient and august lineage. Perhaps Quintus had expected dignity, height, haughtiness, clear eyes, an aquiline nose, an uncreased brow, dark hair and a strong jaw. The face that flashed across his mind — a handsome and chiselled visage that he thought of as bearing all these noble characteristics — was, surprisingly, that of Sextus, a rogue and scoundrel, but with a distinguished air about him.

This man, to his disappointment, was quite small by legionary standards — the box on which he had stood had been necessary to stop the centurions looming over him. He had strangely flat, thinning hair that was an unremarkable shade of brown and was cut in a style that did not suit him. He also had a snub nose and a receding chin. He was overweight, but Quintus guessed from his ragged ears that he might once have been a boxer — or may have at least have practised the art as a youth.

The prefect, a politician, seemed irritable and impatient, forever turning to his freedman for answers to his questions. Quintus did not approve of the freedman having any part in this discussion and despaired of the growing number of people that now had the information about the mine.

Marcus looked up from their conversation, acknowledged the presence of his comrade with a hand gesture, then turned back to the prefect.

'Step forward,' ordered the prefect, 'and tell us what you have found.'

Quintus stepped forward but hesitated to speak, glancing involuntarily at the freedman, who was poised to write on a tablet he held. Both the prefect and Marcus noticed the look and spoke at the same time in justification.

'Records must be kept,' said the prefect pompously, 'for posterity.'

'It is no business of ours what the prefect wishes to record,' said Marcus dismissively.

The prefect and the optio looked at each other and decided simultaneously that it was a point not worth pursuing. Marcus gave a slight bow of his head to prompt the Flavian to speak.

'Give your report,' he demanded. 'What did you find?'

'Sir,' Quintus began, 'we explored all the tunnels and passages of the —' he hesitated and looked at Marcus, but when he received no clue, he continued uncertainly — 'temple, within the mountain…'

'The mine,' the prefect interrupted emotionlessly, 'the goldmine.' He instructed the freedman to write this down and then told Quintus to continue.

Quintus now knew where he stood and carried on with greater confidence. 'We found no enemy in the mountain. They had fled. There is evidence of workings, and there was a food store near the entrance.'

'Anything else?' demanded the prefect, his eyes glistening with anticipation.

The nuggets secured against Quintus' skin were digging into him, and even seemed to have heated up. He was sure that his face was bound to betray him. He knew that Sextus had seen through him and wondered if the piercing eyes of the freedman had the same power. Nevertheless, when he spoke, he did not reveal the presence of the hoard. He would let them find it for themselves.

'Nothing in the mountain. I think the tribesmen have taken much with them. Whilst there were pans, pipes and pits at the front of the mountain and just inside it, there seemed to be only a few tools left behind. There were adzes and chisels and there were barrows tipped over, their contents gone.'

The prefect looked disappointed, and Marcus looked dubious.

'I think,' said Quintus in explanation, 'that all was taken from the rear of the mountain.'

At this, his listeners' attention was once more focused.

'The rear...' began the prefect.

'There is another way out?' Marcus asked.

'There is,' said Quintus. 'The cave goes right through the mountain, coming out into what appears to be a pasture and, beyond that, there is woodland. There were even a few ponies grazing there. We checked the perimeter as best we could by torchlight, but we could not see everything in the dark. There may be a path through the forest. There may be a road.'

'You left it guarded?' Marcus asked.

'We did not have enough men — only our contubernium, and that is incomplete.' He shot a look at his questioner. 'We sealed the entrance instead. There were stones cut for the purpose, to prevent entry from outside. It is shut and can only be opened from within the mountain.'

'Wait outside.' The prefect was imperious, waving Quintus out, and he had turned back to converse with Marcus before Quintus had even saluted.

Quintus went out into the cool of the night. The stars that they had studied so assiduously were now all but invisible, the bright moon making them dim into insignificance. The fires and torches of the cohort were now also obscuring the constellations and the stories that they might tell.

Quintus' other senses were assailed as he watched the activity of the camp. Stakes were being driven in and voices were raised in conversation, laughter and argument. There was the crackle of flame and the smells of burning and cooking, intermingled with sweat and other bodily odours.

At the front and centre of the parade ground, a detail was digging two square holes. The prisoners had seen such preparations before and were aware of the significance of the holes being dug so assiduously. They knew they were to be executed. They also knew that it was often Roman policy to allow prisoners to see the place of their execution before one last round of questioning.

Quintus could see, some distance away, his own people sitting and standing morosely in a semi-circle just inside what he still thought of as the low wall of the temple. Rufus, helmetless, was revealed by his red hair in the torchlight. Even from here, Tullius could be seen twiddling his earring. The silhouette of Crassus' broad back and the two heads together that were Lux and Nox only made Quintus feel even more guilty about the gold he carried. Still, it was too late now; he had given his report.

A hand on his shoulder made him flinch, although he knew that all were friends here — or should be. It was Marcus.

'Good report,' he said. 'The Flavian is pleased.'

'Pleased with me, you, or his goldmine?' Quintus asked, the sarcasm in his voice barely hidden.

'All three, I think,' Marcus replied, not responding to the implied challenge in Quintus' voice. He put his arm around his comrade's shoulder and began to walk him back towards the mountain, towards the rest of the contubernium. 'I had to tell him, Quintus. There was no way that such a thing could be kept a secret. And he will tell our new pilus prior, Antoninus of the Second. He has had the prefect's ear on their march. It will leak to the men. I could not be responsible for this.'

166

Quintus shrugged his friend's arm from his shoulder; he did not feel like such comradeship at present. To him it felt like yet another betrayal, part of a rising tide of deception. He was at the centre of it and unable to hold it back.

'There are blacksmiths like Crassus in the ranks,' Marcus was continuing, not taking the shrug as a rejection, 'but also others who would know — miners, engineers, anyone. I could not have kept it from him.'

'And our captive chieftains? The grandson especially?'

'He knows. I think this is what he intends.' His voice tailed off as he indicated the post-holes. They walked in silence until they reached the man who held Quintus' weapons. 'Return them,' ordered Marcus, 'and let these men go and find their tent. There is no treachery here.'

'Will you come with us?' Quintus asked, as he placed his sword back in its scabbard and the dagger and enemy sword into his belt. The guard had been reluctant to hand back the latter, muttering something about it not being regulation, but it was only covetousness on his part, and Quintus had insisted. He then took back his helmet and shield from Rufus, tucking the helmet under his arm.

'I am between two worlds,' Marcus said, a touch of sadness in his tone. 'I am not sure where I belong.'

Quintus looked sideways at his comrade, raising an eyebrow in question. 'Meaning?'

'Meaning that I am not confirmed as centurion, not yet officially given the helmet and plumes. Therefore, I am optio still, but also decanus to this contubernium. If I lay my head to sleep beside you men —' he indicated the small group that was now standing, waiting for instructions — 'then I may be giving up my chance to be centurion. If I billet with the officers, I may not be accepted — and I may lose friendship here.' He laughed suddenly. 'What will be, will be, I suppose,' he said. 'Sextus, do you see my future?'

'On an empty stomach it is blurred, Marcus,' Sextus replied, smiling. 'You are still decanus and optio for sure, so why not come and eat with us?'

'Maybe later,' Marcus said, then gestured to the group. 'Come, I can at least show you where your tent is pitched. Jovan and Maxim await you.'

Lines of tents, their guy ropes awkward and treacherous in the dark, stretched down the field. It had been cleared of bodies, discarded weapons and the evidence of fighting; straight roads now led between the accommodation, flattened by many feet. It was as if no battle had taken place here. The headquarters tent stood larger than the others, the standards of each century and of the cohort fluttering at its mouth. It was hard for anyone but a Roman legionary to believe that such order had been achieved in such a short space of time. The legionaries expected it.

Marcus indicated a spot to them, then told Quintus: 'You take charge of the contubernium for now. I am going back to see what the prefect is telling Antoninus.' He sighed. 'I will find my place soon enough.'

They recognised the two black-bearded figures of Jovan and Maxim, waiting for their masters beside the tent.

'You have already erected it!' Publius was overjoyed.

'We had help,' admitted Jovan, waving his arm noncommittally, his long fingers encompassing several nearby tents.

'They were happy to help,' Maxim said diffidently, bowing his dark head. 'There was a rumour that you had gone into the heart of the temple and would return with jewels and other riches.'

The men, believing they were still sworn to secrecy about the mine, looked at each other — this was perhaps a little too close to the truth.

'Well, I thank them,' said Rufus, performing a bow in the general direction, 'but now we should eat.'

'There is bread, biscuit and hot pottage,' said Maxim, 'but no meat, I am afraid.'

'And?' Rufus grabbed the slave by the scruff of his tunic, mock-threateningly.

'There is wine, sir. I have managed to save some wine,' said the man quickly, as Rufus released him. 'Your stocks too, sir,' he whispered urgently to Sextus, who smiled.

'There is hot water, too, should you wish to wash and shave,' offered Jovan.

The men were tired, but also pleased to find a fire and food and shelter all ready for them. Whilst some went straight for the fire, and Rufus and Sextus went straight for the wineskins, Quintus first wanted to wash the dried blood and dirt from his face. Jovan held out a bowl and a cloth, offering to shave him, but Quintus was too tired to bother with more than getting clean.

The water was warm, and the cloth that Jovan had brought was not too rough. He washed his face and neck, glorying in the simple pleasure this gave him. He then commanded the slave to unlace his armour. Setting the segmented chest-piece aside, he was about to pull his tunic over his head but stopped, realising that to do so would reveal the gold.

'Enough, Jovan,' he said. 'It is too much effort.' He looked up and noticed Sextus' eyes upon him.

Sextus rose and moved closer to where Quintus and Crassus were washing. 'Well,' he said loudly, making Crassus jump, 'are you going to monopolise our man? We need him to unlace our armour.'

'You could unlace each other's armour,' said Crassus crossly.

Quintus waved Jovan away. 'Take him,' he said. 'We can manage.'

Although Sextus withdrew with the slave, he did not go far.

Visitors came from other contubernia, asking awkward questions about the temple, the mountain, the jewels that were said to be within it. Quintus waved the questions away and told the others to do the same, but he was uneasy. There was more than one secret here.

The men ate, drank and told stories, but there was no doubting the tension between them.

'Tell me what you read in the stars,' Quintus said to Sextus, in an effort to make light conversation as they sat by the fire, 'apart from the constellations. There, for instance — look, a light shoots across the sky.' He pointed to a streak of white that sped out of sight to the south.

'A shooting star,' said Sextus, clearly bored, 'or if you like, the sparks from Phoebus Apollo's chariot still falling to earth.'

'Which is true?' Quintus asked, hoping that he showed a genuine interest.

'Either,' said Sextus dismissively. 'It depends on what you want to believe.' Then he launched into his own inquiry. 'For example, I believe that Crassus and you found something significant in that tunnel: something religious, perhaps, something strange — something that, for reasons of your own, you want to keep from us.' He paused, turning his full dark-eyed gaze on Quintus. 'Perhaps it is to protect us,' he said. 'Is that so?'

'No,' said Quintus unconvincingly. 'We found nothing. There was a rockfall and Crassus stumbled, that is all.'

Sextus shook his head, a crooked smile fixed on his face. 'Then that is the waste from the horses of Phoebus Apollo that streaks across the sky —' his sarcasm was heavy — 'and it falls to earth as silver denarii.'

'There is no need...' began Quintus as his friend moved away from him.

Moving away from the fireside, Quintus tried to subtly investigate what had happened to Marius, the centurion — at least he thought he was being subtle. He asked Tullius, in an innocent tone, 'You were next to the centurion when he fell, were you not?'

Tullius was immediately evasive: Quintus recognised this because it was how he had been with Sextus.

'Centurion?' Tullius muttered, squatting on the ground and barely raising his eyes. He was cleaning his sword. 'What centurion? Marcus says we have a new centurion. Antony, I think — or is it Galba of whom you speak, or perhaps Marcus himself?'

'Marcus was optio during the action this morning.'

'The benefits of being in combat,' shrugged Tullius, turning his back on Quintus, clearly intending to bring the conversation to an end.

Quintus ploughed on. 'Marius,' he said. 'You were next to Marius when he fell.'

Tullius put his tools and his sword down and swung around challengingly, silently warning Quintus to take a step back.

Quintus, like a ship that has lost its rudder and is driven before a storm, carried on towards disaster. 'You must have seen who killed him — you were right next to him.'

'Then so were you,' Tullius spat. 'You were as close as I. Did you see what happened? Did you witness the killing blow?'

'No,' said Quintus quickly, holding up his hands, finally recognising the dangerous waters into which he was sailing. 'I saw nothing.'

Tullius turned his back and returned to the slow polishing of his blade, now muttering angrily to himself rather than producing his usual tuneless hum.

Quintus realised that, though he had learned nothing, he had managed to stir the muddy waters of dissent and unhappiness. Ursus would have been ashamed of him.

Quintus immediately felt some of the loneliness of his station, salted with the guilt that any distance between himself and the contubernium was his own fault. He had built a wall between himself and Sextus, and himself and Tullius, that had not existed before.

Yes, he thought as he grasped the armband beneath his tunic, *Ursus would have been ashamed of me.*

XVII: LIBERATIO

Quintus hardly slept at all, waking before the cornicen signalled the assembly. The first light of dawn was a pale streak, a wan and uncertain promise of morning. The bulk of the mountain was still in shadow, looming over them all.

Jovan, of course, was already up, tending to the fire. He could see Maxim offering some morsel or other to the mule. When did they ever sleep?

'I will take that shave now, Jovan,' Quintus said, and the man was soon able to oblige, with a sharp dagger and a steady hand. Quintus kept his head still, closed his eyes and drifted into thought. As the sun at last rose weakly, apprehensive of the rolling clouds that threatened it on either side, he worried at the threads of the night that had just passed.

He had slept badly because at heart he was an honest man and did not take easily to intrigue. He recognised and did not like the bad blood that was beginning to swirl around the band of comrades.

'Done, sir.'

Quintus dismissed Jovan and his shaving gear with a wave of his hand and stood to survey the camp. There was a film of mist on the ground, snaking between guy ropes and what little grass remained — enough to reach the top of a caliga but no more. There was smoke rising, charcoal greys against an ash-grey sky. There was some noise, muted conversation, the shuffling and complaining of pack animals, the vague crackling and spitting of fires, and the odd curse as someone tripped over a rope or rebuked a slave. This first light was also the signal for the cornicen to sound the assembly. All around him the camp was starting to awaken.

Now it could be seen that at the front of the parade ground, before the headquarters tent, two stakes of wood had been erected, driven deep into the holes dug there, and two cross-pieces lashed to them. Today there would be at least one execution.

Crucifixion, as all the legionaries knew, was reserved for the worst felons: criminals, rebels, slaves who had killed their masters. The law said that any slave who committed such a crime would be crucified, but that so would all the slaves of the murdered owner, however many they numbered, however old, young or valuable they were — women and children too. And the Senate, though there had been outcries when children were involved, upheld the law.

Officially, these tribes had been slaves, so had turned on their masters. Marcus had taken the prisoners with the intention of gaining information from them — their numbers, their leaders, their camps and bases. He was not squeamish about torture — it was a means to an end — but these, Astures and Cantabrians, had proved themselves to be more than willing to embrace death, rather than be disloyal to comrades. Some few had joined the ranks as auxiliaries but, along with most everyone else, he did not trust them.

Sadly, they had managed to lose two of the prisoners already, including the most important one. Flavius was not pleased, nor were the centurions, but there was little they could have done. Quintus' squad had been given guard duty, which he had taken for himself, Crassus with him. They were squatting down near the captives, cleaning blades and armour, when they were surprised by a strange gargling noise behind them. They turned quickly to see one of the captives grinning at them, mouth and teeth covered in blood, then starting to laugh horribly. Crassus was nearest to him, first to see what he had done, and had a blade in his hand. He thrust his sword into the man's neck, cutting off the unearthly noise.

'No…' began Quintus, but he was too late to remind Crassus that they were meant to be kept alive.

'Look,' said Crassus in disgust, pointing.

Quintus could see the long black hair of the grandson shaking from side to side, the boy in the throes of an ugly death, his throat pumping out dark red blood. The chieftain that Crassus had just killed, if that was what he was, had ripped his teeth deep into this man's neck, taking out a clear chunk of flesh, a killing bite. Quintus did not hesitate but drew his own sword and stabbed upwards into the man's sternum, seeking the heart and silencing the eerie sound.

Others, including two centurions, came running at the sounds and looked on amazed at the murdered man.

'Your duty was to keep them alive!' Antoninus cried furiously. 'You should be flogged.'

Galba was not angry but curious. He looked closely at the bite wound. 'The only way to prevent this was to separate them,' he said. 'Did no one order such an action?'

The order, they all knew, should have come from the pilus prior — the role Antoninus had claimed — but he had been busy currying favour with the prefect rather than seeing to the necessities of the senior centurion. Quintus smiled to himself — perhaps Galba was not as stupid as he looked.

'Separate them,' Antoninus ordered. 'We will have no more acts of revenge.'

'I think it was "liberatio", not revenge,' said Sextus thoughtfully.

'Deliverance from crucifixion,' Quintus agreed softly.

'I wish I had not seen it,' said Crassus morosely. 'The one who killed him wore different decorations. He may not have been a chieftain but more of a holy man.' He was already, out of nothing more than habit, relieving the man of his armbands and torc, hoping that they were made of precious metal. The boy wore a gold ring, which Quintus casually cut off and handed to Galba. 'For you or the prefect, sir,' he said.

Antoninus, not included in the 'gift', harrumphed at this and repeated his order that the prisoners be separated. He then detailed Sextus and Crassus to remove the bodies, then stomped off back towards the prefect's tent. Galba smiled, foolishly or knowingly — only he knew.

The legionaries separated the rest and tied them to their own individual stakes. Torture of such men would be unlikely to bring information. The best that they could hope for was betrayal, the Roman presence being seen as a way to settle some dispute between tribes or families. Revenge had brought Rome vital information before now. This incident might have been such a dispute — sadly now settled, but none of the men really believed it so. The prisoner had been saved from torture, crucifixion and shame.

Antoninus' anger would be taken out on the remaining prisoners. He had elected himself as chief torturer, but his insistence that everything be done 'by the book' made him less than effective. An imaginative torturer was something to be feared — a torturer with flair, with invention, who devised new methods of inflicting pain. Antoninus would just break bones whilst asking standard questions — not enough for these captives, although it would help to dissipate his own rage.

Though Quintus knew it had to be so, he wondered who would witness this example other than Roman soldiers. Who would carry the word to the tribesmen? For, to be effective, punishment had to be witnessed. It was only fifty years since, in the Consulship of Lucius Gellius and Cornelius Lentulus, that the longest road in Italy had been lined with crosses carrying the remnants of the slave army raised by the rebel gladiator — and slave — Spartacus of Thrace. It was meant as a warning; slaves would see the suffering and realise that this was not a path they wished to tread. It had worked — at least thus far. But would it with these men?

As sunset approached, on the note played by the cornicen, the centuries were drawn up in parade order, Century One to Century Six, across the open ground. There should have been six columns in total, but Marius' act of combining the Fourth and Fifth had caused confusion and, once the assembly was called, it took the surviving centurions a little time to unpick the lines. They had settled on four columns, each with at least one signifer, one tessararius, and a leader.

Century One, led by its optio, was combined with Century Two, the joint force under the command of Antoninus. Both the centuries had suffered death and injury in the action during the climb: Century One had lost its centurion, who had been pilus prior; Antoninus, though he still limped from the spear he had taken in his calf, had, apparently with the prefect's approval, assumed the position.

Galba, who had kept command of Century Three, had either learned nothing from his experiences or was much wiser than he looked. Either way, he now stood bareheaded in front of his men, helmet under his arm. His century had taken him to their hearts. They had decided — their losses being less than any of the other centuries — that he brought them luck. He was flanked by two signiferi, who, to the trained eye, were protecting him and shepherding him rather than anything else. He puffed out his chest and grinned.

Marcus had taken charge of the combined Fourth and Fifth. He was still an optio, not yet confirmed as a centurion, even though he wore the plumed helmet of the deceased centurion of the Sixth. The Sixth was the other century that was almost complete, apart from its centurion, Valerius, whose shade had taken such an inordinate time — and such a great deal of pain — before it finally stepped into Charon's boat. Though Sextus claimed that its passage would be paid for by the Vestals, his men did not totally believe this and found a coin to place under his tongue. The Sixth's optio, Furius Lentulus, approved by the century's legionaries, now stood proudly at their head.

Quintus was thinking, as he stood at the head of his own century, that the crucifixion they were about to witness mirrored the punishment for any legionary who killed an officer. It would be the sentence for Tullius if his suspected crime ever came to light. Quintus looked sideways at the veteran, trying to see the truth. But he looked just like the rest. The scrubby beard, the torn ear, the earring and the long scar were hidden inside his helmet, and his face was buried in shadow.

Of the short-handed cohort of over four hundred men that had set out, fewer than three hundred remained, not all of them fit for service. One stroke of fortune was that though many of the signiferi had been lost, no standards or banners had fallen into enemy hands, and the bull of the Old Ninth still flew proudly outside the prefect's tent. Though it seemed to take a while, the reorganisation had been achieved within a short period of time, and the men now stood waiting for the prefect. A raised platform had been constructed and the Flavian, resplendent in a uniform that had either seen little action, or had been thoroughly cleaned and polished by his slaves, stepped up onto it. He began, to Quintus' surprise, by telling the men the secret that Marcus had kept so close.

'This is no temple,' Flavius said, and Antoninus repeated his words in his parade ground amplification. 'It is a mine,' he went on, adding truthfully, 'but how productive a mine, we know not.'

The prefect then lied: 'What metal or substance the enemy mined here, we know not. It is a mystery.'

Quintus had not really been listening, but now his ears pricked up. *I think not*, he thought to himself, and guessed that Marcus was thinking the same. A covert glance at Crassus showed that he, too, was nodding his head slightly, unconsciously.

'These men,' the prefect continued, 'thought to hide it from us. They also sought to defy the power of Rome.' His voice had risen, and he hardly needed the centurion's echo — Antoninus continued to repeat after him, nonetheless. 'They were defeated in battle, driven from their lands, their gods destroyed, their chieftains broken, and declared slaves and outlaws by the emperor Augustus himself. In rebelling, they earn themselves the punishment of rebels, and of slaves who turn on their masters.'

XVIII: CRUCIFIXIO

Flavius' speech, the legionaries were pleased to note, was short, any nuances it might have had destroyed by Antoninus' shouted repetition. The men did not really care about the punishment; they had all seen torment and suffering before.

On the prefect's command, a sharp hand signal, two prisoners were dragged across the front of the parade ground. They had been stripped naked and scourged, the first action to increase their shame and humiliation, the second a failed attempt at interrogation. Their hands were mangled, fingers hanging uselessly, and they could not stand on feet that had clearly had toes broken — all part of the process of extracting information.

Antoninus had learned nothing. Through an interpreter, one of the prefect's freedmen, the prisoners had spoken nothing but defiance and pride, given away no secrets or locations, and would not even confirm the existence of their queen. Instead, they offered their bodies and essence to their own gods before they were silenced. Their intransigence — and the habit of their people to sing hymns of defiance even as they were executed — had sufficiently annoyed their questioners that Antoninus had their tongues cut out.

Their once arrogant bearing had collapsed, and their heads were sunk below their shoulder blades; had they ever had intelligence to impart, they could not do so now. Around each of their necks hung a hastily scrawled placard that read 'Enemy of Rome'.

In turn, they were hauled up to a crosspiece, their arms wrapped around it. Their feet stood on a tiny platform fixed to the upright plank of wood, their legs bound to it. Their nakedness made them look even more vulnerable.

The sun would set on their pathetic flesh, lighting it up red and orange. Then night would bring the cold. It would be a long and painful death, as it was intended to be.

The prefect gestured for the two primary standards of the cohort, the pilum and manus, to be brought forward, so that they would be the last images of this world that the prisoners ever saw. Two guards were placed at the foot of each cross — as if the men could ever escape, thought Quintus — and that was it.

There was no point in the legionaries watching them suffer. Instead, the atmosphere changed from belligerence, blind patriotism and vengeance, to order and method and routine. The centuries would have their dispositions decided before these men had died.

Quintus had realised that a further interview with the prefect was inevitable; he still had information to impart. This time, he hoped that it would be in more friendly circumstances. He was expecting the summons when it came.

Flavius was shadowed by his freedman, who seemed intent on taking down every word spoken. Quintus thought that the man tried too hard to please, but what did he know? He had never been a slave. Centurion Antoninus was also present, standing very close to the seated prefect, so that he could whisper advice into his ear. Marcus stood a little way off, his newly acquired centurion's helmet under his arm, but his position in the tent indicated that he was a junior officer — a fact of which both he and Quintus were painfully aware.

'I am interested in the mine,' said the Flavian, as he sipped his wine, 'and in its potential. Gold, you say, but provide little evidence.'

'The pans and workings are at the front, sir,' said Quintus. 'This is how gold is separated from base metal, so my amicus, a blacksmith, tells me.'

'A blacksmith?' Flavius sounded doubtful. 'Then where is the gold?'

'I think they have fled with whatever they have mined, sir,' said Quintus as the nuggets he had concealed beneath his tunic once more chafed against his skin. He felt a tingling as his face reddened beyond his conscious control, the rising heat prickling his neck. He thought that this must be obvious, like a beacon shining out in a pitch-dark night, but no-one else seemed to notice. He did not dare to wipe away the sweat that gathered on his brow.

He was rescued by a call from outside, to which Antoninus responded, and a legionary — one whom neither Quintus nor Marcus had seen before — entered and saluted. Antoninus whispered something to the prefect.

'No need to keep it secret,' laughed Flavius. 'This man is an engineer, one of yours. What does he say?'

In answer the man stepped forward and opened his palm. In it was the same evidence that Crassus had first grasped. Amongst the gritty base of the rock were tiny, shining pebbles. 'Gold, sir,' the legionary said simply, 'and lots of it. The mountain is virtually made of gold. They must have somehow had word and fled with what they had already mined.'

The Flavian put down his wine and looked closely at the open palm. For some reason, he did not wish to touch the shiny metal — it was not his, after all. He and Antoninus both peered closely at the mixture, as if they had expertise in such matters. Marcus would have craned his neck to see but did not dare. Nor did Quintus, who still stood to attention. The centurion waved away his engineer, telling him that he wanted a full report of the ease with which the gold could be extracted, and of the potential of the mine, measured in denarii, sestertii and, he hoped, solidi.

'Where do you think they have taken it?' Antoninus snapped at Marcus, as the Flavian closed the engineer's palm over the gold, making the centurion tear his eyes away.

'They will have taken it down the road at the rear of the mountain, sir.'

'You have seen this road?'

'Not I, but this man and his contubernium saw it and investigated some of it, though it was dark.'

'A road? Where did it lead?' Antoninus turned his attention to Quintus, dark eyes narrowed.

'West, sir,' he said. 'The stars, which my comrade read, said that it headed west, out of the mountains. What we saw was more of a track, but a definite way. We would have a better idea in daylight.'

'Your comrade read the stars?' Flavius asked.

'Both for fortune and direction, sir. It is possible to do both,' Quintus paused, 'or so I am told.'

'Did he say that the enemy had fled this way?' Antoninus probed. 'With the gold?'

'He did not,' Quintus said emphatically, then, seeing the look on the centurion's face, he added, 'but we did not ask the question.'

The Flavian raised his hand for silence. The freedman stopped his infernal scratching and left his hand poised above the tablet. Antoninus started to speak but was stopped by a look from the prefect. He was thinking.

'Our strength?' Flavius asked Antoninus.

'Not a full cohort, sir. We have perhaps four full centuries of fighting men, plus some auxiliaries and the slaves and baggage.'

He was being optimistic. Marcus and Quintus both knew that this was an overestimate. 'And, of course, your personal staff,' he added, although there were only around a dozen infantry — veterans, admittedly — attached to the prefect.

'You,' Flavius began, addressing Marcus but clearly forgetting his name. He leant across to the freedman, asked a quick question and received a quick answer. 'You, Marcus,' he said this time, though not honouring him with any sort of rank, 'when both the existence and the safety of this road is clear, you will take the Fourth and Fifth through the mountain. This man will show us the way.' He flicked a languid hand at Quintus. 'We will follow this road to see where it heads.'

Marcus saluted in acknowledgement but was not yet dismissed.

The prefect addressed Antoninus: 'Hopefully it will lead us to the rest of the rebels, to this woman who plagues us, if she truly exists. We will find and destroy them for good. You will march with us, bringing the Second. The rest will stay here to guard the mine; Galba of the Third will command. The First and Sixth will also remain, veterans and new men, a good combination.' He congratulated himself on his expertise, and the freedman nodded approvingly.

Antoninus saluted his acceptance. He would be the senior centurion seeking battle, but the optio of the Sixth was his creature. There should be opportunities for him to ensure that both their pensions grew.

The freedman leaned in to speak privately with his master. A hurried exchange of whispered words resulted in the prefect doing three things. He had the engineer put the gold dust into the freedman's open hand, picked up his wine cup and drank, then rose and dismissed all but Quintus from his presence, telling the officers to make whatever preparations were necessary. He had one last question for Quintus. 'Your friend who read the stars — does he read good or bad fortune in them?'

Quintus did not know whether to answer truthfully. If anything, Sextus had predicted ill luck, but he had not really been clear. He doubted that the prefect wanted to hear that his enterprise was perhaps not favoured. He opted for at least a form of honesty.

'It was not clear, sir. There were clouds, and the stars faded once the moon rose. But it was west, definitely west.'

Flavius waved him away impatiently, turning once more to the scribe. The last that Quintus heard was, 'Have you written the dispositions?'

'I would have broken their legs long since,' said Sextus matter-of-factly, as they assembled at the call of the trumpet in the morning. 'They are just tribesmen, not rebel slaves. I would have eased their suffering.'

'The whole thing is pointless,' Quintus replied dryly. 'A public death to send a public message, I understand, but only we saw this.'

'I have seen it in Rome,' Sextus added, 'not just judicial deaths, but executions by one gang or another in the Suburra. Demonstrations of power.'

'But who saw this?' Quintus shook his head. 'Only the blind eyes of the standards witnessed it.'

The men had finally died at some point during the night, and their bodies were being cut down and would be carried away, no doubt to be flung to the other side of the ditch, somewhere in the wood. The guards, young men from the Sixth, had not noticed when the last breaths were taken; they had stopped their ears to the groans and whimpers whilst bemoaning the fact that they had drawn this duty. The tribesmen could not cry out, and the legionaries, engaged in night-time activities of gambling, eating, drinking and sleeping, barely cast a glance at the prisoners.

'There will be more executions today,' said Quintus. 'There are two left yet.'

'I wonder what we are proving,' mused his comrade.

'We are proving that we are stronger, mightier, better,' said Rufus, his veteran's viewpoint not unexpected.

Tullius nodded and grunted.

'To whom?' Crassus asked. 'There are only legionaries here; they died in the night, in the dark, unwitnessed...'

'It never worked in Rome,' Sextus explained. 'A gruesome death, torture and mutilation only led the gang that had been "punished" to return with a punishment of their own.' He shook his head. 'Even the state. Tying a boy into a sack with a dog, a cockerel and a viper and throwing him into the Tiber did not prevent parricide. Boys still supplanted tyrannical fathers with violence, whatever the threat.'

'You can only die once...' started Crassus philosophically.

'Stop it, you idiot!' The conversation was interrupted by Cato, who was yelling and slapping Publius on the back of his head. 'You don't know when you've gone too far, do you?'

Publius put on a show of mock humility, dipping his head and smiling to himself — he knew exactly how far to go. He had teased and tormented his friend until he had caused a reaction — the small explosion that was instantly regretted and extinguished by Nox, who once more turned to the front, his face a mask.

'It is a sign of affection,' Quintus said to him, quietly.

'It is a sign of stupidity, of a disordered mind,' Cato hissed in response. But there was no malice in it.

'Do you think they were friends? The tribesman and the comrade who killed him?' Rufus pondered.

'Maybe even brothers,' said Quintus.

'Maybe priest and acolyte,' Sextus suggested.

They all knew about the incident. It had been described to them in gory detail by Crassus, and it had grown in the telling as it spread around the camp. Though only the aftermath of the attack had been witnessed, not the actual biting, Crassus had apparently seen the man's teeth sink into the other's neck and the blood spurt several feet high. In the camp, the men said that the enemy chieftain had turned into a kind of avenging wolf. There were tales of magic, whispers of evil.

The discussion went no further as they were called to attention. It seemed that they would not be witnessing further executions; instead, they were making ready to move out. Quintus and his contubernium had been ordered to show the way. They had traversed the passages before and would act as guides. They would be inside the mountain when the general assembly was called and the next victims were raised to the crosses. Quintus was not sorry to miss the spectacle.

The Sixth century, with their black-bearded optio, Furius Lentulus, at their head, would be with them to start with, but then they would remain at key points, forks and side caves, as guards. Today this century was tasked with keeping safe both the front entrance to the mine and, once the legionaries had passed through, the rear door also.

This morning, it was only just dawn outside, and there were many torches within the mountain. The caves were therefore much brighter, and the workings much more obvious. Tool marks, indentations and deep wounds in the walls — missed in shadowy dark and haste — were now revealed.

Crassus leaned across and whispered in Quintus' ear, 'It will have dried. The wall will have dried; they will not find it.'

'Shhh,' urged Quintus, realising that Sextus could possibly hear them. If they stayed quiet, no-one would know that there was a hoard to find.

As Quintus hushed his friend, Antoninus joined them and demanded, 'What am I not to hear?' He was met with a wall of silence and took this as defiance. 'I command here,' he said forcefully and pompously. 'I demand an answer.'

'It is nothing,' said Quintus humbly, 'just gossip, sir.'

'About centurion Galba and his helmet, sir,' added Crassus.

Antoninus laughed, pleased to see Galba as a figure of fun. 'This is no secret,' he scoffed.

Quintus nodded silent approval at Crassus' quick thinking as Antoninus, still chuckling, ordered them to lead on.

Crassus was right. Though the legionaries peered down the side passages, and though Sextus managed to be the one to show them that particular working, there was no evidence of anything untoward, nothing to raise suspicion. The line where old wall met new had vanished, and Crassus' hasty repair looked like nothing more than a rough patch — and there were many such rough spots in the mine. But Sextus was no fool — he knew that a secret was being kept from him. He was still muttering to himself when they reached the boulders that had been used to block the entrance.

'Not like that,' he told the two legionaries who were struggling with the stones. 'There is an order to it, a mystery perhaps, certainly ingenuity.'

The men stood back and held torches so that Sextus could see. 'There was only one way it went in,' he said, 'so only one way it will come out.'

The legionaries had not spotted the narrow central stone, the one that provided the lock, and they watched as Sextus drew it out and daylight appeared in the gap. 'Now they will move.'

The men saw how the 'lock' worked and smiled; the engineer, the one who had brought the gold dust to Flavius, was particularly impressed. Antoninus inspected the opening and nodded, as if he was also knowledgeable. The soldiers rolled the two large stones to each side, where they sat comfortably in grooves that bore witness to long usage. A pale blue sky appeared, the light flooding in and making the men blink. Quintus waved his group on.

'No,' said Furius Lentulus, holding an arm across the opening. 'The Sixth will make sure it is safe.' He signalled to some of his century, who went through the entrance at a trot. 'Then the centurion has ordered that he be first to step into it.'

Quintus did not understand why, but he stepped back automatically, making room for the Sixth and for some of the big men of Antoninus' century, who passed out into the light with the centurion at their head.

'Why…?' Quintus began.

'If the gold they had already mined was here, he wanted to be first to find it,' said Crassus, conspiratorially. 'Only we know that there is none.'

'Do we now?' Sextus asked, eavesdropping. 'Are we sure we checked it all?'

'Perhaps not,' Crassus agreed meekly, the language of his body shouting guilt — a language that Sextus could read.

XIX: VIA AD AURUM

Furius Lentulus, along with some of his legionaries, followed
the centurion out. With the absence of the optio of the Sixth,
there seemed to be no reason to Quintus why he and his squad
should not leave also. A metal basket for torches was fixed to
the wall, holding a few unlit ones. Into this they placed their
own extinguished lights, then made their way out of the
mountain. Quintus was feeling the pressure of Sextus' gaze,
and he needed to get outside to breathe.

The field that they entered looked different to the one he
remembered from the night-time. It was bigger and greener.
The few ponies that still grazed seemed a long way away, near
to the hedges, which seemed higher and denser. The wood,
too, seemed further away than he remembered and, looking for
the opening, he began to doubt the existence of the road.

Antoninus, two thirds of the way down the field with his
legionaries, waved an arm at Quintus, beckoning him forward.
He assumed that the signal was for all of the contubernium, so
the group jogged, Quintus taking the lead in the absence of
Marcus, with the others two abreast behind him. Furius
Lentulus passed them with a small group of the Sixth, jogging
in the opposite direction, presumably with orders of his own.

Quintus halted the men with a raised hand and waited for
instructions. Antoninus, he thought, did not look pleased —
but then he seldom did. His birch rod was beating a tattoo on
his free hand, betraying his impatience. He asked curtly: 'Is that
your road?'

He was pointing to a low and narrow opening in the trees,
only now spotted by Quintus. The branches formed a webbed

ceiling across an overgrown track. He remembered it, perhaps misremembered it, as being broad and flat and long in the starlight. He was not even sure this was the same place, and he started to look around to see if another such gap existed.

'It is … I think … the same, sir,' he said hesitantly. 'It was dark. I did first describe it as a track. We explored it for only a short way, to make sure no enemy were concealed within.'

With a jerk of his hand, Antoninus ordered bluntly, 'Go, tell us it is still so.'

Quintus' response was immediate: 'Draw your swords, at the double, and follow me.'

He and the squad once more moved into a jog and entered the gap, ducking under the overhanging branches that were low enough to brush their helmets. They kept their swords in their hands. Quintus was relieved to find that within a dozen or so paces the track broadened considerably, though it was still cast in shadow by the trees. He signalled a halt.

'So, we go back and tell him there are no enemy, and the track becomes a road,' said Tullius. He was cursing the overhanging branches, being closer to them than anyone else — aside from Quintus. Twice he had almost lost his helmet, though had he not been wearing it he might easily have lost an eye.

'We should check further, first,' said Quintus. 'We had better be sure; I don't want to anger him. It may narrow again. But now we must walk; we are supposed to be flushing out Astures, and they could be lurking anywhere.' But he said this without conviction, not really believing there were any enemy warriors left here.

They checked a further thousand paces down the road, until the entrance behind them dwindled to a pinprick of light. The road was straight and, from the position of the sun, as they had said, it headed west. Cato had sharp eyes. 'I think I see light where it ends.'

'How far?' asked Rufus, whose eyes were not so good.

'Probably the same distance again, perhaps further.'

'Then we investigate,' Quintus said flatly, 'otherwise we have not done our job.'

They set off again, the low branches whipping them and tugging at them. It was Publius who put into words the question that more than one of them had been asking themselves as they struggled to cope with the encroaching trees.

'What are the horses for? If we legionaries — and not just the tallest — have to duck, it is not possible to ride a horse down this road, so why are there horses in the field?'

'They must have passed this way,' said Cato, equally puzzled, 'unless there is another way out.'

'They are packhorses,' said Sextus, as if it was obvious. 'They were used to transport the gold out of here.'

'Then there could be a hoard at the end of this track?' Rufus asked, suddenly interested in the conversation.

'There could,' said Quintus, 'but we do not know how far, or if it's guarded, or…'

'…if it even exists,' Sextus interrupted. 'If I was an Asturian goldminer, I would have hidden it away by now. It would be secret.'

It seemed to Quintus and Crassus that the word 'secret' was aimed purely at them. They glanced at each other, then looked away quickly, but not so fast that Sextus did not see. Meanwhile, the men were nodding in agreement.

'On, then,' said Quintus. 'Double time, but watch your heads.'

Crouched and uncomfortable, they headed for the opening, which they could all now see.

The light grew ever brighter, the trees thinner, and the entrance — or exit — in front of them grew larger. As they approached it, they slowed and became more wary. They were of course nothing more than a patrol, after all, and had probably strayed too far from the cohort, though they had taken no more than an hour to reach this point. They advanced cautiously and balanced lightly on the soles of their feet, swords drawn, a semi-circle of shields protecting them, with Quintus emerging first from the trees.

They came out into daylight. The sky was bright blue and dotted with fair weather clouds. Before them stretched a rocky plain of umber, in which, for a mile or two, the road was no more than a discolouration of the land, before it vanished into a valley. In the distance and to the south were rolling hills rising into mountains, all shades of the same orange-brown, warm in the Spanish sun. To their relief, there were no tribesman to be seen.

'This is far enough,' said Quintus with conviction. 'I think we have found the end of our road. A short rest, and then we return.'

The march back did not seem as long as the march out had been, and somehow the low branches were not as annoying. They made better time. As they approached the end of the track, they could hear sawing and shouting, the sound of axes and branches falling. There were Romans in the entrance already, clearing the way. Antoninus had called up engineers and surveyors and given them men of the Sixth as labourers. The opening that marked the start of the woodland route was already wider; axes, hammers, chisels and saws were being utilised to cut it back whilst the worst of the overhanging branches were chopped so that the centuries could march at least four abreast.

They passed these men with difficulty, as their work was making the road worse before it made it better. They re-emerged into the field, where they saw legionaries of the Sixth guarding the entrance to the mine and stationed in the corners of the field; some were even succeeding in corralling the horses so that they could be tied. There were around a dozen ponies; they were tame and mostly bays — compact beasts with muscular legs, clearly adapted for the rugged terrain though too small to make good cavalry mounts. Sextus was probably right: these were not for riding.

Antoninus was upon them almost before they had left the wood. 'Your report?' he demanded of Quintus, then gave away his true desires. 'Was there gold? Is it the *via ad aurum*? Did you find gold on the road?'

'No gold, sir, no Astures either, just the end of the forest road, an hour's fast march from here.'

'How does it end?'

'On a flat and rocky plain, sir, barren of life. The direction of the road runs ever westward. We could see for miles along it — there was no sign of the enemy, no sign of anything.'

'Could we build a camp there?'

Quintus gave it serious thought. 'There was no water that I could see, but plenty of timber, of course — and it was raised. The plain sloped down from the wood.'

'There will be water in the wood — there must be streams,' Antoninus murmured to himself, once more tapping his birch rod on his open palm. 'You, follow me. You men,' he said, indicating Quintus' comrades, 'may as well stay and help the engineers.'

The men were tired from the march but would never show fatigue. They were immediately put to work on the road, which rapidly ate into the forest, advancing like a scythe through wheat, cutting a path both flat and wide.

Quintus and Antoninus passed swiftly back through the mountain, the way now organised as Rome would have it. The passages were lit with torches, and soldiers were stationed at regular intervals. Antoninus was especially keen to report to the prefect personally, to take the credit for sending Furius Lentulus back for surveyors and engineers, for sending Quintus down the track, for the ongoing clearing and widening.

The prefect's tent was crowded — guards, slaves and freedmen were all undertaking specific tasks. The centurion began with praise for his efforts on the road. 'The road will be made wide and flat for our marching columns,' he said, 'and it will be made taller.'

'Tall enough to proceed on horseback?'

The centurion was disappointed. 'Not if you want to move soon — it would take time to make it tall enough for riders. Horses will have to be walked.'

The freedman — present and scribbling as ever — tutted, leaned in and whispered something to his master, who nodded and asked Quintus, 'What do you say?'

'It will not be difficult to make it wider, sir, but the branches above are twined together. I think height would be a problem.'

'And its length?'

Antoninus made to answer, but the Flavian raised a hand. 'I will hear it from this man,' he said softly.

Quintus nodded, though the centurion looked daggers at him. 'A two-hour march to the open ground, sir, perhaps less once it is cleared.'

'And is this ground defendable?'

'It is, sir.'

'Good. The prisoners?' This was directed at Antoninus who, not expecting the question, had to think quickly.

'There are two left. We might still have information from them,' he said hopefully.

Again, to his annoyance, the freedman intervened, whispering advice to the Flavian, who nodded acceptance and spoke decisively. 'We will not. They will be crucified before we set off in the morning.' He continued, now speaking to the freedman, 'Take this down. The prisoners, as I have said, will be put on the crosses at first light. Three centuries, the Second under Centurion Antoninus, plus the Fourth and Fifth, are to advance through the mountain. I will be with them.' He looked up at the scribe. '*We* will be with them. The remaining men under Centurion Galba will stay camped here. The Sixth, under —' he paused and consulted the freedman in a whisper, then continued — 'under Furius Lentulus will guard the mine. They will guard our backs also.'

Finished with the dispositions, he looked up and seemed surprised to see the two legionaries still present. 'Go, eat,' he said. 'You have done well. Tomorrow, we will hunt the enemy.'

The two men saluted and left. Quintus returned to an otherwise empty tent to find Jovan and Maxim, seemingly always busy, mending, cleaning and maintaining both the tent and other materials. They were also baking the hard biscuits on which the men relied and producing the porridge into which they were dipped. He ordered them to bank the fire and boil the water, then had his armour and caligae unlaced by Jovan. Carefully, with his back to the slave, he removed his tunic, ensuring that the nuggets were hidden, along with Ursus' will. As he undressed, he had realised that a better hiding place was needed for his secrets. He decided that, sadly, he would not trust the slaves, nor his fellow soldiers, and squirrelled everything safely away in his satchel. Finally, he peeled off his undershorts and sat wrapped in his cloak whilst his clothes, caked with blood and sweat from the past few days, were washed, then hung to dry by the fire. Maxim set to work cleaning his armour and weapons.

Quintus did not want to talk. Whilst relieved that all was hidden, he was also saddened that he had become so untrusting. He sat for some time, staring at the fire.

When the rest of the men finally returned, he was dozing, his head lolling on his chest, the warmth and crackling of the fire hypnotic. Publius spotted him first and put his finger to his lips to hush the others, silently waving Maxim away. He crept up behind Quintus and, with a swift movement, pulled the cloak from his back, waking him at the same time. The men found the sight of their naked comrade snapped from sleep hilarious, he less so, grabbing the cloak back from Publius.

'What if we had been enemy?' Rufus offered, slapping him on the back.

'What if I had been armed?' Quintus snapped.

'You weren't,' laughed Publius. 'Wash day! About time.'

Cato was unlacing the ties his friend could not reach for himself. Publius did the same, then both dumped their tunics and shirts onto Jovan, who soon had most of the clothes of the contubernium steeping in hot water.

Inside the tent, Sextus, having helped Rufus, offered assistance to Crassus, whose own amicus remained by the fire, once more wrapped in his cloak and his own thoughts. Sextus, of course, had an ulterior motive, convinced that the blacksmith had found something in the mine — found it and concealed it. Logic said that it was likely to be gold, and more than the handful of dust he had first held. Though his 'help' included a furtive search, disguised as trouble with knots, he found nothing and remained both disappointed and suspicious. He stamped outside as Crassus finished removing his clothes and handed them to Jovan.

'I will find out for myself.' Sextus sat by Quintus, talking to the air rather than his comrade.

'There is nothing to find,' sighed Quintus, shaking his head, the lie coming more easily than he would like.

'We shall see.' Sextus stood, wrapped his own cloak more tightly, and moved away from Quintus, muttering under his breath, 'I will go and find out for myself.'

'It is guarded,' Quintus could not stop himself from responding.

Sextus turned to face him and tapped his nose knowingly.

Maxim and Jovan draped the clothes over sticks and, whilst they dried, the steam rising off them, they set to work on arms and armour. Only Tullius and Rufus would not let them touch anything of theirs, Tullius through professional pride and Rufus through his distrust of Macedonians in general, and his fear of seeing a sword in the hands of a slave. These two stayed in the tent, whilst the others laughed and joked outside. Quintus, once more dressed, sat apart from them, claiming to be on guard.

Later, as the moon lit up the sky, Publius came to him, calling him fondly by his nickname, Macilentus. He brought food, chattering inconsequentially but not offering to relieve his duty — nor did he apologise for the practical joke. Quintus had not expected him to. It was Lux's way, and it did not dim the affection the others had for him. He stayed where he was, dozing on and off, until the first pale light of morning began to add red highlights in the east. All the while, they wondered what had happened to Marcus.

If the men were to eat, drink, wash, and relieve themselves, then they knew that all needed to be done before the trumpet sounded for assembly. They were soon about their noisy business, shattering the serenity of darkness with the heavy footsteps of the coming day, disturbing Quintus' half-waking reveries

As it grew lighter, the comrades grouped around the remnants of the fire, Crassus using his blacksmith's skills to stir it back to life and Maxim feeding it with freshly cut fuel. Tullius sat apart from the rest, still humming and cleaning his blade and armour incessantly. Rufus and Cato were sharing a joke, which, from the leer on Rufus' face, Cato's deep laugh and Publius' look of confusion, Quintus guessed was a dirty one. With a jolt, he realised that Sextus was missing and looked instinctively towards the mine, wondering how he would slip past the guards. He then saw his erstwhile friend walking back from the latrines, adjusting his belt.

Quintus was not a naturally distrustful person, and he did not like this new side of himself that had emerged. Sextus, it would seem, had read his mind. He waved ostentatiously and, with an insincere smile on his face, he mimed squatting and wiping himself. He then turned to share in Rufus' humour, making a lewd gesture in explanation to Publius and slapping the innocent boy on the back.

Quintus sighed inwardly, then straightened himself and threw off the cobwebs of the night. He had been accepted as their leader in the absence of Marcus — there was no doubting it. But it seemed lonely.

XX: CASTRA

Half the men in this scrubby place that had once been a battlefield knew that today they would be breaking camp. Orders had been given and their tents were already being dismantled. Their pots, quern stones and rations were being loaded onto mules and carts, pegs pulled and stowed, guy ropes coiled, and fires quenched.

The morning held the promise of a fine day, and though there had been swirling skeins of mist on the ground earlier, it was vanishing with the dawn as the cornicen stepped forward and blew the general assembly. It was to be the same as previous mornings in this camp, in that two crosses stood, waiting for a victim each. However, some of the soldiers would not be going back to fires and tents but would instead be marching on in search of rebels.

There was no sign of the prefect, the men were relieved to see, for that meant no speech — of encouragement or otherwise. Marcus appeared from the officer's quarters, and Quintus saw no evidence of shame on his face. The Third — Galba's men, who were remaining — were armed and armoured, but carried no packs and no equipment, and their slaves and animals were all busy in and around their tents. Furius Lentulus stood at the head of a much reduced Sixth, with many of his century on guard at both the entrances and inside the mine, some at this end of the forest road. By contrast, Marcus' men were fully laden. Their mules and slaves were packed and ready to go, standing patiently to one side.

Still, they all had to stand to attention as the standards were brought out, knowing they had to wait for the executions.

Antoninus was the last to emerge, limping from his calf wound, which was still bound. He stood where the prefect would have stood and took it upon himself to provide the men with his thoughts. They were short.

'The enemies of Rome!' he shouted.

The naked bodies of the last of the prisoners were dragged across by their bound hands to their place of execution. They were sorry-looking individuals, half-dead already, all angled limbs and ribs, skin stretched tight across them, like the pattern left by receding waves on wet sand.

Quintus caught Sextus' eye as the men — stripped, humiliated, broken, vulnerable, and certainly no threat — were heaved up onto the cross, where they would spend their final hours in agony. He saw the slight shake of Sextus' head and agreed. He, too, would have broken their legs to shorten their journey to whatever otherworld they believed in.

'Death to the enemies of Rome!' shouted Antoninus, as the prisoners were hauled up and tied to the timber. 'Death to the enemies of Rome!' he repeated, demanding the response that he had not initially received.

The men understood. 'Death to the enemies of Rome!' they called back with the required enthusiasm, though most had grown weary of this daily spectacle.

Antoninus kept the men drawn up in their centuries until it was fully light, waiting — at least the men assumed he was waiting — for the prefect. But it was Flavius' freedman that arrived, scuttling across the parade ground like a self-important crab. He it was who spoke to the centurion, not Flavius himself. With his message delivered, he scurried back the way he had come whilst Antoninus — to his frustration, with half the morning wasted — ordered the men to their duties. It had been a misunderstanding. The centurion had been waiting for the prefect to act. The prefect had been waiting for the centurion to act.

The prisoners dangling in their torment barely moved, although their hearts could be seen still leaping in their chests, as if trying to escape, and their agony was deeply etched onto their faces. They did not cry out, though low and eerie moans emerged from time to time, and they certainly did not sing or offer defiance, which pleased Antoninus.

He was annoyed with the prefect. Through some error of communication, the men had stood watching the crucifixion until half the morning was spent. He was also annoyed with the weather. The promise of a fine day had failed to materialise, the early sun sidling off into banks of cloud. The men stood under grey skies, irritated by a cold wind that veered from north to east and back again.

Antoninus issued commands, first to Galba and Furius Lentulus, who had stood at the head of their own centuries as the morning drew on. The men who were remaining were sent back to their tents, where they waited to be called for exercises, drill and weapons practice.

They endured a further delay as the prefect gathered his guards and servants, before issuing orders to Marcus and to his own century. They marched to the entrance to the mine and began to traverse the passages, the prefect deciding to go first, to Antoninus' further annoyance. He went slowly, stopping to talk to guards as if he was on some sort of inspection or triumph.

It took time to bring all of the legionaries through the tunnels. They were narrow in places, so only one or two men could pass together. It was well into the afternoon by the time that nearly all of the men, the slaves and pack animals, plus the few horses that they had — including the Flavian's — had come through the mountain and were assembled in the field. The Second had brought up the rear and the final dozen or so were now emerging reluctantly into the open. The clouds had thickened and darkened, and a steady rain had started to fall.

'You!' Antoninus did not give Marcus the respect of recalling his name. 'Let's get out of this cursed weather. Lead your century down the road — column of four, at the double. The prefect's party will follow. The Second will bring up the rear.'

Quintus and his contubernium were at the front of the century — or two centuries, the combined Fourth and Fifth — and began the steady trot that was double marching pace. Marcus, splendid in Valerius' helmet, took the front right. Quintus took the front left, with the veterans Rufus and Tullius between them. Ahead of them, the standards of the two centuries bobbed proudly, tassels streaming — those of the cohort who were moving with the prefect.

The track had ceased to be a track and was now a wide road. It had been cleared, the ruts and potholes filled, but still without sufficient height to accommodate a rider.

Antoninus sent some of his own men ahead — to scout for danger, he said. However, Quintus suspected that the centurion wanted to be the first to find any gold. The number who knew it was a goldmine was expanding. Quintus wondered what would happen when the knowledge spread through the entire cohort.

Rain was falling heavily onto the tops of the trees, — it was as if a hundred drums were being beaten far above them. It moved slowly and languidly from the low branches, beginning intermittently and then becoming more and more frequent as the water worked its way through the leaves. It finally collected and fell relentlessly in great, plump drops onto the legionaries' heads and backs.

It slowed them: the ground was easily churned and the branches, heavy with water, became even more of a nuisance than they had been previously. The prefect ordered them to slacken the pace to a normal march. Antoninus was pleased; his injured leg was troubling him, and though he would never have owned up to it, a slower pace suited him. He had received the orders: a normal march would be sufficient.

By late afternoon — though it was hard to gauge the time from within the green tunnel they traversed — they had passed far enough through the trees for the entrance to disappear behind them. They had settled into a rhythm. The initial panting of exertion was replaced with efficient breathing, long and deep, permitting conversation.

'I think our prefect may have made a tactical error,' Quintus said to Rufus.

Rufus agreed. 'We may have to spend the night in this forest. How far is it now, do you think?'

'An hour, maybe more,' guessed Quintus. 'We should be going faster.'

'Our pilus prior has an injury,' said Marcus with disgust. 'He should have excused himself.'

'Or ridden in a cart,' laughed Rufus.

'As you would have done?' Tullius spoke sarcastically, knowing that none of them would ever want to appear weak.

Antoninus knew that this was not an ideal situation. He was already rehearsing his arguments as to why the slow progress was Marcus' fault, and not his. The men had not worked quickly enough, of course; they were lazy, badly led, and their equipment was not up to scratch. Meanwhile, his own century — and himself, of course — were blameless paragons of excellence and industry. And, naturally, it was the prefect that had truly slowed them down — though this could never be said.

Luckily for Marcus — for such accusations had ruined reputations and careers before — the small patch of light that marked the end of the road finally appeared ahead of them and, as it did, the centurion's scouts appeared, jogging towards them.

'Report,' said Marcus, since he was the first officer that they encountered.

'We report to Centurion Antoninus,' said one of them, insolently.

'You report to me, then to the prefect,' spat Marcus angrily. 'Antoninus comes last — he is bringing up the rear.'

'Limping,' muttered Tullius, before looking innocently heavenward, as if it were not he who had spoken.

Marcus shot him a look of warning but said nothing.

'We have seen it anyway,' said Quintus. 'It is a flat plain, sloping into the distance. You do not need to describe it — just tell us if you found...'

'Gold.' This time, it was Rufus who pretended to look blameless, whilst Tullius smiled.

'...enemy,' Quintus finished firmly, as if the interruption had not been made.

'No sign of enemy,' said their leader, a man made anonymous by the helmet and armour worn by all of them, but more so by the cloak drawn over his head against the elements.

'Carry on,' said Marcus dismissively, and the men left, seeking the prefect and their own centurion.

'What do we do when we reach the plain?' Quintus asked. 'Do we stop? Do we camp?'

'We halt and wait for orders. We cannot camp without orders, and the prefect is well behind us.'

Quintus wiped water from his brow with the back of his hand. 'I think it may be drier out of this forest,' he said, 'this rain is coming from the trees, not the sky.'

They did not have to make a decision — before they reached the end of the road, a runner came up fast, a messenger with orders for Marcus.

'We camp,' he told the men on the front rank. 'Pass the word.'

This was all that the legionaries needed to know. Each had his own specific role to fulfil. It meant that some of them would need to break ranks and run ahead of the column, men from the other centuries joining them. These men were surveyors and engineers, whose first job was to decide a position for the camp. It would preferably be high ground — defendable and with a water supply. The earth also needed to be soft enough for a ditch to be dug and for stakes to be driven in.

As the first of the marching column reached the end of the road, the light brightened considerably and the rain, which seemed like a deluge that would last until the heavens were emptied, finally slowed, first becoming a drizzle, then no more than an annoyance. It was true, it was wetter in the forest than out. Already, having found a stream that ran from mountain to plain, and having determined that here the ground was softer than the bare rock, the pioneers, with measured strides, stakes and mallets, had begun to measure and mark out the camp.

Each man knew what he had to do and, as the rest of the column caught up, the camp had already started to take shape. The ditch that would mark its boundary was already partly dug. The principal street, which would run down the centre and contain the prefect's headquarters, was already delineated, and timber from the wet trees had been cut for the gates. The tent lines were staked, so that the slaves could begin unpacking and pitching them as soon as they arrived. The camp would face the plain and would have the forest, and its second gate, at its back. It was not as seamless as it should have been, with the centuries short of numbers, but the men coped, and the camp grew.

The prefect's tent was first to be erected, and his personal guard were amongst the few not assisting the construction. There were other 'immunes' excused from such work, including the surveyors and engineers who directed operations, as well as medics and other specialists. Within a couple of hours, where there had been bare ground before, a defended Roman camp — a sort of fortress or castra — stood.

Whilst Jovan and Maxim struggled with a wet-wood fire, Quintus sat morosely and uncomfortably in his own tent. Here there was no chance to relax, or to wash, or even to remove armour. Caligae might be unlaced to provide some comfort, helmets might be removed, but the lorica laminata — the armour with its overlapping plates like those of the crayfish — remained tied. They needed to be ready to relieve their comrades on guard duty, ready to defend the camp immediately.

Although he — and everyone else — had been professional on the march, there was still distance between him and his companions. He was, awkwardly, once more in charge of the contubernium, Marcus having been called to the Flavian's tent. Just as awkwardly, Tullius was ignoring him, still smarting, it would seem, from the almost-made accusation. Sextus was barely speaking to him, the secret that he had yet to learn eating away at him. His conspiratorial chats with Rufus isolated him further. Even Crassus was sulking, having felt the sharp edge of Quintus' tongue through no fault of his own. Only Publius and Cato seemed innocently unaware of the dark thoughts and suspicions that filled the air. Publius still teased his friend and Cato still took the bait, even whilst they manned their own small section of the palisade.

'Look,' said Publius, pointing west.

'I will not, not this time,' spluttered Cato. 'I am not going to rise again. I have had enough. Give it a rest.' But he caught a movement in the distance, realised that there really was something coming and pushed his friend out of the way to get a better view.

No-one had really expected anything to come this way after dark, and it was already dusk when the camp was finished, but here they were: a broad line of Astures, appearing in the half-light, running from the valley. First had come their horses, apparently loose but all heading in the same direction, towards the fort and the forest. Then, behind them, there were the tribesmen, the dip hiding them so that just their weapons and the arms waving them appeared first, silhouetted against the lighter sky of the west, followed by the heads and shoulders of the men. At first it seemed that there was but a single row of them, but then more weapons and heads appeared, and more again behind them. There were many of them, shouting and armed with the axes, spears and long blades that they favoured. They had no order, no formation, and no discipline.

'An attack!' shouted Publius, sounding the alarm. He was echoed by the other men on watch. As the trumpeters shrilly amplified the call, the prefect and other officers appeared from the headquarters tent, issuing orders for the defence of the camp.

Quintus and the rest of the tent-party ran to their section of the perimeter, helmeted and holding their swords, spears and shields, ready to fight.

The scene that faced them was distorted by the strangeness of the light. Their own small world was encircled by burning torches, regularly spaced on the parapet and marking the gate, the via principalis and the headquarters. Fires were also sputtering in front of tents, the dirty smoke from wet fuel lurking and eddying in the wind.

To the west, the setting sun had gone, but no star could yet be seen. To the east, the sky was black as a raven's wing, and remnants of the rainstorm still lurked. To the south, the mountains were still visible as a dark shadow against a black sky. To the north, in cloudless obsidian, Quintus recognised Draco and Ursa Minor rising. He turned — as he normally would — to Sextus to ask him to name the group of five stars that formed a sort of house, prominent to the west of Draco, but then he thought better of it. Their friendship was fragile at the moment, and he feared sarcasm or rejection.

Instead, he paused and squinted, then joined in with Publius and Cato's incredulous exclamations. 'They are not attacking,' said Quintus. 'They are just running.'

Similar comments rippled down the perimeter, as legionary after legionary realised the same thing. The enemy were running — whether to something or from something was not yet determined.

'They are going back!' cried Cato.

'No, they are stopping,' Publius said.

'They are doing neither,' said Quintus. 'Look, they do not know what to do.'

And it was true: the Astures had been running, as if chasing their horses, and were carrying their weapons rather than

209

brandishing them. They had now stopped at the sight of the fort and seemed undecided about whether to go forward or back. The ponies had halted too, now they were no longer being chased, and stood nervously in a small group to the south.

The tribesmen shouted to each other, their voices carrying in the dark, whilst the watchers in the camp peered, trying to make out what was happening. The palisade that had been built had small steps behind it in places, and it was from these that the legionaries watched the tribesmen approach, then stop. By now it was full night. Draco had risen in the north, but there was not yet any moon. Many men asked each other whether there would be a moon tonight, and a few were able to say, Sextus amongst them.

'A three-quarter moon,' he said. 'It will not rise until late, and it will rise to the east of the mountains. Unless the sky clears, it will be no help.'

'Do we fight them?' Quintus asked no-one in particular. 'What are they doing?'

'They are the enemy,' said Sextus. 'If we let them pass, they can ambush our comrades at the mine. We must fight them.' He may have been superstitious, but he was no coward.

It seemed that their officers had come to the same conclusion, as the trumpet sounded the assembly for battle.

Quintus shook his head. A night battle, with no moon and an enemy on their own territory. What could be worse?

XXI: DECURION CASCA

Marcus strode determinedly past the men as they answered the call to assemble, running from all corners of the camp to take their positions. Quintus, Crassus and the others had been quick to answer the call.

Marcus pushed his helmet firmly onto his head — Centurion Valerius' helmet, brightly polished and with deep red plumes. *No*, he thought, *my helmet — Centurion Marcus*. He tightened the chinstrap and marched purposefully to the front, his eyes fixed straight ahead. He would lead, but not on his own. The standards would go with him, the hand and spear of the cohort, their discs shining and their tassels streaming out behind them. The signiferi were already there, splendid in wolfskins.

Antoninus took up position just in front of him, an unsubtle indicator of their relative status. He was tall, but not as tall as Marcus. Both were easily overtopped by Quintus, the tallest man on the front row immediately behind the two centurions. Marcus' men had been quicker to muster, so they had taken the front of the column, the ground nearest to the gate. Antoninus' century had formed up just behind and to the right, ready to march forward if it were they who were ordered into action.

Quintus could hear the increasingly acrimonious conversation between the two officers, conducted in hoarse whispers.

'You will not lead,' Antoninus was insisting flatly. 'It is my right, and it is my century that will go.'

'But we have fought them before,' countered Marcus, 'and defeated them before.'

'Then whose are these?' Antoninus sneered, gesturing at the field. 'The ones you left behind?'

'You left at least six alive.' The prefect's cultured tones cut into the conversation. He made no attempt to keep his voice down. 'We crucified them.' He, with the ever-present freedman, had stepped between the two officers.

'And we know that others passed through the mountain,' added Antoninus, now not bothering to lower his voice.

'Not this many,' Marcus snapped. The conversation was clearly no longer secret, and he waved his arm in the direction of the shouting. Nothing of the enemy could now be seen, but they could be heard.

The freedman put his mouth close to the prefect's ear and spoke softly. The prefect nodded. 'It is night,' he said, with finality. 'No-one fights at night. There is not even a moon. You...' Quintus was the nearest soldier, and his height made him an obvious target. 'When will the moon rise?'

Quintus exchanged a quick glance with Sextus, also on the front rank. 'Late, sir, not until midnight, but it will provide some light, as it is a three-quarter moon.'

Once more, the freedman whispered urgently in the Flavian's ear, and the prefect added, 'Unless there is cloud. Will there be cloud, legionary?'

Quintus shook his head and spoke with less certainty. 'I cannot predict the weather, sir. But it looks like it is clearing. The moon will rise behind the mountains...' He trailed off; he did not know what else to say. Sextus was more expert than he, but his comrade now stared stiffly ahead, apparently not even taking note of the conversation.

'They are there now,' said Marcus forcibly, turning the conversation to more pressing matters. 'I can hear them. We must stop them.'

The prefect glanced out to the plain. 'They will not attack the camp,' he concluded, then paused briefly, before turning to Marcus for confirmation.

'They do not have to attack the camp,' Marcus said quickly. 'They could pass it by, traverse the road and surprise Galba and his command. It could be a disaster.' He indicated the ranks of legionaries. 'My men are ready.'

'So are mine,' said Antoninus, addressing the prefect. 'My century is complete; his is not. Men of the Fourth are manning the palisade, guarding the camp…'

All this time, the shouting of the Astures had continued, echoing in the darkness. The watchers could see nothing but shadows moving back and forth, spectres in shades of black on black.

Then a new sound intruded: that of the impact of sword on shield. There were grunts of exertion and screams that sounded with animal intensity. And there were hooves, galloping horses, whinnying and neighing.

Suddenly, in the midst of this maelstrom of noise, there were calls of command. A tone of authority could be identified in Asturian, the voice demanding a response. It was a woman's voice, gravelly but strong, rising above the noise. The reaction was immediate — the cries of the hurt and injured decreased and the music of metal on metal died. Instead, the sound of the hoofbeats became dominant, heavier than the light, unsaddled ponies of the enemy. There were gruffer shouts, this time in a language the Romans understood.

'The gate, open the gate!' was the yelled instruction. 'We are horsemen of the Ninth, open the gate!'

A gate had been constructed from hewn timber, not hinged, but braced with thick branches. On the prefect's command, the trumpet sounded the call for the braces to be removed.

'It could be a trick,' protested Antoninus.

'It is not,' replied the prefect. 'I recognise the voice. That is Casca, decurion of our cavalry. Let them in.'

The combined Fourth and Fifth were positioned directly in front of the gate. They needed to move, fast. Marcus ordered them to fall back into two columns, either side of the opening. It was a simple manoeuvre and a straightforward command — his men had cleared the space within seconds. Marcus and Antoninus also knew to move. The big men who guarded the Flavian had to move him; he was slow to realise where he was standing. Even the freedman was faster, flinging himself to the left before his master.

The hurdles that formed the gate were shifted just in time, with the cavalry streaming in and reining to a halt. The mounts turned and dug their hooves into the soft ground. Some of the men appeared injured, some horses too. Their once splendid caparisons showed dirt and damage in the torchlight. At least two mounts were riderless. There were auxiliaries too, who held up open palms whilst controlling their ponies with their knees, lest they be mistaken for the enemy. It did not take long for them all to be let in; they came at speed and not in great number. The last rider turned in the saddle, ensuring that there were no more to follow.

'Close the gates!' he shouted. 'Close the gates behind me!'

It was Casca who gave the command, the man whose voice the prefect had recognised. His hand gripped the standard of the cavalry.

Antoninus repeated the order: 'Close the gates! Prepare for an attack!'

As the cavalrymen dismounted, and the loose horses were brought under control, the legionaries rushed to man the perimeter, swords drawn whilst the centurions barked commands to make sure that the camp was fully defended. The columns dissolved as legionaries rushed to their predetermined positions on the wooden barrier that formed their defences.

But no assault came. Instead, the dust and noise brought in by the animals settled. It was as if a wave had crashed upon the shore of the camp and subsided. The men were ready for a second wave, but it did not come. The decurion dismounted, handed the standard to another soldier and approached the prefect, ready to report, but the Flavian held up a hand to silence him.

'Wait,' he said. 'Listen.'

The rain had long since ceased and the wind had dropped to nothing. In the stillness, they could hear the Astures calling to each other in celebration. Then that female voice of authority intervened and the noise once again subsided, although a low murmur of conversation could be heard. There was no indication of pursuit or attack, and though the men with the keenest eyes scanned the dark from west to east, there was no movement. Suddenly, a fire winked into existence to the north, then another — pinpricks of light on the plain that showed the line of the enemy. They clearly did not care. They had chased the Roman horsemen into their camp and feared no further attack.

It was Marcus' voice that broke the spell. 'You and you, take your squads and guard the entrance to the forest!' he yelled at two men. 'Take torches. Go now.'

The two groups Marcus had selected were from the side where he was standing, opposite Quintus' contubernium, who helped to open the gate sufficiently to let the men out. Other legionaries filled the gaps caused by their departure. Quintus, Sextus, Crassus and Rufus lifted the hurdles, pushed the gate shut, jammed the braces in place, then took their positions once more. Again, they were near enough to hear what the officers had to say.

Only a few feet from them, the prefect lowered his hand and looked for the first time at the cavalry officer, lit by torches held by slaves who had come running. He was covered in ochre dust and one leg was seeping blood. His round shield was marked and battered. He saluted with a fist to the chest.

'Report,' commanded the Flavian.

Casca was a knight, a member of the equestrian class — a patrician, really. Even though he was just a decurion, at this stage in their careers he was not much different in social standing from the man to whom he reported. He removed his helmet to reveal a face that was lined with years. He had grey hair and grey stubble on his chin.

'We did as ordered,' he said wearily. 'We were led by our auxiliaries, who have a better knowledge of these mountains.' He pointed to the few who had come with them. They now stood apart with smaller horses. 'We followed the road west, to try and find a way past the range. As we travelled, we realised we had ridden in a huge arc. The sun, at first setting ahead of us, was then on our left, and two days ago it set behind us.' He stood stiffly, his voice hoarse.

'Bring him a drink,' Antoninus ordered.

A slave ran to fetch a cup of watered wine and handed it over with his head bowed. The decurion emptied the cup, handed it back with a curt 'another' and continued.

'The road travels in a great sweep around the mountains, first west, then south, then east, sometimes broad and flat, sometimes narrow and rocky. Sometimes it is out in the plain, and sometimes it is in deep forest tracks, but it is always there, always heading for the peak at the end of the range.'

'Our peak,' said the prefect softly, 'our mountain.'

'Your mountain?' Casca asked curiously.

'We came at it from the other side. A passage leads right through it. It is a mine — an important one — I will tell you later. Carry on.'

Casca nodded and resumed. 'Our pickets spotted a party of natives from a distance coming towards us on foot, although they led some pack animals. I think they thought themselves safe, as they made no attempt to hide their presence. At their head I was amazed to see a woman in furs and a white headscarf, clearly a leader.'

'We have met her,' said Marcus, then asked flatly, 'You destroyed them?'

The officer shrugged. 'We were in the forest; they were in a narrow canyon that started as the trees ended. We were able to charge them down almost before they could defend themselves.' He added, 'The animals escaped; they ran as if they knew where they were going.'

'They did,' Quintus said quietly to Crassus, as if they were part of the conversation.

'Shh,' replied Crassus urgently, knowing they should not have been listening.

The slave ran up with another cup, and the decurion threw his head back and finished it off. Handing it back to the man, he continued, his voice stronger. 'We left the enemy where they had fallen and gave chase, hoping to catch the ponies, but the Astures' knowledge of the ground was better than ours.' He sighed. 'We captured no horses, and then we were caught in an ambush.' He paused to allow this fact to sink in.

'They waited, a larger group, and as we passed through the gully, they attacked. Their javelins killed a few of us and hurt a few horses, slowing us down. We had no choice but to ride on, only to be attacked again and again.' He bowed his head in sadness and frustration, then continued the account. His tone was factual and unemotional. 'For over an hour we traversed the narrow ravine, no more than two abreast. Over and over, they came and killed one or two, including many of the auxiliaries. A javelin took the signifer, and another felled the man who took the standard from him. I took the sacred banner, and an arrow landed in my leg. A spear missed me by inches and ripped my cloak.'

Antoninus, unable to contain his impatience any longer, asked, 'Could you not have turned around, found another way?'

The decurion shook his head. 'Friend, they were high above us. The sides of the valley were rocky, too steep to ride, too steep to even climb. They could not have chosen a more perfect spot.' He paused, shifted his weight onto his good leg and resettled his helmet under his arm, the plumes brushing his shoulder. 'There was no room to turn our mounts. Though we rode as fast as we could and with shields above our heads, it was not enough.'

'Your leg…?' Marcus asked.

'Will heal,' Casca replied, looking down at the weeping wound.

'Will you?' Flavius asked. A commander who lost his command yet survived would be expected to fall on his sword — all knew this.

'If I expunge the shame,' said Casca quietly. 'I have men left.'

'Success depends on how many tribesmen are camped on the plain,' whispered Crassus out of the corner of his mouth.

'Shh,' hissed Quintus, adding, beneath his breath, 'He has around twenty horses to command, no more, plus half a dozen auxiliaries. It is not enough.'

'Then we should help,' whispered his friend, smiling.

Casca had picked up the thread once more, though he looked increasingly weary and downcast. The physical injury was perhaps worse than it looked, and the mental turmoil now seemed to be taking its toll. 'I think they might have killed us all,' he said dolefully, 'had it not been for the rain. It came hammering down so heavily that we could barely see in front of us, but they could not see at all. They loosed no more arrows. We could only go forward anyway, so it made no difference to us. To them, it meant that they could attack no more.'

'This is the same rain that nearly drowned us in the forest,' said Marcus, to which both the prefect and Antoninus nodded in agreement.

'As the rain lessened, I realised that the sun had set behind the storm so that, as the road widened and the cliffs that the Astures had hidden in flattened out, the dark of the storm had given way to night,' said Casca. 'There were no stars. The cloud lingered until, as the rain finally ceased, we rode out onto a wide plain that sloped gently upwards. But we could see them; they could not hide anymore. And they could see us. I decided to attack. I swear I made the right decision, the only decision.'

XXII: CLEPSYDRA

Quintus thought that it sounded like Casca was trying to convince himself that he had done the right thing. He turned his head slightly so that he could see the decurion. Casca had lifted his chin and was looking directly at Flavius with tired eyes.

'I decided to attack, in spite of the dark. I decided there was time. I could see torches and fires lit in the distance and assumed it was their camp. I decided that if they ever gained it, we would never defeat them.'

'I am guessing that was us,' murmured Crassus.

Quintus nodded. There were lessons to be learned here, but he was as yet unsure what they were. He wondered what he would have done differently.

'I decided to chase them. I knew they would run.' Casca was pleading now, as much with himself as with his audience. 'I have fought Cantabrians, Ligurians and Astures — they always run. They never stand for battle.'

The men who could hear this speech all nodded — officers, legionaries, freedmen, and even slaves. They, too, knew that these tribesmen never fought pitched battles.

'I gathered the riders into a line, and I carried our standard at its head. With the last of the light, whilst we could still see shadows moving, we charged for the centre. We fought them and cut them down, although the numbers were against us. They had spread out thinly, so we could not attack all of them. What could we do but go for the centre? We would have died and would at least have taken the enemy with us, but then a female voice, a voice of command, rose above the noise.'

'We heard it,' murmured Quintus, and Crassus nodded.

'Suddenly, the enemy parted and vanished into the dark. We went straight through them, at full gallop. They chose to fight no more.' Casca put his helmet back on his head and stood proudly. 'Was it a defeat? I think perhaps not, neither for them nor us. It was a running battle, like nothing I have ever known. And they seemed to have leadership.'

He took a deep breath. 'My second saw something familiar, the fluttering of the vexilla, and called out that the camp was ours. I looked where he pointed and saw the silhouettes of the standards. I knew then that this was no enemy camp, though I still do not know why and how it is here. That's when I called for the gates to be opened.'

'All will be made clear, my friend,' said Flavius kindly, putting an arm on the shoulder of the cavalryman. He encouraged him to walk with him, back to the headquarters tent, and the conversation moved out of Quintus' earshot.

'I think they will attack us in the morning, at first light,' said Quintus.

'I think the cavalry will want to attack them first,' Crassus responded.

For the next hour there was heated discussion in the headquarters tent, voices rising and falling. Slaves came and went with plates of food and flasks of wine. Meanwhile, the plain glowed with the lights of many fires, as if the earth reflected the stars.

Although the legionaries listened hard, few words could be picked out. Quintus tried his best to deduce what was being said but failed. Publius had the uncanny ability to imitate the prefect, including his personal tics, and even managed to copy the clipped tones of the decurion, but his attempts at humour hindered the attempts of the others to guess what was being said. He was therefore silenced with a sharp word from Rufus and descended into a petulant sulk. The others of the contubernium fell to speculating over what they would do if they were the prefect. Only Sextus did not take part in this game of conjecture, deeming it pointless.

The line of enemy warriors, marked by the string of winking lights that were their fires, had not moved. None of the legionaries had been stood down, so they were all left manning the defences. Meanwhile, the slaves and the animals they looked after remained warm and well fed near their own fires.

'If I was the decurion,' offered Crassus, uncharacteristically cautious, 'I would wait for morning. I know horses. Horses can no more see in the dark than their riders.'

'Then you would have little honour,' said Rufus curtly, pulling at his moustache. 'It is obvious to me that he should fall on his sword. If I was the decurion, I would have taken my own life already to preserve my name, the name of my family and the honour of my men. Did he not flee from the enemy? Yes, they parted to let him through, but he could have turned and attacked again. Instead, he sought sanctuary.'

'It was dark,' rejoined Crassus lamely. 'No-one fights in the dark.'

'Nox could fight in the dark,' said Publius, his fit of pique forgotten as he crouched behind Cato, tipping his helmet forward onto his nose with a flick of his finger.

Cato turned and swore. He had his sword drawn. Publius was lucky to not feel the flat of it as his friend swung around at where he fancied his tormentor to be. Publius, knowing what would happen, had already ducked low. 'One day,' growled Cato. He settled his helmet again and tightened the strap.

'Will you two stop playing?' Rufus said angrily, pointing at the line of fires. 'Those are our enemy. This is serious.'

Publius shrugged, put on his serious face and asked Quintus, 'What would you do if you were decurion, Mac?'

'Nothing,' said Quintus, laughing, 'for you would never find me on the back of a horse. It's not something I enjoy or am very good at, so I definitely won't be leading cavalry. I prefer firm ground on which to fight.'

'Then if you were the prefect?' Publius asked.

Quintus mulled the situation over for a couple of minutes. 'I would wait until daybreak and take the men out into the field. The battle ground is flat, and we have the benefit of the top of the slope.' He used his hands to illustrate his tactics. 'I would send our century in first, in testudo formation, aimed at the heart of the enemy. We would scythe straight through their centre, then turn and do the same again. I would use the Third to roll in the sides of their line, so that they were hemmed in on three sides. I would then position the cavalry to stop their escape.'

This statement briefly changed the subject of the discussion from what their officers might do, to the poor tactics — in the opinion of the veterans — that Quintus suggested. The testudo was for raising sieges, not attacking infantry. The Third would have to be divided across two wings, fatally weakening it, and the cavalry would not be needed. Tullius and Rufus had fought many battles, and they had no respect for cavalry at all, seeing them as preening, pompous and, above all, unnecessary.

'I would keep them in reserve,' decided Rufus, 'and even then, I would hope not to use them.'

'Pompey's cavalry turned at Munda; that is what lost them the battle. My father told me so, in one of his more sober moments,' Crassus said pensively.

'But the Dictator's cavalry had already taken the centre,' said Quintus, 'or so I was told.'

'My father spoke from experience, not conjecture.'

Quintus accepted the mild rebuke with a nod.

'Who would know what the auxiliaries were doing?' asked Rufus dismissively.

'And if you were Marcus, Mac?' Publius persisted, turning the conversation back to their own situation.

'I would lead the Fourth and Fifth, and I would be a better leader than either bring-me-another or Marius.' Quintus watched to see if Tullius reacted to the sound of the name, but he just fiddled with his earring. Quintus continued, 'I would tell them to follow Valerius' helmet, which I now wear, for he was the best of the three we have lost.'

There was a general murmur of assent and a nodding of heads, even a reluctant grunt from Tullius.

Quintus concluded, 'Marcus will lead us if Antoninus lets him. He is a soldier.'

'He is my comrade,' said Tullius, joining the conversation for the first time, 'but I think he is lost to our squad — otherwise, he would be with us guarding this camp.'

This was too melancholy a thought for Publius, who once again posed a question of tactics, asking, 'Would you abandon the camp?'

'If we go to fight the Astures, it protects our backs if it is manned,' said Cato.

'If it is manned, we have soldiers who have not gone to fight. What use are they?' It was Tullius who offered this observation, then continued, showing his disdain for the slaves, 'I would empty the camp. I would leave the slaves and servants behind. If these became the slaves and servants of the enemy, so be it. If they were destroyed, it could only be because the cohort had been destroyed, so it would be of no matter.'

Crassus picked up on what Cato had said, suggesting, 'You could say that the camp was a haven, a place to regroup.'

'Then you would be saying it is a place to which we would flee, having been defeated,' said Tullius, his voice edged with sarcasm.

'I said regroup, not flee,' Crassus insisted.

'So, it would either serve as a place of safety and "regrouping" —' Tullius pronounced the word as if it brought a bitter taste to his mouth — 'for those who survived, or as a prize for the victors. If the battle is lost, it hardly matters.' He spoke as if his argument was irrefutable and took once more to polishing his dagger blade, a piece of oiled cloth beneath his thumb.

The men were quiet for a while. The lateness of the hour meant that they felt like sleeping, though they knew it was not a prospect. They were beginning to feel the chill of the night; since the officers had departed, they had been standing still apart from the stamping of their feet and the short walk along their part of the perimeter. It was, inevitably, Publius who reignited the debate, asking Quintus, 'Would you fight them before the dawn?'

'I think not,' Quintus scoffed, 'for who would fight at night?'

'Hannibal did,' offered Cato, 'in the mountains of Campania. He tricked the Romans into thinking he had a great force by tying torches to the horns of oxen.'

Tullius looked at him with suspicion. He did not quite trust a dark-skinned soldier who knew what the Carthaginians had done.

Cato noticed and offered a mild justification. 'I learned this in a history lesson that I can barely remember, my friend.' He pointed with mock erudition at the enemy. 'And he was helped by tribesmen from Hispania, maybe Asturian, maybe even these.' He paused. 'And he lost.' His tone caused laughter and broke the tension. He could always defuse a situation when he wanted to.

There was no time for more discussion, as Quintus was suddenly pulled away from them.

'You!' It was the new signifer, the fair-skinned soldier, who ran up to them and called out, 'The tall legionary, you are wanted by the prefect. Come.'

Quintus jumped down and followed the man without question, wondering what he had done wrong, for such summonses rarely carried positive connotations. Arriving at the prefect's tent, he at once questioned the need for speed, as he was left waiting outside. He tidied his clothes as best he could, straightened his helmet and stood to attention.

Fifteen minutes later, he was called in. The air inside the tent was still and stale, filled with swirling shadows amid the smoke of torches. He was immediately too warm, and though beads of sweat dripped down his forehead, he dared not remove his helmet.

The tent seemed crowded. The prefect, his chest armour unlaced, had his freedman close on his shoulder. Marcus, with Valerius' helmet under his arm, stood next to another slave, who carried a flask of wine. The decurion, looking downcast and dishevelled, sat with a cup of wine on a low stool. He was facing a bare-headed Antoninus who, like Marcus, looked to be ready for battle. Two more slaves stood ready to serve. Quintus was surprised to see half-eaten fruit on a platter, and wondered idly from where it might have come. The conversation — discussion, argument, it was hard to define — stopped as he entered, and Flavius addressed him.

'It was you who told us when the moon would rise, was it not?'

'It was, sir.' Quintus wished that he had paid more attention to Sextus' more knowledgeable speeches on the movements of the night sky.

'Tell us again.'

'It will rise a little after midnight over the mountains to the southeast — a little after because it must clear the peaks, though they are lower there.' He hoped he had remembered correctly.

'How long?' Flavius asked his freedman briskly, who was now fiddling with something that Quintus could not see.

The freedman replied, 'Two hours, sir.'

As he spoke, he shifted and Quintus caught a glimpse of a clepsydra, a simple water clock that the Flavian must have carried in his baggage — a narrow-necked vessel wedged so as to drip a coloured liquid into a marked bowl.

'Then you have an hour,' Flavius told Antoninus bluntly.

The centurion saluted, picked his helmet up from the table beside him, and left quickly, taking two of the slaves with him. Quintus could hear him beginning to bark orders outside.

Marcus turned to speak to Quintus, but the prefect was already waving him away. 'You are dismissed,' he said. They were not sure which of them was the subject of this order, so they looked at each other.

'Both of you,' said the prefect forcefully. 'You, go back to your guard duty and you, follow my plan.' He pointed at Quintus and Marcus in turn.

They each saluted with a fist to the heart and left the tent side by side.

'What…?' Quintus began.

'No time to explain,' breathed Marcus urgently. 'You must pass the word.' He gave Quintus his orders.

The camp was already buzzing with the effect of Antoninus' commands. First, the guards by the trees were reinforced, Flavius sending some of his own men to bolster their numbers. Should the enemy break through, it would be up to them to prevent any from gaining access to the forest and surprising Galba. A runner had been sent to warn him, but there was no way of knowing if the message had been delivered.

Second, the slaves were gathered together and told the part that they would play.

XXIII: ZAMA

It was dark when Antoninus signalled — still half an hour before moonrise, if Sextus had predicted accurately. The cloud was thinning, and a few faint stars showed through.

'Open the gate,' ordered Marcus, then muttered a silent prayer to Mars the Victorious.

The legionaries jogged out as quietly as they could, cloaks wrapped around them to make them even less visible. A signifer was at the head of each century, the standard for once held horizontally. The cavalry horses were led out, also in single file. Each man followed closely in the footsteps of the one ahead, relying on him to pick the way. The centurions took up position in the centre, along with the prefect, flanked by the pilum and manus standards of the cohort. For once, the freedman was not in evidence.

The Third took up the front three ranks in skirmish formation, their lines spread, two paces from the next man at the side and behind. They knew that this formation was a dangerous one, difficult to defend. Each line was not exactly behind the other but offset by half a pace so that there were no gaps for enemies to exploit. It felt vulnerable but the formation covered much ground, allowing the line to spread right across the plain.

The final legionary and the signiferi would be closest to the camp, leaving it empty of any but the beasts and those too injured to fight. Torches burned at all the places where they had burned before, but there were few men holding them. The camp looked no different, though it was now open and undefended.

Quintus found himself leading the front rank of the Fourth and Fifth, picking his way north as fast as he could over ground that he could not see. Two paces behind him was Crassus, with the rest of the contubernium strung out to the south. To his right was the new signifer, his standard held down and hidden. The combined century also stretched to three ranks, widely spaced.

Behind them came the slaves Jovan and Maxim, almost invisible in their simple dark tunics. They had no armour and no way to defend themselves should the enemy fall on them. They led a mule loaded with twin baskets containing hastily assembled bundles of birch twigs dipped in oil. There were half a dozen similar bizarre collections positioned at equal intervals behind the legionaries, each with a pair of frightened slaves in attendance. Behind them, nearest to the forest, were the cavalry, also spaced across the plain.

The Dragon chased the Little Bear across the heavens in an unseen pursuit, thanks to the scattered cloud. A few stars of the strange house that Quintus could not name had sunk out of sight. Elsewhere, the skies had cleared: to the north, he recognised the 'W' that was Cassiopeia, and he hoped that this Greek queen would bring bad luck to the queen of the Astures. To the west, he saw the Hunter, the Bowman, headed for his rest. He had no idea how any of these star movements related to moonrise. Apparently, the prefect — or one of his freedmen — did.

The legionaries, in position, stood still and apprehensive in the dark. They had been given two new orders: the trumpet call for 'Zama', an even riskier and more open arrangement than the skirmish formation they were in, and the call that was sounded now. This, a long, single note, blown as all saw two torches cross in front of the gate, was the signal for the action to begin.

The slaves scrabbled to light torches, dashing flint against tinder, and running from legionary to legionary to ignite the brands they also held. Then, trembling with fear and anticipation, they clutched one in each of their own hands. On a signal, the legionaries began the march down the slope, still blind, the torches burning out any night vision that they had gained. The slaves marched with them, each holding two torches aloft. A few came close to panic, but the sight of the standards, now raised and seemingly bathed in flame, and the sound of so many comrades around them ensured their fortitude remained intact.

They had been ordered to make as much noise as possible. Quintus shouted support and encouragement, which Crassus echoed. Publius took it as an opportunity to make crude suggestions about where he would insert his torch in any Asturian he caught. Rufus and Tullius started a song. All around them, legionaries were shouting battle cries.

What the Astures would have seen was a sudden forest of lights advancing towards them. Some immediately fled west. Most were no cowards, though, and began shouting orders of their own, turning to face the flames that flowed inexorably towards them.

A clear trumpet call of two notes, the second falling fast, ordered the legionaries to each take a step to the side, so that they now formed 'Zama', the risky open formation that Scipio Africanus had invented to neutralise the Carthaginian elephants. This time, however, it was not to counter pachyderms, but to allow passage for the cavalry. With their swords drawn and their lances set, the horsemen cantered through the gaps created by the soldiers, then kicked their

231

mounts into a gallop and aimed at the centre of the Asturian line. Their momentum maximised by the slope, they smashed with a resounding crack like rolling thunder into the unprepared enemy. At the same time, the trumpet called again, a reverse of the previous tone with a rising note and then a steady one, telling the men to form three wings — the normal formation for battle and a tighter structure, in which the legionaries fought shoulder to shoulder. In the dark, the men struggled to obey. The pattern required of them was familiar but had only previously been practised when they could see their fellows. Though they shouted to each other and upbraided those who were out of position, the solid blocks of spear, shield and sword that marked the heart of Roman potency struggled to take shape.

Casca, leading the cavalry, was desperate to redeem his honour. He took off the top of one man's head with his first swing and the arm of another with his second. Lying low on the back of his mount, his shield covering his vulnerable side, he then laid about him with his sword, sowing more panic, his own signiferi stabbing with the deadly points of their standards on either side of him. A lance thudded, taking his horse in the chest. It screamed as it fell, rolling and pinning him beneath it. He lay on his back, with his left arm under the beast and his right arm still holding his gladius, still fighting, not even dropping the weapon when he was punctured and pinioned by the point of an enemy javelin. The man who would have dealt him the death blow raised his axe, only to have the sharp point of the cohort's standard thrust into his side. He fell to his knees next to the dying horse before tipping forward onto his face. The prefect, who had galloped in with Casca and his cavalry, protected the decurion as he struggled out from underneath the beast, grabbing him by the folds of his cloak and pulling him from the fray.

He was too late. He saw the wounds and he saw that the light had gone from Casca's eyes. Nevertheless, Flavius dragged him away from the fighting and laid him down gently. Casca had fallen, but he had fallen honourably, and he had taken many of the enemy with him.

Behind the line of combat, the meagre torches of the legionaries had begun to expire, and the men began to think that their tactic had not worked. Their steps faltered, as they could not see the ground under their feet. The formation became more ragged and broken. Some began to look around at comrades who still held torches, seeking help from the light.

Then, as if by magic, the moon appeared above the mountains, flooding the field with eerie white light. It was three quarters full, just as Sextus had said it would be. It was enough to fortify the men and to fill the doubters with relief. The moon, exactly as predicted, rose at around the sixth hour. It rose in the southeast, in what was now a clear and cloudless sky. It cleared the ridged outline of the mountains, lower here as they tumbled away to the east. On the plain, it picked out the silhouettes of the battling tribesmen and the cavalry, casting the struggle into long shadows that writhed against each other.

Though the ground was dotted with torchlight from those brands still held by slaves, it was now the risen moon that provided most of the light. The slaves were encouraged to run, to regain the camp. Many made it, but some did not. Jovan and Maxim were two that made it to the gate, still partly open and manned by soldiers too injured to fight. They laughed with relief and hugged each other as they found themselves once again within the camp, climbing onto the perimeter timbers to watch the progress of the battle.

The first thing they saw was the blocks that the call of the cornicen had ordered finally solidifying, as men found their place. Like molten metal poured into a mould, the shape swelled and filled the corners, its edges straightening and hardening. The men now formed two wings and a centre, each an independent fighting force that became even stronger when all were employed together, as they were now. The men advanced.

After the initial shock of the cavalry charge, the Astures regrouped, prickly with spears and blades, and angry at the trick that had been played on them. The chieftain's voice, silent until now, was once more issuing orders, shouting across the battlefield. The fighters were pulling down and destroying any of the horsemen that were still amongst them. The legionaries, Antoninus and the standards at their head countered the Asturian anger with composure, advancing as patiently as a wave that lapped the sand.

The front of the Roman line presented an unbroken wall of curved shields, topped with a bristling thicket of spears. Now that the enemy could be seen, even if only as shadows, Antoninus could call the advance. The three blocks marched forward, ready to fling their weapons at the Astures when close enough. They needed to be no more than five paces from the enemy for this to be effective; they knew that it took nerve and discipline to hold the line so close to a world of blind rage and fury. Antoninus waited until he thought they were close enough and then signalled to the trumpeter, whose single note unleashed the hail of spears. These halted the advance of the enemy, sowing death and confusion in their ranks.

The legionaries did not need to be ordered to draw swords — that came naturally — and now the wall of shields was broken at each man with a brandished blade. Quintus looked to his left; there was Crassus, as he should be. To his right, he saw the fair signifer, resplendent in his wolfskin cloak. His bright white smile broke across his shadowed face as he raised the standard high and the formation once again marched forward.

Those of the cavalry that had not been killed in the first murderous charge and its aftermath had taken position on the outside of each wing, forcing the Astures into a tighter space. The tribesmen were pushed into each other and not given room to manoeuvre.

The Third clashed with the enemy first; they thrusted, parried and stabbed, not minding which part of an enemy their deadly edges found. Enemy faces exploded, guts were hanging out, and limbs were severed. The Romans sustained their own losses as Asturian axes, spears, daggers and swords did their own bloody work. But the legionaries were also protected by their armour, shields, formation and discipline. Five Astures fell for each legionary that dropped. As the trumpet sounded, the men stepped back, passing through the ranks that opened behind for them. They took their wounded comrades and allowed the next rank to take the front.

Only after three such changes did Quintus find himself face to face with the enemy, recognising Marcus' voice raised in command. Next to him Crassus had come closer than he had been in the skirmish formation, so that the two could protect each other. Further down, he could just make out the figures of Rufus and Tullius, standing firm. They were letting the enemy come to them and killing efficiently.

Quintus was the legionary on the end of the line, with just the signifer to his right. He could see no more than his own small area, a pace or two in front and to the side. He could speak to none but Crassus, but his lack of vision meant that his hearing seemed to have become more acute. He heard the cries of the enemy and the hoofbeats of the cavalry. He heard the noise of swords on shields, spears in flesh, the unearthly screams of injured horses. He heard the voices of command. His sense of smell seemed also heightened: there was the iron-tinged tang of blood, the foetid waft of punctured guts, and the sweat of both beast and man.

Still, it was shadow versus shadow, and the dance of the combat was slow. This was because the soldiers could not see their feet and did not know where they trod. The dark played tricks and would not show who was a foe and who was a friend, and they could not see what was happening elsewhere on the field and so could not react. Riderless horses suddenly reared out of the dark, slaves with torches ran in the wrong direction, and Astures almost fought each other in error. Romans did the same, pushing men who were no foe away with curses. The moonlight ducked in and out from behind the thin clouds that had gathered, forcing the men to reduce their speed.

It was here that their training really came into its own. The training that the boys had undertaken on the Campus Martius had always been with heavy wooden swords and even heavier wooden shields, so that the weapons they now carried felt light by comparison. They held the ribbed grip of their gladii tightly, ready to cut or thrust. They balanced their curved, rectangular shields in their left hands, covering their bodies from shoulder to calf. In their belts, the men also carried long, thin daggers.

Each weapon, if used well, could exploit the weak points of the enemy soldiers.

Quintus found himself face to face with an Asturian. He was long-haired, with furs on his shoulders and a sword cut on his cheek, which was bleeding copiously. The man screamed as he struck past Quintus, apparently seeing an opponent in Crassus. He missed his target but exposed his neck to Quintus' blade. The warrior's hot blood sprayed Quintus' face and his scream became a strangled gurgle. Another stepped into the space he had made.

Quintus looked to make sure that Crassus was unhurt, but in his place he saw a bald Roman soldier, his helmet gone. He did not know him; he was an out-of-position legionary of the Third. His sword arm had saved Quintus from almost certain death, but then he dropped to his knees as he received a blow himself. An enemy's short-handled battle-axe was wielded in a deadly arc, which the legionary parried two-handed by holding his sword before his face. Quintus blocked a blow from his own opponent and was amazed — and gladdened — to see the bald man rise, turn and strike again. He could not see Crassus, or any of his own contubernium, which led a detached part of his brain to think that perhaps it was he who was out of position.

The trumpet sounded again, and Quintus knew that this would be the last time that it sounded this night.

It was the order to fight independently, *contendite vestra sponte*, to break ranks and take on whatever enemy you could find. The melee became chaotic, each legionary fighting one or more of the Astures whilst also defending comrades who they saw threatened.

This order, Quintus knew, should have been a sign that victory was near; it was the equivalent of an order to finish off the enemy, for they no longer posed a threat. However, Quintus did not quite believe this as he parried an enemy weapon aimed at his head and thrust low, under the enemy's defence.

He felt, rather than saw, his sword penetrate the flesh of the man who had raised an arm to him. He realised, with detachment, that the arm held a battle-axe. He ducked as its clumsy swing kept its momentum even as he withdrew the gladius and the man died. He pushed him away with his shield, moving on to the next. His arm was tiring, but there seemed to be no end to the enemy. He realised that he was much further down the slope than the line of enemy fires. Most of the tribesmen that had survived must have been forced back onto the track up which they had come, though some seemed to be fleeing past him in the wrong direction, towards the camp. He realised, at the same time, that the enemy was thinning. He was having to stride to find opponents, picking his way through the dead and injured on the ground.

He found Rufus and Tullius, the latter wounded and leaning on the shoulder of his friend. He could not find anyone else; he was most worried about Crassus, having not seen him for some time.

He lifted his sword in defence as a tribesman rose up in front of him. His arm was injured but steady enough to hold out his weapon, hilt first, whilst dropping to his knees and casting his eyes on the ground. He was the first of the enemy Quintus had seen surrender. The legionary took a step past him and then turned swiftly, grabbed him by the hair and swept his sword across his neck. He was not the only unarmed man whom he sent to his fate this day. It could not be helped.

XXIV: IO SATURNALIA

Battles do not end because the soldiers wish it so, or even because the gods have decided on a victor. They end when the enemy ceases to resist, when they begin to lay down their weapons and raise their hands. But the order the legionaries had been given whilst still in camp did not allow surrender. Their centurions had explained that there could be no quarter given, no prisoners taken — the prefect did not want any more executions, nor did he want any prisoners to feed and water, and these people made exasperating and disobedient slaves.

Antoninus would have tortured a few for information, but the prefect told him that they had all the information they needed, and so no captives would be necessary. If they found the Asturian queen alive, then she could be brought in, but none other.

As the light rose gently in the east, making the last of the stubborn clouds flee, the colours and moods of the spilled blood were revealed — dark and bright, new and old, oozing and dried. It was even evident by the entrance to the forest, where those Astures that Quintus had thought were fleeing in the wrong direction had encountered the soldiers guarding the path to the mountain and the mine.

It was true dawn, and it seemed that resistance had broken completely. The legionaries were either loudly drunk on blood and victory or strangely quiet, and the trumpet was calling them back to camp. The men cast around for further enemy warriors to fight, but few remained, and there were even fewer of those willing to engage. Some prisoners had been taken, against orders; the centurions sent word that if any enemy

239

warriors, apart from one, were found alive, both they and their captors would face execution. There was no choice but to put the prisoners to death.

Quintus returned to the tent to find all but Crassus, Tullius and Rufus. Cato told him that Rufus was with Tullius, who had taken him to have his wound dressed, since it was beyond the crude skills of the veteran. There was no sign of Crassus. He asked after him, but none had seen him since the order to engage individually had been given. But no one had seen him fall, which meant there was still hope.

The adrenalin of victory had Publius and Cato swapping exaggerated stories without really listening to each other. Sextus was curled up silently in a corner, wrapped in his cloak. His face was a mask.

Jovan and Maxim's excitement was both endearing and annoying; they were like two small dogs, jumping up and down and demanding praise and encouragement. They had, after all, taken part in a Roman battle. They spoke of *servos ad pileum vocare*, liberty earned by providing service in battle. They would happily have shaved their own heads to wear the cap of freedom — but the legionaries shook their heads. The slaves had not been armed, after all, and though they would call it a battle, and its importance would grow in their telling of it, the chroniclers, should they ever hear of it, would call it an 'action' or a 'skirmish'.

Men were sent back out onto the field. Medics had to find any legionaries that could be healed, and executioners had to despatch any Astures that lived. Some men went searching for lost companions. Quintus was one of these, setting off wearily in search of Crassus.

Sword in hand, he kicked the bodies over with his foot, generally not bothering with tribesmen unless they lay on top of a Roman. There were many more of the Astures lying here than his countrymen, which demonstrated the tide of the battle. If he found the woman in the furs, she would be brought back alive, but he thought she had either died or escaped. The tribesmen would not have left her behind if she had lived. Roman casualties were light. If he found any enemy warrior who was still alive, he killed him as swiftly as possible, despite any vocal pleas or silent entreaties of the eyes. They died with a thrust to the heart, or a clean stroke across the neck, whatever was more efficient. Quintus was the son of a farmer, after all; he had slaughtered many beasts but had never sought to bring them pain. The order had been no prisoners and no slaves. Not torture. Not cruelty.

Crassus was not the only darker skinned legionary in the cohort, but the fact that he was in a minority should have helped with the search. Sadly, Quintus did not have time to look thoroughly; indeed, he had barely begun his search when a shout went up on the other side, towards the forest.

'Gold!' he heard. 'There is gold!'

Immediately, like a flock of starlings on a patch of spilt seed, there were men around the shouter. Some told him to hush — the fewer men knew about it, the richer those few would be — and others pushed and shoved whilst spreading the word, calling to friends and comrades. The secret quickly became public knowledge.

Men started turning over Asturians, seeking the precious metal. Then a further excited shout went up from the men who had caught the packhorses and were opening their satchels.

'By all the gods, it is a heap of gold — a veritable mountain!'

In the bags was more gold than the men could have imagined: gold nuggets, gold dust, and gold running through rocks. It was thrown in the air and trodden underfoot as they grabbed it and shoved it under their tunics.

The packhorses were loaded with it, including the precious rings that the men had cut from the fingers of the dead and the torcs that they had snatched from their arms. The largest nuggets brought death and injury as discipline fled and the pugio — the wicked knife that all legionaries carried — was pulled. Fights broke out all over the field.

Quintus was nearer to the camp than the forest, at the southern edge of the ground. He watched the fighting, aghast. He listened to the shouts and curses, not sure whether to try and stop the riot or to report it to the officers. But he need not have worried; the decision was not his. Word had already spread, and the prefect had moved to seal the camp. His own guards were preventing any more men from leaving, keeping the rioters outside. The two centurions, along with junior officers, were on the battlefield, shouting and laying about the men with their fists, their rods of office and the flat of their swords.

'Quintus!' Marcus yelled. 'What are you doing here?'

'Seeking Crassus — he is lost!' Quintus shouted over the din.

'Get back to the gate and help to restore order there!' the older man commanded urgently. 'Don't get involved. There will be punishments here. You must find him later.'

The advice proved unnecessary, as at that moment the trumpet rang out and it was everyone's duty to return to the camp and the parade ground. Failure to do so was desertion, and the punishment for desertion was death. The call had the immediate effect of halting some of the men in their pursuit of violence, providing a reminder of who and what they were. Much of the insanity seemed to pass from the field as the familiar triple note, the last tone lingering in the air, brought the men to their senses. Only a few still grappled with each other, apparently oblivious to the martial sound of the trumpet.

One such man was holding another in a headlock, and Antoninus struck him hard across the face with his fist, causing blood to well on his lips. The centurion ordered two of his men to take the fighter captive, pinioning his arms. Two more took the man who had been released from the headlock.

Similar episodes were scattered across the bloodied grass. Fighters were pulled apart, sometimes by their fellows to save them from punishment, sometimes by Marcus and Antoninus, and sometimes by other officers and the men of the prefect's personal guard. Men crowded around the closed gate either of their own volition, seeking to follow the order to assemble, or because they were caught by the arms between two of their burly fellow soldiers. The latter would wish they had obeyed the trumpet.

Finally, a mere fifteen minutes after the first shout, the field was cleared of legionaries. The few who had medical training were still allowed to search for Roman survivors, although the melee had made it increasingly unlikely that they would find any.

Marcus, with prisoners of his own, shouted for the gates to be opened and the men streamed in, eager to form up in their ranks — though many were also keen to get back to their tents and hide their newfound wealth. A line of soldiers at either side of the gate, the prefect's men, prevented this from happening.

In the camp, Quintus could see slaves building up the fires, feeding and watering the mules, cooking and cleaning. There was no sign of any tents being dismantled. It looked like the cohort would not be on the march this day.

He joined the front of the right-hand column of the Fourth and Fifth. Already present were the remnants of his contubernium: Lux, Nox and Sextus. Across from them, half a dozen men, including some with wounds or bruised faces, were sullen as they were gripped by their comrades. Tullius and Rufus were yet to appear, and there was still no sign of Crassus. Quintus listened to the whispered conversations that flowed around him.

One of the cavalrymen — horseless for now, his mount having been killed — had put the discovery of the gold into perspective, and the rumour had spread through the ranks. He had said that the Astures had been coming away from the mountain when the cavalry had first encountered them — coming away with what had been mined. The connection was not difficult to make; it was a goldmine, and if their finds were anything to judge by, a huge one.

'A huge goldmine,' said Sextus sarcastically, looking sideways at Quintus. 'Who knew?'

Quintus looked at him with exasperation. 'I knew it was no secret to you. You were there when Crassus spoke.'

'There is more to you and Crassus than you are saying.' Sextus turned his face resolutely to the front, signalling that the exchange was at an end.

Quintus sighed. How long could this go on? 'Crassus is missing,' he said flatly and was rewarded with an unconscious twitch of Sextus' head towards him.

The trumpet sounded again, this time the signal for silence. Flavius mounted the block placed for him. His freedman almost climbed up with him, then thought better of it. The signiferi were ranged on either side of the raised platform, holding the standards firmly. Antoninus stood by the prefect, ready to relay his words.

'Men of the Ninth,' the prefect began, honouring them with their history, causing the signiferi to raise the standards high and eliciting a cheer that he had not expected before the centurion had a chance to echo the words. After all, this was the first time since their disgrace that they had been addressed as part of the legion.

'Men of the Ninth,' he repeated. This time, the men allowed Antoninus to shout the words, then cheered again. The Flavian continued: 'Today you have won a great victory, but it was not just a victory for you. It was a victory for the cohort, for the Ninth Hispania, for Rome.'

As the centurion repeated the words, to loud acclaim from the men, the prefect pulled his cloak over his thinning hair, the sign that he was acting as a priest. This emphasised his broken nose so that he resembled a hooded raven.

'We lost some men, and we honour them as we honour the gods,' he said. 'We lost Titus Casca Sabinus, decurion, noble knight of the equestrian order. Today we will help his shade across the Styx.' There was nothing prepared for him to sacrifice, but this did not stop him from offering thanks. He lifted his gaze to the skies. 'Our thanks to Mars, to Capitoline Jove, to swift-footed Mercury and to lame-footed Vulcan. Let us feast and pour libations in their honour.' He lifted the long-necked vessel that the freedman handed to him and tipped its ruby contents slowly on the ground in front of him.

'Of course, he thanks the gods of slaves and fire,' Publius whispered.

'But he does not offer freedom,' said Quintus.

Antoninus' voice boomed, repeating Flavius' words: 'Even the slaves and servants had a part in it; perhaps you should cheer for them also.'

The soldiers' response was perhaps not quite as spontaneous and enthusiastic as it had been when they had cheered for themselves, but Publius took it upon himself to at least give the slaves some honour, shouting, '*Io Saturnalia! Io Saturnalia!*' This referred to the festival when slaves and masters switched roles for the day. The proclamation caused laughter and more cheering as it was taken up and repeated. Many of the slaves looked up from their work with curiosity. Some realised that they were being thanked. They smiled and waved, then continued with their tasks.

'We thank Mercury for the trickery, Vulcan for the fire,' said Cato.

'I thank Mithras, who protects soldiers, for my life,' said Sextus, breaking his silence briefly. 'I hope to thank Vulcan for the life of the blacksmith.' The acknowledgement of Crassus' status as 'missing' was welcomed silently by Quintus.

In front of them, the tone had changed. The prefect's head was once again bare. Now he was denouncing them. He spoke shortly. 'This morning, some of you have disgraced yourselves, have disgraced Rome, and have shamed the emperor. You know what you did. You will be punished. Turn about.'

The centuries turned smartly, a parade ground move, so that now they faced the gate and the field of carnage beyond it. The hurdles that supported the two halves of the gate were crude X shapes, two logs lashed together to form a cradle for a longer, central tree trunk that held them rigid. The supports were about three feet apart, meaning that those giving the punishment could use the cut ends of every other one to tie the hands of their prisoners, stretching their shoulders and leaving the middle hurdle pressing painfully against their sternums.

Antoninus rather approved of this arrangement, although a whispered order from the prefect spoiled at least some of his entertainment. 'No deaths, Centurion,' said Flavius. 'We have lost enough.'

The guilty, six of them, had been stripped of their armour, helmets and tunics so that their bare backs faced the men. They were anonymous — delinquents caught in the act of delinquency. Any gold that they might have had concealed had been taken from them. Two of them were naked but for their caligae, their bare backsides demonstrating the rigour of the search.

'This is their crime,' announced Antoninus. 'If it is your crime, too, you will receive the same punishment.' He pointed to a cloak on the floor, with something shiny at its centre. 'You will be given the chance to avoid punishment,' he added, then ordered the legionaries with the switches to give ten lashes to each man — probably sufficient to hospitalise them, but not enough to kill.

Quintus wished he had not been at the front of the line, at the head of the century, for both he and Sextus were amongst those who were handed the wicked knotted leather thongs that would provide the lashes. Both accepted the task as part of their duty. They would perform it efficiently, but neither would take any pleasure from it. It was just something that had to be done. They each weighed the scourge in their hands and prepared to administer agony and admonition.

XXV: MORPHEUS

As Antoninus counted, and the cohort watched, Quintus and Sextus, along with four others, took the skin from the backs of the guilty.

Though neither tried to swing particularly hard, it was difficult not to, as the whips were heavy with a momentum of their own. They also knew that if it looked like they were holding back, they would find themselves receiving punishment rather than meting it out.

They completed the chore efficiently. Once the count was complete, the men had water and vinegar thrown over their backs and were then cut down and helped away. They would not be allowed to die; they were needed to fight.

'Back in line,' Antoninus ordered.

The prefect spoke again. 'If you have any of the gold that was on that field, then you have stolen from the emperor. You will be lashed, but it will not be limited to ten strokes. Hear me and give up the emperor's gold.'

Many of the men looked uncomfortable. Sextus cast a reproachful glance at Quintus.

'You will all get your share,' vowed the prefect. 'Today we rest. The field will be guarded by my own men, and you will do well to stay away from it. Tomorrow, we return to Lucus Augustus, to the legion's headquarters, as men of the Ninth Legion.'

Once more there was a cheer, though not as loud as before the flogging.

'I will speak with the legion commander, and we will take this great find for the empire of Rome to Augustus himself.'

He pointed west dramatically and raised his voice. 'To Rome. He will reward you, and the reward will be yours honestly and officially. To Rome, men. And you will get more than gold: you will get honour, land and retirement.'

'He cannot promise this,' said Sextus, shaking his head. 'He does not have the power.'

'Sextus, look on the bright side,' Quintus said softly. 'We will go home.'

'I have no wish to go back to Rome.'

Antoninus amplified the prefect's final words before he stepped down. 'All stolen gold will be returned. Any found after this assembly has dispersed will be considered as having been taken from the emperor personally. Thieves will be punished according to the law.'

The men muttered amongst themselves but no more than that. They were weary; many of them had survived the night on fear and excitement. Now they were hungry, thirsty and chastened by the sight of the convicted gold thieves being dragged away.

Marcus and Antoninus each led their centuries in single file from the assembly area. Between the two lines, a cloak was held out by the prefect's own men. Into it, on pain of a flogging or worse, the legionaries were ordered to throw the gold that they had looted. The amount was such that the eyes of the soldiers accepting it grew round with amazement; the cloak they held filled up so quickly that it had to be removed and a second cloak was brought out. The men were naturally reluctant to part with their fortunes, but the sight of the hurdles and the splashes of blood on the ground helped to persuade them.

Many of the men had not been into the field at all that morning, so they had not shared in the bonanza. Publius and

Cato were two such, able to pass the cloak without dropping anything into it. Although innocent, each managed to look guiltily at the other as they passed. Quintus, too, passed the cloak with his palms empty and open, feeling rather than seeing the accusatory look from Sextus that burned into the back of his neck. He felt the heat rising up his face, and he dropped his head to hide the guilt that seemed obvious to him.

Finally, back in their tent the men were greeted with joy — and hot food and watered wine — by Jovan and Maxim. Sextus refused both and hunched in a corner, his face once more a mask. Jovan pointed to the already sleeping figures of Tullius and Rufus, wrapped in their cloaks on the floor.

'Master Tullius is injured,' the slave offered humbly. 'He needs his rest.'

'And Master Rufus?' Publius asked.

'Uninjured, sir,' Jovan said meekly, 'as far as I know.'

'We shall see,' said Publius, shaking the redhead awake.

Rufus came to groggily. 'What is it…?' he asked.

'How bad is Tullius?' Quintus asked quickly, before Publius could derail the investigation with some sort of jocularity.

'Almost hamstrung,' said Rufus, propping himself up on one elbow, 'but not quite. He has been returned to duty by the medics. Their tent is over full.'

'I had not thought to look there!' exclaimed Quintus, slapping his hand against his forehead. 'What a fool.'

Rufus, still not fully awake, shook his head in confusion as Quintus, still cursing himself, rushed from the tent.

Those trained in medicine had been busy with the injuries of the night, and the tent allocated to them was indeed full, with the three tables used for treatment each occupied. On one, a man lay on his back with his eyes bound, seeing nothing, but otherwise looking uninjured. The other two contained bodies that were face down, seemingly already dead, waiting to be removed by the slaves. Squatting in a corner, his face turned away, was one of the partly clothed men who had been flogged, recognisable by the criss-cross lesions on his back. Somehow, he seemed to have suffered more than the others, though all would be expected to return to duty today.

With a start, Quintus recognised the curly black hair of his friend on one of the prone bodies. He was dressed only in undershorts that were stained with blood at the waistband. There was a wound on either side of the base of his spine, as if he had been stabbed twice simultaneously. They appeared to have been cleaned and bled no more.

Quintus reached down and turned the head gently, seeing Crassus' flat nose and full lips below his closed eyes. As he held his friend's lifeless head in his hands, his grief welled up from deep within him. Tears blurred his vision, whilst the urge to cry out was almost impossible to contain. Keeping his hands from his eyes to avoid showing weakness, he pushed the hurt back down into his soul and took a deep breath. He could not believe that his friend lay here. He could not believe that he had failed to protect him, failed in his duty, and worst of all, failed to fulfil his promise to Ursus.

He had seen death, of course, and had meted it out himself, both in the heat of battle and this very morning, when the efficient disposal of prisoners was the priority. Those deaths were part of his job, part of his life as a legionary. They were not part of his life as a person or part of his soul, as this one was. He understood why, in some tribes, the bereaved wailed to the heavens or threw themselves onto their dead lovers' burning pyres. He understood why they would cast around for someone to blame, someone to take responsibility. But he knew that Crassus' death was his fault.

He took another deep breath and, laying the head softly down, he forced himself under control. He did not know what to do.

The blinded man moaned, seeking someone's attention, and the flap of the tent was opened briskly by an older man. He was grey-haired and did not wear armour, but was dressed simply in a light brown tunic and belt, both splashed with blood. Quintus thought he was a slave and adjusted his intonation accordingly.

'You can take that one,' he said, indicating the prone figure on the table, 'and that one wants some attention.' He pointed at the man with the bandaged eyes. 'That one —' he flicked his eyes towards the flogged man — 'I do not know.' He put his hand on the back of Crassus' curly-haired head and continued sadly, 'This one you can leave. I will take him.'

He made to turn his friend over, but was shocked by the voice that cut through his self-indulgence. The man was definitely not a slave.

'Do not touch him, you fool! Do not move him. The bleeding has only just stopped. Let it settle!'

Quintus stepped away quickly, as if he had been stung.

'That one will see again if he just leaves the bandages alone,' the man in the tunic said briskly as he pointed to the patient with his eyes bandaged. 'That is why his hands are bound.'

Quintus, who had not been paying attention, now noticed this for the first time.

'This one,' the man continued, indicating the legionary sitting on his haunches, with the lash marks on his back, 'is attempting to avoid duty.' He leant down so that his mouth was next to the whipped man's ear and spoke loudly. 'If he does not go, and go soon, I will treat his miserable back with salt.' The legionary understood the message and, with snivels and whimpers, scurried out. 'His friends can treat him, or not — I do not care. The wounds will not fester; that I have made sure of, at least.' He pointed to the other prone body and shook his head. 'This one, you are right about: he has reached the end of his days, though I do not know why, for he appears to have no wounds.' He clapped his hands together and two slaves appeared to take the body away.

Finally, he turned to the still form of Crassus. 'This one, whom you might have killed if you had lifted him up —' his tone was accusing, but he spoke more kindly when he saw the shocked expression on Quintus' face — 'this one rests in the arms of Morpheus. His wounds have stopped bleeding, but I have not yet bound them. I am waiting for them to dry. If you lift him before the wounds are bound, you will open them again.' He stroked the long, dark line of the backbone from Crassus' neck to the base of his spine, letting his hand rest gently between the two wounds, then said softly, 'This one, amazingly, sleeps.'

'He lives?' Quintus exclaimed excitedly.

'Morpheus is the son of Somnus; in sleep he mimics death. You need to look more closely before you pronounce someone dead. He breathes, does he not? It is harder to know, since he is lying on his front. If he were on his back, you could see his chest rising and falling, or the beat of his heart. But he breathes, and there is colour in his skin.' He pressed his thumb and forefinger into the soft flesh on the side of Crassus' arm. His thumbprint showed briefly lighter, then blood flowed back to restore the colour. 'This is an easy test. My thumbprint would stay if he was dead.'

'I am such a fool...' Quintus began.

The man, freedman or legionary — medic, anyway, Quintus realised — ignored the remark and spoke pensively. 'At first, I thought him unconscious and likely to die from his wounds, but he seemed a strong young man. So, I laid him down here, cleaned the cuts, gave him water and wine and, when I returned from another foray after all this gold nonsense, I found him no longer unconscious.' He pulled down the skin below one of his own eyes so as to reveal the white of it. 'You can tell from the eyes,' he said. 'He is not unconscious, but asleep.'

'I am not sure I understand the difference.'

The man tried to explain. 'One is a state of protection — forced on the body, involuntary, and sometimes ending in death. The other is voluntary — a restorative that ends in healing, strength, and recuperation. We do not fully understand, though Morpheus seems to rule both.' He placed his hand gently on Crassus' forehead and said softly, 'The difference is in the eyes.' He became brisk again. 'He sleeps now. I can wake him if you wish — we could do with the room — but I would advise against it until I have bound the wounds.'

As he finished speaking another injured soldier was carried in, arms supported on the shoulders of two legionaries. 'Where do you want him?' they asked curtly.

'That table,' said the medic, nodding towards the newly vacated surface. He then indicated the blind man. 'You can move him outside. He can sit or stand; he does not need to lie down.'

The new patient was dumped none too gently on his back on the table, and the men led the unseeing legionary out. Two new medics, both younger men, entered and began to cut the armour and clothes from the latest arrival.

'May I stay?' Quintus asked.

'No, but you may come back, or even wait outside. I will not be too long with him.'

Quintus stood outside the tent, noting the various people coming and going busily. From time to time, the slaves carried out a body, but many of those who went in supported by their comrades managed to come out on their own. This was not the worst of it. During the night, there had been men with much more serious injuries brought in. Not all could be saved.

Eventually, Crassus came slowly from the tent, a binding around his middle. There was a large and clumsy bag over his shoulder, seemingly made from a cloak, but otherwise he was clothed in just caligae and undershorts. If Crassus had kept the gold on his person, Quintus thought, it would surely have gone. He unfastened his own cloak and draped it over Crassus' shoulders. The sun was high now, and it was a reasonably warm day, but his friend looked like he might need it. Even if he did not, it was an acceptable sign of friendship and affection.

'Let me take the bag,' Quintus said. 'What is it?'

'I do not know,' Crassus said as he passed the bag across, 'but he said it was mine.'

Quintus looked inside — there was a helmet, chest armour, and the remnants of some cloth.

Crassus thanked him croakily for carrying it, his voice hoarse and ragged, but he refused to take up the offer of an arm to lean on. 'Thank you. I am fit for service,' he said proudly. 'I will walk on my own two feet.' He stopped and turned his eyes on Quintus, smiling. 'Though I may be a little slower than usual.'

Quintus smiled back and nodded in understanding. They did not always need words.

They crossed the parade ground in front of the gates, Crassus looking at the bonds and blood with curiosity. 'What happened here?' he asked.

'The tribesmen were transporting gold, and the legionaries found it. They discovered that the mountain was not just a mine, but a goldmine. They fought over it.'

'You fought over it?'

'I did not have the chance to be involved; the centurions and the prefect's men arrived.' Quintus held his hand up quickly. 'I would not have been involved even if I had had the chance,' he insisted.

Crassus did not immediately reply. When he did, it was in a very quiet voice, almost a whisper. 'Sextus said it was cursed, and perhaps it is. As you can see, I have no gold concealed.' He lifted the cloak with his left hand so that his almost naked body was revealed to his friend. He then dropped his arm, letting the cloak cover much of him once more, and indicated the bag that Quintus had slung over his shoulder. 'I doubt it is in there. I have lost what I had.' He paused. 'I think I am glad to be rid of it.'

'It was not the gold that injured you,' said Quintus peevishly. 'It was an enemy blade. Perhaps it was good fortune that you were not killed. You can look down on fortune from above, or up at it from below. The outcome will be the same whichever way you look.'

'As you wish,' agreed the blacksmith, in a tone intended to put the argument to rest.

XXVI: PUPILLUS SEXTILIUS ESQUILINA

Some men slept, some ate, and some warmed themselves at fires. But what should have been a joyous — and raucous — celebration of victory, had been all but snuffed out by several factors. Firstly, since the battle had been at night, tiredness was making the men irritable and short-tempered. Secondly, some had lost friends and comrades. Thirdly, and most heinously, men had fought and injured each other over mere gold, and they had once again been accused and punished for poor behaviour. Still, as far as they knew, they were going to march to headquarters in the morning, and then they were going to Rome, so this mood would not last for long.

Arriving by their own fire, Quintus found Nox and Lux deep in conversation. Joyfully they chorused, 'Crassus! You live!'

'By the will of Jove and the hand of Vulcan,' Crassus said formulaically.

'And the skill of a medic,' added Quintus.

'But what happened to your clothes?' asked Cato, concerned.

'This bag seems to contain his armour and helmet,' said Quintus.

'It was cut off, I'm afraid,' Crassus said apologetically as he took it from Quintus and peered inside. Slowly, he handed it to the slave. 'It will need mending and polishing.'

Maxim pulled out the remnants of a bloodstained tunic, with a belt hanging from it. 'I think this may be beyond my skill,' he said.

'I have just what you need,' said Publius happily. 'I have a spare tunic in my pack.' He jumped up and went to fetch it, returning with a pristine piece of clothing. 'Never worn,' he said.

Crassus needed help to put it on. His back injuries were by no means healed, and his ability to bend and stretch was much compromised, but he felt better, more whole, once he had managed.

'I will wash the belt,' Maxim said. 'I can at least fade the bloodstains.'

Crassus thanked them all, then lowered himself gingerly onto the ground. A question from Cato was enough to start the conversation about his morning, what had happened and how. Quintus looked inside the tent for the rest of his contubernium. Rufus and Tullius slept within. Sextus sat cross-legged in a corner, his cloak pulled around him, apparently dozing. Quintus let the flap fall and went to speak to Jovan, who was feeding the mule.

'We return to Rome?' the slave asked.

'We march for Rome,' said Quintus, checking the hooves and haunches of the animal for injuries. 'Tomorrow morning, we will first head for Lucus Augustus, then for Rome.'

Maxim joined them, having put Crassus' belt into a pot of hot water. 'The armour will require the skills of both of us,' he told his cousin. 'You will have to come and help me.'

Once the men had rested, they spent the afternoon telling tales of heroic deeds and daring. The stories of the two Macedonians — though they were slaves — were listened to with indulgence. Tullius, awake now, told of how he had been cut from behind by an Asturian axe, almost severing his hams, an injury that would have incapacitated him and meant an end to his service.

'It is shameful that anyone could be craven enough to kill a man without facing him,' Quintus said pointedly, seeking a reaction from Tullius.

'Romantic nonsense,' Sextus scoffed, giving Tullius time to frame his response, or to decide not to respond. 'I have killed many an enemy without seeking eye contact. And what about the cavalry, striking down?'

'Well,' said Cato, 'they are cavalry after all, not real soldiers...' The conversation then meandered off in a different direction.

Still, Quintus looked hard at Tullius. He would get to the truth of it eventually.

In between the tales, and a certain amount of dozing, both slaves and men were busy with the tasks that were essential. The injured were resting. Maxim, having cleaned the belt as best he could, had set it to dry and was now baking biscuit. Jovan had exchanged his task of mending with another slave, who had arrived seeking help for his own masters in writing letters of condolence. The other legionaries were cleaning and sharpening equipment. For once most of the men had been allowed to rest, but without wine or women they did not really know how to do so. Even now men were out in the open, practising sword strokes with each other, sparring with open hands, stretching and exercising.

Quintus and Crassus were playing knucklebones: the outcome would decide who would receive the next haircut from Maxim. Sextus moved across and sat down next to them, deliberately knocking the astragali from Quintus' hand.

'You spoil the gamble,' Quintus complained. 'Why?'

'Because I cannot get you to see the danger, either of you.'

'The danger in gambling?' Crassus asked innocently.

'The danger of keeping secrets from friends.'

'We have no secrets,' Crassus said, believing it now that he no longer had the gold.

Quintus stayed quiet.

Sextus looked at them noncommittally, then said, 'My life started as a secret and has remained so. I have never liked it. I have no knowledge of who my father was; I think my mother probably did not either. But I had no knowledge of her either.'

'You were a foundling?' Crassus asked, interested.

'I was. A foundling in Rome. I have no desire to return there, Crassus. I know you do not either.'

'Then we stay in Lucus Augustus. You can introduce me to the prefect's wife!' Crassus laughed.

Rufus arrived at Sextus' back and put a hand on his shoulder. 'I would be happy to stay there,' he said, 'but I would like my share of the gold.'

'It is not so easy; something tells me we should not go there either.'

'What tells you…?' Quintus asked.

'The stars, the moon, a betrayal made, another to come, my history — a history of secrets and betrayal.'

'Tell us your fears,' said Crassus, as Publius and Cato ducked under the flap of the tent to join them.

'Jovan, a drink,' Sextus ordered. As the man hesitated, he added, 'Yes, from my own stock. For all.'

There was a hiatus as Jovan vanished then reappeared, holding a full wineskin. Sextus indicated that cups should be filled for everyone.

'We won a battle today, after all,' he said, then settled into his story. 'I am a foundling,' he started, 'a survivor. I was left in the summer, so I was warm enough in swaddling clothes on the steps of the temple of Capitoline Jove — an offering, perhaps…'

'So, you could be noble-born?' Rufus exclaimed, laughing. 'Left at a temple rather than thrown on a rubbish heap! I thought you had an air about you.'

'I could be the son of Marcus Antonius and Cleopatra Philopator, or of a butcher and a whore. Which do you think is more likely?'

'You look more like the general than a butcher,' ventured Cato. 'I hear he was very handsome...'

'As are some butchers,' Sextus added firmly, narrowing his eyes. 'Shall I continue?'

'Carry on, carry on,' chanted his audience. Almost all of the contubernium was now listening.

'Very well.' Sextus took a long drink and continued: 'I was taken in by the Vestal Virgins —' he held up a hand quickly — 'and no, I don't know why but they found me a wet nurse and allowed me to grow within the walls of their temple. I had but two things to my name — a swaddling blanket of, I was told, exceptionally good quality, though I never saw it, and a label that was tied to one foot. It read, "Save him. He is a citizen." My name attests to my beginnings, Pupillus Sextilius Esquilina — my parents were considered dead, I was born in the month of Sextilius, and my tribe was taken as being the hill on which I was left.' He became pensive. 'There is either nothing of me in my name, or everything. I cannot decide. I did not decide to shorten it — others did that.

'I grew. I learned to walk and talk. I thought I was happy, but I had no brothers, no friends, no playmates; the girls that were dedicated to join the Vestals were serious, aloof. When I was around seven, I began to ask questions of the old women, for Vestals grow old, very old to a youngster's eyes. My questions soon tired them. I became an annoyance, and when I ran off into the streets and sewers of the Suburra, they did not come

261

after me.' He paused to drink again, and a smile flickered on his face. 'Well, they did the first three or four times — then they tired of the game and abandoned me. My fault, really. My choice.'

'At seven?' Cato whispered.

'Boys can be very brave — or stupid,' said Sextus, 'especially at seven.'

'Go on,' Quintus encouraged, fascinated despite himself.

'Some people maintain that level of stupidity well into adult life, Mac,' Sextus threw at him pointedly, then took a deep breath. 'I became a runner for the gamblers, a thief for the robbers, a pimp for the harlots. The women and their handlers frightened me to begin with. They were big and loud, and they smelled of sweat, urine and bad wine. I took many knocks and blows, but they could not stop me from growing. They could not stop me from finding out that I could control them, manipulate them, with a smile and a downward glance.'

He smiled, his even white teeth showing, then dipped his eyes like a virgin bride on her wedding night. His long lashes shadowed his soft brown eyes. 'This warded off many blows,' he added, turning the coquettishness back into something more masculine with a soft laugh. 'I see the question on your lips, Rufus,' he went on, 'and you are right. I was a good-looking young boy in the steeps and brothels of the Suburra, that maze of tenements and inns beneath the Servian Wall. Of course, I was used and abused. I fought when I could and submitted when I couldn't…'

Publius, a picture emerging in his mind's eye, sniggered. Without really thinking, he made a lewd gesture using his finger and fist.

'You would not like it, Publius, if it happened to you,' Sextus snapped, his voice sharp. Then, with a heartfelt sigh, he added,

'Lux, my friend, you would not jest and snicker about such a thing if you knew what it meant.'

Publius was immediately upset. Once more, he had managed to overstep when he thought he was being funny. Cato comforted him.

Sextus picked up the thread, his voice once again even. 'I was very quickly not a child, not a boy, but not a man either — an inhabitant of some half-world in between, knowing far too much about adult things and too little about innocence. I was never innocent.' He opened his arms wide, palms upward, and turned to look at everyone in his audience. His eyes seemed to pierce each of their souls. 'So, I learned. I learned many things that a boy should not know, and some that even a man would shy away from. I learned many secrets and have used them when I must. I learned to read the stars, to make predictions.' He nodded wisely. 'The stars are the only things that have never let me down.'

Quintus could not stop himself from objecting, 'We have never let you down.'

'You will, if you have not already,' Sextus said flatly. 'I sense secrets. I also sense betrayal and disaster. I feel the evil in the gold.' He paused. 'I have no love for Rome, but it would be better than the legion's base. Calamity awaits us there; I am sure of it.'

Although he believed in the gods and their capriciousness, Quintus tried not to believe in fortune, fate, or what could be read in the stars. But it was difficult; he shivered at Sextus' words. The future should be hidden and uncertain, not predicted as calamity, and he wondered what would truly befall them.

The weather was, as ever, in the shadow of the mountains, unpredictable. Without warning, throughout the day, there had been sharp showers, carried on a brisk easterly wind. They sprinkled rather than drenched as they passed quickly over, barely staying long enough to drive anyone under cover. Even the wild hares, rabbits, boars and wolves merely shook their fur and continued about their business, the latter waiting for night so that they could slink onto the battlefield slope. In between the showers, the sun cast long shadows from the mound of enemy bodies, reaching across the field like fingers grasping for the forest path.

As the light dimmed, the trumpet sounded once more. The note that followed the call to assemble was long and mournful: the assembly was for the benefit of the dead.

Outside the gates of the camp, a pyre had been raised by those who had not been afforded the luxury of rest, and legionaries stood by it with torches lit. Inside, they once more faced the podium and the prefect. His head was covered as he recited the eulogy for Casca, decurion, member of the equestrian order, who had bravely and honourably fallen in battle. The freedman, Quintus guessed, would have written the eulogy, and it would be he who wrote the account that was sent back to Casca's family. From what Quintus had been told, he had died recklessly rather than heroically. He had courted death, having borne the heavy shame of retreating from this enemy less than a day before.

A hunting party had been out and had finally captured a roe deer. This was to be the sacrifice that would placate the decurion's shade and give him peace once Charon had ferried him to Pluto's realm.

The men were glad when the sacrifice had been made and the signal was given to light the pyre. Assisted by the oil that had been splashed, the flames quickly ate into the timber and leapt skyward into the deep blue of the darkening sky as the trumpet sounded the dismissal. The last thing that the Flavian said was a reminder: they were to march at first light, which meant dismantling the camp by moonlight. Then they would head first to the legionary headquarters, then to Rome.

XXVII: SIT TIBI TERRA LEVIS

'You said Rome, sir?' Maxim dared to ask his master. 'I thought we were heading for the camp of Legio IX Hispania — for Lucus Augustus?' He bowed his head and added, 'I only ask because Rome is a long march, and I am not sure that this animal is up to it.'

Quintus had just finished inspecting the beast. 'It is fine,' he said. 'It is doing well under your care. I try to talk with it —' his smiled flickered — 'but it seems short of conversation. But you are right: we will go to Lucus Augustus first, where perhaps we may pick up new animals and lead this one to pasture, and then to Rome.'

A voice cut across from the back of the tent. Sextus stood there, in all his coiffed and preened glory. He looked did not look as if he had fought in a battle, slept on the ground and been bored at a funeral; he looked as if he had just come from the baths and the barbers. Quintus still did not know how he did it.

'You know that we will never be marched to Rome if we go to the legionary camp first, don't you?' Sextus said with confidence. 'It will not happen.'

'You are so certain?' Quintus asked.

'The gold makes it so,' Sextus said simply.

'The gold?'

'You know as well as I do that some men have held on to their gold — once the Astures' gold, now the emperor's gold — and thus have held on to the ill luck that goes with it.' He looked directly at Quintus, his sharp brown eyes boring into the soul of the legionary. 'Some have carried that curse since even before the battle; others will carry it with us until it destroys us all. I have warned you. We will not go to Rome.'

'You wish to stay with your woman is all.'

'Any of them — I do not deny it. But I fear that will not happen either.'

'What have you seen?'

Sextus turned away, throwing a parting shot at Quintus. 'You think that I just tell stories, but I see bad fortune. I see an oathbreaker. I see someone who made a promise, took on a task that Ursus laid on him. I see someone who swore the *ius iurandum*, to die to protect his comrades, but who perhaps did not believe it. Marcus is gone from our company. Tullius is injured. Crassus is injured. We all head for death and danger. What do you think I see? Who do you think I see?'

Quintus' eyes followed him, his mouth gaping. Maxim had bowed his head low and dropped his shoulders; this was not an exchange for the ears of a slave.

The sound of the trumpet and the hoarse tones of the officers interrupted them. The notes played by the cornicen came far too late, for the men were used to rising before Sol himself and could not have slept anyway. The trumpet barely managed to assert itself over the noise of the camp being dismantled.

There was a chill in the air, but fair-weather clouds inhabited the high heavens in the fading moonlight. The area of the headquarters, in the middle of the via praetoria, was already alight and more timbers, taken from the temporary walls and fences, were being added to the blaze. Presumably, the prefect was being cared for elsewhere. There were guards stationed on the perimeter, each contubernium responsible for a section. Cato and Publius guarded their own portion, having volunteered to take the place of the injured Tullius and of

Rufus, who had been chosen for the duty by lot. Sextus had now gone to join them, his face still hard, claiming that he would rather do his duty than stay with the tent.

The full light of morning would come later, by which time they would be on the road. They expected to set off before night had truly passed. They were victorious in battle, discoverers of a goldmine, and accepted as part of Legio IX Hispania. Now, they were on their way to the city of Romulus and Remus, the city of women, wine, sun and sin and, for some of them at least, of family and friends. Some of the men even had the good grace to feel sorry for the centuries led by Galba and Furius Lentulus, who would be left behind to guard the mine, but they comforted themselves with the thought that these men would be rewarded as soon as they were relieved.

'We are going to the legionary fort first,' said Crassus, as he pinned on his new cloak. It had been mysteriously acquired by Sextus; Crassus presumed that it had once belonged to a fallen comrade. His old cloak had been made into the bag he'd carried from the medical tent, and fixing it was beyond the skills of the slaves. 'Mac, we might even be paid,' he added hopefully.

Quintus smiled and bent low inside the tent as he packed away his own kit. 'At least being in the town means we might have somewhere to spend it.'

'Sextus is adamant that we should not go there — even though his woman is there.'

'Sextus says we should not even go to the fort, let alone the town,' Quintus snorted.

'He is usually right,' offered Crassus diffidently.

'But not always,' insisted his friend, ducking out of the tent to tie his bundle where there was more room, and where Crassus could place no more doubts in his head.

Any slave worth his salt had kept his squad's fire burning and a pot of something hot over it, even though they had much to pack away whilst the men had only their personal effects. The men would at least help to strike the heavy tent, though they were unlikely to assist with loading the cart, having their own armour and weapons to deal with. Most also helped each other to tie their segmented armour, rather than ordering a slave to do so. It was a question of priorities and good sense — when a slave was available for such tasks, he could be used; when he was busy with tasks that were more important to the unit, the men used each other. Haircuts, beard trims, shaves, cleaning, mending and maintenance had all happened the evening before or not at all. The slaves had then slept a little but risen at midnight to ensure the efficiency of the departure.

The centuries formed up on the gate, or at least where the gate would have been had it not been merrily burning on the fire. The air was beginning to warm up, and the night sky was pale. The moon, which had been such a beacon the night before, was milky and insubstantial, heading for its rest and easily outshone by the bonfire.

The men formed up four abreast. The signiferi were at the front with the standards raised, and the legionaries held themselves as still as they could in the mountain air. Antoninus and Marcus were in some sort of heated conversation nearby, the tesserarius of the Second standing stoically a pace behind them. Of course, the Second should have taken precedence, although it was the prefect and his own guard that would lead them all out. The cavalry — consisting of around two dozen horsemen, including auxiliaries, who were now led by the duplicarius, decurion in all but pay until his battlefield promotion was confirmed — would bring up the rear, after even the carts, slaves and mules. The Flavian wanted a rearguard in these uncertain lands. They formed up now to one side, beasts scratching and pawing the ground in anticipation.

As the flames grew high with the last of the fuel, the back of the column, the men of the Fifth, could feel the heat and see the light dancing on the armour of their fellows. They saw the prefect, splendidly cloaked, helmeted and armed on his horse, trot out past them, his own guards jogging on either side of him. They took up position at the head of the column.

Quintus dared to look quickly behind him as they moved out, heading west. He shook his head; this was not what he had been taught was the legacy of Rome. To the south, the conflagration burned, lighting up an area that was churned and rutted in shades of black and grey. The square outline of the camp could still be seen, as well as the line of the via praetoria, the regular rectangles where the tents had been and the myriad patches of individual fires, many still smoking. All around was ruin. Trees and bushes had been felled or uprooted. Mounds showed where latrines had been, or horse lines, or defensive ditches, or their own dead.

Glancing the other way, to the north, Quintus could see the outlines of the several mounds that he knew to be the bodies of enemies. He knew that these had been visited by crows, vultures and other carrion birds in the daytime, as well as wolves, boars and rats in the night. But no animal would be there now. The noise of their departure — the call of the trumpet, the tread of the men's caligae, the hoofbeats of their horses, and the clink of their armour — would be enough to make even the grizzled grey pack leader of the wolves press himself to the ground until the racket subsided.

They trudged off the open plain and into the narrow defile that held such ugly memories for the cavalry. On an order, they dropped down to two abreast. Scouts rode ahead, yet still the men started at any shadow that moved on the heights to either side, afraid of another ambush. The walls of the valley grew ever steeper and rockier, and Quintus could see that it had been a perfect spot to attack the cavalry. They could not turn or manoeuvre. The men were made even more nervous by the several halts they had to make.

'What is happening?' Crassus asked Quintus, though he was glad of the rest. His injury was clearly troubling him. He walked stiffly and gave the occasional involuntary yip of pain, quickly cut off.

Quintus, his height allowing him a view, saw a dead horse being dragged to the side of the track. 'It is the slain men from the attack,' he said. 'They block our road. I can only see a horse being moved, but wager there are dead men too.' He saw Marcus smiling grimly. As centurion, he had taken his position ahead of Quintus and Crassus. 'I bet he is glad the Second took the lead,' Quintus added. 'It saves us from such work.'

After each short halt, they marched on, past the grim remains of beasts, torn by boars and bears, and the mostly unrecognisable remains of men. The Astures had been down and stripped them of anything useful — armour, weapons, cloaks and tunics. The only thing they seemed to have no use for was caligae. The birds had followed, their first task being the removal of unprotected eyes and any flesh that had been opened. Other animals had gnawed after that, and now great clouds of flies buzzed around the dead. The result was that, as they marched past, they could see a butcher's shop of flayed flesh. Parts of horses were identifiable, as were parts of men. Other parts looked nightmarish: white bone protruded from grey flesh, eye sockets gaped, and jaws hung open in fiendish grins. The stench, in the narrow ravine, was overpowering. Publius retched, and others quickly stuffed their focalia — the scarves that protected their necks from the chafing of their armour — into their mouths or wrapped them around their noses. Quintus saw a legionary of the Second bending over and assumed he was vomiting. However, the man straightened up and opened his hand, throwing a handful of red dust over one of the bodies.

Quintus nodded knowingly and followed suit. 'Help their shades find rest,' he ordered those that marched behind him. Many bent to the ground to provide the barest form of burial for these men, mouthing '*sit tibi terra levis*' as they dropped soil lightly on the fly-blown corpses. The Vestals might have paid their passage, but they needed more than that. Clearly, they were not going to get a pyre, as the cornicen blew the order to quick march. Dawn light would take its time reaching into this cleft. The night was still raw and close around them, like a cold hand clutching at their breasts. The prefect had decided to get out of here as soon as possible.

As they came out into more open country, daylight spread across the eastern sky behind them. Though wooded, the trees were not thick enough to conceal an army, and as colour slowly returned to the landscape, their spirits rose. The quick march was ended, and a normal pace resumed. Permission to talk and sing was granted after a request was sent to Antoninus, which was then passed to the prefect by an auxiliary on horseback.

The road bent round in a great arc, skirting the mountains and both the deeper forests and the broken ground. In places it was poorly maintained, narrow, or blocked by rockfalls; in others it was wide and flat. It was the road used by the Astures to and from the mine, with the secret being kept by the stones rolled across its entrance and the thick forest at its foot. Surveyors were already plotting its course, noting where it would need to be widened or strengthened and compiling reports. Engineers were discussing which trees would need to be felled, which depressions filled, and which rises flattened. It was already an adequate road, they admitted, but not yet Roman.

All the talk in the marching columns had now turned to Rome. Songs were sung, bawdy songs, which some of the younger men joined in with without really understanding their meaning. Veterans explained in great detail how they would greet womenfolk and girlfriends. They were back marching four abreast; Quintus and Crassus were joined at the front of the century by Publius and Rufus. Rufus was surprised to see Publius without his amicus and took the opportunity to bait him. He said something under his breath to Crassus, who laughed knowingly, then repeated it in a whisper to Publius, whose face beneath his helmet turned bright red from neck to crown.

'What did he say?' asked Quintus, smiling.

'I cannot repeat it,' complained Publius, then looked at the other two with curiosity and disbelief. 'Anyway, I do not think what he said is possible.' He turned to Rufus and changed the direction of the conversation. 'Surely you are not married? You are not allowed.'

'The emperor Augustus, as we must now call him, has forbidden his legionaries to marry. But I was a soldier before he became emperor, and I had a wife of sorts. I still have a wife of sorts — not the same one,' Rufus laughed, 'a newer one, with a house in Lucus. The legions accept married men, but once my name was entered on the roll, I was considered unwed — I could be married to the army, I was told.' He laughed again. 'How can a man screw the army? By Jupiter, they even squeezed my balls to prove I had some, then ordered me not to use them. Doesn't make sense, boy.'

'Crassus objected to them weighing his,' said Quintus, laughing at the memory. 'When our group was allocated, he was in front of me when he stood to have his name entered. He yelped when the freedman, the legionary clerk, put his hand beneath his tunic and grabbed his balls. He was an old man, bald and wizened, I think this was the only pleasure left to him!' Crassus remained stony-faced as Quintus finished, 'At least it warned me to stand clear and show him mine — from a distance.'

'I remember myself,' said Publius quietly. 'I had to part my tunic and lift my undershorts to show the clerk. Very embarrassing.'

Quintus looked around conspiratorially, making sure no one else was listening. 'Before we took the oath together, I saw what he wrote on the roll next to Crassus' name. For most men it was "red-haired" or "scar to cheek" or "birthmark in the shape of Italy on his back" or something similar — what they called "distinguishing marks". For Crassus, he wrote just one word, "*asinus*" — and it did not refer to his intellect!'

They all laughed heartily, though Publius joined in a little late, not exactly sure where the humour lay.

'And to think we shared the *ius iurandum*!' Crassus shook his head.

'I mean nothing by it,' laughed Quintus. 'I would still defend you.'

'"One up, two down," the old man cackled, far too loudly,' said Crassus stiffly. He then looked sharply at his friend. 'But that was not what he wrote down, Quintus — he just made a mark.' It was not his favourite memory of the army.

'That's always been the formula,' said Rufus, 'one rod, two balls, which sometimes meant a little feel was necessary — enough to make anyone yelp. Women had been known to try and infiltrate the ranks — for what purpose, only they would know. Their only use would be for pleasure, and rough pleasure at that.' He shrugged knowingly. 'Some women are like that.'

Publius bathed in the glow of being treated like a man for once, instead of a boy. However, as the talk got dirtier and more graphic, it became no longer amusing. He once more exchanged places, so that he was back beside Cato.

Publius' place was taken by Sextus. Quintus was surprised to find himself marching by the man who, as far as he knew, was still not speaking to him. He looked straight ahead and marched on. The talk of women, sex and such had quickly subsided without Publius as an audience. Though an inveterate conversationalist by character, and thus one who hated silences, Quintus held his tongue. He refused to be the one to breach the wall between himself and Sextus.

Finally, Sextus sighed. 'You must speak with Marcus,' he said softly. Marcus was marching half a dozen paces ahead, conversing with the signifer.

'And tell him what?' asked Quintus, much more sharply than he had intended, for which he was sorry.

Sextus sighed again, in exasperation. 'Tell him that we must not go anywhere near the legionary fort, or Lucus Augustus, or the town. Tell him to speak to the pilus prior, or to speak to the prefect. Tell him we should go straight to Rome.'

'I thought you did not want to go to Rome.'

'I don't, but I can cope with it. There is something dangerous waiting for us in Lucus, I am sure of it.'

'What of your woman, Julia?' Rufus asked.

'She must wait. I would rather be late and alive than early and dead.'

'You would miss our chance of being paid? And of taking Lux on a tour of the town?' asked Rufus, trying to take the sting out of the conversation.

'Yes,' Sextus confirmed.

'What worries you, Sextus?' Crassus asked with concern.

'There is an avaricious legate with more power than our prefect, a commander with the might of a veteran legion behind him. Our part in the discovery will be forgotten. We will be a nuisance, an embarrassment. We will be disbanded and discarded.' He turned to Quintus. 'I know the gold brings with it a curse. I have seen it in the stars; I have fought against it in my dreams. I just do not know how the curse will strike. I know that you and Crassus carry a secret, and a part of the curse.' He buried his annoyance and pride. 'Please, Quintus, you are in danger.'

Quintus believed his comrade when he was so earnest. He did appear to have the sight, or something like it. 'I will ask Marcus the next time we halt,' he said, 'but I think I already know the answer.'

They marched on in silence. Crassus concentrated on moving in such a way that his injury was not aggravated, Sextus wondered when Quintus would finally share his secret, and Quintus planned what he would say to Marcus. The task that Ursus had left him was at the forefront of his mind; he knew that only a visit to Rome could fulfil it.

XXVIII: FUSTUARIUM

The sun was beginning to drop when a rest stop was finally called. All knew that the halt would be brief, but it gave the men an opportunity to take off their helmets, wipe sweat from the back of their necks and to relieve themselves in the sparse woodland. Quintus approached Marcus.

'Sextus thinks we should not go to the fort; he says we should march straight to Rome. He thinks that you might persuade Antoninus, then the prefect.'

'His tongue is more silver than mine,' laughed the big man, as he removed his helmet and used his scarf to wipe the sweat from his eyes. 'I do not have such skills.'

'He is serious,' said Quintus. 'He truly believes that we face disaster if we go to Lucus Augustus.'

'It cannot be helped.' Marcus spread his arms in a gesture of futility. 'Not only could I not persuade them, but to enter Rome as armed troops!' He laughed again. 'The last time any armed men marched on Rome, they were led by the Dictator. But Caesar had a legion, whereas we are less than half a cohort. And the Senate was nowhere near as nervous as it is now. Do you suggest we cross the Rubicon?' He patted Quintus on the back. As the trumpet called for the men to reassemble and for the march to continue, he finished with a single, firm, 'No.'

As they fell back into line, Sextus gave his comrade a questioning look. Quintus replied with the slightest shake of his head. At this, Sextus stomped back to the second rank and roughly pushed Publius back to the front.

Quintus sighed. What more could he do?

That night, though the making of the camp was thorough and efficient, the contubernium was not comfortable. The men appeared to be possessed by bad spirits of some sort, making them irritable and argumentative.

Rufus ribbed Publius mercilessly about his supposed virgin status and how he could be 'broken in', as he put it, once they reached the town and its many brothels. Publius took it out on Cato; Lux and Nox almost came to blows over the relentless — and deeply unamusing — nature of his teasing. Sextus sat in high dudgeon, locked into a sulk that would not have disgraced a maiden jilted at the altar. He refused to talk to anyone, and would not even look at Quintus.

Tullius, as ever, seemed to be in a world of his own. He polished his sword, helmet and armour with devoted and mechanical efficiency. He and Publius seemed glad to be the ones who were on guard duty. Publius would have preferred someone with whom he could have a conversation, but he was relieved that it was neither Rufus nor Cato who had drawn the lot.

Quintus made the cardinal error of attempting to lighten the mood by referring to what the legionary clerk had written about Crassus. They all knew the truth of it, since they had all bathed and swum together, but Quintus' attempt to turn it into a joke was ill-judged and ill-received — and not just by Crassus, who swore at his friend and limped off to sit by the fire rather than inside the tent.

The slaves walked around as if they were treading on hot coals. Maxim had already been cuffed by Tullius, who did not like Macedonians anyway, and was shouted at by Publius. 'Of all people,' the dark-skinned slave muttered to himself. Crassus had ordered Jovan to change the dressing on his injury, which he had done carefully, removing the bloodstained bandage and washing the wound beneath.

'It is healing well, master,' he told his patient. 'I wonder if it would be better left to the air?'

'Cover it,' commanded Crassus. 'I have to wear a tunic and armour over the top of it and march. It will not feel the air until I am back at camp, or until it is dry. Is it dry?'

'It is sticky to the touch, master, not yet quite dry.'

'Then bind it,' he insisted. 'Do as you are bid, not as you wish, and keep your advice to yourself.'

This was so out of character for the blacksmith that the slave peered at him, to see if he spoke in jest, and Cato looked up in surprise.

'Bind it,' said Crassus, more politely. He had not intended to be short with Jovan, but he was not about to apologise. Though they almost shared the same skin colour, the man was still a slave.

Three were now by the fire: Rufus and Cato were sitting, while Crassus was kneeling, finding any other position painful. Jovan was busy with paperwork of various kinds — lists of supplies or letters home — and was also helping officers to write their reports on their men. To have a slave that could read and write was a rare luxury, and other squads took advantage of him in return for favours.

A mist had swirled up out of nowhere, covering the ground to a height of a couple of feet. It muffled sound, somehow making men wary and anxious. It was a mist in which evil could lurk, including enemy tribesmen, and no-one liked it. Though the air above it was warm, in the fog it was cold and clammy. Men did not want to sit or lie down by fires; it seemed wrong somehow, as if the breath was being sucked from them.

They felt that if the whole cohort climbed high enough, out of this valley and towards the moon, they would come out of it.

Quintus was once more conversing with the mule. He had yet again unrolled the dog-eared note from Ursus, although he could recite what it said from memory, and he stared at the copper armband that he treasured. He was not convinced that they would get to Rome, even if the prefect managed to persuade the legate to send them. The more he thought about it, the more he came to believe in Sextus' forebodings. They were a cohort at half strength, with an inexperienced prefect and one skilled centurion, who had fought off a few tribesmen and found a goldmine. The scales were balanced by the negatives: they had lost three centurions — including one of the finest and most promising — two thirds of the cavalry and a good proportion of the men. They were also tainted with cowardice and had suffered the punishment of decimation and degradation.

At best they would be combined with other centuries, with a new commander. At worst they would be split up entirely and posted to other units — or even accused of crimes and executed. It was possible. There was no way they would march to Rome on their own, and there was no way Quintus could find time for Ursus' legacy if they did. It was, he told the mule sadly, an impossible situation.

He looked around furtively, making sure that no-one was there to witness what he did next. He felt deep inside his tunic, finding the leather pouch that hung down inside his undershorts. He had decided earlier that morning that the safest hiding place would be on his person. He drew it out and opened the thong at the top, looking at the three gold nuggets inside. Was the mine truly cursed? He showed them to the beast and even let it sniff at them. When it tried to lick his hand, he pulled it away swiftly, scared that the animal might eat his treasure. It gave him an idea.

'What would you do with such wealth?' he whispered, but he only received a twitch of the ears in response. 'I know — I should have left it where it was.'

He started at a movement nearby and quickly closed his fist over the gold. But it was only Maxim, coming to tend to the mule. He waited patiently for Quintus to call him forward.

'Come,' he said, beckoning, 'he is more used to your care than mine.'

Leaving the slave with the mule, Quintus made his way up to the perimeter. Since he wished to be by himself, he offered to relieve Tullius. Tullius would not normally have accepted such a favour — he did his duty whatever situation he found himself in. But tonight, for once, he was glad to be able to limp back to the tent, where he could ease his leg by taking the weight off it. He managed to show no gratitude, merely grunting a noise that could easily have been interpreted as him doing Quintus the favour.

Publius was glad to have someone to talk to and would have started up his usual inane chatter, had he not caught the black look on Quintus' face, a look that told him he wanted peace. The boy subsided again, wishing he had not been so hard on Cato. He vowed to make it up to him, but though he knew that they would reconcile, he also knew that he would push his friend too far again. It was what he did, and he could not deny his nature.

Later they were relieved by Sextus and Rufus, who appeared, much to Quintus' chagrin, to be talking comfortably to each other. He nodded to both as they exchanged passwords and places, receiving a warm enough response and a word of greeting from Rufus, but nothing at all from Sextus.

'Come, Publius,' Quintus said, 'it is cold up here.' He was not referring to the weather; on the raised step, they were almost out of the mist. 'We will perhaps get a few hours' sleep in the warm,' he added. Publius was reluctant to reply; he had been knocked back enough times and by enough people during this last day and a half.

As they walked in silence back to their pitch, the familiar quiet was suddenly shattered by the call of the trumpet — long and short notes that died away on a long, high call, like a wolf serenading the moon. It was a call to wake, and to action. They broke into a run, reaching the tent as the flap flew open and a drowsy head poked out.

'What is it?' Tullius asked. 'An attack? Do we fight?'

'An assembly,' said Quintus breathlessly, recognising the start of the trumpet's summons, 'though not the normal one.' He was searching his memory for a clue as to what call had been blown. It was one he remembered hearing, but only vaguely.

Crassus, who had been struggling to put on his armour, poked his head out. 'Find me that slave,' he demanded. 'I cannot do this on my own.' He was about to duck back inside when he realised that he had not explained the call to them. 'It is a call to assemble,' he said. 'We need to be in full armour, with helmets and swords but no spears. It is a call to form a square, to witness punishment.' Again, he stopped with his head halfway back inside. 'We must be presentable; it is a legionary punishment. Find me that slave, Publius.' This time he disappeared, and Publius went in search of Jovan.

Quintus remembered that the call had been made when he was still a probationer. It had been a legionary punishment — a flogging for a man who had stolen from the commander's wife. However, there had been a rumour that the soldier had done more than steal from her, and the sentence had been her way of punishing him for boasting rather than staying silent. He wondered who was to be flogged this time.

It was still dark, and the legionaries wondered what made the punishment so urgent, and why it could not wait until daylight. Jovan was found — he had been writing letters home for a neighbouring contubernium, and Maxim was dragged away from the mule. In the flickering light of the fire and the uncertain moonlight, the legionaries managed to don their armour, helping each other as well as utilising the slaves. Publius and Quintus, returning from guard duty, were already armed and armoured, so Publius turned to help Cato, using the time and proximity to apologise for his earlier behaviour, whilst Quintus and Jovan gently eased Crassus into his gear. Tullius, reluctantly and with bad grace, accepted assistance from Maxim. Sextus and Rufus remained on guard.

They had been ordered to form a hollow square. It was not a regular formation and took some time to complete to Antoninus' and Marcus' satisfaction. At regular intervals, about five paces apart from the corner, men held torches. The central area, trampled grass and dirt, was half-hidden by the thickening mist, lying within the square like asses' milk in a brothel bath.

Two sides of the square were formed by the combined Fourth and Fifth. The Third almost made up the other two sides, apart from a gap in the corner. Through this opening, three men were dragged in by men of the Third. The captives had no weapons and were dressed only in tunics, which hung down below their knees. The men forced them to kneel in the red dirt and then turned to Antoninus, who had followed them in. He was fully uniformed, the crest on his helmet splendid, the birch rod of his office in his hand. Behind him, equally splendid, rode the prefect. His horse was caparisoned and wearing a chamfron on its head, and he wore his cloak and helmet. However, to Quintus' eyes, he looked less confident and less proud than the centurion. His shoulders drooped and there was an air of disappointment about him. Marcus stood beside him, also cloaked and crested.

'What are they?' Crassus whispered to Quintus. 'Are they Astures, or farmers, or what?'

'They are ours,' Quintus whispered back. 'Look at their feet: only the legionaries of Rome wear such hobnailed sandals. They are ours, men of the Third.'

'They are to be punished?' Crassus continued in a low voice. 'What is their offence?'

'I do not know. Shh, the centurion will tell us.'

Antoninus had stepped into the centre of the square. 'These men,' he began, 'were caught trying to run away. They had with them some of the emperor's gold, Rome's gold. They have been found guilty of being not only thieves, but deserters.'

In the ranks of the Third there was movement, as a number of men began to divest themselves of cloaks, helmets and weapons, handing them to slaves.

'What is happening?' whispered Crassus.

'Fustuarium,' said Tullius. 'I have heard of it, but I have never seen the sentence carried out. It is up to their comrades, their tent comrades, to carry out the sentence. It can be swift or slow, depending on how they view it. They are allowed no weapons, but they can use clubs to speed up the process.' He looked at the men approaching from the ranks. 'These have decided not to — it will be a long and painful death.'

Marcus stepped forward and pronounced the sentence. 'On behalf of their comrades, the prefect, the legion and Rome.'

Quintus was glad that it was dark. Though the torches provided a ring of light around the square, they did not quite reach to the centre, where the brutal sentence was being carried out. He did not want to see the details. He could hear enough — fists landing, soft or hard depending on where they were aimed, bones cracking, and the muffled grunts that with most men would have been screams. This was not meant to be a clean death: it was a dishonourable death for dishonourable men, delivered by those who had been their friends and comrades.

A legionary aimed a kick at one of the condemned who had curled up into a ball on the ground, then grabbed his hair and pulled him upright so a comrade could sink a fist into his guts. The man's face was pulp and gore already, his nose spread across it. One eye was hanging onto a cheek by a sliver of something, the other closed amidst a mass of flesh. Blood had dripped down his tunic below his chin. The stench that reached the watchers told them that he had soiled himself. He drooped like a stringless puppet in the grasp of his tormentor. He was not yet dead, and they were not yet prepared to despatch him. A sickening crunch told of a leg destroyed as a third man put his caligae on the victim's knee and trod down hard. The legionary holding him let him go. He tried to crawl away — an instinct for survival still flickering deep inside his tortured soul — but the first soldier again swung his hobnails, and the deserter stayed still. 'Not yet,' his tormentor grunted, as he turned to help with the other two. 'Not yet.'

Quintus heard Publius whisper, 'Why?'

'They have committed theft,' reasoned Tullius, in a rare moment of lucidity. 'Theft from farmers, natives and townsfolk is acceptable; it's a part of soldiering.' Quintus nodded in agreement. Tullius stroked his scar and scratched at his stubble. 'Theft from friends and comrades is not acceptable.'

'Unless they are dead,' interrupted Cato, an uncertain grin shining in the darkness.

'Unless they are dead,' agreed Tullius philosophically, with a smile. 'Then they are fair game.'

'And...' prompted Quintus gently.

Tullius was fiddling with his ruined ear. The length of the conversation was clearly proving difficult for him. 'And ... desertion, running from fellow soldiers and weakening the unit; that is never acceptable. Theft is just a crime — bad when it is visited on a friend, but still just a crime against a person. Desertion is worse; it is a crime against the fellowship and ultimately against the legion and Rome herself.' The man ran out of breath.

Quintus thought that he had rarely heard Tullius speak with such anger nor, more surprisingly, for so long. It doubled the effectiveness of his words. Quintus allowed a pause for the import of what Tullius had said to sink in. 'It must be discouraged, therefore, by those whom it most affects — friends and comrades — and in as brutal and terrible a way as those comrades decide. There is no honour left to these men.'

By the time the terrible beating was concluded, night had opened the door to day. Dawn stood nervously on the threshold, not yet daring to cross, the light bleak and uncertain, the mist thickening. The moon was waxing still, not quite full, but shrouded by thin and swirling cloud.

The prefect turned his horse and left. Antoninus followed. It was Marcus who gave the order: 'A swift breakfast, break camp and be ready to march in an hour.' He then commanded the cornicen to blow the dismissal.

The bodies of the deserters were thrown unceremoniously into a ditch at the edge of the woodland. Their heads, barely recognisable, were placed on sharpened sticks and left as a feast for the morning crows.

XXIX: LEGIO IX HISPANA

It was not long before the centuries were once more on the march. The prefect was mounted at their head, Antoninus led the Third on foot, and Marcus was at the head of the combined Fourth and Fifth. The cavalry brought up the rear, after the baggage train.

Maxim and Jovan had put out their fire and packed the tents, pots and quernstones away in almost total silence, whilst the legionaries took down the tent. Even Publius and Cato had managed to work together without sparking off each other. Sextus and Rufus had not seen the worst of it, remaining in their guard position when the square had been formed, but they had heard and had seen the bodies dumped. Now, as they left the campsite behind, they saw the mounted remains of the heads.

'Done without weapons,' said Rufus, looking at the ruined features. An unkind listener might have detected admiration in his tone. 'It almost doesn't seem possible.'

'Men are capable of incredible evil,' Sextus responded. 'There is nothing I would put beyond them.'

Rufus looked at him quizzically, but Sextus kept his face as impassive as ever, giving nothing away as he stared straight ahead.

They marched not with the joy of a possible visit to Rome, or with songs or jests, but in a cloud of despondency that seemed to have spread from the prefect outwards. As the morning unfolded, the irresolute light of the early dawn had been taken over by heavy cloud that had rolled in from the north, and fat drops of rain had begun to fall. One look at the deep black heavens was enough to tell anyone that this day would be blessed if it saw any sign of sun.

The way Flavius was slumped in his saddle spoke volumes to the men. He was wet, cold and uncomfortable. His armour was heavy, his cloak saturated and bedraggled. His helmet seemed to be directing a stream of rain down his back, so that his tunic would be damp and chafing. There would be itches that he could not scratch, and his muscles would be aching. He was deeply disappointed in the deserters. The legionaries knew it.

'At least it will not be a long day,' Quintus told Crassus, who marched beside him. 'Those men were taking their last chance to escape, knowing that we would reach the fortress today.'

'Were they truly deserters?' Crassus asked. 'Or just thieves?'

'They were men who had no regard for the common good,' offered Sextus, marching on the other side of the blacksmith, 'who would steal and keep secrets from their comrades. Such men exist, you know.' He looked at Quintus.

Quintus could not escape his guilt. Tullius, who was the fourth in the row, said nothing, though he had appeared to be in quiet conversation with Sextus since they had set out. This was unusual for him, making Quintus paranoid that they were concocting some plot against him — against his mission for Ursus, against his role as decanus.

As they crested a rise they saw the fortress, looming spectrally out of the mist, its walls and towers forbidding in the rain. Antoninus sent a message down the line to the signiferi, ordering them to see to the standards. The signiferi understood and snapped the banners, making the rain spatter from them. The change was temporary, though, as the sodden cloth drooped again within minutes and the pennants and banners of the force hung like limp cabbage leaves from the lances on which they were mounted.

'Keep them dry,' ordered the centurion. The signiferi continued to shake the rain from the standards at intervals, though they were baffled by the impossibility of such an order in the downpour.

'We will be under cover soon,' said Crassus, hopefully, 'to a fire, warmth and wine, I hope.'

Quintus nodded. 'We all hope so,' he said.

The gate of the fortress was reached by the front of the column almost before they realised it, and Antoninus ordered the cornicen to sound the halt and for the standards to be grounded. The prefect, too proud to shout up at the sentries himself, waved the centurion forward.

'Get us in,' he grumbled. 'I need to get off this beast and put on dry clothes.'

Antoninus saluted and trotted to the gate, ready to demand entry and appropriate treatment for the men.

The legionaries could only hear snatches of the conversation. They managed to pick out 'Legio Nine Hispana', and hoped that it referred to them, and they heard the prefect's full name given, Titus Flavius Pusio, with a great deal of gravitas. But they also heard the demand for a password and the obvious answer that they could not have today's password, as they had only just arrived. The men guessed that the delay, as they became ever more sodden, was due to the sentry sending for advice. As the wait grew, they began to complain, voices rising until Marcus felt that he had to silence them. Antoninus looked round sharply, seemingly surprised by the sound of Marcus' voice.

'Keep them quiet,' he ordered. 'Keep them in order.'

Marcus knew that he had been doing just that, but bit back any retort.

Finally, a command came from the gate to Antoninus, who relayed it to Marcus. 'Step them back,' he said. 'They say they are too close; step them back by twenty paces.'

'Turnabout!' ordered Marcus, using his voice rather than a trumpeter. 'Retreat twenty paces!'

'Twenty paces would not make a lot of difference to them if we were going to attack,' muttered Rufus, as they turned on their heels and counted twenty paces back down the hill.

'I think we are a nuisance, rather than a threat,' Sextus said sardonically. 'I think we are interrupting someone's meal or entertainment.' He shook water from his cloak. 'I think, Rufus, like it or not, we are insignificant.'

'Wait until they receive our news,' replied the redhead, 'then we will not be insignificant.'

'I will not hold my breath.' Sextus' tone was caustic.

Once the men had withdrawn, though not the prefect and not Antoninus, one of the great gates opened partially and six mounted men trooped out in full cavalry uniform, armed with lances and long swords. A brief conversation took place between their leader, the pilus prior and Flavius. Voices were raised and objections were made, but with the beating of the rain on the ground and the extra distance between them, no-one could really tell what was being said.

They did, however, see the result of the argument. The six men on horseback surrounded the prefect and escorted him inside — none could tell whether he was a prisoner or a guest. The gates closed firmly behind them and Antoninus was left standing somewhat foolishly alone. He stomped down the hill to where the centuries waited, past the Third so that he could talk to Marcus. The conversation was carried out in low tones so that, once again, no-one knew what was being said. Antoninus went back to his own century, Marcus to his, and the cornicen blew. They were moving, but not inside the fortress.

To their horror, they found themselves marched just a short distance to the same field that they had been in after their punishment and shame not that long ago. The river ran at the bottom, fuller now. The gate into the space had clearly been temporarily repaired and then made good again, and the ground where they had lit their fires had barely recovered. The hedges were thicker and greener, and the trees seemed closer together. The rain dripped from them, making the whole place look even more dreary than they remembered it.

For Quintus it brought back vivid memories of Ursus, and of the charge that had been laid on him by the dead man. He clutched the copper armlet where he wore it hidden. It must, he thought, have been even harder for Marcus, who had been forced to kill his friend. He smiled as he remembered the way that they had acquired slaves who were cousins, and how they had tricked the officer. Then he remembered with sadness and a flash of nausea the flogging to death of an innocent man.

The grass was soaking wet, slippery and treacherous. Quintus spotted the patch that had been the temporary home of their contubernium, but he did not think that they would be camping.

Worst for most, but mostly for Tullius, was the site of the flogging. Though the post had been removed and the posthole filled in, the grass had refused to grow, and the black square stared at them in mute accusation.

'See that? Nothing will grow there,' Quintus said quietly, nodding towards the bleak spot.

'I see it,' said Crassus. 'What of it?'

'It is accursed,' offered Sextus from his other shoulder. 'That is why nothing will grow.'

'It was dug too deep; that's why nothing will grow,' said Crassus dismissively.

Tullius was in one of his reveries; Sextus had to prompt him twice to elicit a response. 'Cursed, Tullius? Or badly engineered? What do you think?'

Tullius turned his head and looked at the spot as if seeing it for the first time. 'Cursed,' he said with finality. The rest fell silent as the veteran returned to his fantasy world.

Despite all that the legionaries had recently achieved, they were marched in and lined up as if they were on some sort of punishment detail. There was no victory parade, no songs and, as Rufus wryly noted, no pay.

Marcus led the combined Fourth and Fifth, proudly wearing the plumed helmet to denote his assumed rank — a helmet into which he had incised his own initials next to those of its previous owner, Valerius. It was the prefect's responsibility to write the report to Valerius' family, but the task had proved to be beyond him. He had therefore passed it to Marcus who, in turn, had deputised Quintus. Eventually, it had been Jovan who had written the words that would comfort the centurion's family and appear on the stone that they would erect in his memory. The report told of his bravery, the love and loyalty of his men, and his honourable death.

The men were drawn up in ranks of six, almost as if for action, but there was no enemy to be seen; instead, they were just standing in the deluge, getting wetter and wetter. The baggage train had arrived and was lined up parallel to the river. The slaves, without helmets, looked even more bedraggled and miserable than their masters.

Some of the men, including all of the cavalry, were part of the additional forces that had been added to strengthen the cohort after the decimation. They therefore knew nothing of this field apart from what the others had told them, but they could understand their comrades' dejection. They had witnessed the fustuarium along with everyone else, and they knew that a decimation, though rarer, must be a terrible thing.

Their prefect was not with them and, though all knew that the pilus prior was the real commander, they also knew that they needed a politician if they were going to get any recognition or any recompense for their efforts. It was the Flavian who would make sure that they were paid, not the centurion. At least they had been left with their banners. The signiferi held the standards high.

'What do they intend for us this time?' Rufus asked angrily. He had hoped to be able to sneak out and into the arms of his Octavia. This now seemed unlikely. 'At least we are still armed. They cannot be intending to punish us, or they would have taken our weapons.'

'We still have our standards,' said Quintus. 'That should give us hope that we are to be kept together, at least.'

'Look at that standard,' said Sextus. The bull of the Ninth Hispana was faded on its deep red background, but at least it could still be seen. 'Six silver discs for six centuries. Do you not think that we should prise at least two of them off?' He laughed, though the others did not see the humour in his jest.

'Does Marcus not know anything?' Cato demanded. 'Quintus, can you not ask him?'

'I have asked,' said Quintus. 'He knows no more than we do.'

'Are we going to Rome?' Publius dared to ask, doubt in his voice.

'We are not,' said Sextus forcefully. 'I warned you that the gold is cursed. I have not even touched any of it.' He held his arms out wide. 'Many who have touched it are injured —' he looked at Crassus, as if he knew, then referred to the fate of the thieves — 'or dead by the hands of their own contubernium.'

Quintus could feel the weight of the leather bag against his leg.

'And was I cursed before any gold was found?' Tullius asked suddenly, with fervour. 'Or did my bad luck come about because of some other curse, one of which you are not aware?'

Sextus was taken aback by the force of the veteran's response, and he would have raised his hands to ward off the invective had they not all been called to attention.

'Not all curses are linked to gold,' Publius said softly.

'And not all gold is cursed,' said Crassus. 'It was my own lack of skill that got me injured, not the gold.'

'You think so? Injured in the back through a lack of skill?' Sextus scoffed. 'The gods are laughing at you even now.'

Crassus was silent. His injury still troubled him, and it *had* been ill fortune to receive such a blow. The conversation died as they realised that something was going on at the gate to the field. A messenger on horseback, but not the prefect, was talking to Antoninus. They strained their ears as best they could, but the rain, and now the fresh wind that had sprung up, muffled the exchange.

They found out what the message had been soon enough as the cornicen sounded the order to camp. The signiferi underlined it by planting the standards, and the surveyors began to pace out the site. The slaves led the mules and started to trudge the carts up the hill.

'Why do we camp here?' Publius asked pathetically as they hauled the tent up once again, trying to keep the inside of it dry. 'What happened to our trip to Rome?'

'Why are you so keen to go to Rome?' Cato asked him. 'Friends? Family? A woman, perhaps?'

'Family, yes,' Publius answered quietly, 'but little else. I think my friends think me foolish for joining the legions. I just want to be anywhere but here, though I think others are keener than I.' He indicated Quintus and Crassus, who were pegging out the guy ropes.

'Not I,' said Crassus, shaking his head.

'Nor I,' said Quintus, as he hammered in a peg.

In the grey of the evening, the rain finally ceased, whipped away by the breeze. As they yet again pitched the leather tents and sent the slaves on an almost hopeless search for dry kindling, the light began to fade, and thicker cloud once more gathered on the horizon. The billowing mass was depressing; it succeeded in blocking the last of the day's light until, almost magically, the sun squeezed its way out from between the cloud bank and the horizon. The light that shone from it was harsh and low, throwing long shadows across the field.

Quintus shivered involuntarily.

XXX: LUCUS AUGUSTUS

The legionaries had glimpsed the rooftops of the settlement through the rain as the centuries had marched up the hill to the fort. As the sun dipped below the horizon, and the shadows faded, there was a commotion at the entrance to the field. Half a dozen veterans, accompanied by a couple of junior officers, were trying to leave, but were being held back by the armed legionaries sent from the fort. The gate was closed firmly against them.

On the other side of the gate, coming down the long hill, was a small crowd from the town. At the front were merchants with samples of wines, oils, breads and cheeses. Behind them were blacksmiths with sharpening stones and mercers with cloth, furriers and cobblers. They were followed by entertainers, prostitutes, vagabonds and a gaggle of mischievous boys at the rear. They had all noted the arrival of a new source of income and clamoured to be allowed into the field. If the men within were under no sentence of disgrace, why shouldn't the townsfolk be allowed to trade with them, to entertain them? Sextus and Rufus hoped that Julia and Octavia were amongst these people.

Quintus watched with amusement from a small hillock. It was clear, from the instructions they had been given, the attitude of the fortress sentries, the closing of the gate and the guard that had been placed on it, that they were not going to be allowed to interact with the townsfolk. It seemed that they were also not going to be permitted to enter the fort or to engage with its occupants; the guards on their gate seemed to have been ordered not to talk to them. Quintus scratched his head at an emerging thought. It was as if they carried some sort of disease — one that could be passed by word of mouth.

He smiled as he bore witness to the townspeople showing insufficient respect for the soldiers at the gate. The guards were getting ever more frustrated — Quintus guessed that they had been ordered not to strike the inhabitants as, on more than one occasion, a hand was lifted in anger and stopped by the touch of a comrade. There was a centurion present, his birch rod twitching and his crest bobbing up and down. He was clearly itching to move the mob away, but he restrained himself and lowered the stick. Instead, he used his voice to keep order as the merchants, entertainers and harlots shouted invitations at the party of putative escapees, which included Rufus and Sextus.

'Rufie, is it you?' The call came from a large woman, black-haired and full-chested, in a plain brown tunic distinguished only by its low-cut neckline. She had recognised Rufus' shock of red hair from her place in the throng and now waved furiously to catch his attention.

'Ockie!' he shouted back, himself waving excitedly. 'You are here! I hoped you would be.'

'What are you doing?' Octavia demanded. 'Why do they keep you there?'

'We do not know! None of us know!' he yelled. 'Try asking these idiots!'

The idiots to whom he was referring were in the process of stopping anyone making contact, pushing the crowd back. 'You, woman,' called their centurion, 'get back to your home and leave these men alone.'

He spoke swiftly to a soldier, who pushed his way through the crowd and took Octavia by the arm, forcibly leading her away. Rufus was furious, shouting and desperately trying to break through. He, too, was firmly prevented.

A couple of the boys had managed to sneak behind the legs of the soldiers and had begun to climb the gates. These were, under the circumstances, treated mildly, being merely grabbed by the scruff of their necks and thrown back. The gate remained steadfastly closed, the guards resolutely facing away from it. Gradually, and none too gently, they forced the townsfolk back whilst receiving ever more withering insults regarding the nature of their fathers, the habits of their mothers, and their own lack of manly equipment.

The centurion came to the gate and spoke angrily to the junior officer, the tesserarius who had thought they would be allowed into the town. His message was sufficient to make the group turn around and dejectedly make its way back into the camp.

Rufus tried calling after Octavia, but the distance was too great, though they did manage one final wave.

In the growing dark, and as the rain started once more, she and the other folk could be seen trudging their way back to the town, herded by legionaries with their swords drawn.

'Did you see Julia?' Rufus asked, as they made their reluctant way back along the track.

'No,' said Sextus, wiping the rain from his forehead with a sleeve. 'I saw your Octavia, and I saw you both wave. I am not sure if that is harder for you than me…'

'At least I saw her,' said Rufus. 'I know that she lives.'

'What did the centurion say?' Quintus asked Rufus as they returned, knowing that the rift between him and Sextus would likely prevent a report from that quarter.

'That none are allowed to visit us, or even to speak with us, on pain of death. That our trying to leave, and encouraging the townspeople, was putting his men in danger of being flogged or executed…'

'…and we wouldn't want that, would we?' Sextus added with heavy sarcasm.

'You're right, we wouldn't really care,' said Rufus, as he climbed up onto the hillock with Quintus. 'We don't know them. But I am glad I saw my Octavia amongst the folk.'

'And I am sad that I did not glimpse my Julia,' said Sextus, unhappily.

'We do care,' Quintus offered in mitigation, whilst looking disapprovingly at Rufus. 'They are, like us, just soldiers, just innocent bodies.' He sighed. 'I hope that they are just being cautious with us. The prefect will sort it out. We must wait until morning.' He shook his head. 'But I must admit that I don't see the point of keeping us here, or of keeping you from your women.'

By now it was fully dark, the rain had again abated and some of the stars could be seen cautiously peeping through the lattice of thinning cloud. There was still too much cover for Quintus to make out the Little Bear, or any other constellation. He was not going to ask Sextus, who was still not talking to him unless he was forced to in the course of his duty.

Sextus and Rufus began to plan how they would manage to get out and spend the night in the town, then re-enter the camp unnoticed in the morning. But there was no real fire in their conversation, no serious attempt to come up with a strategy. They knew that it was hopeless and that they might as well wait until morning. One more night would not make any difference. It would, they convinced themselves, actually make the reunions sharper and more pleasant.

The centurions had made sure that the camp was properly set up and guarded — this could be some kind of test, after all

— although there was no building of perimeter fences, digging of ditches or construction of gates. By general agreement amongst the officers, these details were unnecessary so close to legionary headquarters, and with reinforcements on the other side of the gate should they be needed.

Antoninus took overall command and, though he pretended to be aware of what was happening with the prefect, the other officers knew he was not. They did not, however, betray him to the men. Returning to the tent and their own fire, smoking terribly with the wet wood it had been fed, Quintus, Sextus and Rufus faced a barrage of questions.

'What was happening at the gate?' asked Tullius. 'It looked like the townspeople wanted to trade with us.'

'Never mind trade,' snorted Rufus. 'They had women, real women, with them.'

'And how would you have paid them?' Cato asked innocently. 'We have not received what is owed yet, and we are owed a great deal.'

'These were our women, mine and Sextus', not whores!' Rufus emphasised the point by clipping Cato's ear.

Cato muttered an apology whilst rubbing his ear, but he persisted with his question. 'What about our pay? When will we have what is ours by right?'

'Some of us have taken our pay already,' Sextus said mysteriously, his face half in shadows.

'Not that again,' said Cato, crossly. 'We are not party to your secrets, Sextus.'

'What did that centurion actually say?' Publius asked.

'That if we try to leave, their own men will be executed or flogged,' said Rufus.

'Not us?'

'Not us, them.' Rufus shook his head. 'Strange, eh?'

They agreed that it was strange, and still wondered why they were being made to camp rather than being allowed back into barracks. Quintus shared his earlier thought — that the men were being treated as if they had a disease.

The talk around the fire gradually petered out as each legionary left to bed down in the tent. But for most of them, sleep was elusive, and the night was a long one. The fire sputtered, but the slaves managed to keep it alight by drying wood out next to it and by watching it in shifts, used to taking their sleep when they could. It meant that it could be built up when the first of the contubernium, Cato, woke and wanted something hot to eat, and it was kept that way whilst they fed the rest.

It became easier once it was light and the drizzle had ceased. The mist vanished with the dawn chorus. The morning itself broke fine and clear, the sun rising into a bright blue sky. Finally, it was going to be a warm day.

'Maybe it is summer at last,' Cato said to Maxim, who was in charge of the porridge that boiled on the fire. 'Maybe yesterday's downpour was the last of the spring rain. Maybe summer here is like it is in Rome: hot, dry and carrying on forever.'

'Who mentioned Rome?' Quintus asked, ducking out from under the tent flap, rubbing his eyes at the brightness.

'I was just wishing for summer sun and warmth,' said Cato.

Crassus joined them, his wounds on the way to healing, although they still restricted comfortable movement and itched unbearably. 'Is our trip still on, do you think?' he asked.

'I think that is why we are here,' said Cato, conspiratorially. 'Quintus said they were treating us as if we had some sort of disease. I think they are; I think it is gold fever.'

'Gold fever?' Tullius repeated dully, as he emerged from the tent, stiff-limbed. 'A poor excuse.'

'I think so,' said Quintus. 'I thought about it last night. They do not want their own men contaminated with it. They are not to communicate with us, so we cannot tell them and they cannot be infected. They would not even let us talk to the townsfolk. I think that they want to send us off to Rome before we share the news.'

'That would explain why we are here, and why I was prevented from talking to Octavia,' said Rufus. 'I hope she is all right.' He had just risen, along with Publius. They yawned and stretched as they made for the fire.

'All the soldiers came back,' offered Quintus. 'I saw them. So, she was not detained.'

Rufus nodded, his mouth already full of grain porridge.

'Orders?' Publius asked no-one in particular.

'Not yet,' said several voices.

Last to emerge was Sextus, whose pact with Apollo appeared intact. His tunic was immaculate, his hair was combed, and his cheeks were smooth. Apparently, he still sulked. His mouth was downturned as he asked, 'Rome? What of Rome?'

Rufus passed him food and drink as he finished his own mouthful. 'Quintus thinks that we are here so that the legionaries in the fort do not know that we ride for Rome.'

'I said this would be a disaster. It is turning into one. I would like to stay here just long enough to collect Julia, then find a farm. I would be happy never to return to Rome.' He frowned as he salted the gruel. 'Julia is young, bright and loyal; I would take her to wife and settle.' He winked lewdly. 'I would even forswear the Flavian's fragrant wife.' The smile that followed seemed sad. 'I have no love for Rome. It may be where I was born, but it is also where I was abandoned and abused. I have no love for this place either.'

'But you had a life there, in Rome,' Rufus exclaimed. 'You have told me of the exciting times in the whorehouses.'

'The place is a pit of vipers,' Sextus said. 'I would rather fight the Astures; I can predict their behaviour with greater certainty.'

'Not the stars again,' his friend objected.

'The stars do not lie,' he said simply, casting a significant look at Quintus. 'They speak of curses, and of betrayal.'

'We would never betray each other,' said Publius, shocked at the notion.

'We might,' said Sextus. 'Never is a very long time.'

Quintus once again felt for the familiar comfort of the gold beneath his tunic, even as he denied any thought of betrayal. 'We will not,' he insisted. 'We are brothers in this contubernium.'

Sextus opened his mouth to respond, but as he did so, the blast of the trumpet put an end to all conversation.

'An assembly,' said Publius.

'Officers only,' said Rufus. 'I have heard it often enough before.'

'And look,' said Crassus, who had quietly kept eating whilst the tale was told, 'our prefect is here.'

Coming into the field was Flavius, sitting on his horse and accompanied by half a dozen armed and armoured riders. A centurion walked ahead of the little group, a standard bearer behind him. It was hard to tell if the prefect was an honoured guest or a guarded captive. The gates were shut behind them.

'You go,' Crassus urged Quintus. 'You are our optio, after all. Find out what is happening.'

XXXI: SIGNIFER

Quintus hurriedly finished his drink and handed the cup to Maxim. Jovan offered to help him dress, but a glance at the men heading for the bottom of the field showed that there was no need for armour. Quintus' gladius was already scabbarded at his belt, as if it was another limb.

He jogged down to where the other officers were gathering around the prefect, who remained mounted. Most were just in tunics like him, although both centurions had their crested helmets with them. Antoninus was carrying his, and Marcus was wearing his despite the growing heat of the day. Quintus was excited, hoping for orders to march to Rome.

Antoninus stood by the prefect's heels, ready to relay the message, but when Flavius bent down and spoke to him, he took a reluctant step to one side. Since the gathering was reasonably small, Quintus guessed that the prefect wished to address them himself.

The group included two centurions, two optiones, of which Quintus was one, the newly promoted decurion of cavalry, six signiferi, the cavalry and — most importantly, Quintus thought — the pilus and manus standards of the cohort. They showed the discs of the six centuries, indicating that the cohort was still whole and part of the legion. In addition, two with the duty of tesserarii had survived. There should have been three, but no-one had seen the need to fill the gap left by the tesserarius of the Fourth, an extremely unpopular and pompous man who had fallen in the first assault on the mountain. A single cornicen, the only one to survive the same assault, had blown for the assembly. At least they outnumbered the escort sent from the fort with the prefect as they jostled for space so that they could hear what he had to say.

The centurion who had accompanied the escort offered some assistance to the prefect, but he was batted away with harsh words. He withdrew several paces from the Flavian and his officers and tersely ordered the mounted men to do the same.

The prefect, his balding pate gleaming with sweat in the morning sun, spoke from his horse. He used a normal tone so that his escort, deliberately moved away, would know that they had no part in these matters.

'Men,' he addressed them, 'I have been a guest of the legion commander in the fort. Do not think I would not have joined you in camp if I could have done so without causing offence to my host. We have been chosen for a great mission, a secret mission.'

This is it, thought Quintus. *We will be ordered to head for Rome.*

'We are to take the centuries we have here to create a bridgehead for the emperor Augustus.'

The listening officers heard 'Emperor Augustus' and made the connection: their information about the goldmine would be delivered to the great general directly. They began to smile and pat each other on the back. Their fortunes were made.

Then one or two began to ask questions. Why would Octavian, now elevated as Augustus, need a bridgehead to Rome? He had Rome at his feet, the Senate was packed with his supporters, and his family held all the key posts. What could have happened? It dawned on them that this was not going as they had planned.

'A bridgehead to Rome?' Quintus dared to ask, his voice small.

'Not to Rome, optio, no,' the prefect laughed nervously. He then bent down so that he was even closer to the men. 'We are sent to Britannia, to build on the work of divine Caesar, to open the way for Augustus to expand the empire into the north.'

'Britannia!' sputtered one of the signiferi in horror. It was the new, younger man who had taken on the role. 'My father was in Britannia; he told me of it.'

'Not so loud,' said Flavius, raising a finger. 'It is a great secret and a great honour to be chosen.'

'It may be a secret, but it is no honour,' spat the signifer. 'The place is cold, damp and diseased, full of shades and sorcery…'

'Quiet!' ordered the prefect, his voice rising. 'Centurion, silence this man.'

Antoninus stepped forward and raised his birch rod threateningly.

The signifer, armed with nothing but his standard and his wolfskin cloak, stepped back, but continued muttering. 'What about the mine? Who will tell the emperor of the mine?'

'The legion commander will tell the emperor,' insisted the prefect. 'The commander knew of the mine already; it was not news to him. We are not the first. He may have already sent a deputation to Rome.'

At this, several voices were raised at once.

'How could he know?'

'It was our secret!'

'We discovered it!'

'He knew,' confirmed the Flavian. 'Word had arrived before we did. He knew. He has claimed the right to take the message to Rome. He has the men; he has the authority.' It sounded final, though the prefect seemed a little beaten rather than uplifted by the honour bestowed on him. He changed his tone, almost pleading for their support. 'I am trusting you, my officers. You must tell the men that we are on a special mission, a secret mission. You will tell them that we go to help expand the empire — that we go forwards, not backwards. Tell them we are heading to Rome.'

'They will realise soon enough when we start to march west, not south,' Quintus said, under his breath.

Those closest to him heard and agreed with nods of their heads.

'Antoninus,' the prefect said, addressing the centurion, 'give the order.'

Antoninus nodded. He commanded the cornicen to sound his trumpet, to order the camp to be dismantled and the men to be ready to march.

The man was hesitant at first, then realised he had no choice and unenthusiastically put the long, curved instrument to his lips. Ahead of him, men's necks jerked up and they ceased whatever they were doing, ready to drop into the time-honoured routine. Behind him, the prefect had ridden across and was dismissing the centurion from the fort and his mounted escort, although the legionaries noted that they went no further than the gate.

The group of officers, uncharacteristically, did not snap into action. Instead they still stood around, stunned and with many questions on their lips. Quintus asked Marcus, innocently enough, 'Whatever the orders are, why not just tell the men? They will know sooner or later; why not now?'

'It is your job to tell the men, Macilentus,' said Marcus, lifting his chin to talk to the optio, 'and you must do it subtly and quietly. The prefect could not address the camp without soldiers from the fort hearing. They must not know.'

A number of voices asked, 'Why not?'

'It is a special mission, one of great honour. They would want to take it from you.'

'Surely we will be receiving reinforcements — the other centuries, new cavalry, men to replace those we've lost?'

'We go with what we have,' said the centurion, 'to keep the mission subtle and secret. The fewer that know, the better. Tell them quietly but firmly.' He made to walk away.

'He is afraid of their reaction.' It was the fair-headed signifer who had spoken before. 'He thinks if it comes from you, the men will accept it more readily.' He was dismissive, contemptuous. 'Our prefect is exchanging Rome, home, for Britannia. Of course, he would rather it came subtly and quietly from you.'

'Enough!' spat Marcus furiously, his patience gone. 'Whatever the truth of it, the prefect has his reasons. You do not need to know what they are, nor guess what they might be.' He looked hard at the signifer. 'Go, tell your men.'

The group broke up resentfully, the officers heading in twos and threes for their own centuries. Some, including the cornicen and the outspoken signifer, dragged their feet, letting others spread the tidings first.

Antoninus had gone over to the troop of cavalry and was talking with the centurion from the legion; Marcus decided that there were enough people to tell his own century, so he could supervise from a distance. He did not want to be the one to tell the men.

As the news was shared, the voices of the legionaries, who had already begun the process of packing up the camp, were raised more and more in protest and dissent. They had expected to go to Rome.

As the grumbling grew, the work of dismantling the camp first slowed, then ceased. The men converged on the hillock that Quintus had claimed the evening before, their leader seemingly the signifer. His standard was firmly fixed in the ground.

'My father served in Britannia,' he was saying. 'It is a place of mists and melancholy, marshes and monsters…'

'Then we should refuse to go!' a shout went up.

'What did your father find there?'

'Did he come back rich?'

'Did he come back at all?'

Then there were complaints:

'What about our gold?'

'What about our reward?'

'What about our pay?'

The noise of the men was proving to be a magnet to the rest of the legionaries. From all over the field, they streamed towards the hillock. By now, no-one was listening to the signifer. Some were even throwing jests at him. Others had seen the opportunity for a fight and were seeking out and squaring up to those with whom they had disputes — whether over dice games, women, debts, or accusations of thievery and cheating. Any excuse would suffice.

Quintus, as an officer, should have been at least partly responsible for quelling the violence, but he froze. He knew, where these veterans were concerned, that he did not have the authority. At the bottom of the field, the prefect had ridden across to the cavalry contingent from the fort, with Antoninus at his side. It was clear that they were seeking help and that, if nothing was done, there would be panic. Blood would be spilt — and it would be Roman blood spilt by Roman soldiers.

Suddenly, Sextus was at his side. 'Give me the gold,' he hissed urgently. 'Stop hiding it and give it to me.'

'W-what gold?' stuttered Quintus.

'The gold you have hidden, the gold that you and Crassus shared! Give it to me — or some of it, at least. Quickly, there is not much time.'

Quintus, amazed at the accusation — and the truth of it — was not able to think of any further denials. He reached under his tunic and drew out the leather bag, thrusting it into his comrade's hands. Sextus closed his fist around it and jumped up onto the knoll, taking hold of the standard and waving it around, despite the objections of the signifer.

'Here is your pay,' Sextus shouted, holding the leather bag aloft. 'No need to fight over it.' He opened the drawstring and drew out a nugget of bright gold. 'Look, comrades, there is gold with which to pay you. Flavius has given me this as a token to show that you will get your pay.' He hissed at the signifer, giving him a shove, 'Get down you fool.'

At the mention of gold and pay, all thought of marching to Britannia instead of Rome became secondary, as did the individual disputes. The prefect, with a cavalry escort, was riding up the field, the horsemen with their long swords drawn.

'Look!' shouted Sextus. 'Here comes Titus Flavius Pusio, our prefect, to honour his promise!'

'Sir,' Sextus addressed the prefect directly, shouting over the heads of the legionaries, 'I told the men about the gold we collected from the Astures on the field of battle. I told them that was enough for them to be paid.'

The Flavian was hesitant, jittery, and this was passed on to his horse, which pranced and pawed at the ground. The cavalry horses were behind him, ready to charge. He settled his beast with an oath and took in the situation. Then he shouted: 'I would have paid them by now, had some not kept the gold! I cannot pay them until I have it all!'

There were mutterings amongst the men, many accusing friends and comrades, but the moment for violence had passed. The fire, if it had not gone out, at least now only smouldered.

Quintus fervently hoped that the prefect could also read the mood and that he would not go back on what he had said.

'As long as the gold is not legitimate, it is cursed,' Sextus announced imperiously. 'You must hand it in, so that it can be shared fairly.'

Antoninus and the centurion from the fort had caught up and had taken in what had happened. With his birch rod in his hand and his helmet firmly on his head, Antoninus snapped out orders. 'You, signifer, be glad that I do not relieve you of your post. Take the standard and get back to your place.'

Sextus uprooted the sacred object and put it into the man's outstretched palm.

'You, optio,' Antoninus addressed Quintus, 'tomorrow night, you will arrange a secret way for those men who … accidentally failed to hand over the Asturian gold to deposit it. Then you will hand it to our commander.' His eyes and the sweep of his arm included the mounted prefect. 'You, legionary,' he said harshly to Sextus, 'get down from there. You look like a second-rate pimp trying to get a better price for a third-rate harlot.'

This brought general laughter, which Sextus took in good part as he jumped down from the rise. Quintus offered an open hand to help him and was surprised to find the leather bag, not empty, thrust into it.

'We may need it yet. Put it back into that sweaty place from where it came.' Sextus smiled. 'Come, we should not be here. We have embarrassed our commander.'

They melted away into the crowd, which was already dispersing. Legionaries returned to their work dismantling the camp whilst discussing how much pay they were owed and where and how they would spend it, forgetting that most of it would vanish in dice games and brothels before it ever made it back to Rome.

The prefect spoke quickly and secretly with Antoninus and voices were raised, but the centurion appeared to get his way and issued orders to the cavalry escort. They, in turn, had a heated conversation with their own commander, who, after a brief exchange, waved them off towards the gate and the fort.

Sextus heaved a sigh of relief. 'They are going to collect the gold,' he said confidently, 'or at least enough silver denarii to cover the pay that is owed.'

'How do you know?' Quintus asked.

'I just do.'

'Where is the gold?'

Sextus harrumphed. 'It went into the fortress with the prefect. It did not come out with him. The legion has the gold — the legate, I would guess — but I think enough has been said in public to ensure that the men are paid.' He shook his head gently, disturbing his faultless locks. 'Politics!' he grumbled. 'The legate has ambitions to be governor of Hispania. His Senate career is all but over. He has few clients and few supporters, but out here he has the chance to be a ruler. He thinks the news of the goldmine will secure him the post. He wants to make sure that he is the one to give the news to Augustus, preferably in person.'

'But how did he find out?'

'My guess would be the freedman. He was once the permanent shadow of our Flavian, but I have not seen him for days.' Sextus was pensive. 'I think that we will probably never see him again. The usual reward for such a betrayal — and by a former slave — is to have his head quietly removed from his shoulders.'

Quintus nodded. He knew it to be true.

The two ducked and dived through bodies back to their own fire — or where it had been until Maxim had extinguished it. Quintus was still desperate for information from his friend. 'How do you know all this? Politics? Intrigues? Secrets? How did you know about my gold?'

Sextus just tapped his nose knowingly and smiled.

XXXII: AQUILA

As they walked, Quintus asked Sextus, 'So, are we talking now?' He hoped that the rift between them was finally closed.

'It was the secret that lay between us, nothing else,' Sextus replied unemotionally as he ducked back into the tent. 'We should arm,' he added. 'I would have felt safer down there had I been wearing armour.'

Quintus agreed. He thought that Sextus had turned out to be a better leader than him.

'Here,' said Sextus, 'help me we this.'

Sextus was jiggling his way into his armour and needed another pair of hands to tie the leather bindings. Quintus finished the job quickly, then required Sextus to do the same for him. The others of the contubernium were also dressing and arming, congratulating Sextus on winning them their pay as they passed to and fro.

As soon as they were alone, Quintus persisted, 'You always knew about the gold, didn't you?'

'I had a hunch, no more.'

'And you leapt up onto that hillock on the back of a hunch, to stop a mutiny?'

'Perhaps a strong hunch would be a better descriptor. I watch, I listen, I calculate. I read faces and the language of the body. Your face tells me more than you ever could in words. You were scared, you were indecisive, and now you are relieved. It is not difficult to work these things out.'

'True — I was scared and I froze,' said Quintus in a small voice.

'You see, it is not hard to share secrets, and you feel better for it.' Sextus pushed his hair back so that it sat in its perfect wave on his head. 'You should trust me. Tullius has shared his secret with me. It has lightened his load. You and Crassus could have shared.' He said this so matter-of-factly that its full weight took a moment to register with Quintus. But before he could say anything, Sextus continued, 'Of course, I am not telling you what Tullius confided in me.'

Quintus frowned.

'You should trust me,' Sextus repeated. 'I like Tullius, but you are even more important. I must protect you so that you can protect Ursus' legacy.'

Quintus was about to ask how Sextus knew of that secret also, when the signifer approached their tent, still carrying the standard. Shaking his head in wonder, he instead addressed the newcomer. 'You were ordered away.'

'I am on my way.' The signifer had to stretch his neck to catch Quintus' eye. 'I wanted to thank you. To thank you both.' He turned his head to Sextus. 'I know what I thought to do was foolish, but I went ahead and did it anyway. You saved me.'

'And your father? You are proud of him. Who did he save?' Sextus asked.

The signifer snorted. 'It is why I am named Aquila,' he said. 'My father saved the Dictator, forty years ago in the year that Crassus and Pompey were Consuls. He was famous for saving great Caesar.'

'Go on,' said Quintus.

'He was more than a signifer; he was the aquilifer to Caesar's Tenth. He carried Caesar and Rome's most famous eagle, the eagle of Legio X Equestris. Caesar took nearly a hundred ships across the water from Gaul to Britannia, including cavalry, but he could not land as the cliffs were too steep. They had to row until they found a beach. But the Britons, allies to the Germanic tribes, stopped them and would have repelled them, until my father jumped into the water with the eagle and urged them to follow it. Caesar would never have landed had it not been for my father. The world would have turned out differently.'

'A brilliant story. I hope it is true,' laughed Sextus.

'It is true,' the storyteller insisted, 'though I do not tell it often for fear of disbelief.'

'You should be proud of your father,' Quintus said briskly. 'He is a hero, and you are too. You may have nearly started a mutiny, but at least you made sure the men are paid. They will come to remember you for the latter.'

The signifer saluted them both and left with a heartfelt, 'Thank you.'

'A brave man,' said Quintus.

'And a foolish one,' responded Sextus. 'He could easily have lost his head. We could have found ourselves fixed to crosses by nightfall.' Whistling tunefully, he walked off to where the slaves were loading the pack animal and cart. Quintus, too, began to pack up his gear.

Marcus had left the other officers to give his century their marching orders, reasoning that there were enough of them, so his voice was not needed. He strolled up the field, officiously checking on the progress of various tasks and glorying in Valerius' splendid helmet. As he approached the place where Quintus' contubernium was now unpegging the guy ropes on their tent, he called across, 'Optio, I may need you with the century rather than here.'

317

Quintus was not used to being addressed by his rank, especially by Marcus, but he said nothing, merely waving an acknowledgement.

Marcus persisted, 'Optio, did you not hear me, or do I have to persuade you to leave your men?'

'Persuade?' hissed Quintus under his breath. 'You could not even persuade a river to flow downhill, or a tree to drop its leaves in autumn. Persuade!'

'What did you say, optio?'

Quintus repeated himself, this time more loudly.

Marcus looked nonplussed, not exactly sure what he had said to deserve such an undoubted insult. He began, 'What…?'

But Quintus interrupted him. 'I asked you to persuade the prefect. I warned you that we should bypass this cursed camp. Now we are once more leaving the legion. You did not even try.'

'I tried,' said Marcus, opening his hands in a gesture of helplessness, 'but his mind was already set. He did not know he would be betrayed.'

'He did not, but you did. Sextus knew, and you did not believe him. You could have saved us from this "adventure".'

'I have duties,' said Marcus, turning away, not willing to argue. Yes, he could have made more of an effort to persuade the prefect, but he had known that it would be hopeless.

'You have duties, too,' Marcus said, starting to stroll down the slope, but Quintus was not finished.

'You need to take responsibility,' he said angrily. 'It is your fault that the whole cohort, or what is left of it, is off on a fool's errand.' He spat contemptuously and swept his arm to take in the field and its occupants. His face had reddened, the flush starting from his neck and quickly flooding his cheeks, his anger sparking in his eyes. He reached out and pulled at

318

Marcus' cloak, making him stumble backwards and sending his precious helmet awry, pricking his dignity.

Marcus turned automatically, arm raised, and struck Quintus hard with the birch rod that he gripped in his hand. He had not lost his temper but had been governed by instinct. He had not thought what he was doing, or to whom he was doing it; in fact, he had not thought at all and, even as the birch rod whipped and made contact, he was immediately ashamed and sorry. But he was unable to make amends in front of the men, many of whom had stopped to watch this incident out of curiosity and for entertainment. He stood rooted, praying for Quintus not to react so that he could square things with him in private.

But Quintus' anger had got the better of him. He took one step and used a forearm to smash into the centurion's face. Valerius' splendid helmet went flying, and, as Marcus staggered and dropped to one knee, blood spurted from a split lip.

Quintus had committed a crime against discipline and order. He was guilty of striking a senior officer, the sentence for which was anything from a flogging to death. It depended on no written set of laws and punishments, instead on caprice and inclination, on how well the prefect had dined for breakfast, or on who it was that whispered in his ear that day.

Sextus knew all this and ran to intervene. He grabbed Quintus by his shoulder, pulling him back and shouting at him to calm down and think.

Others had run across and now lifted Marcus up, who wiped his bloody lip on the back of his hand and looked sharply at Quintus. Marcus was as angry at himself as he was at the optio. He was about to speak to Quintus when their eyes were drawn to Valerius' helmet, no longer on the ground, but instead held in the hands of Antoninus, its crest waving softly in the breeze. The pilus prior smiled a crooked smile.

'Well, centurion,' he said, dripping scorn, 'this is how you discipline your optio, is it?'

The two combatants stared at him, Quintus finally calming down, although he still breathed heavily. Marcus noted the crowd of legionaries standing behind Antoninus and knew that the centurion could choose this moment to be diplomatic or to be cruel.

Antoninus chose cruel. 'I would let it go,' he said, rationally enough, 'but it is too late. Look, the men have seen. They have seen two officers brawling like schoolboys.' He kept his tone reasonable, but it had an edge. 'The men of the Sixth have seen the venerable helmet of their revered centurion thrown in the dust and treated disrespectfully.' He held the offending item aloft, then continued, 'The men of your own century have seen their optio disciplined by their centurion, the centurion in turn attacked by the optio.' He shook his head, as if in sadness. 'I would have let it pass, but the word is already spreading around the camp. You must report to the prefect. You, too.' He pointed at Sextus. 'I will keep the helmet,' he added to Marcus, twisting the knife. 'You are not worthy of it.'

He turned to the men behind him. 'Escort these three to the prefect,' he said.

'We need no escort,' Sextus began.

'But you are criminals, so you do,' Antoninus said, then addressed his men. 'Disarm them. Tell the prefect that they come for sentencing. I will be there presently to describe their crime.'

The little party marched towards the corner of the field where the prefect had set up his headquarters. They did not speak to each other. They were, naturally, worried about their fate. The freedman having vanished, it would be the pilus prior, Antoninus, that whispered into the prefect's ear.

The legionaries delivering the prisoners could not help but, under questioning, tell Flavius something of the crimes of which they were accused. However, they fell short of giving advice on the sentence, which could have rebounded on them.

'Sir,' said Sextus, stepping forward smartly, 'we admit what happened and we would have your judgement so that we can return to our duties.'

Quintus realised that Sextus was being clever, but also taking a risky gamble. Without all the details, without Antoninus' no doubt negative intervention, they might avert disaster; however, the prefect might not take kindly to being rushed into a decision. He was already flustered, missing his right-hand man.

'We do not have time for this,' he said in exasperation. 'We march now, this morning. I am not going to put you in chains for a whole day only to punish you tonight.'

The prisoners held their breath as they realised that, for convenience, the Flavian was considering summary execution.

Then, like the sails of a ship as the wind changes, the prefect's decision altered, and the scales tipped in their direction. Sextus gave silent thanks to Minerva, to whom he had prayed for wisdom.

'Centurion,' he said shortly, 'did you strike your optio?'

'I did,' Marcus admitted.

'Did he deserve it?'

'He did.'

The Flavian turned his attention to Quintus. 'Optio, did you strike your centurion?'

'I did.' Quintus knew that, despite this being a possible capital offence, he had to tell the truth. There were too many witnesses, as well as the centurion's bloody and swollen lip.

'Centurion,' Flavius went on, businesslike now, 'do you wish this man flogged or executed?'

'Neither, sir,' Marcus said with horror, having forgotten that the fate of his underling was at least partly in his hands.

Flavius turned to Sextus and snapped, 'What is your role in this?'

'It was an honest argument, sir. I merely stepped between them. They are friends; there is no enmity…'

'I do not want a lawyer. The facts will do.' Flavius turned to Marcus and Quintus. 'You two, be thankful there is no gladiator school nearby. I reduce you both to the ranks.' He turned to a scribe. 'Record their names.'

Quintus and Marcus were both amazed that the punishment had not been worse, and they were keen to be away from the prefect before he could change his mind. They both gave their full names to the slave, then saluted smartly. Though desperate to leave, they had to remain until they were given permission to go. 'You,' Flavius said, addressing Sextus, 'where is the gold that you waved about your head?'

Before the legionary could answer, Antoninus breathlessly bundled into the area. He had heard the lenient sentence, but it was too late to change it.

Sextus ignored him and addressed the prefect in respectful tones. 'Sadly, sir, there was none. It was mere sleight of hand. I am a conjurer from the Suburra; I have need of such tricks. Search me. You will find no gold.'

'Search him,' ordered Antoninus, cursing the soft-hearted prefect and trying to contain his own fury. 'Do it thoroughly. And search these two also.' His mouth compressed into a thin line. 'Do not be gentle. Search in their secret places also.'

It was the worst that Antoninus could do under the circumstances. What he ordered was more of an assault than a search — but no gold was found.

As they readjusted their clothing, Antoninus put his face close to Quintus, so that the soldier could feel his hot breath on his cheek.

'You I have already tasked with retrieving any gold from the men. You will report tomorrow night with all that you manage to collect. Now go.'

The three left swiftly, glad to be out with their lives, if not their positions.

Miserably, Quintus said, 'It is not over for me. I will be accused of stealing, whatever I provide tomorrow. My father always said that my temper would be my undoing. It is true.'

XXXIII: JULIUS QUINTUS QUIRINIUS

The trudge back up to their tent was a long one. Marcus was nursing his lip and no longer willing to offer the hand of friendship, the enormity of his loss weighing on him. Sextus was dealing with the dark and troubling thoughts that the rough search had awoken in him, and Quintus was worrying deeply about the gold that he still had concealed in the tent.

Before they had left the prefect, Antoninus had intervened with him and had managed to appoint two of his cronies to the now vacant positions of optio and centurion of the combined century. The prefect had hardly noticed that anything had happened, being too busy with all the things that his freedman would normally have taken care of for him. He demanded that Antoninus stay and help him, which the centurion was obliged to do. He still managed to bark out an order to the three culprits that their contubernium would march at the rear of the century, and that Valerius' helmet would be given to the new appointee.

The patch where their tent had been was now bare, apart from the men's personal packs and poles. Everything else was either on the shoulders of their companions or on the cart. The looks of disappointment and disaster on the faces of the three stopped the others from asking what had happened. That Marcus was rejoining them — without the splendid crest — was sufficient for them to guess at least the initial extent of the punishment.

Finally, Rufus plucked up the courage to ask, in a doomed attempt to lighten the atmosphere, 'You escaped death, then?'

Crassus put a restraining hand on his arm, whispering urgently, 'It may come later, you fool.'

'No, Crassus,' Quintus confirmed. 'We escaped death; we escaped even a flogging. The prefect is drowning in all the things that his freedman used to do and was half-hearted in his judgement.'

'Although I am fairly sure that he thought about instant death just for convenience,' Sextus added with a half-smile.

'But you lost your rank.'

'And the pay that goes with it,' said Marcus sadly, 'but the shame will be hardest to bear. Ursus would have been mortified.' He paused and looked disapprovingly at Quintus to ensure that he had taken the point. Then he turned to the men he had once led, who were all now gathered within earshot. 'And we march at the back of the century. We are now considered the worst of the squads instead of the best. I am sorry.'

Publius and Cato exchanged a look and, in unison, shrugged their shoulders. They did not really care. Tullius' face was impassive, and Rufus tried and failed to hide his annoyance. He had served a long time, almost eleven years now, and was quietly proud of being in the front rank; those at the back were rewarded with the worst jobs. His pale golden eyebrows were raised in question. 'For how long?'

'I think for as long as Antoninus is pilus prior,' said Quintus dejectedly. He put his head down, hot tears of shame welling in his eyes. 'It is my fault,' he sniffed, trying hard to control his emotions. He felt the strong arms of Crassus steering him away so that his hurt should not be seen.

'Pathetic,' spat Marcus with undisguised contempt.

Publius and Cato followed Crassus' lead, wanting to comfort Quintus, as did Sextus. They were a little surprised by Marcus' insult, but Tullius and Rufus sided with him, agreeing with his assessment.

'I had the right to strike him,' Marcus continued, 'and he did not have the right to strike me.' He was becoming increasingly indignant, his soft voice adding power to his wrath rather than detracting from it. 'Now I have lost my position, my pay, and even my helmet. I should appeal.'

'I would not,' Tullius said impassively, his first contribution. 'If you do, you die.'

'He is right,' said Rufus. 'You cannot question a commander's decision. Besides that, he will have forgotten all about you by this afternoon and he will not wish to be reminded.'

'The new centurion may die in action,' Tullius suggested innocently, eyebrows raised. 'Such things happen.'

'As may the pilus prior,' said Rufus. 'You should once more be our decanus, our contubernium's leader — that at least would take out some of the sting.' He addressed the group around Quintus. 'What do you boys think?'

'Quintus is our decanus,' said Crassus, supporting his amicus. Publius and Cato nodded their agreement.

'This is no time for change,' Sextus put in. 'Quintus may have been foolish, but we have all done foolish things.' He let his eyes meet those of Tullius. The veteran's gaze initially flashed defiance, before he looked at his feet once more.

'Keep him,' Marcus hissed, then hawked on the ground, 'but let him try to order me...' The threat was left hanging, incomplete but potent.

Maxim had approached as meekly and as humbly as he could, not knowing who to address. 'We are moving out; we should join the century.'

'He is right,' said Crassus. 'We should move.'

Hardly a unit, they walked down the slope in three separate groups. Marcus was accompanied by Tullius and Rufus, all of them ready to take on any legionary who tried to make fun of the former centurion, their glares making this clear. Some, at least, were saddened. Marcus had been a good officer, and there were few that had complaints against him. The century would be worse for having lost him as its leader.

Sextus walked with Publius and Cato, his features frozen and unreadable.

Quintus and Crassus walked together, Quintus staring hard at the ground, Crassus staring challengingly at other legionaries. They formed up at the back of the century and immediately received a sharp rebuke from the new optio — a saturnine character and clearly a veteran of many years — for their slovenly approach.

'Looks like latrine duty for you men,' he concluded merrily, leaving the squad to grind their teeth in frustration.

As they waited for the order to move out, they said nothing, each in his own private world, each coping with the situation as best he could. They hardly listened to the prefect, who could not resist a speech-making opportunity.

'We are honoured,' the Flavian began, and laughter was suppressed in the ranks. The men knew the sort of honour they were receiving. 'We are sent by Augustus to establish a bridgehead for his new province of Britannia.' This brought some murmurings; many of the men had served with the general — or against him — when he had been mere Octavian. 'The Dictator himself, the emperor's revered father, used the very city to which we march to send transports to its southern coast. He landed there in force, made treaties, made alliances, and established friendships. I have taken the auguries and they show us favour.'

'If they are so good, why take them in private?' Sextus grumbled.

The prefect added a final flourish. 'We will be famous, we will be rich, and we will be welcomed.'

'With fire, swords and spears,' muttered Rufus, though no-one reacted to this, as few but his own contubernium heard him.

Apparently finished, the prefect kicked his horse to the front of the column and the cohort once more found itself on the march, its line snaking out of the field and along the banks of the river before climbing onto higher ground. The Flavian had decided to keep the river on his left flank. His engineers and scouts had told him that the ground was better here on the east bank. It would still mean crossing watercourses, but not as many as on the opposite shore. It also meant crossing the river first at one of the many places where it was wide and shallow, with islands and trees in the central stream. As they crossed, they could see the hills rising up to both the west and east. Those on the west were softer, rounder, but cloud topped. Those on the east were jagged and threatening. Their passage lay between them.

Quintus sighed as he looked at their route from the island. The ground was churned, muddy and wet as they pushed the carts, their wheels misbehaving and sticking. The front of the column stamped about impatiently. *That*, he thought, *is where we should be.*

Progress was not fast. Although the road had been used before, it had become overgrown — it was early summer, after all, and the trees and brambles had decided to colonise the track on which they marched. Still, when it was clear, they marched well, those at the front singing, those at the rear mired in their own private misery. They had started late, so there was no stop for noon, but the column came to an untidy halt an hour or so afterwards.

'This looks fun,' Publius said to Cato, daring to break the silence.

'What is it?' Cato asked, craning his neck to see. 'Tell us, Mac; you have a head start on all of us.'

Quintus had decided he was not going to participate in any conversation, but Cato had never offended him. He stretched his neck. 'It is a river crossing, Cato. Wide, shallow, fast flowing. The men could make it easily — the horses maybe, if led. The carts, never. Our surveyors will have noted it in winter, but now the snow melts down from the high ground. The whole area looks like it may flood.'

He was right. It was wet and marshy, the ground squelching under their caligae, and the column became spread out as the legionaries sought higher and drier ground. Neither the prefect nor the centurions were worried about this arrangement, although it showed a certain lack of discipline. This was Roman territory, and it had been for many years. There would be no attacks here.

'They are sending cavalry up the eastern bank. Hopefully they will find a ford.' Quintus looked up at the sun, already sinking in the west and ready to hide behind the hills and trees. 'I think this is as far as we will go today.'

'This is no place to camp.' Crassus, the fourth on their row, joined the conversation. 'We will have to either cross or retrace our steps.'

'We will cross,' said Quintus, turning back from looking north. 'The horses are returning; they must have found something.'

'There,' said Cato, finally catching a glimpse of the confluence through the ranks ahead of him. 'It is fast flowing but clearly shallow.'

A bend in the river had caused it to silt up, and there were even grasses and spindly trees attempting to grow on the various islands dotted across the water. The men could wade, the horses would be led, and the carts, they realised, would have to be manhandled across by the most junior legionaries of the most junior century — now them.

The order to march followed quickly, although it was slow for their century, who were tasked with helping the slaves and equipment through the sludgy ground. Muscles straining, they shouldered, lifted and pushed the carts, whipped the pack animals and drove the slaves, until eventually, with their legs caked in mud, they gained dry grassland.

The job was not unusual, nor particularly difficult — it was just that they would not have been the ones chosen had Quintus and Marcus not been caught brawling like a pair of juveniles. Rufus, Tullius and Marcus made their displeasure plain with their looks, muttered insults, and their taciturn refusal to help any of the others in their contubernium with their tasks. Sextus found himself assisting wherever he could, so that even he began to look ragged, but the three veterans remained firm in their resolve to complete only their own part of the undertaking.

Even when, finally, the cohort had found dry ground and was making camp, they managed to somehow divide the tent into two distinct sections — the veterans and the others. Quintus considered issuing orders in his elected role as decanus of the squad, but he did not dare, fearing the scorn that he believed would be thrown at him.

He now sat on the bank of a small stream that fed a tributary, desultorily washing the mud from his legs. He had considered stripping off and swimming — some of the other men had already done so, using it as an opportunity to also wash their tunics — but he decided he could not be bothered. The noise of them splashing each other and laughing just downstream annoyed him, though he knew it should not have done. He was, if truth be told, feeling sorry for himself and wondering how he might heal the breach with Marcus.

Sextus was one of those who had swum — he could not stand to be dirty for any longer than was necessary. He approached now and sat on a stone, careful to make sure that it was clean. Confident that they were on friendly territory, he wore just his tunic, belt and gladius. Jovan had managed to find a comb from somewhere and, amazingly, the legionary was once again clean-shaven. His tunic had dried and was spotless. *Of course it is*, thought Quintus to himself, but he welcomed the company.

'The gold?' Sextus asked.

'Hidden.'

'Well hidden, if that search was anything to go by. I am glad to have washed at least some of the distress of that invasion away.'

'I can fetch it if you need it,' Quintus offered, beginning to rise.

'Not necessary.' Sextus put a hand on his arm, gently pushing him back into a seated position. 'You must heal the rift with Marcus,' he said. 'Ursus would have wanted it so.'

At the mention of Ursus, Quintus slipped further into his depression. 'I wanted to go to Rome to fulfil my duty to Ursus, and to his memory. I think his shade wanders still, restless and unhappy. I want to carry out his wishes, but other than that, I have no wish to go to Rome. Like many here, there is nothing there for me.'

'Tell me,' Sextus said. 'Our new centurion is in the water with the men, the optio I know not where. I think that we may avoid duty a little longer.'

Quintus sighed, glanced sideways at his friend's impassive face and nodded. 'Very well. You have a knack for extracting information.' He felt a need to unburden himself. 'I was, as you know, brought up on a small farm, with cattle, goats, chickens and crops. There were market days in their right season. My father was away fighting for Octavian in Perusia, so it was run by my uncle and five or six slaves — slaves who, as I grew older, I realised were making fun of their master, even stealing from him.'

'How so?'

'My uncle had been a soldier. He fought with Ventidius in Parthia and was there when the shame of Carrhae was finally avenged. But he was wounded first by a Parthian arrow, then by a kick in the head from a cataphract —' Quintus lifted his head to offer an explanation — 'a Persian cavalryman.'

'What did you do about the thieving slaves?'

'I was ten years old, or thereabouts, so nothing,' Quintus said simply, 'although I did let them know that I knew, and that seemed to put a stop to some of it.'

'Did you not tell your uncle?'

'He would not have understood, or would have become depressed, or would have worked himself into a rage. The depression was the worst; it was as if he opened the cover on a well of despair and plunged in headlong. He would be gone for days, sometimes weeks. His nights were full of terrors, and his days were full of forgetfulness and anguish. He sought oblivion in anger, wine and tears. One day, he walked to market — or so we thought — but he never came back. I know not what became of him. My mother was not strong, and the slaves treated her badly. I was powerless, and I vowed revenge when I was older.

'My father visited when he could. He served in Legio VI, fought for the Dictator, and was offered land in Arelate and Beneventum, but he could not settle. He was supposed to be retired, but he answered the call of Octavian and ended up in Perusia. The army was his life.

'I was born when my father was away. I was the fifth child, hence Quintus. But I am the first to survive. I was weak, spindly and long — look at me, Sextus, I am no Adonis. She wrote to him to say how hard I fought, how I battled to stay alive, how each step of my continued existence was such a struggle. I think that when he returned home, he expected better. From her letters he had built a picture of a strong and handsome boy, a young god or hero. When he was faced with me, mewling, skinny, barely alive, he could not hide his disappointment. He demanded another child, a replacement for me.

'She had a difficult pregnancy and gave birth early. My sister, a tiny thing, survived just a few days.'

Quintus fell into a reverie at the memory of his baby sister, his face a mask of grief. His eyes misted, staring straight ahead into the swirling waters. The noise of the men in the river barely touched his consciousness.

'Go on,' encouraged Sextus tenderly, wanting to put an arm around Quintus' shoulders but not daring. He saw that his friend barely had his emotions under control, and he was scared to release them.

Quintus took a deep breath, gathered himself, and gently closed the door to the dark places of his soul. 'My father grieved and carried her tiny body out to bury her in the far field with the daisies and the other lost babies. At the time, I did not understand, but I could feel his loss.' He turned to face his comrade. 'He tried, Sextus. He tried so hard, but I just would not do. He took me to market with him, but I was of little use. Other farmers had strong sons, gruff and dark, not pale and skinny with the hair of a girl.' He ran his hands through it. 'He smiled at me riding the cart and indulged my wish to be a soldier like him, with my wooden sword and a stick for a spear. I remember being happy. I remember him being happy.'

He paused again, picturing the sunny scene in his mind's eye, seeing it through a rainbow prism. With a sniff, the happy father and son vanished, and he was businesslike again.

'A few weeks later, my mother was with child again. She gave birth to Proculus, my younger brother. He took the life from her, took the last of her strength and made it his own. He was robust, lusty and upright. A slave was found as a wetnurse, my beloved mother all but forgotten — as was I. He took my place. This time when my father returned, he encouraged my ambitions and sent me to the Campus Martius. He wanted me to join up; he was desperate to see the back of me so that he could lavish attention on my Achilles of a brother. He was overjoyed when I was accepted, and he could not hide his delight when I left.'

He stood, using Sextus' shoulder as an aid, and set his lips into a grim smile. 'So you see, my friend, I have no desire to go to Rome. I don't think I would be welcome at home.'

Sextus rose also. He was about to speak when he realised that a tesserarius was approaching, a wax tablet in his hand, calling a name. He was accompanied by a standard bearer, the standard drooping in the still evening air. With a start, Quintus realised that it was his name, and that maybe the prefect's judgement would be revised after all. For a moment he considered hiding, deserting even, then Sextus said to him, 'Is that not your name he is calling, Julius Quintus Quirinius? I think your gold-collecting task is upon you.'

Only then did Quintus remember, with a wave of relief, that it was not a revised sentence. This was followed by a wave of despair at the job he had to do.

XXXIV: BRIGANTIA

Quintus was delighted to see that the signifer who gave his unwelcome job legitimacy was none other than Aquila. He had been tasked by the centurion to stay with Quintus on his quest as a sort of punishment, but he was actually glad to be helping. The tesserarius, his job done, departed, leaving the young signifer behind.

Crassus agreed to help him too, although he was still stiff from his injury. Though it was healing, was doing so slowly — too slowly for the blacksmith. Quintus used Jovan and Maxim to pass an announcement: a cloak would be laid by the riverbank, where the men had earlier been swimming, and this was the place designated for the emperor's gold to be returned. He did not expect much, but he hoped for at least a little so that he could prove he had done his best to complete what he considered to be an impossible undertaking.

The message was simple: the prefect had declared that anyone caught with the emperor's gold was a proven thief and would face the consequences. At any time between sundown and sunup, legionaries had to deposit any gold they possessed at this place. They could do so — at this time and place only — without fear of punishment.

Aquila planted his standard and stood impassively facing the river, his back to the cloak. Crassus and Quintus, with occasional help from Sextus, took it in turns to watch the cloak from a distance to ensure that, should any man leave gold here, it was not stolen by the next.

By dawn, half a dozen men had slipped past and deposited small items taken from tribesmen and scant handfuls of gold dust; dozens more, Quintus surmised, had failed to come forward, trusting in Fortuna rather than in Flavius.

As the sun rose, Quintus went to where the pack animals were tethered and returned with the nugget that Sextus had shown the men. Adding it to the rest made it look like a half-decent haul. He showed the collection to Crassus and Sextus whilst Aquila saluted, ready to march off.

'I would prefer it if you stayed with me until this is delivered,' Quintus said, recognising the power of the vexillum carried by his comrade.

'Until it is delivered,' Aquila agreed.

'I have seen that before,' said Sextus softly, pointing at the nugget, the largest piece of gold. He spoke so that only Quintus should hear him. 'It is the one I showed the others, so none of the men put it here.'

Quintus almost spoke, but then decided to keep his silence.

The contents of the cloak were tipped into a leather bag and the little party, minus Sextus, made its way towards the command tent, in search of the prefect. Instead, the men came across Antoninus, who was checking readiness for the day's march and ensuring that the camp was well on its way to being dismantled. He was about to reproach the men, always ready for an opportunity to punish them, but he was given pause by the presence of the standard-bearer, fully uniformed. Instead, he greeted them with mock politeness. 'And what have we here, so early in the morning?' he asked, his voice singsong.

'Gold from the men for the prefect,' said Quintus, saluting.

Antoninus held out his hand for the bag, insisting with a hard look that Quintus let it go when he seemed reluctant. He weighed it in his palm and smiled. 'Not enough, I would say. A duty failed.'

Crassus was indignant. 'The task was completed. We can no more make the men put their stolen goods in it than we can make this standard fly away.' Then he realised that he had spoken disrespectfully and lowered his head.

It was Aquila who intervened. 'He is injured, sir. He sometimes does not know what he says — and it was this one's task, not his.'

Quintus nodded in agreement.

'Take it,' ordered the centurion, smiling a cruel smile, 'though I doubt you will see the commander — it will be a slave or a freedman or one of his personal guard. There is no guarantee that the bag will not end up even lighter than it is now.'

'I will take it,' said Aquila. 'I will put this bag, unopened, into the prefect's hands.'

Agreement between them all was swift. Quintus wanted the task to be complete. Crassus wanted to be away from the centurion. Antoninus wanted to be about his business, and Aquila was confident that he could access the prefect. They departed in separate directions, relieved that this particular assignment was over. Crassus apologised for speaking out, and Quintus was quick to forgive him.

By the time the copper disc of the sun had fully cleared the horizon, the men were once more marching. It was not a difficult march, but was made more wearisome by Marcus' refusal to engage with any of the contubernium except Tullius and Rufus. Tullius took the isolation in his stride, but Rufus was finding it difficult. He had worked hard to gain the trust and respect of his fellow legionaries; for ten years he had ridden the tide of jests and insults relating to his flaming hair and sun-baked skin.

He had found comfort in the auburn-haired woman who had been his wife, though no marriage had ever taken place before priests or witnesses. He had lost her when, two years ago, he had been fighting with General Agrippa against the Cantabrians, finding himself — along with the rest of the army — close to death as the enemy had proved to be more intractable and cunning than any had thought possible. He had been hurt and was laid up for just long enough for her to think him dead. The injuries he had taken were not to the face, so they were not obvious to his companions, but many blows to the head had caused him dizziness, forgetfulness and confusion. Before recovering his wits, he had been visited by phantasms and terrors of the imagination and had sent up prayers to his family gods, believing himself about to die.

He did not die, but the headaches and the proximity of defeat made him now careless of his safety, as if he had already laid the path to his own death. To keep his thoughts from returning to such dark places, he craved companionship, and Marcus was denying him this, testing his loyalty and stretching him between the two halves of the squad. He did not like it.

This day the legionaries had two tributaries to negotiate. One was a difficult incline, the stream running through a deep cleft in the rocks. At its base, the water was fast flowing but the gap was narrow and easy to cross. The other tributary was wider, muddier and harder. It had slow-flowing water, shallow for the most part but dotted with dips, pits and hollows that caught out the unwary. In the reeds and mud, huge water birds were disturbed and flapped away, squawking. They spooked some of the mules as they crossed, forcing soldiers who had already gained the far bank to return to the cold depths to help the struggling slaves with the beasts.

Apart from the crossings the march was uneventful, the steady tramp of the heavy caligae punctuated by jests and songs that rose and fell as verses were exhausted or the singers became bored. Orders to halt or change pace were shouted for no reason that the legionaries — except perhaps those at the very front — could ascertain. Formations were squeezed or misshapen by carters or traders who were also using the track, or by scouts riding up and down the column. They checked ahead, checked that the rear was keeping up, and reported back to the centurions and the prefect.

Sextus, marching beside Rufus, tried to talk to him, but though Rufus was desperate for conversation, he was also painfully aware of Marcus' impassive gaze and answered only in monosyllables. He did not care that Marcus was no longer decanus, but he also saw no need to cause offence.

Tullius, his wound still troubling him, gritted his teeth and, battling silently against the pain, was unable to speak anyway. At the end of the day, he needed respite and, as soon as the tent was erected, Quintus — as decanus — excused him from further duties and let him rest. Marcus muttered that he — as decanus — had already done so. The two glared at each other, but neither spoke. For the contubernium, it meant that the tent was once more home to Marcus' faction, whilst the fire and the ground outside was the resting place of the other five. They did not mind; the night was warm, and the ground was dry.

As Quintus and his comrades lay under the stars, a few of which he could now recognise, he complained to Crassus about his situation.

'I never wanted to go to Rome,' he told the blacksmith. 'It was never in the stars.'

Crassus grunted noncommittally.

'Perhaps I am cursed? First I fell out with Tullius and Sextus, and now Marcus isn't speaking to me.'

'Stop complaining,' Crassus muttered, recognising the peevishness of the boy still alive inside the man that his friend was becoming.

'Perhaps you were injured because you were cursed,' Quintus tried.

'Sleep,' Crassus commanded. He then turned onto his side to put an end to the conversation, though it pulled at his wounds and hurt him to do so.

Quintus, realising that no one was ready to listen to him, sulked himself to sleep.

By the end of the next day's march, once clear of the heavily forested slopes, the men could see their destination. The sparkling blue sea flattened the horizon. They appeared to be making for what initially looked like an island, although on closer inspection there was a long sandbar that gave access from the shore. Brigantia, the place was called. It was a village, or perhaps a small town depending on where you came from yourself. For a Roman from the city, it was tiny, hardly a settlement at all. For a farmer like Quintus, used to single-street villages or the local market town, it was, if not a metropolis, at least a decent sized settlement. It had more than one street; it had a bakery, a harbour, a brothel. It also had a few municipal buildings and temples — still wooden, but no doubt with plans for stone. Apparently, to the joy of the men, it had a bath.

The Dictator had visited it in the year of the Consulship of Calpurnianus and Messalla, after divorcing his wife due to the scandal of the Good Goddess. It was a story that Sextus was happy to relate, with many added details of his own, supposedly gleaned from his time with the Vestals. Caesar had realised that trading vessels from Gaul, Britannia and Lusitania all visited the natural harbour and had sent Roman triremes and quinqueremes to make contact with those shores.

The Dictator had found an abandoned Celtic hill fort, once home to the Artabrians, and had made this his headquarters, establishing a small garrison and expanding the harbour. This had grown — although more into a town than a fortress, centred on the old hill fort. In addition, inevitably, the army had left behind veterans, wounded men and even deserters, along with camp followers who saw a better life here, seeding the population with almost all the layers of Roman society. There were no patricians, but those who made money off the backs of others would soon fill this niche.

It had become a profitable trading port and many ships, from small coastal cogs to seagoing vessels, now bobbed at anchor in the natural bay formed by the shape of the land.

The men stopped outside the town, but were only stood at ease, rather than being allowed to go and make camp. Quintus scanned the scene, able to see over the heads of the men in front of him. *So, this is where we are embarking from*, he thought. The prefect, he knew, needed ships to take the cohort's troops, baggage and animals. They would need either a few big ships or many small ones. Quintus could see a few small vessels, but only two large ones; the way the land curved and fell prevented him from seeing the whole anchorage. He had no idea how the commander would go about obtaining the transport that they required.

The men began to discuss the sea voyage with apprehension, sharing tales of storms, sea monsters and Neptune's fury. Although few had been to sea, many seemed to know someone who had had a bad experience on the water. As he and Sextus disagreed over who would be the sickest, Quintus was surprised to hear a messenger calling out the name of one of the contubernium's slaves — Jovan.

Quintus called to both the messenger and the slave. In terror, the slave identified himself to the messenger, pulling off the headband that hid the tattoo on his forehead — the mark of his slavery. He dropped to his knees and bowed his head, wondering what he had done wrong.

'Up,' the messenger ordered tersely. 'You are to bring your skills, not your dread. You are to be used by the prefect, not punished. Who is your master?'

Jovan was confused; the army — this small part of it — was his master.

'The decanus of your contubernium?'

Marcus shook his head, willing none to name him. He did not wish to come to the Flavian's attention again. 'It is him,' he said, indicating Quintus with a sneer, happy to see Macilentus once more obliged to enter the prefect's tent. Quintus, for his part, accepted the title with some trepidation, wondering what the prefect wanted with them.

They hurried after the messenger with the eyes of many men following them, assuming both were to be punished. On the word from the messenger, the guards let them into the tent. Jovan at once fell onto his belly, his arms splayed out on either side. He had learnt many years ago that this was how you greeted high monarchs and generals.

'Get him up,' said Flavius tersely, annoyed to be shown such deference and seeing the sly smiles already beginning to grow on his soldiers' faces. 'Listen, slave,' he went on harshly, 'you will end up like that, but on a cross, if you do not please me.' His tone became a little more conciliatory. 'My freedman would have dealt with these issues, not me. You will take his place.'

Jovan held his nerve and bowed his head. Quintus had not yet dared to speak.

The prefect turned to his clerk. He was a literate slave whom he had thought of freeing, but was dissuaded every time he saw the man's dark eyes and the threat of rebellion in them. Slaves should be humble, not have eyes that sparked a challenge every time they met yours. 'My freedman is gone,' he sighed as he indicated the slave with a wave of his hand. 'This man brings me the lists. Can you read them?'

Jovan nodded. 'I can read them.'

'Good, give them to him,' the prefect ordered his clerk.

The slave passed the lists across reluctantly. The two could have had a conversation, Greek to Macedonian, but they did not dare. Instead, both stood meekly waiting for orders.

Flavius was exasperated. 'You,' he ordered his slave, 'go.' Then he turned to Jovan. 'You, tell me how many ships we will need.'

Jovan scanned the list, seeing not just men, but beasts and carts and all that they contained. 'I cannot say, sir, until we know the size of the vessels. It could be as many as thirty.'

'And can we pay for them, or must we requisition them?'

Jovan had no idea how to answer this, so he stayed quiet.

The question turned out to be rhetorical. 'We do not have the manpower to requisition so many,' the prefect answered himself. 'We must pay for them. We have enough gold.'

Again, there appeared to be no question to answer.

The prefect nodded absentmindedly to himself, took the list from Jovan's trembling fingers and scanned the tally of men, material, horses, mules and carts. He knew his force was much depleted, but still there were many here. 'You have skills,' he said to Jovan, who bowed his head. 'See, on the lists you have this mark by your name. This indicates that you can read, but it is this in which I am most interested.'

Jovan looked where his finger was pointing at his own name, then followed it across to the column detailing former occupations and skills. Many of the slaves had nothing in this column, and some had 'V' marked there. Jovan knew that this stood for 'verna'; these men had been born into slavery and been the property of the army from birth. Next to his own name was 'L' and 'F'. The 'L' he guessed was for 'litteratus,' literate, but did not know what the 'F' indicated.

'Factor,' the prefect said, noticing his confusion, 'your former profession?'

Jovan nodded.

'So, manager, businessman, trader — most importantly, negotiator.' Flavius smiled at his own discovery. 'You will take our gold and negotiate ships for these men and supplies. Your decanus will go with you, as will four of my guards. They may help negotiations.' He clapped his hands and another two slaves rushed forward, each holding out a leather bag. The smaller one, Quintus recognised as the one containing his own overnight collection. The larger must have been the rest of the gold that the perfect had managed to retain after their visit to Lucus Augustus — minus whatever he had kept for himself.

The prefect handed the bags to the senior member of his guard. 'Try to bring one of these back,' he ordered, 'preferably the heavier one.'

The negotiations were not easy and were conducted in a half-words half-numbers language that Jovan and the shipmaster's representative seemed to understand. However, Quintus and the accompanying legionaries had no idea what was being said, which worried them tremendously.

Jovan advised that the larger bag should be kept out of sight, but after over an hour, he reported to Quintus in hoarse and desperate whispers that the smaller would not be enough. The guards had lost their concentration; they were busy watching the comings and goings of the port rather than the negotiations, and Quintus was able to slip one of his own nuggets to the slave.

'Add this,' he urged.

It was enough. Only the small bag was passed across, the large nugget apparently clinching the deal for eighteen ships, complete with helmsmen and deck crews. The ships were mostly powered by sail, although there were banks of oars should they become becalmed. Unlike warships, the oars were not manned all the time, and it was explained that the legionaries would need to row if their use was necessary. This, Jovan explained, was one of the reasons why he had been able to negotiate a better price.

The prefect, pleased with the deal and even more pleased with the return of his gold, decreed that it was to be an early start. The legionaries would therefore have to be aboard by the evening and would sleep on deck. The ships would sail with the morning tide, the wind taking them eastwards along the coast. He made his wishes clear to the centurions: once boarded, the men would stay put. There would be no visits to the town, neither baths nor brothels. Boarding would commence at once.

XXXV: CALDARIUM

Rufus, craving friendship and conversation, came over to where Publius and Cato sat talking. They were with Quintus and Crassus on the forward deck, sitting and lying around a small fire raised up on stones — one of many on the decks of the ships — which had been constructed by Maxim. Sextus had dodged the half-hearted guard detail on the quay and was off, with both slaves in tow, seeking comforts for the voyage. Quintus would not be surprised if he managed to return with a slave girl or two. *If only*, he thought.

Rufus was not as bothered as Marcus about ignoring the others. He did not really care who was decanus, as he would be unlikely to take anything other than battle orders from them whoever they were. He did have a soft spot for Lux, though, and had taken it upon himself to help the lad lose his virginity. Publius, for his part, was not as keen as Rufus thought he should be; he seemed to want to lose his virginity in his own time and in private.

'We are going into town,' Rufus announced, 'just for a little while. Will you come with us?'

'The prefect has forbidden it,' said Quintus, with what he hoped was a stern note.

'I know,' replied the redhead, 'but I have already heard that Antoninus and his friends are going. If they can go, so can we.'

'Marcus would not have it so,' said Publius.

'But I would. We could go together, you and I.' He winked. 'You know I have a little undertaking for you. Marcus can have Tullius for company.'

Publius looked at Cato, who gave the slightest shake of his head. He then turned to Crassus, who was noncommittal, and to Quintus, who was more definite. 'If Antoninus is in town, that is as good a reason as any for us to avoid it.'

'Then you miss out,' said Rufus, shrugging, unwilling to try to persuade them further. 'I will go with the others.' He left them and headed for the other end of the ship.

'They intend to make a night of it,' said Quintus. 'Baths, brothel and probably a brawl.'

They had been allocated to a small trader, powered by a single sail and half a dozen oars when necessary. They had a grumpy helmsman who seemed to be too old to be doing anything as important and as physical as managing the tiller. The other member of the 'crew' was a half-naked boy who seemed to be lacking at least some of his wits. He scampered about, coiling rope and testing the ship's moorings. His tasks apparently complete, he sat in the prow on a pile of rags next to his sleeping employer, staring unblinkingly out to sea.

As dark enveloped the harbour, with just dim riding lights showing where other vessels lay, the men could see, from their position on the raised part of the deck, many shadowy groups disembarking and vanishing north towards the town, including some that were meant to be stopping this flow. Those ships that carried the largest numbers, including the prefect's vessel, one of the bigger ships, had officers aboard, able to prevent such movement. For them there were guards on the quayside, the prefect's own men, serious about their duty. The smaller ships, theirs included, could surely be trusted to follow orders.

Once the exodus appeared to be over, the last of the groups scuttling up the hill like little boys playing truant, there was little else to see, and they turned to throwing dice. But it was a miserable sort of game, only half-heartedly played, and with no real stakes to gamble. Publius threw four twos, a definite 'dog' to Cato's 'Venus', and then stood up to look over the ship's side, the lights of the town winking not so far away.

'We should go,' he said quietly.

'We should,' agreed Cato unexpectedly, arriving at his shoulder.

They were going to ask the other two, in the full knowledge that Quintus would oppose, but Crassus had already joined them. 'I agree,' he said, and half turned towards his friend. 'Even if Mac does not want to go, we should take the opportunity.'

'Someone needs to watch the fire,' Quintus responded, knowing that he was outvoted and giving himself an excuse.

'Maxim will do that.' The confident voice of Sextus joined the conversation from the quay, the two slaves with him, each carrying a bag. 'Wine and food for when we return,' he announced.

Quintus, even though he knew that the argument was already lost, still tried a rearguard action. 'Don't blame me if anything goes wrong...' he began, but he was cut off by Sextus' encouragement of the others, beckoning them to come silently, his finger to his lips.

A few short instructions to the slaves and, within minutes of their arrival, they were tending the fire and their masters were no longer on board. Sextus led and Quintus, somewhat reluctantly, brought up the rear.

The five young men made their way up the hill and carefully navigated the streets of the little town; they were aware that they were not the only legionaries to decide that a little relaxation was a just reward for their march. They dodged various small groups that flitted to and fro in the dark like bats in a barn. They were all heading for the baths, the prostitutes, or both.

Quintus' group found the baths. They were inside a wooden building, not large, but one from which familiar sounds and smells were emanating — the grunts of those exercising or being massaged, the wheezing of those not used to such activity, the crack, slap or thud of the masseur's hand on flesh, depending on whether he was using an open palm, a heel or a pummelling fist. There were the low tones of those talking business and the raised voices of those telling raunchy tales; there was the smell of sweat, perfume and olive oil. Threaded through all was the sound of water, splashing, running, dripping, trickling and gurgling. For Sextus it smelt and sounded like home. It brought back mixed memories, some warm, some less so.

They changed quickly out of their tunics, leaving them with the slave in the apodyterium and taking the square towel offered by him in exchange for a small coin. Quintus told his companions to wait whilst he peered into each of the rooms, intent on avoiding both Marcus and Antoninus. The natatio was the size of a fishpond and the exercise area, where they found a bench on which they could sit, was no more than beaten earth. The other rooms were all through doors and Quintus needed to see who was here. As he opened doors and looked, he was assailed by billowing steam, cold blasts of air or wafts of olive oil. He acknowledged men he knew with a brief wave or a nod. The place was busy, and not just with legionaries. There were many prostitutes, both male and female, offering their services.

Pushing a door open a crack, he spotted the three veterans through the steam of the caldarium. Tullius was being massaged — or rather, pummelled — by a slave, and the other two were relaxing nearby. Marcus was scraping Rufus' back with a strigil, neither of them fully facing the door.

Quintus withdrew. He was fairly certain that he had been seen by at least Tullius, if not the others, and he was relieved that they were being ignored, rather than teased and baited or, worse, driven from the place. There was a sort of uneasy truce between the various groups, as they managed to move around the baths, small as they were, without interacting. Each party pretended that it had not seen the other.

When Quintus returned to his group, Sextus raised his eyebrows, silently asking if he had found Marcus. Quintus replied with a twitch of his head in the direction of the hot room. Sextus shrugged. 'So we will have to wait to open our pores,' he said. 'It is not too bad here.' They found two empty benches in the tepidarium, where the five of them could sit facing each other, so that only their backs were visible. It seemed safer that way.

'The centurion?' Sextus asked, head cocked to one side.

'Not found,' Quintus confirmed.

'I am not going to enjoy this until they have gone,' Publius complained, at which the others chided him for whining.

'It was your idea,' said Crassus. 'We could have still been throwing dice.'

'Leave him be,' Cato said, coming to his defence.

'Once there was a satyr, so well-endowed that rich ladies travelled miles just to look at him,' Sextus said incongruously, then paused. 'A story, perhaps?'

They all nodded agreement and Sextus began telling a long and involved tale about three whores, a rich lady, a satyr and a competition — which a cynic might deduce was designed to make Crassus feel uncomfortable. Then, with horror, Quintus looked up and saw Antoninus and three of his cronies entering from the western door, heading directly for the caldarium. They were bound to spot the three veterans. The usual form — as with all the other legionaries present — would be to pay no heed to any other soldiers; the more junior men who were breaking curfew would just give way to their superiors. If Antoninus came into the tepidarium, Quintus and his friends would be expected to quietly move; if he entered the caldarium, Marcus would be expected to do the same. The dance was a silent one; no-one would actually 'see' anyone else.

'We had better move,' said Publius, nervously.

'Why?' Crassus asked. 'He is not approaching us.' He was right. The centurion headed straight for the caldarium, his companions closing the door behind them.

A series of muffled shouts, bangs and yells signalled that all was not well. The door shook and rattled, and two men tumbled out, locked together, one with his forearm around the other's throat in a wrestling hold. Rufus' bright red hair and long moustaches made him easy to recognise, and it was his arm that was throttling the other.

As they crashed to the floor, two more men fell through the door behind them. Marcus, with the muscular arms of a wrestler, was holding Antoninus in a bear hug, squeezing the life from him. He held the centurion from the back, pinning his arms to his sides and lifting him almost from the floor, but his opponent was slippery from the oil and it was hard to maintain a grip.

A grunt from inside indicated another bout. Tullius was apparently being tipped off the massage table by an assailant, who was then free to help his comrade escape Marcus' grip. As Antoninus squirmed and kicked, his companion cracked a fist into the back of Marcus' head and the centurion slipped the hold, turning to smash his own forearm into Marcus' face.

The tables were turned in a moment, Marcus now being held whilst Antoninus rained blow after blow upon him. Tullius emerged, shouting and flailing, heedless of his injury. He hurled himself at the centurion, knocking him flying onto the beaten earth floor.

'Don't be stupid,' urged Cato, but it was too late. Quintus and Sextus had already launched themselves across the room. Crassus, nursing his healing wounds, was slower but still close behind. The numbers were now in their favour, and Marcus, freed from the man's grip, planted a blow on Antoninus' chin that made the centurion's head rock and his eyes mist. The next split his lip, so that fresh blood now entered the wrestling arena, mingling with sweat and oil.

Cato put his hand on Publius' arm as he also began to rise. 'No,' he said urgently and firmly. 'You stay out of it.'

He need not have worried, for it was over. The baths' guards had waded in with batons, separating the combatants and threatening to throw them out into the night if they did not behave. Quintus, supported by Crassus as they were ushered away, found himself laughing. He was amazed that Antoninus and Marcus were too.

Sextus had somehow managed to avoid both blood and oil, and had slipped the attention of the guards, joining Publius and Cato back on the bench with a smile.

'Is this not a death sentence?' Publius asked, horrified at what had happened.

'No uniforms, no rank, no fight,' Sextus smiled. 'All is well, but some demons have been laid to rest.'

'Tullius risked his life as if he did not care.'

'There's a reason for that,' said Sextus, knowing about the dread shadow that lay on Tullius' conscience like a dead animal in a pond, spreading disease. 'But it is between Tullius and his gods.'

Quintus and Crassus watched as the others brushed themselves off, Antoninus having to wipe the blood from his lip. This was the point at which it could turn serious, but the centurion just smiled and signalled to his companions to let things lie. Marcus did the same, though he knew that he had the advantage of numbers if Quintus and Crassus fought with him, five to Antoninus' three.

'A gentleman's disagreement,' said the centurion, mumbling through swollen lips and holding out an open hand, 'and a very enjoyable one.'

'So be it,' said Marcus, accepting the olive branch offered.

Still, Antoninus and his friends deliberately sauntered across and occupied the caldarium in which the veterans had been ensconced, to show who was in charge. Marcus, over the complaints of Tullius and Rufus, reluctantly accepted this and shepherded them away to a different room. Before he followed them in, he grunted a word of appreciation and thanks to Quintus, the first sign of a thaw between the two.

'He what?' Marcus was beyond incredulous, spitting out the wine that he had just gulped.

'He is going to report us,' Quintus repeated slowly. 'He seeks revenge.'

'To whom? Why?' Rufus joined in.

'The prefect, I suppose. He wants to see us flogged.'

'But why? It was nothing, and we were all civilians when it happened.'

'Vengeance for his hurts, spite, who knows?'

'It is just my ill fortune following us,' Tullius added sadly. 'Mal Fortuna, indeed.'

'It is not your fault,' Rufus reassured him. 'It was just a brawl; I have been in many such. And we were out of uniform.'

'He says he was assaulted; he says he was attacked by soldiers breaking the curfew,' said Quintus.

'Then what was he doing there?' Marcus demanded.

Quintus gestured with open palms. 'He will say he was checking the baths and town for deserters and legionaries breaking the rules. He will say he was on official business disguised as a civilian.'

'By Mars and Jupiter, he lies!' Marcus' rage was close to boiling over. His face had reddened and his words had become slurred; he was on his feet, ready to storm over to the prefect's ship. 'I will go to him. I will tell him it was just a rumble, a dispute amongst friends.'

Quintus knew that he would have to restrain him if Rufus or Tullius did not; he knew also that he would likely receive a bent nose for his troubles. Tullius had dropped into one of his fugue states, muttering to himself and shaking his head, oblivious to events around him. Rufus spotted the danger and rose to help, putting a restraining hand on Marcus' shoulder.

'He will not know of what you speak,' he said calmly. 'He is a Flavian, a politician. Don't be fooled by his face; his boxing was done with rules, with limits, not in a street brawl.'

Marcus moved to disembark, Quintus blocked his way, and Rufus gently turned his shoulder.

'Rage is no friend to justice,' he said coolly. 'Reconsider, my friend. Here,' he passed him the wine cup.

Marcus took a long pull, and then let out a deep breath, like air escaping from a pig's bladder. The deep redness faded first from his cheeks, then from his neck, although both remained pink and hot. Finally, the madness in his eyes died, the fire extinguished.

'Leave, Mac,' ordered Rufus, waving him away. 'I will come and talk to you soon.'

Quintus had received the news of the proposed accusation against them from one of the centurion's cronies, drunk but delighted to pass on the bad tidings. The man had been on the waterfront, relieving himself against the side of the boat, when he had spotted one of his adversaries.

'We'll see you flogged, you lanky bastard,' he slurred, as he leaned back and directed a bright amber stream at the timbers. 'Antoninus is bringing a charge against you.' He squinted through one eye and pointed, the action encouraging the last of the amber stream to soak his feet. 'We were there legitimately, seeking rule-breakers like you, or so Flavius will believe,' he laughed. 'Better bare your lanky bastard back.'

He staggered off into the darkness, laughing harshly. Quintus had dismissed him with a rude gesture and then hurried from his place in the prow to the stern of the ship, where Marcus was.

He returned from the veterans with nothing but abuse and invective in his mind — a toxic mixture when coupled with the reproach he levelled at Sextus and the disappointment he felt in himself for involving Crassus. Sextus, he blamed for persuading them to go, and he both admired and detested him for slipping out of the reckoning. Crassus, in his opinion, would not have been there if he had insisted that they stay on the ship, so the blacksmith's involvement was all on his head.

Then, unprompted, the thought of the Bear crossed his mind, and the disappointment he would have felt at such foolishness and poor judgement. Quintus shook his head to clear it of the image of Ursus, but the vision would not fade.

As a sliver of pale light defined the horizon, Ursus held out his fists. He opened the left to reveal a white stone on his palm, then the right to reveal a gold nugget, a nugget which Quintus recognised. A tear wet his eye as Ursus smiled a crooked smile, full of pity.

Mal Fortuna, indeed, thought Quintus darkly.

XXXVI: HYDRA

On the ships the moans from the hungover were mixed with cries of anguish from those who only now realised that they had been robbed, or cheated, or both. They knew that there was no chance that they would ever catch the culprits — something the crooks knew only too well.

Dawn seemed, to many of the carousers, to arrive early — too early for their sore heads, dry mouths and red-rimmed eyes to be able to cope. Not all had made it back from the town; if they did not appear before sailing, they would be marked on the lists as deserters, a capital offence. Those who were still drunkenly lying in a shop doorway or at the foot of a whore's bed would be fugitives for life. Latecomers could be seen stumbling down the hill, themselves likely to receive a flogging for their rule-breaking.

What Quintus' contubernium did not know was that, though Antoninus had managed to speak to the prefect and had even managed to have the offences recorded, there would be no time to carry out any punishment. The prefect was overwhelmed with tales of deserters and rule-breakers, which had been brought to him by every officer — many covering their own backs by accusing others. Flavius, still missing his freedman, found that there was not even time to inform the accused of their fate.

'Record them,' he ordered. 'Record them all. I will deal with them later.'

The tide was turning with the dawn, and the various helmsmen were shouting to their crews and to each other. The wind was freshening from the west and, as the dawn light grew, small clouds could be seen scudding across the sky, as if rushing for home.

On their own little ship, preparations were already being made by the boy, who was stronger, more skilled and more agile than Quintus had previously given him credit for. He seemed to be everywhere at once, lifting the hawsers from the quay, coiling the ropes, pulling on lines and raising the sail, all the time maintaining a bright grin on his face as if this was the best day of his life. *Perhaps it is*, Quintus thought.

The men, used to being rudely awoken but not used to being passengers, tried to keep out of the way of the sailors, but they still called on slaves to find them something to break their fast. These calls ceased abruptly and turned into a series of groans as each ship crossed the bar of the harbour, transitioning from the still calm of the protected waters to the tossing and churning of the restless sea. Quintus had thought that the short voyage from moorings to open water had been pleasant, not realising that within the confines of the harbour, it always would be. He had never been to sea, but he had heard men's tales of nausea and dizziness occasioned by the roiling waves and the unpredictable motion of the boat. Once they crossed the bar, he realised what they had been talking about. The ship pitched and rolled and he immediately heaved, gaining the side just in time to see the red tinge of last night's wine hurled into the water.

The sailors smiled; it would not do to make too much fun of their guests, but they secretly enjoyed the discomfiture of the Romans. For them, this was a good start to the morning; there was a favourable tide, a brisk wind and waves that were merry without being dangerous. They revelled in the feel of open water as prows cut creaming bow waves and sea creatures danced in their foaming wake. Most of their passengers had never even seen a dolphin before and were sufficiently amazed and distracted by their antics to stop vomiting, at least temporarily. Quintus found that if he stood on deck, allowing the wind and the salt spray to splash his face, he felt less nauseous. He was unbearably cold and wet, it was true, but at least he wasn't throwing up.

Jovan staggered from man to man, offering dry biscuit to each. Mostly it was refused. Quintus tried to talk to him. They had a shouted conversation that was mostly whipped away by the wind, and he learned that Maxim was with the mule and the others were finding their own ways to cope. There was little any of them could do, except find a place that was vaguely comfortable and stay there.

It was a long day, a hard day for the helmsmen and crews, who worked until the sun touched the horizon. They took soundings, noted landmarks on the coast as it hurried past, held course with the tiller, and fought and then rode the wind. The morning had seen them sail north, trimming sails to use the strong westerly, until they were past a wide river mouth. This was a frightening experience for the legionaries — an hour or so with no land in sight. They were then able to give the vessels free rein to run before the wind, east along the coastline, rounding headlands and capes.

It was a hard day in a different way for the cavalry horses and pack animals. Some were docile and unconcerned, while many were scared and trembling, adding to the chaos by emptying bladders and bowels. It was a hard day for the men, unable to help since no oars had been needed in the brisk wind. This state of idleness was unfamiliar to them and they were not prepared for it. They would usually spend such unusual leisure time dicing, whoring or fighting, not hanging on to timbers or heaving their guts up over the side of a ship.

The setting of the sun, red and gold in a cloudless azure sky, was the signal for the ships to heave to and anchor. They would not land ashore, not on this first night, nor on any other night when there were rocks, treacherous currents and possibly enemy tribesmen to navigate. They were at the beginning of the voyage, fully stocked with fresh water and food. The helmsmen knew of safely sloping sandy beaches where they could later top up water barrels and take respite.

Though anchored, the ships did not stop moving and the men had an uncomfortable night under the bright stars of a clear sky; the moon, a mere sliver, rose late and rode into the morning. It was full dark by the time the ships were secured, and they would start at the first glimmer of dawn. At least it was a short night, the spring equinox having passed whilst they were on the march, the lengthening of the days already felt. The legionaries slept badly, if at all, even though most of them were exhausted. They had not realised how much energy they had expended just by gripping on.

On Quintus' ship, Sextus stayed awake, stargazing and telling his listeners some of the tales of the heavens. It was still and quiet but for the soft caress of the waves against the hull, and, although the separation between the two groups still held, an outside observer would have been hard put to notice it. He spoke of the various gods sufficiently offended or grieving to place enemies or loved ones in the stars — of the hunter, the Greek queen, the two bears. With an expansive gesture, He outlined the longest of the constellations, the water snake, or the Hydra, in the west — the monster of many heads slain by Heracles, though in the sky it had but one. *One head is sufficient*, seemed to be his message, as he looked pointedly at Marcus and Quintus.

The men knew that they must have at least dozed when in the morning they opened their eyes to find themselves surrounded by a cold and clammy fog — a thick miasma that prevented them from seeing all but those boats closest to them. Some of the other ships, like ghostly creatures hung with flickering lights, rode in and out of view.

Quintus stood up in the prow, trying to use his height to see over the mist, but to no avail. He could no longer see any land. The others huddled for warmth around the fire, wrapped tightly in their cloaks, plaintively asking him what he saw, to which he just shook his head. Marcus and the veterans still kept their own counsel.

The ship's boy, still in no more than a loincloth but seemingly immune to either cold or wet, summoned Quintus to follow him with urgent gestures. He had few words of Latin, so he tended to communicate with his passengers by waving his arms. Quintus followed, knowing that he was being taken to speak to the helmsman, who was also the captain and shipmaster.

'We must man the oars,' said the old man gruffly. 'The boy will take one.' He caught Quintus' doubtful expression. 'He is stronger than he looks.' He laughed through the gaps in his teeth. 'There are ten of you and a mule, I suppose the animal cannot row, but you can take turns on the other oars.' He grinned at the lad and said something in his own language, at which the boy flexed the muscles of his arms like a prize-fighter. 'He will not need a replacement,' the helmsman stated.

'And you?'

'I will steer.' The man leant on the tiller.

'Where? There is no sun, there are no stars, and you cannot see land. Should we not wait until this fog lifts?'

'Not my decision.' The old man spat over the side. 'Your little fleet is already moving.' He pointed to where, amongst the swirling mist, a noise could be heard. Quintus recognised it as the sound of splashing oars. 'Someone knows where they are going. If we do not follow, we will be marooned.'

Maxim and Jovan had been dividing themselves between the two groups of men and the mule, trying not to show favouritism. At the moment, Maxim was with the beast, Jovan tending to Marcus' fire. They were, of course, not trained to legionary standards of fitness, but they might come in useful.

We can use them later, thought Quintus, *when we can see what we are doing.* For now, the strongest meant Crassus, although his injury might trouble him, Tullius, for whom the same applied, Rufus, himself and Marcus. He needed to speak to Marcus and the veterans at the other end of the boat.

He approached their fire gingerly, although Rufus greeted him as a friend. Tullius appeared to be asleep, and Marcus was staring out to sea — or at least into the fog. Quintus spoke to the air above Marcus' head, while Rufus signalled encouragement silently.

'We need to work together,' said Quintus. 'We need to man the oars. Crassus and Tullius carry injuries — perhaps it would be best if you and Rufus joined us.'

Rufus half rose but was frozen by Marcus' hard stare.

'And this is your decision?' The voice was cold.

'It is what is best.'

'As decanus, it must be your decision.'

'Then that is what it is.'

'So be it, then. Come, Rufus, it seems we must row.' Marcus stood up smoothly, leaving his cloak where it fell on the deck. Jovan rushed to pick it up.

'I can row,' said Tullius, emerging from what had seemed like a trance. 'It will do the injury good to stretch it.'

'Then if we can persuade Sextus to dirty his hands, we have our crew,' said Rufus.

There were leather wrappings for their hands, though they were old and salt-encrusted. The ship's boy, who had already hauled in the sea anchor, patiently demonstrated how to use them to best advantage, all the time scratching his head at these world-conquerors' lack of nautical skills. There was some jostling for position — Marcus and Quintus did not wish to be next to each other, and Sextus felt that he should be at the back so that no-one could witness his inadequate ability. There were also more rowing stations than there were oars — the ship had once had a bigger crew.

The boy, with much sighing and arm waving, finally had them seated appropriately. He then sat down himself, slid his oar into the water, and began to sing a song of some sort, with words that the legionaries did not understand. However, they were not so stupid that they did not divine its purpose — there being no piper or drummer, the boy was providing a signal, a beat for their strokes. After one or two missteps, they established a rhythm and suddenly felt the joy of the boat moving smoothly under them like an ox finally persuaded to put its back into ploughing. Quintus, to his amazement, forgot his sickness for a while, even though he was in the evil-smelling dark and damp innards of the boat.

After what seemed like an age, but which was, in truth, under two hours, the helmsman called down from above. The boy stopped singing, shipped his oar and signalled to the men to do the same. The reason, he explained in a mime that involved him blowing through his cupped hands and pointing skywards, was that they had found a wind — hopefully, Quintus thought, a favourable one.

They unwrapped the leather bindings from their hands and rubbed them, whilst jiggling their shoulders to iron out knots and cramps. It took Quintus a while to even stand straight. Tullius rubbed the backs of his legs, but when Rufus looked at him quizzically, he nodded.

'It is good,' he said. 'It has done them good.'

On deck they could at once feel the reason for their release. The wind was fresh and gusty, whipping up whitecaps and chasing the fog away. The blanket that had covered the water was torn and tattered, as if a pack of wolves had fought over it, and it was now fleeing to the east in shreds, swirling briefly like smoke on the water before vanishing completely.

Their little fleet appeared scattered: they could see seven or eight other boats, but none of the larger ones. The biggest ship — the one that might once have been a trireme and had now been commandeered by the prefect — was not in sight. It was as if the head, the many heads, of the fleet had been cut off.

Quintus had a strange feeling about the scene. Had not Sextus forecast something of the like in one of his stories? When he looked to the east, the sky was light — not blue, but light enough to see the baby clouds against it. To the west it was dark; there was no horizon, as cloud and sea melded together in one grey-black mass of terror, lit intermittently by flashes of Jupiter's fire.

Crassus put his arm around Quintus' shoulder and took Publius under his other arm. His touch was reassuring in the eerie hush, punctuated only by the roll of far-off thunder. Other than this it was silent; they heard no call of seabirds and saw no sign of frolicking dolphins. The sea itself bubbled like a pot on the boil.

'What is happening?' Crassus asked. 'Do we sail on? I think I could row.'

'I do not know what is happening,' said Quintus. 'I taste something strange in the air, and there is a tingling on my skin. I have never known the like.'

'Nor I,' Publius admitted in a small voice.

If they had thought that by now they would have their sea legs, they were quickly disabused. The sea changed character again. Great dark lines stretched across it, each topped with bright white foam.

Suddenly the ship lurched, as if Neptune's sacred hand had grabbed it from below, and tipped into the trough of a wave — a wave whose sister broke way above their heads, crashing into the sea astern. Shock was soon replaced by a familiar nausea, as the deck plunged and jolted beneath them. They were raised up on the next crest, and had they been able to stand and stare they would have seen the greens and browns of the shore to the south, the trees and mountains of safety improbably dappled with sunshine — but there was no time to look. Instead, they plummeted into the depths of a salt-soaked valley where it was as if they had been flung into Hades, all light extinguished.

As they began to rise again, the helmsman could be heard yelling at them over the sudden roar of the waves. 'Get below!' he shouted desperately. 'Get off the deck and look to your beast and your possessions! Look to your slaves and your companions! Pray, my friends, pray, but get below!'

Crassus turned his two comrades towards the hatch, waiting as Marcus and Tullius dropped down. Rufus then halted for them. Still sick, Cato had stayed below, Sextus ministering to him. Maxim and Jovan were terrified, but had stayed with the mule, attempting to calm it.

Last to drop down was Quintus, trying to pull the hatch closed as the noise of the wind began to rise.

XXXVII: BRITANNIA

The next few hours passed in a haze of terror. The legionaries were thrown from one side of the little ship to the other, bruising themselves against the timbers. The ship groaned and cracked, and more than once they thought that it would split apart and spit them into the waves. Water poured through the hatch, which Quintus had been unable to properly secure, and, if the ship leant over far enough, water splashed through the holes meant for the oars. As it collected at their feet, they were soon soaking wet and trembling with cold. They could do little but cling on to the nearest piece of timber, and each other, whilst the storm giants fought a great sea battle above their heads.

The wind howled across the deck, and they could hear the sail flapping, knowing that the speed of the storm's approach was such that the boy had been unable to furl it. Ropes whipped and twanged, thunder rolled and bright flashes of lightning could be seen through the opening, briefly illuminating Maxim as he clung to the mule, and the cowering figures of the other men, holding on to anything solid.

Some of the cargo, inevitably, broke its moorings. Warnings were shouted as heavy sacks and splintered crates flew around the hold.

'Crassus, look out!'

'Rufus, duck!'

'Tullius, behind!'

Finally, the movement of the ship became less violent, the flotsam settled, and the men began to relax, flexing their frozen fingers. They heard the thunder rolling away into the distance, becoming more of a low growl. The flashes of lightning that lit up the square of sky visible through the hatch become less frequent, less intense. They began to feel their limbs for bruises and breaks. Jovan went to comfort Maxim, and Quintus went to check on Cato. The men dared to speak, to inquire after each other.

The little daylight that was managing to find its way through the hatch dimmed, and darkness fell outside the hold as well as in it. With the night, the Titans seemed to tire of their game. The ship settled, sitting low in the water and spiralling gently. The mule had been flung against the side and lay dead, its neck broken. Maxim cradled its head in his hands. Jovan had left his cousin and was trying to salvage some of the contents of the mule's pack, despairing as everything came up soaking.

No-one called down from above, so Quintus dared to climb the ladder. Sextus followed, claiming keener eyes. Before the tempest had raged all around them, they had been able to see the bobbing lights of the rest of the fleet. Now there were none.

'Quintus…?' Sextus began to ask in a whisper, his voice catching in fear.

Quintus did not let him finish. 'I know.'

The rest of the men emerged slowly, collapsing onto the deck in heaps. The strange, soft glow of the whitecaps was all around, the sea still simmering gently, but they could see no riding lights, no boats.

'There is no land to be seen.' Sextus' disorientation was complete. He had never been out of sight of land; with the lack of stars or sun, he did not know where he was. 'We are alone.'

The quiet was uncanny, the waves making only soft sounds against the hull, the wind gently tugging at the sail, the colour of the sky casting a pall over everything.

The wind had dropped to merely steady, as lighter clouds thrust the darker ones out of the way. In the west, the thunderheads still stretched from the sky to the sea, lit now and again by ominous flashes from within. They were like the glimpses of a sunny morning seen through a thick forest, or the light of forges marked from the bank of the Styx as shades waited for the Ferryman. In the east, thick cloud still prevented the stars from emerging. The water rolled and heaved, as if some leviathan swam just below the waves, ready to breach the surface.

It was night — not the black of a moonless night on land, but a vista lit by a strange, pale light, more green than white, that came from the ocean. It allowed Quintus to see that there was no-one at the helm, and he feared the old man had been swept overboard. He looked around for the ship's boy, then heard him. Following the voice, he saw that he had lashed himself to the mast and was now gesticulating and shouting loudly in his own language. He pointed to the spot where the cloud was starting to break up, a few stars showing through.

'The end?' Quintus asked, searching for the right words in the boy's tongue. 'The calm? The finish?'

The boy shook his head violently, indicating his bonds with desperate hands, trying to communicate the reason for them.

Quintus wondered what was meant, then watched as the window on the heavens, a sign of such hope, quickly closed. He looked around in panic, seeking the comfort of a star or the familiarity of the moon in the firmament, but there was suddenly not a single light in the sky. There was no North Star to guide them, and neither the Little Bear nor the Great Bear could be seen. There was no memory of Ursus, nothing for Macilentus — the soaked and frozen skinny soldier — but failure.

At that moment he felt the bite of the freshening wind on his cheek and realised with a start what the boy was telling them. He shouted down the length of the boat at the shadowy figures on the deck.

'This is not the end of the storm, but a pause! There is more to come!'

The first reaction was an unexpected one from Sextus. He appeared out of the dark and grabbed Quintus by the shoulders, shaking him furiously, his face so close that their foreheads almost touched. He screamed desperately. 'Fling it! By all the gods, get rid of it while you can!'

Quintus understood. Needing no further urging, he pulled away from the maniacal grip and scrabbled beneath his soaking tunic, finding the offending object still within. He pulled out not Ursus' charge, nor his armband, but something else, a nugget still bright and full of evil. 'You do it,' he said hoarsely, handing the gold to Sextus.

Sextus took it, breaking his vow never to lay hands on the cursed stuff for the second time, and flung it into the waves. He then locked eyes with Quintus. 'Survive,' he pleaded. 'Tie yourself to something. Do it well. We need you. More than that, Ursus needs you. Save yourself.'

Quintus returned the gaze, looking deep into Sextus' soul. This was no jest. He tore himself away. 'Find rope, men!' he shouted past Sextus at the indistinct figures of his comrades. 'Tie yourselves to the boat! What we have suffered was not the end of the storm, but the beginning!'

The silhouette of the ship's boy could be seen tugging theatrically at the bonds that bound him to the mast, as if in demonstration of what to do.

'You think that we will suffer worse than what we just went through?' Crassus shouted.

Wet, bruised and cold, Quintus twisted the rope in his hands around a stanchion, then wrapped it around his wrist. 'So the boy thinks!' he called back.

Sextus spoke excitedly, pointing into the waves. 'Look, Quintus, the sea is boiling where the nugget landed. It was as I said: it was cursed.'

To Quintus, the sea was no more boiling where Sextus pointed than anywhere else. He shrugged — cursed or not, it was gone now.

'We need to tie ourselves?' Marcus asked, looking at the clouds and waves, not seeing a storm.

'The boy thinks there is worse to come, and he should know.' Quintus squared his shoulders, took command and shouted to his comrades from his position near the tall prow: 'Tie yourselves well! Marcus, Sextus, you too!'

The men accepted the order. They lashed themselves to rails or stanchions, crouching in expectation of another lurch like the first one, of another battering. A minute passed, then five minutes, then longer. They waited like rabbits caught under the shadow of a hawk, but the storm did not come.

The clouds remained thick and the wind remained steady, but it did not strengthen to how it had been before, and the waves stayed lively, rather than dangerous. They seemed to be held in relative calm, a solitary shivering ship held tightly in Ocean's grip.

A band of curiously hot air passed over them, like the heat of a summer's day being let into a tavern. Quintus shuddered; he did not know the moods of the sea. The darkness and danger of the storm seemed to pass to the rear of the boat; there was lightning within it, a crackling of thunder, but still it did not reach them.

Quintus could now just make out the horizon to the west. Turning his head, he could see a hint of dawn light to the east, though it looked not hopeful, but sickly. Still he could not see a single other ship. They were completely alone, being pushed along by the flapping sail in whatever direction the wind had chosen.

Sextus had tied himself further down the ship. Now, with a long rope fastened to his waist, he made his way gingerly back towards Quintus, hands gripping the gunwale. 'Is it over, do you think?' he asked. 'Has it passed?'

'I do not yet know. The boy was saying that that storm was just the beginning.'

The dawn crept up on them slowly. On land, it would have brought them colour — greens, browns and the bright shades of flowers. Here, it merely seemed to increase the range of greys: the agitated grey sea, the unbroken grey cloud.

'Are we safe?' The question was called from one of the men near the mast.

'Not yet!' Quintus called back. 'Wait just a little longer, until we are sure.'

A gash appeared in the unbroken cloud and, as it opened, a pale orange light filled the space, highlighting the sharp edges of the boat and colouring the tips of the whitecaps in the yellow hue of bruised skin.

Quintus looked out in wonder. Sextus' gaze followed his friend's stare. He shook his head and spoke with incredulity and fear. 'I have never seen the like.'

'Nor I,' said Quintus in a whisper. 'It is like the world's end.'

'Are we still in the waking world? Have we passed beyond?' Sextus kept his voice low, as if Dis himself might be listening.

Quintus pinched himself. 'I still feel,' he said. 'My skin still reddens at the touch ... but maybe that would be the case if we had passed beyond.' He was thoughtful. 'We are leaving our world, remember. We are crossing the ocean.'

In the light Quintus had half expected to see the black edge of the world, an abyss into which the ocean endlessly poured. But instead of a precipitous drop into a void, a set of shining yellow and white teeth grinned at them. They were framed by a thin line of white below and a thin line of green above, and were mobbed by flocks of whirling seabirds. They were the white cliffs that guarded another world.

As they watched, the tear in the clouds grew, as if a divine hand had taken hold of the edges and pulled it apart. Through it, the sky was blue.

'What is it?' Sextus asked.

'Britannia!' Quintus said in awe. Though he knew that divine Caesar had crossed the water before and had set foot on the strange land, he was never quite sure that he believed the tales that had come back to Rome — of a wild land full of mists and monsters, and a wild people, tinged with magic.

He offered a silent prayer to Ursus: *We are all safe. I have not failed you.*

He then turned to smile at Sextus. 'It is our destination, Sextus. All is well. It is where we should be.'

HISTORICAL NOTES

The Quintus series is set in a Rome that is coming to terms with autocratic rule, yet still in the process of recovering from a seventy-year-long series of civil wars. These finally ended with Octavian's defeat of Antony and Cleopatra at the Battle of Actium, and their joint suicide, although echoes of revolt continue for some time afterwards. It is now 17 BCE, ten years since Octavian named himself Augustus Caesar, with lifetime powers.

The year 17 BCE would of course have made no sense to our Romans; to them it was the year of the Consulship of Gaius Furnius and Gaius Julius Silanus, or the year 737 AUC (*ab urbe condita*, i.e., from the founding of the city). The months of the year and even the way the Romans referred to different times of the day would have been equally alien to us. I have tried to compensate for this for the sake of the modern reader.

At the end of the civil wars there were around fifty legions under arms, meaning there were over a quarter of a million men loyal to one or other of the generals. Antony's final defeat was, in great part, due to many of his legions switching sides. Augustus retained twenty-eight legions, renumbering some of them. There was no logical numbering of legions — if I were to raise a legion and you were to raise a legion, we may well give them the same number or symbol. The Ninth Hispania, to which Quintus belongs, was one of Julius Caesar's legions, later disbanded and reformed, possibly as part of the Tenth Gemina. Whatever designation it had, it is not unreasonable to think that the men kept 'old' loyalties and symbols.

The men of a 'tent party' or contubernium would have had slaves to cook and clean for them. These may have been treated well or badly but, so embedded was slavery in Rome, they would have been very unlikely to revolt. Our modern sensibilities can barely comprehend the nature of such an institution. Anthony Trollope's *The Life of Cicero* mentions that a master might be a friend to slaves: Roman life admitted of such friendships, though the slave was so completely the creature of the master that his life and death were at the master's disposal. Quintus, I hope, is fair to these men.

The Roman goldmine — the largest in the Empire — existed at Las Médulas, in the modern province of Leon. The fantastic landscape there today bears witness to their method of mining — using water to crack the rock and destroying the mountain (*ruina montum*) in the process.

A NOTE TO THE READER

Dear Reader,

I cannot thank you enough for taking the time to read the first Quintus novel. I hope you enjoyed it. Although each novel in the series may be read as a stand-alone, the next in the series, *Decanus*, resumes the adventures of Quintus and his comrades in a new land. I hope you will continue to follow them.

The start of the story arose when I came across the idea of 'decimation'. Surely common sense says that it would be a punishment that was inefficient in the extreme? Further digging revealed that Polybius, the Greek historian and Plutarch, in his *Life of Antony*, both describe the process in detail (although, in Antony's case, it seems not to have had the desired effect) and there is an attested instance (Crassus, during the Third Servile War against Spartacus) in 72 BCE.

Other examples are either in Rome's distant past or reported many years after they supposedly happened but it is clear that, as a punishment, it existed. As to method, numbers, and aftermath, these are conjecture. Suetonius (writing around 100 years after the events in this book) claims in an often quoted passage (*Cohortes, si quae cessissent loco, decimatas hordeo pavit*) that Augustus used decimation — but provides no dates or examples. The event in Hispania could well have happened, and would have left no evidence.

If you find any errors, I shall be delighted to hear from you. I will always endeavour to respond, and if you're right, correct future editions, but remember, though I try my best to be accurate, this is a work of fiction, not history.

Reviews by knowledgeable readers are an essential part of a modern author's success, so if you enjoyed the novel I would be grateful if you could spare the short time required to post a review on **Amazon** and **Goodreads**.

Neil Denby

Sapere Books is an exciting new publisher of brilliant fiction and popular history.

To find out more about our latest releases and our monthly bargain books visit our website:
saperebooks.com

Printed in Great Britain
by Amazon

26153449R00215